Lucky Number 11

By Jess Kitching

KINGSLEY

P U B L I S H E R S

First published in South Africa by Kingsley Publishers, 2023
Copyright © Jess Kitching, 2023

Kingsley Publishers
Pretoria,
South Africa
www.kingsleypublishers.com

A catalogue copy of this book will be available from the
National Library of South Africa

Paperback ISBN: 978-1-776431-6-2
eBook ISBN: 978-1-776431-5-5
Hardcover: 978-1-776431-7-9

Also by Jess Kitching

How To Destroy Your Husband
The Girl She Was Before

To my fellow survivors -

I want to say something inspiring here, but all there is to say is you've got this, even on the days you think you don't.

I found out recently that I enjoy watching people die.

Does it alarm you to hear me say that? Do you want me to take the statement back?

Well, I can't.

Like most people, I was taught from a young age to say sorry if something I said or did caused distress, but I was also taught never to lie. So I'm afraid I can't apologise because the truth is that I do enjoy watching people die. I enjoy it more than I've ever enjoyed anything before.

You see, there's something beautiful about witnessing someone fade into an eternal rest. A purity shines through all the blood and gore. There's this moment, this split-second of deliciousness right before the lifeless, glassy film coats their retina, where a flash of something so raw and so honest bursts into existence. I'm not religious, but seeing it is the closest I've ever felt to God.

In its simplest form, it is a moment of utmost peace. In this world of chaos and sadness and pain, how often can a person say they are at one with peace?

If you ask me, the moment is made all the purer when the person is dying against their will. When they finally surrender to the violence they've spent their life pretending doesn't exist. When they feel themselves bleeding out and give up on looking for an escape route, the fight in their muscles ebbing away into nothing. That bright, shiny future they imagined for themselves evaporates and then... then they're gone.

Death, a universal experience we will all share one day.

But some deaths are more imminent than others. Yours, for example. It's creeping closer and closer, like a car turning a corner at the same time as a pedestrian stepping out onto the road.

Unavoidable.

Inescapable.

Final.

Death... it's coming for you. Can you feel it?

The *White Tent.*

Leaving the dregs of his coffee in the car, Conrad walks with purpose towards the tent at the top of the hill. Pop-up white structures remind most people of wedding marquees and fancy parties, but not Conrad. To him, they mean something else entirely.

"A dog walker found her," explains the officer who greets him halfway. She does her best to sound professional, but the wobbly undercurrent in her voice gives her away.

Conrad glances at the pale, drawn woman. She doesn't look a day over twenty-one. Her uniform still has that fresh-from-the-packaging crispness to it.

She must be new, he surmises. *Maybe this is the first body she's ever seen.*

The urge to wrap a blanket around the officer's shoulders and steer her away from the scene overwhelms Conrad, but he shakes it off. Protecting innocence is not his job. No, he comes into the picture long after innocence has been eviscerated.

Conrad shoots what he hopes comes across as a supportive smile at the officer, but he suspects his permanently downturned mouth doesn't perform the gesture correctly.

The pair walk in sync towards the tent, their sensible black shoes sinking into the wet ground with each trudging step. Conrad's breath puffs before him in little bursts of fog. His knees creak, the effort it takes for him to reach the summit of the hill enormous. Then again, everything about this job feels like a walk in the mud to Conrad these days.

"Forensics are ready for you to take a look now," the officer informs him.

Conrad nods and peels back the opening to the tent. Together, they step inside.

Figures in white all-in-one suits acknowledge Conrad, but he doesn't return their greeting. He can't, not when his attention has been captured by something else – the naked, bent out of shape figure on the floor, their hand outstretched as if reaching to him for help he is too late to give.

Even with almost thirty years in the police force and a history of managing cases that would make the most hardened heart wince, Conrad has never gotten used to seeing a dead body. There's something about the way their eyes stare at him he finds hard to shake off. It's like they see through to his soul, even the murkiest bits. Especially the murkiest bits. His failures, his vices, his useless hope that he could live in a world where dog walkers didn't stumble across maimed corpses on drizzly Thursday mornings.

Nowadays, even copious amounts of alcohol can't keep the pleading gaze of the lost at bay. Fellow officers would claim 'bullshit', but Conrad swears he can remember the eyes of every victim he's ever seen. They come to him, seeking him out. They catch him in their flat, lifeless field of vision and beg to know why he didn't do more to save them.

"I'm sorry!" he wants to shout, but what use would it be? He's too late. They are gone, lost to the violence of their final traumatic moments, and their eyes will forever stare through him as though he is nothing but smoke in the air.

This one has brown eyes, although Conrad can only see one of them. The other is closed shut thanks to a blow to the head that looks to have broken their right eye socket.

Conrad scans the rest of the girl's battered body. He tries not to imagine her last moments, but he can't help it. Was she thinking of the exams she would never get to sit? The wedding dress she'd never try on? Or something simpler, closer to her everyday life, like the parents she'd never again get to kiss goodnight?

Conrad does his best to swallow the sour taste these thoughts have brought to his mouth. He looks at the body again, methodically this time.

There's a shiny coating to the girl's skin, a different consistency and sheen to the rain she's been left out in, as if something has been poured over her. Bleach, potentially, given the faint smell of it inside the tent. There's something in her hand. It looks like a folded piece of paper. Conrad's stomach drops, already dreading reading whatever is written on it.

Continuing his assessment, Conrad takes in the wounds obliterating the girl's smooth skin. His eyes linger on the deep gouges across her slender wrists before continuing to track the rest of her maimed corpse. They come to rest on two violently etched markings beside her navel.

Conrad's heart stops, his body filling with the same empty life force as the girl laid out before him. "Is that…"

"A number thirteen," the officer confirms in a small voice.

If Conrad could fall to his knees without losing all sense of superiority here, he would.

Willing himself to remain composed, he pulls on a pair of gloves and removes the paper from the girl's hand. Once it's unfolded, he comes face to face with an image that has haunted him for the last ten years, and one that will continue to haunt him until the day he dies.

Conrad's coffee repeats on him, the bitterness burning the back of his throat as his worst fears are confirmed.

It's happening, he thinks. *It's happening again.*

Conrad knows more than anyone what that means. Everything changes from here.

Chapter *One.*

"Fears are growing for missing schoolgirl Gabriella O'Hara. The fifteen-year-old was last seen crossing Fitzroy Street at around 4pm on the twentieth of February, placing her last known whereabouts in the Huntington area. Her parents alerted the authorities when Gabriella failed to return –"

I bustle into the living room, a knot of anxiety already - and that's before I see what's on the TV. "Can you turn that off, please?"

Dragging his sleep-crusted gaze from his laptop, Joel glances at me. "Huh?"

"The TV. Turn it off," I repeat, turning my back on the red and white banner at the bottom of the screen and the misery it details.

"Sorry, I didn't realise it was on." Joel riffles through the documents surrounding him on our dining-table-turned-Joel's-office. Working from home, a post-Covid hangover that my introverted partner adores, even if his setup is the least ergonomic space he could work from.

Locating the remote, Joel points it at the television. The screen turns black, our apartment falls silent, and my jaw unclenches.

"Thank you," I say, then I focus once more on my desperate search and rescue mission, yanking back sofa cushions only to throw them down in empty-handed defeat moments later.

"What are you looking for?" Joel asks.

"Stefan's copy of *Dracula*. I told him I'd bring it back today. I could have sworn I left it on the coffee table last night…" I scan the living space of our apartment, hoping for the book to jump out at me from the sea of framed art prints and potted plants.

"I'll help you find it. What does it look like?"

"It looks like a book," I tease. Joel shoots me a withering glare, but he can't fight his smile. "It has a black cover and a red spine."

"Black cover, red spine, got it. You know, I think I saw it last night. In fact, I definitely did. I put it somewhere…somewhere safe…"

I try not to show my panic at this. "Where?"

Joel grins. "Now that, Hannah, is the question."

I swear, if he weren't so loveable with his tatty bedhead and old-man-style slippers, Joel's illogical tidying methods and general messiness would make me scream. Luckily for him, those deeply-etched dimples are enough to make even my most 'why can't everything be organised?!' bad mood fade.

Joel joins me in ransacking our apartment until he locates the copy of *Dracula*, tucked behind our peace lily, of all places. He holds it in the air like it's a winning lottery ticket.

"My hero!" I cry, grabbing the book and placing it in my handbag well away from my lunch. Stefan treats his books better than most people treat their relatives, and I for one am not going to let my strawberry yoghurt burst all over one of his classics.

"You've got to admit, that was a safe place," Joel says, flashing me a cheeky grin.

"It was a classic example of Joel tidying, let's put it that way. But when it comes to Stefan's books, please leave them where I can find them. He'd never lend me anything again if I lost one. You know how literature students are about their books."

"Do I? I haven't been to university in ten years. Have you got a secret boyfriend you've confused me with?"

"I can't believe I've let slip and told you about him," I joke as I snuggle into Joel. He smells of coffee and toast, his fuel of choice ahead of a stressful day of deadlines.

Since signing comedian Art McArthur as an ambassador last month, the animal welfare not-for-profit Joel works for has experienced a dramatic popularity increase on social media. With the sudden rise of the company's profile comes the need for more content to be created. As the only graphic designer on the team, that duty falls on Joel's shoulders, which means my poor partner waking up at sunrise to create another (hopefully) viral image. Joel's working hours have never been longer, and he's never had more meetings and dinners with donors to attend - events he begrudgingly goes to in the hope that his hard work will result in a generous pay rise.

"I suppose I'll forgive you for having a secret lover if you promise to check out the property links I sent you this morning," Joel says after failing to stifle a yawn. "I found some great houses while you were in the shower. Mum's even sent me one to show you."

I pull out of the hug. "You've got Jackie in on the property hunt too?"

Joel shrugs. "She wants us to stop throwing money away on rent and settle down."

"Is that the not-so-subtle beg of 'please make me a grandma soon' I hear," I joke as I slip my coat on. "I'll look at the links when I'm on the bus, but I have to check - are they promising leads or your usual 'we could live here... if we earned double what we do now' ones?"

"Real, genuine, promising links," Joel confirms, and I squeal with excitement.

"Maybe this time we'll find our new home!"

"Maybe. I mean, surely the hundredth house has got to be 'The One', right?"

"We've not seen that many," I laugh, then I grab my handbag and prepare to leave the cosiness of home. "Don't work too hard today, okay? Remember to eat some lunch, and not at your desk. I'll be back after seven tonight, but I will check the fridge."

I mean it as a joke, but the atmosphere shifts at these words.

"Back after seven, ready to start the next chapter of your life," Joel says. He reaches out and, even though it's time for me to leave, I accept his invitation. Encased in his embrace, my heart flutters the same way it did when we first met three years ago.

We were the only people under the age of fifty to attend a talk about the impact of violence in mainstream media. Joel, a film buff who wrote movie reviews as a side hobby. A man who wanted to challenge filmmakers to create roles for women outside of the silent wife, rape victim, damsel in distress or fuckable temptress who dies two scenes later. Me, working through the trauma so many said would define me by trying to figure out how to live in a world where aggression was so neatly woven into everyday life.

I couldn't even attend a talk about violence in mainstream media without something happening. Someone on the back row shouted 'bullshit' and stormed out when the host said action movies tell men two things – kill or be killed – and women another two things – be saved or be killed.

"I think someone got lost on the way to the monthly misogynists meet up," Joel commented as the door slammed shut behind the outraged departee. Everyone laughed, the tension in the room faded and for the first time in a long time, I looked a stranger in the eye and smiled. We went for dinner after the talk, met for brunch the next day and the rest, as they say, is history.

"Hurry home so we can celebrate. I'll be waiting with a surprise." Joel winks when he's finished speaking, then his gaze flicks to my lips. His eyes trace the curves of my mouth, the tiredness in them melting and giving way to something much more appealing.

It's tempting, so tempting, but I pull away. "If I don't go now, I'll miss the bus."

"Damn that bus," Joel groans. "We'll celebrate tonight, okay?"

"Deal," I call over my shoulder before scampering out of the apartment.

The air in the corridor is stale, nothing like the warm, toast-scented environment of home. Zipping my coat up to my chin, I make my way down the stairs. Threadbare carpet leads the way and scuff marks line the walls, the tell-tale signs of furniture removals from residents long gone. No matter how shabby the communal areas are, though, I wouldn't change this place for the world. After all, I've made some of my happiest memories here.

The chill outside has permeated through the front door, so much so I can see my breath when I reach the ground floor. It's felt like an eternal winter, my weather app seemingly frozen on a screen promising nothing but rain, dark clouds, and bitter cold for months on end. Today is no exception. The little early morning light there is filters through the frosted glass, the world still rousing from its slumber.

There won't be many people around when you leave here, I remind myself. Not until I reach Robson Lane, at least. A scream could be blown away in the wind as easily as a piece of litter.

Balling my hands into fists, I push open the front door, braving the cold and my intrusive thoughts.

An icy wind whips my cheeks as I step outside, but I push on, sidestepping puddles while making note of the people I see. A bald man reversing a car out of a driveway, a downtrodden woman loading her backseat with bags. Other than their presence, I'm alone with only the echo of my footsteps for company. It's enough to make me quicken my pace.

The bus is already coming up the road by the time I reach Robson Lane. I break into a run and make it just in time. Once seated, I check out the property links Joel sent. Four houses, each with three bedrooms, at least one bathroom and the promise of a new beginning. I message Joel to say that the third is my favourite, ask him to apologise to his mum for not liking the one she sent - one that turned out to be three streets away from her house - then turn my attention to life outside the window.

I could narrate this route with my eyes closed. Right at the end of Robson Lane, down Haworth Road for three minutes (five if the bus stops to let people on). Travel through three sets of traffic lights that always seem to turn red as the bus approaches. Two more left turns until you pass a multistorey car park and the local university's science block, then it's time to get off the bus. A ten-minute journey away from my apartment, one I make for the five days a week I work as a waitress and barista.

The fading blue and orange sign for Break Time, my place of employment for the last two years, greets me from further up the road when I get off the bus. The paint could do with a touch-up and there are more wobbly tables than sturdy ones, but Break Time always has a steady queue of customers, even after a chain coffee shop opened a few doors down. Close to the city for commuters and practically on campus for students, it's in the perfect position.

Pushing open the rickety front door, I squeeze through the morning rush of customers and wave to Ellen and Stefan who are already busy serving behind the counter. With an ever-growing queue and no time to waste, I duck into the cramped backroom, swap my coat for my apron then join them on the café floor.

"Looks like it's going to be a fun one today," Ellen says as I take my place beside her.

Break Time is Ellen's labour of love. Turning her partner of fifteen years leaving her into the opportunity to chase her dreams of owning a café, Ellen is an incredible woman to work for. Short-haired, short in stature, but not short in patience, Ellen is the kind of boss who makes you want to come to work. She's also lived in this city forever, knows everything about everyone, and bakes the most addictive sweet goodies for us to sell.

"What did you think of the book?" Stefan asks after handing a woman with neon-pink hair a chai latte. Before I can speak, the next customer begins reciting their order. Stefan nods along, but I know his attention is on my response. He can compartmentalise conversations like that, whereas I'm more of an if-I'm-talking-while-serving-I-will-forget-the-order kind of waitress.

"I loved it. The story didn't feel dated at all. You know, I don't understand why I haven't read many classics before. Each one you've recommended has been great."

"Right? People get put off by the label 'classics', but to me, that means the story is timeless. Most of the messages in them are as true today as they were when they were written, and those stories still have such an influence over pop culture. I mean, how many people have heard of *Dracula*? How many people have dressed up as him for Halloween? But as for reading the book? Well, that's a different story."

Ellen bags up a croissant and rolls her eyes. "This isn't one of your fancy lectures, kid. There are customers to serve and coffees to pour."

The people in the queue smile, Ellen's telling off the opposite of stern.

Stefan offers Ellen a mock salute. "Yes, Ma'am," he says, before whispering to me, "I still think you should consider enrolling at university, you know. You'd love my course. You already know more about literature than half the people there."

"Maybe one day," I shrug, because vague platitudes are easier than outright dismissal.

I don't tell Stefan about the prospectuses I downloaded out of curiosity the other month, or about how reading them made me feel.

University, along with many other things, had once been on the cards for me, but that was a long time ago. Back when social media wasn't the centre of everyone's universe and people asked for iPods for Christmas. I used to dream of being a teacher. I thought maybe one day I'd even teach abroad. Now I'm just grateful to be behind this counter, milk-splashed apron and all. My life might not be Instagram-worthy to some, but dishing out coffees and pastries is more than enough for me. University and everything it offers can remain what it has for a long time – a daydream of a different life.

I serve the usuals – professors in need of a caffeine fix, hungover students clambering for a snack before lectures, and suits looking for a pleasant location for their latest meeting. My smile stays fixed, the tip jar is steadily topped up, and the day runs smoothly. By the end of my shift, my feet throb and my back aches, the hum of exhaustion a feeling of being alive I've come to adore.

"What a day," Ellen says as she counts the money in the till. A healthy stack of cash, I'm pleased to note, one I hope brings Ellen closer to the Mediterranean cruise she's been saving for. "You two head off, let me finish up here."

"Are you sure?" I ask, hovering by the coffee machine that I'm only halfway through cleaning.

"Positive! You haven't stopped all day. Go on, go home."

"Thanks, Ellen," I say, dropping my cleaning supplies and following Stefan into the backroom. "You've got that Contemporary Fiction essay to write tonight, haven't you?" I ask as we grab our stuff.

He groans. "Did you have to remind me about that?"

"Of course! Isn't part of being a good friend teasing the people you care about?"

As we walk back through to the café, I check my phone. A message from Joel wishing me luck waits for me, as does one from Danielle.

Will you save me a seat tonight? My bitch of a boss won't let me leave on time so I'll be late (AGAIN!!). Why does she make out like no one will hire a rental car if I'm not there?! Remind me again why I need this job...x

Smirking at her theatrics, I type a response.

Because your mortgage won't pay for itself, I'm afraid. But consider your seat saved x

Beside me, Stefan shakes his head. "I swear, you're the only person I know who's still smiling after a full day at work. Can I tease you about that?"

"Not on my watch. Hannah knows the value of a job well done, don't knock it out of her," Ellen jokes. "Don't forget your brownies, Hannah."

"Thanks," I say, grabbing the box that Ellen's left on the counter for me, my usual Thursday order. As I wrap one of the brownies separately, I turn back to Ellen. "Is there anything leftover from today? A croissant or sandwich, perhaps?"

I've barely finished speaking before Ellen hands me a sandwich she's already wrapped, a knowing look glinting in her eye. "Now go, the pair of you, and thanks for all your hard work today."

The air is even brisker than it was this morning when we step outside, and it slaps my face to tell me so.

A few doors down from Break Time, I spot Robbie. Curled in a sleeping bag in the doorway of the electrical store that went out of business two months ago, he looks more tired than usual, but he perks up when he sees me. "Good day, Hannah?"

"Not bad, although I did break another plate," I reply with a grimace, then I hand over the food parcel. "One sandwich and one slice of calorific, chocolatey goodness for you."

"God bless you. After the day I've had, this might just save me."

I look down at Robbie's cup, so sparse of donations I can see the bottom of it. "Is there any room at the shelter tonight?"

Robbie stops tucking into the sandwich to shake his head and my chest twinges. He can't be much older than I am, but Robbie spends more nights sleeping on the street than he does in a bed. A family fallout and a run of bad luck saw him end up homeless, but a lack of stable support keeps him trapped in his predicament. The hoops he has to jump

20

through to access basic help would be enough to make anyone scream, but somehow Robbie finds a way to keep smiling.

Distress must be written all over my face because Robbie points at me. "Don't worry about me, Hannah. I've got dinner and a view of the stars – what more could I need?"

"As always, Robbie, your way of looking at the world gives it more credit than it deserves," Stefan says. "Have a good night, okay?"

Robbie waves goodbye and Stefan and I continue down the road. "I can't believe the shelters are full again," I groan. "How can anyone be expected to sleep outside in this weather?"

"That's what happens when the government only cares about the top two percent of earners," Stefan says dryly. "Can I give you a ride home?"

I shake my head. "I'll get the bus. Thanks, though."

"I wouldn't mind driving you home, you know. You can't live that far away."

"It's not that. I've got a thing tonight, that's all."

"Ah, I forget – your mysterious Thursday night thing!" Stefan replies, using a spooky tone like he's a bad actor performing on Halloween. "Remind me what it is again?"

"It wouldn't be very mysterious if I told you, would it?" I joke. In the distance, I spy the number 74 bus and quicken my pace.

"I bet that you're a superhero and this is the night you meet with all the other local superheroes to figure out how to stamp out crime."

"That's it, you've figured me out. They call me Super Coffee Girl."

"Clearly they've never seen you burn milk." Stefan breaks from my side to cross the road. "Enjoy your night, mysterious woman. See you tomorrow!"

"See you tomorrow," I call back, then I put my headphones in and blast the same punk rock music my mum used to wince at me listening to as a teenager.

Once on the bus, I balance the brownies on my knee and apply a coat of lipstick, the bright slick of colour reassuring me that I am in control tonight. After all, anyone who can successfully apply cosmetics while riding public transport can do anything, right?

Lipstick on, I watch the world from the window as the bus takes me further away from home. The opposite direction to where I want to be.

This is the last time you'll make this journey, I remind myself, a thought that makes me sink into my seat like I'm plunging into a warm bath.

Five songs in and with the second church on King Street in sight, I stop the bus. No one else gets off it when I do, a fact that feels lonelier than it should. Tucking my chin inside my coat, I walk past a row of businesses closing for the day until I come to a stop outside the building that has been a constant in my life for ten years now.

It's a generic, rundown structure. Nondescript, boring even. The battered red bricks it's built with give it a factory feel, but it's not a place that produces anything creative or exciting. From the outside, you'd think nothing of it. You'd probably pass it without a second thought, never once imagining that this is the place where strangers come together to spill their secrets. Where horror stories come to life and where even the worst nightmares seem tame.

The headquarters of Sisterhood of Support, in the flesh.

Chapter *Two.*

Pushing my shoulders back, I head inside and climb the staircase to level two. The lights are off in the room on the left of the corridor, a space that hosts mother-and-baby classes, but the room on the right is lit up. Muffled chatter fills the corridor from its inhabitants, my fellow Sisterhood of Support attendees. I'm ten minutes early, but for those who view tonight as their lifeline, you can never be early enough.

Through the small rectangle of glass in the meeting room door, I spot the usual eager suspects – Karolina, Dipti, Carla, Paula, and Amrita. They lug stacks of chairs into the centre of the room and arrange them into a poorly-formed circle.

I used to scoff at the rounded setup of Sisterhood of Support meetings. Organising our chairs in such a way felt like we were recreating a movie set, some group therapy session in a tearjerker that had hopes of winning an Oscar. Only in our circle, there was no one shouting 'cut' whenever someone's tears were too heavy or a story became too distressing to listen to.

But even if I hated the circle, I respected it. I respected it because I knew what it meant to the people who attended and, once upon a time, to me.

Founded by Tanya Goulding twelve years ago, Sisterhood of Support is a group for women who have experienced violence, abuse, sexual assault, and every other horror imaginable. What started as Tanya seeking a place where she could meet fellow survivors has grown into an important hub for so many.

Originally, Tanya ran peer-based support meetings on Thursdays and Saturdays from a church basement, but, thanks to her ambition and dedication, Sisterhood of Support has evolved into an institution that works with survivors every step of the way. As well as continuing the Thursday and Saturday peer sessions, Sisterhood of Support offers one-to-one counselling with Tanya herself at either the headquarters or Tanya's home, legal support for court cases, and a range of classes such as self-defence and art therapy. Some women travel well over an hour to attend and discover a place where they are heard, believed and supported.

For ten years, I have attended group sessions. I know their routine like I know every freckle on my face. We start with a guided meditation and then open the circle for pressure-free, guilt-free conversation. No one here can eradicate anyone's trauma, but they can listen and, most importantly, they can understand. After what we've been through, finding anywhere that offers that is rare.

Not that I saw Sisterhood of Support in such a positive way at first. To me, it was an unwelcome probe ransacking the worst time of my life and sharing its findings publicly like an open reading of a diary. My years here have been the toughest of my life, but they saved me, and tonight they will come to an end.

I check my phone for the passcode that was emailed to everyone half an hour ago, a security measure set up to ensure meetings are as safe as can be. Typing the four-digit code into the intercom, the double door buzzes, access granted.

Everyone choruses warm greetings as I walk into the room, then Dipti eyes the box in my hands and grins. "I swear, I only come to these meetings for the brownies," she jokes.

"Well, I only come so I can bring them to you," I reply.

"What was it that Mary Poppins said – a square full of sugar makes the misery go down?" Amrita quips.

"Something like that," I reply with a grin, then I make my way over to the refreshments table and set down the box.

With its neutral paint, wooden floor and stackable chairs, there's something about the meeting room that reminds me of a school assembly hall, but the framed prints hung on the walls tell you something very different to Parents' Evening is hosted here. Call me old-fashioned, but I can't remember a poster in my primary school that read, 'Fuck the patriarchy'.

Brownies deposited, I head towards the group, but Tanya exits her office and makes a beeline for me before I can reach it. Styled in all black, as always, Tanya's had a haircut since the last meeting. It's blunter than most people could pull off, but the severe crop works on her angular face.

The new haircut does nothing to conceal the jagged scar across Tanya's throat, a physical reminder of her ex-husband Andrew's failed murder-suicide attempt, but Tanya doesn't hide her injury. She never has. She leads by example, unashamed and encouraging us all to be the same. She even has a headshot from a photoshoot she did with a national newspaper framed above the fireplace in her living room. Her scar is fresh in the image, red, angry, and commanding. Her eyes challenge you in the photograph, daring you to say she is anything but a survivor. The power of the image takes my breath away every time I see it.

"I love the haircut," I say when she intercepts me.

Tanya fingers her hair, an air of self-consciousness about her. "Thanks. I'm still getting used to the length. You know me, I've never been one for long hair, but this is a whole new level. I might as well have shaved it off!"

"Well, it looks great."

"As always, Hannah, talking to you puts me in danger of growing a very big ego."

I laugh because, despite how adored she is, Tanya is the least egotistical person I've ever met. "Do you want me to help with the setup or is it all under control?"

"Actually," Tanya begins, putting her arm over my shoulder. "Can I have a word with you in private?"

I open my mouth to respond but she steers me away before I can answer.

The room falls silent as we leave, unease clogging the atmosphere. Secrets aren't big at Sisterhood of Support. They lead to tension and anxiety, an unnecessary addition when most of us here are already anxious enough.

Before heading into Tanya's office, I offer everyone a friendly smile that settles most of the nerves. Carla still glares at me, but that's to be expected. Ever since I interrupted a story about her ex's penchant for violence whenever his favourite football team lost because I was having a nosebleed, that's the only way she looks at me.

While Tanya closes her office door behind us, I take a moment to study the room I know almost as well as I know my own home for the last time. The bookcase filled with volumes on violent behaviours, overcoming trauma, and the power of sisterhood. The photographs of members past and present. The box of tissues on Tanya's desk, always there, always topped up.

How many times I've been in this room. How many tears I've cried.

"I see you still haven't hired a personal assistant," I say, indicating to the wilderness of papers on Tanya's desk.

"They wouldn't understand my filing system."

"That's because your filing system is chaotic."

Tanya laughs. "Trust me, there's a method to my madness."

I smile. "You're just like Joel. A loveable mess."

"As long as the word loveable is in that character description, I'll take it," Tanya replies. She takes a seat and indicates for me to do the same. When we're both sitting, she beams at me, her smile shining with a warmth that no one else quite receives. "How are you?"

"I'm okay, thanks, but I don't think you invited me into your office to find out how I am," I joke.

"You're right, that's not why I asked you in here," Tanya admits, then she leans her forearms on her desk, a seriousness cloaking her features that makes my stomach flutter. "I have a favour to ask of you. We have a new girl starting today, Riley Hunt. Have you heard of her?"

I shake my head. Tanya's thin eyebrows raise, but I'm not sure why she's surprised. She knows I avoid the news. Other than the stories told in this circle, I know nothing of the pain in this world and I'm more than happy to keep it that way.

"It's her first session today. I want you to keep an eye on her and make her feel welcome," Tanya says.

Now it's my turn to raise my eyebrows. "Are you sure I'm the best person for this? Today's my last session, after all."

Tanya flinches at my casual delivery of the news that broke her heart when I announced it a few weeks ago. "You're still sure about that?"

"Positive."

Sadness glints in Tanya's eyes, but she clasps her hands together, professionality restored. "Well, I'm still going to place Riley next to you in the circle. After everything she's been through, I feel like you're the person who will most understand her right now."

I try not to react to Tanya's words, but I don't do a very good job of it. Being chosen because you understand someone's experience at Sisterhood of Support is never a good thing. It means their story links closely to your own, which is often a fate you wouldn't wish on your worst enemy.

"As long as she doesn't get too attached," I shrug, turning away before Tanya sees the burn on my cheeks.

"Thanks, Hannah. I knew I could count on you. Now, I think we'd better go back outside, don't you?"

Tanya places her hand on the small of my back as we leave her office, then goes with Karolina to make tea and coffee for the meeting. I stand with Dipti and Amrita, chatting about Amrita's son's football game at the weekend.

"I swear, I've been to every muddy field and stinking sports ground this city has to offer," she jokes. "If you ever need a location for a secret outdoor rave, you know who to ask!"

When more people arrive, I take it as my cue to duck out of the conversation and reserve seats using my handbag and coat, a move that Carla pounces on. "You can't do that, Hannah. It's a support group, not a popularity contest," she snaps.

"I've been asked to save these seats. Danielle's running late."

"So? Are we supposed to let you do what you want because you're Hannah Allen?"

"Carla, please," I sigh, "it's my last meeting. For once, will you leave me alone?"

Carla folds her arms across her chest. "How am I supposed to do that when you're treating this circle as if you own it?"

As if summoned by the rising tension, Tanya appears at Carla's side. "Ladies, are we almost ready to begin? I sense there's a lot to talk about tonight."

Carla glowers at me for a second longer but, as always, Tanya's presence proves to be magic. Carla takes a seat beside Karolina, her bottom lip stuck out.

We're all settling into our seats when the meeting room door opens. In walks someone I've never seen before, but someone I instinctively feel like I know. The anger she radiates catches at the back of my throat, reverberating through my core as if it's my anger, my hurt, my rage.

She's young. Too young to know of the hurt that's created a space for her in this circle. Icy blonde roots shine through her poorly-dyed black hair, hair that's framing a face so sour it looks like it was born scowling. She's dressed as though she's raided an older brother's wardrobe and put on the biggest, baggiest clothes she could find. Her arms wrap around her torso, holding herself together even though everything about her screams that she wants to fall apart.

An older woman in a smart beige trench coat nudges the girl forward. "Go on," she instructs.

She must be the girl's mother. They have the same upturned nose and thin lips, not that you notice those features on the angry girl at first. To be fair, they're not the first thing you notice on the trench coat woman either. How could you when so much pain lines her features?

"I'm Sarah, and this is Riley," the mother announces to the room.

My heart aches. 'This is Riley', words Sarah would have once said to introduce her daughter to friends or work colleagues but are now said to acquaint her with strangers with horror-filled pasts.

As Riley takes a minuscule step into the room, I find myself on the verge of tears. I don't need to hear her story to know it, to have lived it. She looks nothing like me, but she is me. Me from ten years ago. A teenager whose innocence was stolen. Someone people call a survivor but who is desperately searching for a way to go back to being the person they used to be.

Even Sarah transforms before me so that when I look at her, I see my mother. A woman who has all the markers of someone who was once full of life but now just looks eaten alive by worry.

When my mum died six years ago, the doctors said it was cancer that killed her, but the truth is that what she was forced to live through did more damage to her than stage four breast cancer ever could.

"Riley," Tanya chimes, gliding towards the newbie as if the moment isn't teetering on a knife-edge. "We are so pleased you could join us! Come in and make yourself comfortable. The others can't wait to meet you! Please remember, Sisterhood of Support is a safe space."

A curl of a snarl appears on Riley's lips. I can almost read it. *Safe space?* she wants to spit. *Is there such a thing anymore?*

"I've chosen a seat for you next to Hannah," Tanya continues.

Upon hearing my name, I find myself on my feet and walking over to greet the new girl. "Hi Riley, I'm Hannah. Hannah Allen."

The girl's eyes widen in recognition, my name and my story known to her long before she was old enough to understand what any of it truly meant, but Sarah knows. She'd have been a woman with a young family when Peter Harris was roaming the streets. No doubt she'd have been petrified by the idea of being one of his victims. She'd have seen my face on the news when I was taken, and when I was found, and she reacts accordingly.

"Oh my," she gasps, her hand raising to her lips as if to hold in a scream.

I ignore her shock. After ten years, horrified reactions don't sting like they once did. Not when I've worked so hard to put distance between Hannah Allen then and Hannah Allen now.

I gesture to the seat taken up by my handbag. "Want to sit with me?"

Riley shrugs, but she moves of her own accord this time. I drop my handbag to the floor, and she plonks into the vacant chair.

As Sarah dithers before eventually being convinced to leave by Tanya, I watch Riley from the corner of my eye. Even though she slumps as if she's given up on holding herself upright, I know that if I tried to grab her hand, she would break my wrist clean in two. Ready for anything – the survival stance, the way most of us at this meeting are sat.

We wait a few more minutes, accepting five more of the usuals including Danielle who rushes over in a whirlwind of rainbow coloured clothing and perspiration. "The traffic was a nightmare," she complains as she ties up her mound of hair. "If I didn't have to drive home, I'd suggest going for a drink when we finish to calm my nerves."

"Now, now, you know Tanya doesn't encourage the use of alcohol to deal with stressful situations," I scold playfully, my humour glossing over the fact that, even if we both could, I wouldn't go for drinks with Danielle after the meeting anyway. I've not met anyone from Sisterhood of Support socially for months now. A gradual withdrawal, my usual tactic of isolating myself enough to make goodbyes easier. One of my worst habits, one Tanya's never been able to break, even after ten years of working with me.

"Yeah, well, Tanya's clearly never navigated this city in rush hour. I need a double vodka just to lower my blood pressure." Danielle laughs at her own joke then spots Riley beside me. She outstretches her arm to shake Riley's hand, her sleeve rolling up to unveil the scar across her wrist from her first suicide attempt. "I'm Danielle, nice to meet you," she says. Riley glances at Danielle's scar, then turns away.

I jump in before Danielle is hurt by the snub. "I've got to rush home tonight, otherwise I'd say yes to that drink," I lie. "Joel's planned a surprise for –"

Danielle holds her hand up to stop me. "If you're going to finish that sentence by saying 'my last meeting', I don't want to hear it."

Amrita must have been listening to our conversation because she speaks up. "Danielle, don't be silly – Hannah will never leave us. She can't. After all, how can we carry on without her kindness and wisdom?"

"Kindness and wisdom? I don't know about that," I joke, but Amrita shakes her head.

"Don't dismiss it, Miss Allen. You are the glue of this group. After ten years, how could you not be? So you can't leave, because what will happen to us if you do?"

Amrita's words close around my throat, bringing with them the overwhelming urge to cry. I don't want to come to these meetings and hear the kinds of stories I go out of my way to avoid anymore, but as much as I'm ready to leave, the thought of what comes next is terrifying. Even though I've been withdrawing for weeks now, imagining a life where I don't hear about Amrita juggling motherhood with a demanding law career or Paula's bravery while stepping back into the world feels like imagining the life of a stranger. Sisterhood of Support has been a cornerstone of my life for so long now. What will take its place when it's gone?

But you're ready to find out, the rational part of my brain reminds me. That's the part of myself I can listen to when I'm not face to face with people whose friendship saved my life.

My inner spiralling is interrupted by Tanya clearing her throat. "Everybody ready?" she calls.

Collectively we inhale, then we nod, and the meeting begins.

Chapter *Three.*

"I've had a lot of bad days this week. Remember the other month when the doctor lowered my medication dosage? I think it was too soon. Still, I've tried. I've been going out more, but I can't get used to people looking at me or the things they say. Just the other day, a group of kids were on the bus and one of them called me Cyclops."

A pity-tinged murmur rings out around the room, but it ends quickly to give Paula the space to continue.

"I suppose I should be glad the boy knew something from Greek mythology. It means he's learning something in school, right? Still, it hurt my feelings," Paula sniffs.

In a world where anything short of airbrushed perfection is ridiculed, life for Paula is tough. Her missing right eye and the scars obliterating her face make her an easy target for an ignorant stranger's cruelty.

Everyone at Sisterhood of Support sees Paula's beauty, but we know more than most that the average person isn't always kind. We've lived through the stares, the comments, and the heckles. We know how deep they cut. How when you're alone at night, you relive the verbal attacks, picking at the scab on your soul until it bleeds.

As the circle floods with sympathy, Paula raises a tissue to her eye and dabs away her tears.

"Thank you for sharing your experience with us, Paula," Tanya says. "I hope you know that in this circle, you are surrounded by people who admire the strength in your candidness and in all you do to push yourself to step outside of your home."

The group nods in agreement. Well, everyone apart from Riley does. Instead, she glares at Tanya like she wants lasers to shoot from her eyes and tear through Tanya's skull.

"People can be so cruel. My own son tells me I'm hideous. He forgets his daddy gave me these scars," Karolina says, tugging the sleeve of her jumper over her hand. I've never seen what's beneath Karolina's thick layers of clothing, but seeing as one of her ex's parting gifts was to pour a pan of boiling water over her, I can guess.

"Do you feel like you're hideous?" Tanya asks.

Karolina blinks. "How else am I to feel?"

Tanya leans back in her seat to address the group. "Who else here feels like they're hideous?"

Most of the women in the circle raise a hand, but the proud self-love advocates keep their arms firmly by their sides, as do I. I've spent far too much money on hair dye and clothes to label myself as anything other than well-presented. Riley doesn't raise her hand either, although I predict her reason for not participating is more to spite Tanya than because she doesn't think she's hideous.

Tanya surveys the group. "If that's the case, my next question would be – who here thinks anyone else in this circle is hideous?"

Every hand that was up is now down.

"See? We are our own worst critic. No one is hideous. We may carry marks from our traumas, but we still shine. Marked, scarred, bruised… beautiful, strong, survivors." Tanya turns to Karolina. "Your scars don't make you hideous, Karolina. Beauty is so much more than perfect skin or shiny hair. You *are* beautiful, inside and out. You might not think so right now, but there will come a day where hideous is the last word you would ever use to describe yourself."

Beside me, Riley scoffs, a sound so full of scorn it blows the gentle atmosphere wide open.

Tanya turns to Riley, smiling. "Is there something you want to add, Riley? Because it's okay if you do. All contributions are welcome."

The room waits with bated breath, ready to hear the newbie's response and officially welcome her into this circle of pain. A circle Riley so clearly doesn't want to be part of.

From the corner of my eye, I watch Riley dig her thumbnail into her forefinger. There's an aggression to the gesture that unnerves me, and I notice her hands are already heavily scratched. Any second now, she's going to rip through one of those scabs and start bleeding.

Stop, I think, turning to Tanya and willing her to notice my nonverbal cues, but her gaze remains fixed on Riley.

"You'll find that everyone here is very supportive," Tanya continues. "You have experienced unimaginable pain, I know, but you're here, in this moment with us. Together we will work towards helping you find peace with your past and hope for your future."

That's when Riley loses it. She jumps to her feet so quickly that her chair skids out behind her and clatters to the floor.

"Peace with what happened?" she hisses. "Is that a joke? I lost *everything* that day. You want me to walk out of here thinking everything happens for a reason and that these bad things we've been through are lessons in disguise? Well, fuck you and your twisted school! I didn't want to enrol. No one here did. Do you honestly think Paula looks at her missing eye and thinks, 'I'm so glad this happened to me'? Do you really think Hannah doesn't look back and wish she'd walked home from school a different way that day?"

I jolt at the mention of my name, then burn at Riley's words. I burn because she's right. No matter how many Sisterhood of Support sessions I attend, the truth is that if I had the chance to change one moment in my life, the moment I was abducted is the one I'd pick. I'd leave school five minutes later, catch a bus home, go to a friend's house. Anything to make sure I was never walking alone on Clifton Crescent, never in Peter Harris's line of sight. No amount of time or therapy will ever change that desire.

"Fuck you and fuck the lies you tell," Riley spits. "You're as sick as the monsters who hurt us if you think we will ever look back and think otherwise." With that, she pushes her way out of the circle and heads for the door.

Tanya makes a move to go after her, but I jump to my feet. "I'll go," I say, then I run to catch up with Riley. She lets out a snarl when she hears the meeting room door close behind me and kicks the corridor wall.

"Go away, Tanya!"

"Riley, it's me. It's Hannah."

Fat, black tears stream from Riley's eyes as she faces me, her heavy eyeliner staining her cheeks. "I'm not going back in there. You can't make me."

"I'm not asking you to. Trust me, it's not where I want to be on a Thursday night either."

Riley snorts and wipes her nose on the sleeve of her hoodie, then she scuffs the floor with the toe of her shoe as if trying to burrow her way out of here. "I hate it. Everyone in there knows who I am. They keep looking at me with big, sad eyes like I'm pathetic."

"No one thinks you're pathetic, Riley."

"No? Well, they should. I won't even go to the bathroom on my own these days. How pathetic is that?"

With that, Riley leans against the wall as if standing is suddenly too much. A single black tear makes its way down her cheek and drips from the tip of her chin.

"You know what I hate the most?" she whispers. "That everyone in there knows what happened to me. At least they think they do, but they don't *know* what happened. No one ever will. No one will ever be able to understand what it was like."

Riley's words twist my soul. For the second time, our similarities strike me like a bolt of lightning.

I take a step towards her. "You're right, they won't, but they can understand what it's like to be hurt in a way that no one should be. After what we've lived through, we don't find that in a lot of places. But what you experienced? That pain? That's yours to carry."

Riley fixes her gaze on me, her blue eyes piercing. "No one's ever said that to me before. All they say is, 'I know how you feel'."

"That old chestnut," I reply, rolling my eyes. "How could anyone know what surviving hell is like unless they lived through it too? Even in your worst nightmares, you can't picture it vividly enough."

"Exactly. My mum keeps telling me she understands, but how can she? She's been with my dad since she was sixteen. She was never… that never happened to her."

My heart twists at the scorn in Riley's voice, a mirror of the same scorn I would speak to my own mum with. When she was nearing the end of her life, all I wanted to do was apologise for the way I'd treated her, but I didn't know where to begin. Day after day, I went to the hospice and watched the body that had held me tight on my worst days shrink as illness consumed it, but I still couldn't find the words. The way Mum gripped my hand, though, told me she knew what I wanted to say. It told me she understood, she forgave me, that she'd take every insult I threw at her if it meant I found my way back to being okay again.

With a cough, I clear the emotion that comes from remembering that time from my throat. "You're right, she can't understand, but if she could trade places with you, she would. She'd take this hurt from you in a heartbeat."

A heaviness sweeps over me as one of the most painful memories with my mum echoes through my brain. Me slamming my bedroom door in her face, her on the other side of the wooden barrier screaming, 'If I could take away your pain, I would. I'd take it all'.

Defeated, I sit on the floor and tilt my head to look up at Riley. "I don't know your story, Riley. I really don't – I don't read the news – but if you're here then it can't be a good one. All I can say is I'm sorry you went through that, and I'm sorry you feel pressured to talk about it, but you don't have to say anything in these meetings unless you want to."

"I don't want to say anything about it ever, that's the point."

"Well, that's fine too. At the end of the day, you're the one who decides what you need to do to be okay."

Riley studies me, her eyes brimming with tears. "What if I don't know what I need to do to be okay?"

"Then that's okay too. You don't have to have all the answers right now. In fact, you don't need any answers right now. You're here, you're trying. That's all anyone can ask for."

Riley slumps to the floor beside me. "How did you get through it?" she asks after a beat of silence.

"Time, I guess. It's taken a long time to get to where I am today," I admit, but then I remember who I'm talking to. "It sounds cliché, I know, but it gets better. I don't wake up consumed by what happened anymore. It doesn't control me like it once did. It wasn't easy, but I got there. I surrounded myself with good people, I talked, I attended meetings."

Riley shoots me a sideways look.

"I know it feels like the last thing you want to do, but talking to people who understand even a fraction of what this feels like helps more than you think. We all need to know we're not alone, especially when that's how we've been made to feel."

"I just hate that Tanya's trying to make me think what happened is okay."

"She's not doing that, Riley. What she's trying to do is show you that it's not the end."

Riley nods. After that, we don't speak. We just sit side by side, lost in our own thoughts, close but not touching, until the sound of chairs scraping across the floor pulls us from our silence.

"The meeting has finished. Everyone will be coming out in a second," I say, stretching to awaken my stiff back. "Do you want to go back in before they leave?"

Riley shakes her head. "I don't want them to see me again after I stormed out."

"Okay. Come with me," I say.

I lead Riley to the bathroom at the end of the corridor and lock the door behind us. We listen to the meeting room doors swing open and the group leave. They file down the corridor towards the stairs, chatting amongst themselves. I can tell from their voices that some have cried, but even with a door between us, I can hear how relieved they are to have shown up.

When everyone's gone, I turn to Riley. "Should we go into the meeting room while we wait for your mum?"

"I'm not sure Tanya will want me there after I shouted at her."

"Trust me, Tanya's the most patient person ever. The first time I met her I was nothing short of horrible, but she still ended my session saying she couldn't wait to see me next time. She'll welcome you back with open arms, I promise."

"Even if I don't deserve it?"

"Even if you don't deserve it."

Riley hesitates, but she unlocks the bathroom door. I follow her back to the meeting room where we find Tanya stacking chairs. She smiles when she sees us. "I told the others to let me tidy up. I've not been to the gym in months, I could do with the workout."

"Do you... do you want any help?" Riley offers.

"That would be lovely," Tanya says. She turns her attention back to tidying, but as Riley gets to work, she catches my eye and mouths, 'Thank you'.

The sound of stacking chairs narrates the stillness between the three of us. There's something oddly peaceful about the rhythmical clinking of metal and plastic. I close my eyes, listening to my goodbye Sisterhood of Support lullaby.

You've done it. You never have to attend a meeting again.

The strongest wave of peace overcomes me at that thought. A smile dances on my lips, one that's only wiped away when the meeting room door buzzes open and Sarah rushes into the room. "I'm so sorry I'm late," she pants. "I went to the supermarket to pass the time and got stuck in a queue. I didn't forget you, Riley, I promise."

Sarah's frantic upset jars with the serenity we've coexisted in. I watch Riley shrink away from it, disappearing back into her baggy clothing.

Tanya notices too. She approaches Sarah and rests her hand on her forearm. "It's okay. These things happen."

Sarah's shoulders fall and, for a moment, I think she's about to collapse. "I can't believe I'm late picking her up. After everything that's happened, I wasn't here when she needed me."

"Hey, it's not your fault. There's nothing you could have done to change the way the night's gone," Tanya soothes, her words carrying so much weight given the circumstances.

Sarah's lips twitch before she looks at Riley. "Did you… did you have a good time?"

"I guess," Riley replies. She flashes me the faintest smile before walking towards her mother. "Can we go now?" Without waiting for an answer, Riley leaves the room.

Sarah turns to Tanya as if she has more to say, but she scurries after her daughter instead. Inside my chest, my heart breaks all over again.

When the door closes behind them, Tanya lets out a long, steady sigh. "Well, that was an interesting session!"

"Never a dull moment at Sisterhood of Support."

"Never," Tanya laughs as she runs her hand over her cropped hair.

"Do you think Riley will be back?"

"Yes," she answers without hesitation. "How about you? Will you be back?"

I shake my head. "I'm done, Tanya. I'm okay now." With the meeting over and no Riley to act as a haunting reminder of who I used to be, those words finally feel true again.

"Oh, Hannah," Tanya replies, disappointment coating her features. "I was half-hoping meeting Riley and seeing how much you could help her might change your mind."

"Riley's got you. She's got all the help she needs."

"Maybe, but still – you spent your entire last meeting outside! We didn't get to say a proper goodbye."

"It's better this way. You know I'm terrible at goodbyes, and saying goodbye to everyone here? Well, that's too much to handle." My voice cracks at the end of my sentence, and I hate myself for it.

It's as if the realisation that this is it hits Tanya too because her eyes suddenly fill with tears. "Sorry," she says, waving her hand in front of her face. "I promise I don't usually get like this! It's just... I feel like we've been working towards this day for a long time, only now it's here I'm not sure I want it to be. Ten years I've known you. Ten years of watching you grow. I think of you as a friend, one I can't imagine not seeing twice a week. Silly, isn't it?"

"It's not silly. I think the same of you too, but seeing me twice a week when I've nothing to talk about sounds boring. I mean, who wants to listen to a story about how I almost broke Break Time's coffee machine again?" I joke, nudging Tanya with my elbow.

She splutters on an empty laugh. "You know I'd listen to you tell me what you had for breakfast, Hannah. You don't have to talk about what happened to keep your place here."

"I know, but there are people who need your help more than I do. They deserve your energy. It's time for my seat to go to someone else."

Tanya nods, but sadness still seeps from her. Suddenly, the pain of saying goodbye to my mentor is too much. I think of my history with Tanya – how she took every angry word I fired her way, how she wiped away every devastated tear and helped me after Mum died and I fell into the habit of taking pills until I forgot I'd lost her. My bottom lip wobbles and for one fearful moment, I'm about to change my mind, but then Tanya takes my hand in hers.

"Ignore me, Hannah. This is a good thing. You wanting to live your life on your own terms is all I could ask for! It's what we've been working towards for so long now, and I couldn't be prouder that you've got there. Just promise me one thing?"

"Anything."

"Promise me you'll visit. Even if it's only once a year, come back and visit me. After all this time, I'm not sure what my life looks like without Hannah Allen in it, and I don't want to find out."

I'm too choked up to respond, so I let my body do the talking by pulling Tanya into a hug. I hold her close, squeezing as if the pressure I exert can let her know how much her guidance has changed, and saved, my life.

The way Tanya holds me back tells me she knows.

Sniffing back my tears, I pull out of the embrace. "I'd better go before I start crying and leave a trail of snot on your jumper."

"Something to remember you by?" Tanya jokes. We laugh, our upset momentarily pushed aside so I can maintain the courage to walk away.

I locate my handbag on the floor in the centre of the room, exposed now the chairs have been tidied away. I sling it over my shoulder, ready to leave, but as I'm about to take my first step into freedom, there's a knock at the door.

I look through the window of glass and instantly wish I hadn't.

A foreboding figure peers back at me. The same foreboding figure I wake up every day wishing never to see again.

Detective Inspector Conrad Wallace, a man who, ten years after we first met, has somehow found himself back in my life, which can only mean one thing – something is terribly, terribly wrong.

Chapter *Four.*

Tanya fusses around, setting up a formation of chairs for us to sit on and pouring glasses of water even though no one asked for a drink. Conrad and I don't bother exchanging pleasantries while she does this. We both know I'm not pleased to see him and, judging by the agonised expression on his weathered face, he wishes he wasn't here as much as I do.

When there is nothing else for Tanya to do, she takes a seat. Her hand brushes the top of my back in reassurance, but I'm so thrown off by Conrad's sudden reappearance I barely notice the gesture.

"Conrad," she enthuses. "It's been a while!"

As Conrad nods in response, I take a moment to study him. The time that's passed since we last met hasn't been kind to him. His dull skin sags sadly, his wrinkles deep, his shoulders slumped as if carrying an invisible burden. An air of defeat surrounds him. He's nothing like the spirited detective I once knew, the one who cut me free of the gardening wire that bound my wrists and ankles and told me I was safe.

Sitting opposite Conrad in this worn-out state, you'd be forgiven for thinking he was the victim of trauma, not me. After all, I've spent years carefully crafting my image so that if we met, you would never suspect I was the girl who survived a fate no one was supposed to live through.

I wonder if Conrad is surprised to see me like this. So settled, so normal.

Long, brown hair I use a conditioning treatment on weekly. Nails I get painted in muted shades of pink at a local salon. A wardrobe of modern, stylish clothes.

But more than how I look is the life I lead. The life I built for myself, brick by brick. A job I'm good at, one I enjoy, one I attend even on bad days. Colleagues I call friends and a support network I can rely on. Living with a devoted boyfriend in a home filled with precious memories and knickknacks. Plans for buying our first house that we will hopefully fill with a family one day.

When Conrad found me, I remember shouting at him that I might as well be dead. Well, look at me now, Conrad. I'm living. I'm really living.

Or at least I was until he showed up.

"Why are you here?" I ask before Tanya can continue to fill the silence with awkward small talk.

As Conrad's tired eyes meet mine, I try to steel myself for whatever he's about to say, but nothing could prepare me for the news he delivers.

"I'm here to speak to you about someone. Gabriella O'Hara, I'm sure you've heard of her?"

I shake my head.

"Hannah doesn't watch the news," Tanya explains on my behalf.

"Well, Gabriella O'Hara was a missing schoolgirl, like you," Conrad explains. "She disappeared, like you."

An unexpected burst of fury bites me. "I didn't disappear – I was taken."

Conrad's cheeks flush at his faux pas. "My apologies, Hannah. You didn't disappear. Neither did Gabriella. Unfortunately, unlike you, she didn't make it."

The air is strangled out of the room. Tanya holds my hand in hers, but I take no comfort from it. I'm too focused on the thought of an empty seat in a classroom. Too aware that somewhere out there in a messy, poster-lined teenage bedroom lies a bed that a girl called Gabriella O'Hara will never sleep in again.

But Conrad isn't done with his bombshells. As I watch him struggle under the weight of what he's trying to tell me, my lungs constrict.

"There were some… interesting details at the crime scene. Details I need to make you aware of. I know the last time we met, you asked to be left in peace but I'm afraid that's no longer an option."

The hairs on my arms stand to attention. "What do you mean?"

"The discovery of a body is going to be all over the news tomorrow. Once we confirm publicly that it's Gabriella O'Hara, we can only keep details of the crime scene under wraps for so long. I wanted you to hear it from me first. There's no easy way to say this, Hannah, but there are significant similarities between the Peter Harris murders and the killing that's happened now."

"Similarities?" I ask, my voice barely a whisper. "What similarities?"

Conrad's pained expression deepens.

"Conrad, what similarities?" I ask again.

This time, Conrad concedes that he must tell me more. "Like with Peter Harris's victims, there was a numerical brand on Gabriella O'Hara's body, only this time the number wasn't tattooed onto her. This time it was carved into her skin."

Beside me, Tanya gasps. My reaction isn't audible but it's just as horrified. My skin burns hot and cold all over, the ink in the number eleven tattoo on my abdomen bubbling into life. The brand Peter Harris forced on me the day I was taken.

"Gabriella O'Hara was number twelve?" I hear myself ask.

Conrad shifts in his seat. "With this being an active investigation, I can't discuss –"

"Conrad, don't," I cut in, suddenly furious at him for bringing this unwelcome news into my life. "I'm not someone you can palm off with a vague line about police procedures or confidentiality policies. After everything that's happened to me, after everything we've been through, we don't have that relationship. If you're here to tell me something, then

I deserve to know it properly."

I hold Conrad's gaze, my stubbornness so different to the version of me he last met.

Conrad gives a small nod, then he clasps his hands together so tightly I can see his knuckles beneath his skin. "Gabriella wasn't branded with a number twelve. She was branded with a number thirteen."

My eyebrows furrow. "But if I'm eleven, how can Gabriella be thirteen? Why would someone skip a number?"

When Conrad's face remains impassive, it hits me.

"They didn't skip a number," I say, sitting back in my seat. "You've just not found number twelve yet."

"We have officers searching –"

Fury bites me once more. "How can someone go missing and no one notice?"

"There are lots of reasons, Hannah. They could be someone without a fixed address, they could be prone to bouts of disappearance or someone who lives alone. They could –"

"I've heard enough," I say, shaking my head. "I don't want to be part of this."

"Hannah," Tanya says, but her measured tone infuriates me.

"No! Don't you get it? I don't want to have this bullshit in my life again!"

"Hannah, I know it's hard to hear but there are things you need to know," Conrad says. "I had to come here and inform you. This information is something we're going to keep from the press for as long as we can, but it's important you know now. Gabriella had…" Conrad lowers his gaze so he doesn't have to look at me when he delivers his next blow. "Gabriella had a copy of your missing poster in her hand when she was found. Written on it were the words, '*The story continues*'."

Conrad's words pin me to my chair. The news swirls around my brain, distorting and jumbling until I'm blinded by the fear of what this means.

"But... but Peter Harris is in prison, isn't he?" I hear myself ask. "You told me he was going to be in prison for life. He killed ten women, he abducted and raped them, he –"

"Peter Harris is in prison," Conrad confirms. "This isn't his doing."

"So it's someone else?"

"Yes, Hannah, it's someone else."

With that confirmation, the bottom of my world falls away. I free fall, waiting to be caught by a safety net that never arrives while scouring Conrad's face for a trace of uncertainty I never find.

"Why would someone *do* this?" I cry. "Peter Harris is a monster. Why would... why would..."

"Hannah, breathe," Tanya soothes, rubbing circles on my back with her palm before turning to Conrad. "You must be able to tell us more, Conrad? I know this is an active investigation but please, this is Hannah's life we're talking about. Once the press finds out about the missing poster and the brand, they will be all over her. Hannah needs to know what she's walking into."

Conrad pauses for a moment then slips his hand inside his coat pocket. He pulls something out, holding it up for all to see.

Instantly, I recoil.

Peter Harris's evil eyes stare back at me, drilling into my soul just like they did when I was his captive. Over the top of his dark, slicked-back hair, the words '*Peter Harris and the Unlucky Eleven*' scream in blood-red text. Then, written on top of his ornately tattooed neck, is the name of the man I have come to detest almost as much as I do Peter Harris – Nathaniel Clarke.

Nathaniel Clarke, the author of the most sensationalist book ever written. A man who saw the ten-year anniversary of a serial killer's arrest as something to cash in on regardless of what rehashing that pain did to those who knew his victims. A man who saw no harm in harassing me with calls, emails, and letters for a year, doing all he could to try and coax an interview from me. A man who, in my opinion, deserves to be sitting in the cell next to Peter Harris. His crime? Not having a decent bone in his body.

And now his book is in front of me.

"Get that thing away from me," I whisper.

When Conrad doesn't move the book straight away, Tanya pushes it into his chest. "She said to put it away, Conrad."

Conrad slips the book back inside his coat, but I can still feel Peter Harris's eyes staring at me through the material of the jacket. Eyes I've fought to forget. Ones I thought were going to be the last thing I ever saw.

I shudder so violently that for a moment I think I'm going to be sick. Tanya squeezes my hand. I grip on to her, the bones in her hand hard against the bones in my own.

"I know you refused to give Nathaniel Clarke an interview, and I can't say I blame you," Conrad continues. "This book is… well, the less said about it the better, but we believe it explains why these killings have started now. We're operating under the guise that it's not a coincidence that a mere three months after this book was published, we have a killer out there copying key parts of Peter Harris's methodology."

I gulp at Conrad's choice of words. "His methodology?"

When Conrad nods to confirm his statement, I break inside. Peter Harris's methodology flashes through my mind in short, sharp bursts of tortured memories. Small but brutally deep cuts that would heal but scar. Showing you his instruments of torture before using them so you knew exactly what was coming and how much it would hurt. Smiling at every desperate plea for help, those dazzling white teeth flashing like it was all a game, one only he knew the rules for.

Peter Harris's methodology – pain, suffering, surrender.

"Whether Nathaniel Clarke intended to write it in this way or not, his book is almost an A to Z of what Harris did to his victims," Conrad explains. "It details everything from his preparation before abductions to why each individual was chosen. We think someone is using it like an instruction manual."

Conrad's eyes lock on mine and, despite his best efforts to mask it, I see the fear in them.

"I came here to warn you, Hannah. I know you distance yourself from what happened, but I'm afraid there is no distancing yourself from this. Whoever is doing this is carrying on Peter Harris's story, and you, I'm afraid, are a part of that."

"But I don't want to be part of it!"

Conrad caves in on himself. "I know, Hannah, I know."

Tanya leans forward, shielding me from the upset of the man who is supposed to keep Peter Harris and everything to do with him out of my life. "Is Hannah safe?"

"Yes," Conrad replies, a little too quickly for me to fully believe him. "This visit is just a precaution. With our history, I wanted to tell you what was going on myself. I came here on my own because I knew you'd appreciate the discretion, but I'm not the only person working to protect you, Hannah. With this case being so high profile, we are going to throw everything we can your way to keep you feeling safe."

"Like what?"

"I have a panic alarm here for you to wear whenever you are home, and one for your partner too. If you push the red button, the police will be at your door within minutes."

Conrad presents me with two plastic devices, but my arms won't move to take them from him. Tanya accepts them for me.

"You want me to wear a panic alarm? And Joel too?" I ask. When Conrad nods, I close my eyes. Joel, sweet Joel. Stressed about deadlines and trying to save the world, one abandoned puppy at a time. Joel who must now be weighed down by the noose of a panic alarm, all because he fell in love with me.

"What else have you put in place?" Tanya asks.

"Usually we'd offer counselling, but I know Hannah attends regular sessions here. You can keep up with these or I can arrange for additional support, the choice is yours."

I keep my eyes shut, trying to blot out the fact that ten minutes ago I was leaving therapy altogether, and now I'm being offered more.

"I've also asked for officers to intermittently visit your place of work to see that you're okay and report any issues. Tomorrow I'm going to come to work with you and explain to your colleagues what's happening –"

My eyes snap open. "But I don't think my colleagues know who I am. I've never told them."

Conrad's face twists. "I'm sorry, Hannah, but they're going to have to find out."

That's the moment I crumble. Ellen, Stefan, and the customers who give generous tips and ask how my day is going... never again will they see me as simply 'Hannah the waitress'. I choke on a sob. Everything I have worked for, the life I fought so hard to create... gone.

"It's okay, Hannah, it's okay. It's better they find out now, not later via a headline," Tanya soothes, but I barely hear her over the sound of my cries.

Conrad shuffles awkwardly. He never was good with emotion. "What time do you start work tomorrow?"

"Half past six," I sniff.

"Well, we'll get there at quarter past. Text your team to come in a little earlier. They will need to be aware of what's happening so they know to keep an eye out for you."

"Keep an eye out?" I echo.

Conrad winces as he sees the depths of my fear. He tries to give me a reassuring smile, only coming from him, a smile is anything but comforting. "We have no reason to believe you're in danger, Hannah. I cannot reiterate enough how this visit is simply precautionary. These measures are simply for your peace of mind. Please try to continue as normal. Things will be okay – you have every resource in the police force on your side."

I want to believe him, I really do, but I was meant to be safe walking home from school, wasn't I? Only Peter Harris saw to it that I wasn't, and now there's someone out there, continuing what he started. Knowing that, how can anyone expect me to believe them when they tell me I'm safe?

Chapter *Five.*

Despite my protests, Tanya insists on driving me home once Conrad has left. I begrudgingly accept her offer, all the while doing my best to ignore the relief I feel from someone taking care of me.

We leave Sisterhood of Support together, walking in sync until we reach the ground floor. I pause and look through the glass in the front door, taking in the darkness waiting for us on the other side.

"Are you okay?" Tanya asks.

My grip on my handbag tightens as I slot my brave face into place. "Why wouldn't I be?" I reply, then I force myself to leave the building.

Stepping outside is like stepping onto an alien planet, one that looks like home but couldn't be further from it if it tried. Menacing shadows linger where the streetlights can't quite reach. The beat of unease that's not existed in my life for so long now once again thumps in the air.

I take in this new, strange reality in disbelief. Hours ago, I had put enough distance between myself and what happened to attend my last Sisterhood of Support meeting, but now here I am, living a new nightmare.

Tanya unlocks her battered red car, the flash of its headlights rousing me from the grip of fear. "Here we are," she says, opening the passenger door and removing a stuffed tote bag from the footwell. "Sorry it's a little messy."

Climbing into the car, I can't help but laugh. Messy is an understatement. Empty water bottles, random papers, and discarded items of clothing are strewn across the backseat. "Tanya, this car is almost as bad as your desk!"

"Earlier you said mess was loveable, okay? Let's keep it at that," Tanya grins, then she starts the ignition and sets off.

Melodic music filters through the speakers as Tanya drives. She's a firm believer in the restorative power of music and, as the gentle sound washes over me, I succumb to her school of thought. The tightness at the base of my neck eases and I turn to look out of the window.

The city I know so well passes by, flashes of life here for a second then gone in the next. This northern landscape of high-rise offices and grey skies is my home. The place I grew up. The place I refused to leave despite what happened to me here. With time, I've reclaimed these streets. I've walked them as a studious schoolgirl, as a headline-grabbing victim, and as the woman I am now.

But who am I now that the past is being re-lived? I thought I'd progressed beyond being known as 'Lucky Number 11'. I thought I'd reclaimed the name Hannah Allen.

An aching claws at my insides, one that doesn't let go, not even when Tanya slows to a stop outside my apartment. "Do you want me to come in with you and tell Joel what's happened?" she asks.

"I think it's best coming from me. Thanks, though."

Tanya nods and takes hold of my hand. "It's going to be okay, Hannah."

I almost laugh at her confidence. "What if it's not?"

"It will be. You have your friends around you, a partner who loves you, and me. I will never leave your side. You know that, don't you?"

Despite everything making me feel like doing the opposite, I smile. "I do know that. Thanks, Tanya," I say. "I should go inside before Joel starts worrying about where I am. Thanks for the ride."

"Anytime."

I exit the car before the reassurance Tanya filled me with leaves my head. I'm so focused on making it inside that I only notice someone walking out of the building at the same time I'm walking into it when our bodies collide.

"Oops, sorry," I say, stepping back to let the woman pass. Her stressful energy swipes me, jarring with my own equally frazzled state.

"Thanks," she says, manoeuvring the pram she's pushing through the front door. Once outside, she glances at two young boys giggling in the foyer behind her. "Jake, Ollie, whatever you're doing, stop!" The woman turns to me, her patience fried. "I swear, if they're not falling out with each other, they're getting into mischief."

I smile politely then look at the two boys. They're nudging each other and giggling like they know a secret that we don't. As I take in their cheeky faces, I remember who they are, and who the woman is. She's the woman from apartment one, the parent of the two pranksters in our building. Last month's antic was to knock on people's doors and then run away before they answered. The month before that, they posted unflattering portraits of residents under their doors. Joel's portrait is still stuck on our fridge, the nose they drew on him so comically large we couldn't bear to throw the picture away.

"Come on! We've got to get to and from the shops before bedtime," the woman snaps. The change in her voice does the trick and the boys scurry after her. After flashing me an apologetic grimace, she leads her family away.

I watch them go, the gate of the apartment building swinging shut behind them. As soon as they melt into the darkness, an oppressive loneliness constricts me. I don't give it a second to set in before I spill into the building with such momentum that my handbag slips from my shoulder and lands at my feet.

When I reach to pick it up, I spot it – a poorly folded piece of paper on the doormat. The second one that's been there this week and the sixth I've found in total.

My blood freezes, the stark white paper taking on a new significance after the events of the day, but I shake myself from my paranoia. 'Danger exists but it doesn't exist in everything' is one of Tanya's favourite sayings. I repeat it to myself as I collect the note.

It's another drawing, this one just as odd as the rest of them. It depicts a stick person running with the words '*Let's play hide and seek*' written above it. The other notes were poorly drawn cartoons accompanied by a short, game-related phrase too. And, like the others, there's no name on this note to indicate who it's from or who it's to.

My body shudders like it always does when anything unusual interrupts the contented equilibrium I exist in, then I move my gaze to the door of apartment one. The home of two boys with a love of pranks. Two boys who stood in this spot seconds ago, giggling.

You're doing it again – you're looking for danger in everything, I warn myself.

Screwing the paper into a tight ball, I race upstairs to my apartment, but as soon as I open the front door, a loud bang rings out.

Instinctively, my fingers clamp around my key, ready to stab it into someone's flesh should I need to, but then I blink in the scene. Multicoloured streamers float through the air, grazing against my skin as they make their way to the ground. A homemade banner hangs from the wall, boasting the word '*Congratulations*' in bright pink letters.

Then, through the rainbow haze of streamers, I see him. Joel, stood tall and proud, a glass of champagne in his outstretched hand.

Joel who is still under the illusion that tonight I have broken free of the binds of my past.

"Surprise!" he cheers. "You did it!"

Joel's happiness flattens me in a way he will never know. As I crumble to my knees, he rushes to my side and wraps me in his arms.

"Hannah, what is it? What's happened?"

I choke on my tears, unable to breathe, never mind reply. Joel tucks my hair behind my ears and searches my face for answers. Plucking up the last scrap of bravery I have left today, I speak.

"There's… there's a copycat killer."

That's all I need to say to find myself in Joel's embrace once more. I try to focus on the way his arms encase me or the feel of the carpet against my feet, but my mind is elsewhere. It's with the schoolgirl who didn't make it home and the unknown figure who ended her life before it had the chance to start.

Chapter *Six.*

The dregs of the champagne Joel bought to celebrate my new freedom sour my mouth. My head pounds already, a hangover most definitely on the cards, but the numbing effect of alcohol is worth whatever pain tomorrow will bring.

I drain my glass and rest it on the coffee table, then check my phone. Tanya's sent me a list of breathing exercises to do if I struggle to sleep tonight, and the Sisterhood of Support group chat is full of notifications from people wishing we'd had the chance to say a proper goodbye. My eyes burn with tears as I read over their kind sentiments, a message from Amrita particularly sticking with me.

Hannah, I refuse to let tonight be my last meeting with you!!!! COME BACK OR THERE WILL BE TROUBLE xx

The words 'last meeting' mock me from the screen.

"I came so close to leaving it all behind," I say, the sadness of my words catching at the back of my throat.

From the other end of the sofa, Joel reaches for me. "Hey, this doesn't change anything," he says, but my eyes drop to the panic alarm around his neck. The one he insisted on wearing even though I refuse to wear mine.

Joel rests his hand on the plastic casing to conceal it. "What's happened is a huge shock, but it doesn't have to alter anything if you don't want it to. Think about it this way – do you want to go to another meeting?"

Even with the events of the night clouding my vision, the glimmer of my Thursday evenings and Saturday afternoons being my own once more shines through. "No, I don't."

"Then nothing has changed. You're still leaving like you planned to. How was the meeting, anyway? We can talk about it if you want to. You decide – a hug and a chat or a bar of chocolate and some time on your own?"

I can't fight my smile. Joel and I came up with that code early on in our relationship, and it has saved us from many miscommunications along the way.

Years of therapy and a few short-term relationships had helped me learn what I did and didn't want in a partner by the time I met Joel, but intimacy was still something I struggled with. Luckily for me, Joel was kind and patient. Our first kiss was on our sixth date, surrounded by Christmas lights after we watched them being turned on for the first time.

"Well, that was more than worth the wait," he whispered when we finally broke apart.

But even with Joel's considerate nature and the gentle pace of our courtship, emotional intimacy didn't come naturally to me. It still doesn't, to some extent. With my feelings boxed away, I can live an ordinary life. I can put on a nice dress and smile or serve coffee to people I used to know from school without wanting to cry. This way of living has ensured my survival, but loving someone who's constructed a wall like that isn't always easy.

"We need to come up with a way of letting the other person know if we need space or time together. Something silly, something only we use, but something that shows me how I can best be there for you, and how you can best be there for me," Joel said. He suggested the line 'a hug and a chat or a bar of chocolate and some time alone'.

"That means we'll always have to have chocolate on standby," I replied.

"I can think of worse things to always have in the house."

And just like that, our code was invented.

One of the things I love most about Joel is how he never presses me for details about my past or pushes me to speak if I'm not ready to. For most people, as soon as they find out I'm *the* Hannah Allen, they can't help themselves. Within seconds of uncovering my identity, unwelcome questions tumble from their lips, but that never happened with Joel. The first thing he said when I told him about my past was, 'At least you're not telling me you're famous for being on reality TV'. A terrible joke, but one that cut the tension of my confession.

"There's a bar of Dairy Milk in the fridge if you need it," Joel offers, poised as if he's ready to run into the kitchen should I say yes.

"Honestly, I'm okay. There's not much to say about the meeting – I didn't spend a lot of time in it. There was a new girl. She shouted at Tanya then walked out, so I sat with her in the corridor."

"Poor Tanya. She won't have known what to do when someone didn't worship her."

"Well, Riley definitely didn't worship her," I grimace.

"Riley?"

I nod. "Riley Hunt."

Joel does his best not to react, but his face pales at the mention of Riley's name.

"What is it?"

"Nothing," he replies, a tell-tale blush creeping up his neck.

"Joel," I say, my voice carrying with it a warning tone.

Joel wavers, but he knows me well enough to know he can't stay silent now. "Riley Hunt is the new girl in your group? Wow, Hannah. That poor kid."

My throat closes. "What happened to her?"

"I... I'm not sure I should say."

"Tell me."

Joel meets my gaze, his expression agonised.

"Tell me," I repeat, more forcefully this time. My brain screams at me for making this demand, but there's something about the way Joel's body collapsed in on itself at the mention of Riley's name that I can't ignore.

Joel reaches for my hand. "A few weeks ago, Riley Hunt went to a house party. Apparently, her parents banned her from going, so she snuck out. You know how it is when you're seventeen and just want to be around your friends, but her doing that was enough for some people to say she deserved what happened to her."

As Joel shakes his head sadly, my lips twitch into a knowing snarl. I'd love to be like Joel, innocent to that toxic side of humanity and outraged whenever it rears its ugly head, but people choosing to blame the victim rather than the person inflicting the pain isn't news to me. I was a fourteen-year-old girl abducted on her way home from school, yet a subsection of people found a way to make what happened my fault.

"She shouldn't have been walking home alone."

"Have you seen how short schoolgirls' skirts are these days? They're asking for trouble going around dressed like that."

"You mean to tell me she wasn't flattered by the attention of an older man? Of course she was! She probably jumped into that car."

Those people would tell you what Peter Harris did was wrong, of course, but only after reciting all the ways I could have saved myself. Because surely every fourteen-year-old carries a rape alarm? Surely they've taken self-defence classes to learn how to fight off a grown man? Surely they know which routes to take and which ones to avoid, how loud to scream to attract attention, and what to wear to hide from predators?

Blame the girl, the route, the outfit. Anything but admit we've allowed evil to breed in this world.

Joel's voice cuts through my anger. "Riley Hunt was a kid who wanted to go to a party, we've all been there, but when she did it? Well, when she was walking to her friend's house, a guy called Phillip Reynor pulled up and asked for directions, then he dragged her into his car."

My blood turns to ice, and immediately I am back where my nightmare began.

I can feel a gloved hand on my forearm, the grip so strong I can't wriggle free. My legs clench. I try to run but I'm unable to move. A scream is trapped in my throat, one that stays in my mouth forever because a hand clamps over my lips and holds it there. Then I am being pulled. Wrenched from reality and bundled into an unknown vehicle by a stranger intent on taking me with him.

"Riley Hunt was held captive for two days before someone who got lost on a hike walked past the house and heard her screams." Joel speaks softly, but the gentle delivery does nothing to protect me from his spiked words.

We sit in silence, Joel's hand on mine. I hold tight. Reality is safe. Joel is safe. My mind, my memories, are not.

"The good thing is she was saved. That's always something, isn't it?" Joel says after a few moments, his bright tone trying its best to lift the heavy mood.

I don't reply. I know better than anyone that surviving doesn't always feel positive. You don't want to be saved after the bad thing has happened – you want it not to occur in the first place.

Sometimes, even years later when life is good again, the thought that slipping away in the middle of all the pain and fear would have been easier than pushing past it creeps into my consciousness. I never tell Joel, never tell anyone but Tanya, but that thought lives in me. The seed is planted for life, thanks to Peter Harris.

I sigh and stretch, my tight muscles shocked by the sudden movement. "I think I need to go to bed. Put today behind me, you know?"

"I'll come with you," Joel says, rising to his feet.

Neither of us comments on the fact that we usually go to bed an hour later than this. We keep silent about the fact that I check the door is locked twice, and that Joel gets out of bed to check it once more too. In fact, outside of 'Goodnight, I love you', we say very little to each other, but the silence between us speaks volumes.

Joel sleeps with his body wrapped around mine as if he can take my pain away by being my human blanket. The gesture brings tears to my eyes, but it doesn't work. Every car that drives past, every groan and ache our apartment makes, has me trembling.

I know that I could wake Joel and he would stay up with me all night if I asked him to. He would watch over me while I slept and do everything in his power to keep me feeling safe, but I can't wake him. I refuse to. For ten years, I have fought to be a woman who can fall asleep without needing a weapon by her pillow. For ten years, I have clawed my way back to normality. I can't go back on that now.

But in the darkness, flinching at every sound, my ability to stay in the mindset of Hannah Allen as she is today wavers. My mind wanders to the place I don't like it to go. To Peter Harris and the past I so firmly avoid.

I remember my first Sisterhood of Support meeting. Three weeks after being found and a few days after my name stopped being a daily fixture in the national newspapers. 'Hannah Allen – Lucky Number 11.'

"Lucky?" I would scowl. "There's nothing lucky about what happened to me."

But of course, to everyone else I *was* lucky. I was the sole survivor of Peter Harris's house of horrors. Unlike the other women he took, I escaped with my life. Sure, I had mental and physical scars, not to mention the crudely finished number eleven tattoo he etched onto my stomach, but I was alive, wasn't I? I was free. I'd get to live the life that for the entire time I was captive I was sure would be taken from me. I was *lucky.*

Only try telling that to a fourteen-year-old girl whose innocence was ripped from her in the most brutal manner. Try telling that to a teenager who has started to wet the bed again, who is so scared to go outside that she will scream and cry and make herself sick to avoid it. Tell her she is lucky.

Lucky – how one word can mean completely different things to different people.

Each time I close my eyes to try to sleep, flashes of Peter Harris's basement burst into my brain.

I don't remember the whole ordeal. I've learned through counselling that the brain can block out severe trauma. It's amazing how it knows to wrap a thick, amnesia-like bandage around certain moments to save us from crumbling irrevocably.

The parts I do remember turn me to stone even all these years later. The dirty mattress where previous victims had also laid to sleep, to cry, to be tortured. The dark stains on the floor, ones I convinced myself were bloodstains. Ones that were later confirmed to be my worst fears. The creak of the door as Peter Harris opened it, inviting a sharp slice of light to cut through the darkness. The slow, methodical sound of his footsteps drawing closer as he made his way down the stairs…

By the time my alarm goes off at 5:15am, my bloodshot eyes are already staring at it.

"Did you sleep okay?" Joel whispers.

"Better than I thought I would," I lie. I make a move to get up, but Joel grabs my face before I can flee the bedroom.

"It's going to be okay. No one is going to hurt you. They won't get the chance to, not with me around." Even in the darkness, I can see Joel's dark eyes boring into mine and willing me to believe him.

I push myself free from him before he can feel my damp cheeks. "My hero," I whisper, kissing Joel's forehead and leaving the room.

I get ready for work in a trance. My limbs move like ghosts, stirring a cup of tea I forget to drink, then packing a lunch I know I'll have no appetite to eat.

But it's when looking in the mirror that I see the real disconnect between myself and my new life. Applying makeup to the pale face staring back at me is like painting the face of a stranger. I almost convince myself it is a stranger until I touch my cheek and gasp at my fingertips brushing against my skin.

You're a mess, the voice inside my head sneers. *You've not looked this tired in years.*

Clenching my teeth, I force myself to apply a coat of mascara. First to my left eye, then to my right. Instantly, I look more alert. Next, I run a stick of lip balm across my lips, tingeing them pink.

This time when I look in the mirror, my reflection does its best to smile back at me.

Then, at 6:00am, the intercom buzzes.

Joel had slipped back into sleep, but the jolt of sound shakes him awake. "I'll get it," he says, rushing past me so he can reach the door first. I notice the panic alarm swinging around his neck and something inside my chest fizzes.

"Joel, it's only going to be Conrad."

"I know, but I'd rather check instead of you doing it," Joel replies. He holds down the intercom's speaker button, an undeniable fear in his eyes. "Hello?"

"It's Conrad."

Joel's relief is so strong I taste it. Appeased, he buzzes Conrad into the building then waits by the front door, his hand coiled around the panic alarm, just in case.

When a knock at the door sounds, Joel opens it to unveil Conrad, who somehow looks even more tired this morning than he did last night. The pair introduce themselves, shaking hands and sizing the other up.

When Conrad's finished his assessment, he eyes my neck. "Where's your panic alarm?"

"You said to wear it at home. We're leaving in a second," I reply.

In reality, my panic alarm hasn't graced my body once since Conrad gave it to me.

"Does this mean you're ready to go?"

"As I'll ever be," I shrug.

Joel holds me for longer than usual as we say goodbye. "Have a good day and text me as much as you can, okay?"

Nodding, I force myself out of the hug, then Conrad and I leave the apartment to face a day I'd do anything to fast forward.

Conrad leads me to a sleek, black car parked outside. The plush interiors are a comfort on such a cold morning, the car almost obsessively tidy. I'm not surprised. Conrad strikes me as a man who doesn't have much of a life outside of work, leaving him with plenty of time to keep his vehicle in perfect order.

As Conrad starts the ignition, he clears his throat. "Joel seems nice."

"He is," I reply, and the conversation dries up from there.

With Conrad being the man who led the team that saved my life, people probably expect us to have an unbreakable bond, but we don't. How can we, when all we see when we look at each other is failure?

Conrad's a detective and a good one at that. When the body of Peter Harris's fifth victim was found, he was called in to save the day.

Only he didn't. He couldn't. Peter Harris was too clever, so the bodies kept mounting, and with them the level of Conrad's failure.

Then I was taken.

A fourteen-year-old child, the youngest victim. The innocent schoolgirl. The life ruined before it was lived. Peter Harris should have been off the streets ages ago. That's why they called the big, bad Conrad Wallace in, isn't it? That's what he was supposed to do, right? Catch the bad guy and save the innocents?

But he didn't.

He couldn't.

The only reason Peter Harris was stopped is because a woman working at a garden centre noticed a young man buying gardening wire every few weeks.

"He had the cleanest, softest hands I'd ever seen. And his nails? Well, I never saw a speck of dirt in them. A true gardener would never have hands like that! So, I asked myself, what does he need all that gardening wire for? Why does he keep coming back for more?"

That was the quote blasted all over the media the day Peter Harris was arrested because it turns out, those questions saved my life.

Sure, it was Conrad and his team who stormed Peter Harris's home and found me in his basement torture chamber, but my safe return wasn't Conrad's victory to claim. Finding me had been a fluke. There was no police work or detective genius that solved the case, just a lady in floral overalls who asked questions.

I was the greatest shame in the wonderful Conrad Wallace's career, and he was the biggest disappointment in my life. Once you know that's how someone looks at you, there's no room for a warm, glowing relationship, even if that person did carry you out of the depths of hell.

With the early morning traffic light, we reach Break Time in minutes. Conrad pulls into the almost deserted car park opposite. "Who are you on shift with today?" he asks.

"Ellen and Stefan."

"Are they the only people you work with?"

"We have two part-timers who fill in the gaps when needed, but it's usually just us three. We're all full-time. Ellen's the owner and Stefan is a student."

Conrad frowns. "If Stefan is a student, how can he work full-time?"

"He's an international student from Germany. They charge him even higher fees than they do people who were born in the UK, so he needs the money. Besides, he's only in class for six hours a week."

Conrad's eyebrows raise. "And how much does he learn in those six hours?"

"Enough to know he shouldn't be paying as much as he is for the course," I joke, and Conrad smiles. It's nice to see his face looking not quite so worn out, but then the reason we are together again hits him and his smile fades.

"Are you ready?" he asks.

Part of me debates answering 'no'. It would be the truth, after all. Conrad was there the first time. He would understand why Peter Harris being back in my life is something I could never be ready for, but what good would telling him 'no' do? What would it change?

So, even though it breaks my heart, I nod, and together, we exit the car to take a sledgehammer to the last slice of normalcy in my life.

Chapter *Seven.*

The sky is coated in darkness as we head towards Break Time, the world around us only just waking up. The sounds of kettles boiling and wide-mouthed yawns echo out across the city.

I think of those lucky people still savouring the last moments of sleep before their day starts. Some of them will be dreading the workload that awaits them. Some will be having morning sex. Some will be flicking through notifications on their phone, building themselves up to brave sticking a leg out of the duvet and into the icy air.

I bet none of them are going into work early to tell their colleagues that someone is recreating the worst time of their life.

As we cross the road, I check the doorway of the electrical store for Robbie, but he's already moved on. Ahead, Break Time's lights are on, the glow they emit inviting on such a dull morning. I spot Ellen wearing her usual polka dot apron and setting up tables. She sees me through the window and waves, but her friendliness falters when she notices Conrad beside me.

Her reaction kills me. *Don't let this be taken from you,* my heart screams, but even if Conrad doesn't tell Ellen and Stefan what's happened, they'll still find out. The news can either be delivered by us or by the press. I know which one I'd prefer.

The smell of freshly brewed coffee greets us as we enter the café. Stefan looks up from behind the counter. His eyes search me for answers about what's going on, but I avoid his gaze.

"Morning, Hannah," Ellen says. She sticks her arm out to Conrad. "I'm Ellen, the owner of this fine establishment, and you are?"

"Conrad Wallace." Conrad shakes Ellen's hand and, for once, I catch a glimmer of the man he is when he's not around me. He stands taller, his chest puffed forward. A man you'd have no trouble believing could solve the case.

Too bad when I look at him, I see the opposite.

"Conrad's a detective," I detail.

Ellen nods slowly, the gears in her mind ticking into overdrive. "Please, take a seat," she says, gesturing to the nearest table.

Conrad complies. Once seated, he takes in the cosy décor. "It's a nice spot you have here."

"Thank you. It's not easy going up against the big chains, but we're doing well. I've worked in hospitality all my life. Bars first, then cafés. Food and drink are the only things I know, so I'd better know them well."

"Ellen's selling herself short," I say. "This place, and Ellen, are local legends. I doubt anyone knows this city as well as she does."

Ellen waves her hand to bat my comment away. "Hannah, as always, is being far too kind. I'm just a woman who enjoys food too much and wants to share that love with the world."

Conrad's droopy features lift in acknowledgement of our interaction, but his attention is caught by an approaching Stefan.

"I made you a cappuccino, Mr Wallace. I hope that's okay," Stefan says, setting four drinks down on the table. He slides a second cappuccino towards Ellen and a hot chocolate towards me. There are two pink marshmallows on the saucer, the only ones I like.

"You remembered my marshmallow order," I say, dropping the sugary lumps into the liquid.

"I'm a barista, isn't that my job?" Stefan laughs, but then he catches Conrad's eye and his happiness vanishes. He takes a seat quickly, his eyes fixed on the table.

"So," Ellen says, wrapping her hands around her drink. "It's not every day a detective comes into my business. What's all this about?"

The jovial atmosphere that existed dies the moment Conrad leans his forearms on the table. I look away as an unexpected barrage of tears prickles my eyes. No one at work has seen me cry before, and I'm determined that is not going to change today.

"As I'm sure you are aware, you work with Hannah Allen," Conrad begins.

Ellen flashes me a pitying smile that kicks me in the stomach. She's never looked at me like that before, never treated me differently. Even when she read my name on my CV during my interview, she didn't react. She just said it, paused, and then asked why I wanted to work at Break Time. At the time, I wondered if she knew who I really was, if she could see my childlike features underneath my makeup and hair dye. She never let on if she did, but now it's confirmed – Ellen's known all along. A nagging part of my brain chimes in, asking if she only ever hired me out of pity.

"We are currently working on an investigation that I cannot discuss in detail, but it involves Hannah. More specifically, it involves Hannah's past. A serious crime has been committed, one that has echoes of the Peter Harris murders."

Ellen presses her lips together in a tight, straight line. She looks so pale that I want to wrap my arm around her and tell her to go home. Stefan, on the other hand, doesn't react as strongly, his eyebrows knitting together the only sign that he heard what Conrad said.

"While we have no reason to believe Hannah is in danger, it is because of the link to Peter Harris that we want to keep a careful eye on her. It's also the reason we are meeting this morning."

"Oh, Hannah," Ellen exhales. Her sorrowful reaction makes the tears in my eyes burn harder. I dig my nails into my palms and focus on that pain instead of her potent sympathy.

"I'd like to stress once more that there is no reason to think Hannah is in danger," Conrad continues, "but we will be monitoring her. This is where we will need your help. First and foremost, if members of the press ask for interviews, which I can assure you they will, say no. No good can come of it. This is Hannah's place of work, a place where she should feel safe. Secondly, there will be daily drop-ins from police officers to check on Hannah. These will be brief, informal visits at different times throughout the day when she is working."

Ellen nods, but Stefan looks more confused than ever. "I'm sorry, what's going on here? Is Hannah in trouble or something?"

His innocence breaks my heart. "Stefan, I'm Hannah Allen."

"I know your name, Hannah. I just don't get what's going on."

I tilt my head, studying the puzzled face of my friend. "Do you not know who I am?"

"You're Hannah," Stefan says. He looks around the table, noticing how everyone is watching him like they can't quite believe what they're hearing. "What?"

Astounded, I sit back in my chair. No one has ever not known what 'Hannah Allen' means before. No one. Anonymity was one of many things Peter Harris stole from me. My face was such a fixture in the daily news that when I ventured out into the world after I was found, hushed voices seemed to narrate my journey. Finishing puberty and discovering cosmetics did enough to distance me from the photograph on my missing poster, but my name still tells whoever hears it my story. To this day, handing over my ID results in the colour draining from a cashier's face. When first meeting me, many people have said, 'Imagine if you were *the* Hannah Allen', their faces filling with horror when they realise, actually, I am *the* Hannah Allen.

Yet Stefan has no idea who I am. I don't know whether to laugh or cry. Conrad looks to me to fill in the gaps in my own words.

"Stefan, have you ever heard of Peter Harris?" I ask. Stefan shakes his head. "He's a serial killer. He was nicknamed 'The Ghost' because it took so long for him to be caught. Maybe you've heard of that?"

Again, Stefan shakes his head, and again, I am bowled over by the strange sensation that overcomes me at the idea of being known only as myself, not as my past.

"Peter Harris murdered ten women. I was… I was abducted by him as a teenager."

Stefan's eyes nearly pop out of his skull. "What?"

"I was supposed to be his eleventh victim, but I was saved before it got that far. Conrad saved me," I say, even if giving Conrad the credit isn't entirely accurate.

"Oh, Hannah," Stefan whispers. "I had no idea."

Conrad leans further forward on the table, his imposing frame casting a shadow over Stefan's white t-shirt. "How old are you, kid?"

"I turned twenty in December."

"And where did you grow up?"

"Freising. It's not far from Munich," Stefan replies, glancing at me as if to ask what's going on.

"But you've been in England for a while now?"

"Almost two years, yes."

"And in that time, you've never heard of Peter Harris or Hannah Allen?" Stefan blinks. "No, sir."

Conrad grunts then glances at his watch. "I know you're opening soon so I won't keep you for much longer, but please don't be alarmed by what we've discussed. As I said, there is no reason to suspect Hannah is in danger. All I'm asking is for you to help protect her privacy."

"Of course, anything for Hannah," Ellen replies.

I catch her eye and notice how the sympathy that doused her features before is no longer there. In its place is nothing but love. Only upon seeing that do I exhale.

Conrad reaches for his wallet, but Ellen bats him away. "It's on the house," she says, then she stands and walks towards the counter to continue getting ready for the day. Stefan follows her, his gaze downcast and his shoulders tense.

When Ellen and Stefan are out of earshot, Conrad leans close. "Are you okay if I leave now?"

"Conrad, I'm fine. Don't worry," I reply. I lead him to the door, then reach for his arm before he leaves. "Will you tell me if you find the other body?"

Conrad nods, then he exits Break Time. I watch his solid frame shrink as he heads towards the car park opposite. Before he goes inside, he turns back to Break Time. From the look on his face, I can tell he didn't expect me to be watching him. He attempts a smile and I wave goodbye, then he turns and disappears inside.

Now he's gone, I should get on with my day. Act normal, keep busy, and force myself to carry on like everything is fine. Instead, I watch the traffic passing outside. The rush of tyres on the tarmac is a soothing symphony. I sway to the sound, letting it wash over me, but then a thought crashes into my chest – somewhere out there in the city I call home, someone is hunting and murdering women in Peter Harris's name.

This terrifying truth submerges me, pinning me down as it swirls around my head, until out of nowhere, a hand rests on my shoulder.

"Hannah? Are you okay?"

I turn to find Ellen behind me, watching my reaction closely. Stefan hovers at the counter doing the same. The room beats with tension, something I don't think the walls of Break Time have ever felt before.

I force a smile. "I'm awake when it's not even seven in the morning. How could I possibly be okay at this time?"

Ellen claps me on the back. "That's the spirit. Now come on, let's run through today's specials. I know you'll need me to say them twice before you remember them!"

I laugh even though the joke isn't funny because laughing means it's just another day at work. Laughing means life is normal, even if the warning bells in my mind tell me normalcy is now a thing of the past.

You'll have heard about me by now. The police will have had no choice but to tell you of my existence. I left too many clues, gave too many signs that it was you I wanted to alert, for them to keep you in the dark. The dark, the place you like to live. The place I'm pulling you from so you can step into the light of the truth. Your truth.

What must you think of me, I wonder?

Admiration?

Fear?

Hatred?

Each day I can convince myself it's something different. Something good, something bad, something indifferent, but then I realise it doesn't matter what you think of me. All that matters is that you think of me. That you can't stop thinking of me.

When you're walking home, the car beside you driving a little too slow, a little too close.

When you're home alone and you're sure the door is locked, but the hairs on the back of your neck prickle as if someone's watching.

When you're in bed at night and you swear you see a shape in the corner of the room, a figure drawing closer, a hand outstretched... you think of me.

You think of me as much as I think of you.

Chapter *Eight.*

As the first customers trickle in, bleary-eyed and hunting for caffeine, I remind myself of my purpose at Break Time. Without my friendly greeting, without the coffee I serve, people's day could start poorly. Who knows what the consequence of that might be? It could be the blow that sends someone over the edge, pushing them to hurt themselves or someone else. After all, who knows what's really going on in someone else's mind?

With a renewed sense of belonging inflating my lungs, one of my favourite customers approaches the counter. Roy, a grey-haired lecturer whose severe eyebrows make him seem far more unapproachable than he is. With sleep still crusting his eyes, there's a warmth to Roy's smile saved purely for the person who can provide him with the coffee he craves.

"Roy! How are you today?" I ask brightly.

"All good, Hannah, although these early mornings aren't getting easier."

"I thought it was only students who complained about early starts?" I tease.

"That's the myth we lecturers like to project. We've got to keep the upper hand, but really, we're more tired than they are."

"In that case, I'll make sure your coffee is extra strong today! I'll even give you a free brownie alongside it in case you need a mid-morning sugar rush."

"You, Hannah, are a lifesaver. My favourite barista, bar none."

Laughing, I reach for a takeout cup as Roy fumbles in his back pocket for his wallet. He rests the newspaper he's carrying on the counter. Despite my 'no news' rule, I glance at it, wondering which poor soul the media are profiting from today. The headline '*Remains Found in the Hunt for Missing Schoolgirl*' shouts from the front page.

My blood runs cold.

Gabriella O'Hara, the missing schoolgirl I know to be dead.

Dead at the hands of Peter Harris's copycat killer.

Trembling, I complete Roy's transaction then he moves to the end of the counter to wait for his order. I stare after him, the newspaper now held under his bicep, pinned against his body. The headline is no longer visible thanks to the sleeve of his coat, but part of a photograph is. A photograph of a girl with deep brown eyes.

My fingers itch to grab the newspaper so I can find out what the media already knows because as soon as they discover this case is linked to Peter Harris, they will come for me. They will come for me like they have done so many times before.

The sound of impatient clicking interrupts my panicked thoughts.

"Excuse me? I'd like to order?"

I turn to the source of the irritated voice. A mid-forties woman, her lips pursed, her right eyebrow raised in challenge.

"Sorry! Early mornings, you know?" I rush. "What can I get you?"

I fumble through the morning in a haze of paranoia, jumping every time Break Time's door opens. Every customer I don't recognise, I study, waiting for them to bring out a notebook and request an interview. I eye every person tapping away on their phone, wondering if they're Tweeting that they've been served by *the* Hannah Allen.

People don't know who you are. They haven't seen your face since your missing poster, I remind myself. *This is all in your head.*

But the illusion of everything being in my head is firmly broken when two police officers enter Break Time a little after ten.

"Miss Allen?" they ask. "Everything okay?"

"Yep, everything's great," I reply. I don't look up from wiping the counter, continuing as if everything is normal, even though my hands are shaking and I've messed up three separate orders already.

Ever the hostess, Ellen bustles over. "All good here, officers. Now, can I interest you in anything before you head off to save the day? A slice of cake for the road?"

The officers make the usual, 'Oh, I really shouldn't' faces, but they leave a few minutes later with a muffin and a coffee each. Ellen squeezes my arm as she walks past and the surge of gratitude I feel towards her nearly bowls me over.

As the end of my shift draws closer, I almost convince myself that I can make it to the end of the day without another jarring moment, but then Break Time's landline rings, a rare sound in the days of mobile phones. The mechanical ringing sets me on edge, my tension only heightened when Ellen brings the receiver to me. "It's the detective from earlier. He wants to speak to you," she says.

The temptation to hang up instead of accepting the call is strong, but I take the plastic device and head into the backroom. "Conrad, is everything okay?"

"I tried calling your mobile. Did you leave it at home?"

"It's in my bag. We aren't allowed to have our phones on us at work. Why, what is it? What's happened?" I ask, terror gripping me.

"I'm calling to let you know we've found a body. We've found number twelve."

I sink onto a chair. "Who is it?"

"We don't know yet. They need to be formally identified."

"Were they… are they…" I can't find the words to express the millions of thoughts and questions racing through my mind, but somehow, Conrad understands me.

"They're an adult female. They were found in woodland. That's all I can tell you at the minute."

"Okay. Thanks," I hear myself say.

The thin tone of my voice must concern Conrad because he sighs like he's angry at himself for making this call. "Hannah, I'm only telling you this because you asked me to, not to worry you. Try not to think about it too much, okay?"

"I'll try," I lie. I go to say goodbye, but Conrad speaks again before I can.

"Oh, and Hannah? Keep your phone on you from now on, okay? Just in case."

Conrad doesn't expand on what he means by 'just in case', but he doesn't need to. The subtext is etched into this entire exchange – don't worry, but keep your phone on you. You're safe, but you're not.

As we say goodbye, the mixed messages repel from each other and the true horrors of what Conrad said echo in my brain.

Two bodies. Twelve and thirteen.

Two bodies.

Twelve and thirteen.

A dark fog descends around me, one I remember so well from the first few years after I was found. That time of my life is hazy, the cloud of grief and trauma so much of what I could see, but I remember how isolated I was, how alone, how lost. Some of my friends were made to stop speaking to me, their parents afraid of how the pain embedded in me might impact their child. The others I chose to cut off, not wanting to be reminded of the life I had before Peter Harris changed the course of it forever. Then I truly shut myself off from the world by dropping out of school so that my mum could home school me.

"What's the point in being around other people? I'll never be like them again. It's useless me even trying," I spat whenever Mum tried to convince me to go back into mainstream education.

It was Tanya who helped me find a way out of the darkness, her hand reaching through the fog and guiding me to a place of peace. She made a home for me at Sisterhood of Support. She reminded me of laughter, of friendship, of small moments of happiness. She taught me how to breathe again.

Sitting in the backroom of Break Time, I focus on my breathing once more. *You're safe,* I tell myself as I fill my lungs with air. *You're safe, you're safe, you're safe.*

I pray that saying the words enough times makes them true.

Chapter *Nine.*

When the lunch rush is over, Stefan appears at my side, carrying a plate with one of Ellen's famous brownies on it. "Take this and sit down," he orders.

I sigh. "Stefan, please, I don't want any special treatment."

"Tough, you're getting it. Now sit." Stefan rests his hands on my shoulders and steers me to an empty table.

Despite myself, I laugh. "Fine, I'll have a break if it means this much to you."

As I take a seat, my muscles unclench and I give into the joy of an impromptu rest. Tucking into the brownie, it takes all my might not to groan in satisfaction. For the first time since Conrad's sudden reappearance, my mind allows itself a moment to settle.

I'm on my fourth bite of chocolatey goodness when a woman with the glossiest hair I've ever seen enters Break Time. Every head in the room seems to turn when she walks in. Even though she looks close to my age, she carries herself with such assurance you'd be mistaken for thinking she was older. She's dressed in the kind of business clothes I used to imagine I would wear as a grown-up, back before my version of being an adult meant overcoming significant trauma first.

The woman beams at Stefan, showcasing a row of impressive white teeth. "Hey there," she says. "It's my first time here, what would you recommend?"

All the men in the café watch the woman open-mouthed, but Stefan serves her like he would any other customer. I bite back a smile at this. With his perfect skin and long eyelashes, I've seen Stefan get hit on more times than I can count, yet every flirtatious signal goes over his head. One time a woman gave him her number and he actually asked what she wanted him to do with it.

"A customer favourite is usually our brownie, but we have healthier options if that's what you're looking for. Are you a sweet or savoury fan?"

"Oooo," the woman coos, drawing out the vowel while she scans the counter. "I can't decide what I am when it all looks so good!"

"I'm glad you think so."

The woman grins, her smile flirtatious but her eyes still roving the room. As I watch her crane her neck towards the backroom, my senses tingle.

Stefan follows her line of sight and frowns. "Can I help you with anything else?"

"Actually, there is one thing," the woman simpers. "I'm looking for someone who works here. You might know her – Hannah? Hannah Allen?"

As my heart lurches in my chest, Stefan flusters, doing everything he can not to look in my direction.

"You know her, don't you? I can tell," the woman pushes. "Is she working today?"

Stefan glances to the backroom as if doing so can signal Ellen to come and save him, but I find myself on my feet, ready to do the saving myself. "It didn't take you long to crawl out of the woodwork, did it?" I snap.

The customers beside me jump at my outburst. They stare at their food like it's suddenly the most interesting thing in the world, but I see them watching from the corner of their eye. They heard the woman ask for Hannah Allen, and the promise of juicy gossip is too strong to resist listening to.

The woman lights up like a Christmas tree when she sees me, her gushing attention now focused on me. She approaches me with a glossy business card in her outstretched hand. "Of course you're Hannah Allen. I can see it now – it's the eyes. They've got the same spirited shine to them as they do in photographs."

"Well, that's good to know," I reply sarcastically.

The woman titters, but we both know she didn't find my comment funny. "Hannah, it's an honour to finally meet you. I'm Raja Kaling from The Daily Reporter. I'm sure you've heard of us?"

I pick up my half-eaten brownie, my appetite now nowhere to be found. "I've heard of your newspaper, and I've heard of you. You were the same person filling up my voicemail a few months ago when Nathaniel Clarke's book came out."

"Well, a ten-year anniversary interview with Hannah Allen would have been a big scoop," Raja shrugs, following me as I head towards the counter. "I won't keep you while you're working, but I'm sure you've heard the sad news about Gabriella O'Hara?"

"I have, and I'm sure you're cut up about it," I say, taking my place behind the counter and shooting Raja a withering look. There's a barrier of muffins and pastries between us now, but it's not enough. I want miles, oceans, continents separating me from this vulture.

"Oh, we are," Raja pouts, but I can see the glint of a story in her eyes. It takes everything in me to not grab a pot of coffee and launch it at her head.

Raja clears her throat, but I raise my hand. "I'm going to stop you there – the answer is no."

"You don't know what I'm going to ask."

"Yes I do, and the answer is no. The same as it was ten years ago, the same as it was a few months ago, and the same as it will be at any point in the future. Now please leave."

"Hannah, I really think –"

"She said no," Stefan interjects, stepping in front of me.

Raja opens her mouth to protest, but at that moment Ellen enters from the backroom. She sees us squaring up to a customer and puts two and two together. "Is this one of them? Is she after a story?" she snaps, throwing a towel over her shoulder and pushing her way onto the café floor. "You need to leave. Now."

"I'm just —"

"You're just nothing, not to my staff, not in my café. Now get out of here before I call the police!"

Everyone in Break Time is watching now. Raja notices. She glances around before fixing a dazzling smile on her face. "Okay, I'll go," she shrugs. Before she leaves, she slides her business card across the counter towards me. "In case you change your mind."

"I won't."

Raja smirks like she knows better then walks away. Only when I see her cross the street do I exhale.

"Are you okay?" Stefan whispers, his hand on the top of my arm.

"I'm fine," I reply, but I'm trembling.

"Why don't you sit down?"

I shake my head. I don't want to sit down. I don't want to do anything other than live my life like I have been for the last few years, only looking around the room, I realise that's not possible. Every eye is on me. Some people are whispering, my name on their lips, the horrors of my past being shared without a second thought for how hearing the recount might make me feel.

My wobbling bottom lip threatens to betray me, but I won't cry, not here, not in front of everyone. "I'll empty the bins," I say before stumbling away.

In the alleyway behind Break Time, I stand in the cool air on quaking legs and wrestle to regain my composure.

I can't believe Raja found me already. I thought my inconspicuous job with no name badge and no 'about our team' webpage would save me from being discovered. That anonymity was one of the things that made waitressing so appealing when I first decided to throw myself into the world of work, but how naïve of me to think I could remain in the shadows forever. I should know by now that if they want to write a story, a journalist will sniff out every lead until they find you for a quote in it.

Defeated, I lean against the wall and focus on my breathing. Inside, the café is bustling again. The coffee machine whirs, the sound of cutlery on porcelain rings out. Normal life resumes. For everyone else, at least, but not for me. Raja's appearance has ruined my day, but it's also confirmed another terrifying thing – it's only a matter of time before the whole country is saying my name once again.

Chapter *Ten.*

My hands sting, my skin raw from using such strong cleaning products, but mostly from my desperation to scour away every stain in Break Time. I scrub the sandwich press, my knuckles hitting against the machine until they bleed, but the metal is still not silver enough.

A shadow falls over me. "Hannah, stop."

When I don't comply, Ellen rests her freckled hand on top of mine. "Stop. That's an order."

With no more fight left in me, I drop the cloth I was using then rest my palms flat on the counter and lean against it.

Ellen's face twists with sympathy. "Why don't you go home early today? Stefan and I can finish up here."

"I'm okay to stay. I want to stay."

"Well, I'm going to put my foot down and insist you go. It's almost closing time, we've got this. Go home. Spend some time with Joel, read a book, have a bath, whatever you need to do to unwind."

I open my mouth to protest but Ellen shakes her head.

"This isn't a debate, Hannah. Go home and take care of yourself."

Ducking my head, I trail into the backroom to grab my stuff. Ignoring the multitude of notifications from Tanya and the Sisterhood of Support group chat, I text Joel to say I'm leaving work early and then drop my phone in my handbag.

Stefan looks up from the coffee machine when I enter the café again. "Has Ellen finally convinced you to leave?"

"Well, she told me it was an order, so I didn't have much choice."

Stefan laughs and presses the lid onto a takeaway coffee cup. "After the day you've had, leaving early is the least you deserve. I'll see you later, okay?"

"See you tomorrow," I reply as I head for the door. "You too, Ellen."

Ellen frowns. "Hannah, you're not working tomorrow."

Her words stop me in my tracks. The weight on my chest intensifies, pushing on my lungs until they're about to burst.

I know this feeling so well. The prickle of sweat, the clammy palms, the blind panic. I've lived it once before, but I can't live it again. I spin around, desperation written all over my face.

"Please don't push me out, Ellen. I know what's happening isn't great, but I'm a good employee. I work hard, I show up on time, I cover shifts at the last minute. You've never once looked at me like I'm Hannah Allen before. Please don't start now."

Ellen breaks away from the table she's clearing and comes to me. "Hannah, you're not working tomorrow because you have Saturday off this week, remember?"

Hot, sticky shame floods me. "I forgot."

"That's okay," Ellen soothes, but the softness of her tone hurts me in a way she'll never understand.

"Take some food to Robbie when you finish, okay?" I say to Stefan, then I leave Break Time before I say anything else foolish.

The busyness of the world outside hits me like a train. People seem to be everywhere, rushing past each other as if where they're going is more important than where anyone else is heading. I stumble through the crowd, panic oozing from every pore until the sight of the bus home saves me. I climb aboard and take a seat I'm lucky to get at this time of day, then rest my head against the window. The cool glass kisses my forehead, reminding me what is real and what is not.

Halfway through the journey, my phone rings, Joel's name appearing on the screen. "Where are you?" he asks as soon as I accept the call.

"I'm on the bus. Why?"

"Oh good, you've not got off yet," Joel exhales, relief punctuating his every word. "I was worried I'd missed you. I'm coming to meet you at the bus stop."

"Why? You've never met me from the bus before."

"I want to make sure you get home safely, that's all."

It takes a moment for me to digest what Joel's saying. When I do, I close my eyes. These simple words, this simple act, proves once and for all that everything has changed. Even Joel, the man who saw me as someone who could take on the world and win, doesn't think I can make it home on my own anymore.

Maybe you can't, the darkest part of my brain nags when I hang up the phone.

Joel pounces on me as soon as I step off the bus. I try not to fall into his arms, but after the day I've had, the sight of someone who cares is impossible not to crumble at. We walk back to the apartment hand in hand, but the gesture lacks any romantic feeling. It's more like a parent steering a child home after they've been scared by a dog, all kind words and soothing reassurance.

Still, I've never been more excited to see my apartment building. Joel opens the front door for me to head inside first. "Any notes from our favourite in-house artists today?" he jokes as I brush past him.

I glance at the doormat, but only crushed brown fibres stare back at me. "None today."

"That's a shame. I've been enjoying their doodles, especially now they're not depicting my nose as something so big it could be seen from space."

I laugh as we climb the stairs. Once home, we lock the door on the rest of the world.

Joel runs a bath for me. I lean against the sink while he fills the tub and watch him select my favourite products from the shelf. The water turns pink, the air around us now tinged with the scent of roses.

"This bath has got that many salts and lotions in it, the water must be worth thousands," I joke.

"Exactly. I defy anyone not to feel relaxed after soaking in it," Joel replies, turning off the tap and grinning at me. "Enjoy," he says before kissing me on the cheek and leaving the room.

When he's gone, I peel my clothes from my body, shedding my workday with every item I discard. Once naked, I move towards the tub, but then I catch sight of myself in the mirror and freeze.

There it is, exposed and reflected back at me – my number eleven.

I wince, the dark ink against my pale skin almost as confronting as the memories it reminds me of. As I rub my thumb over the bumpy numbers, a familiar swell of bile rises in my throat.

The day Peter Harris forced the brand on my body, the needle cut deeper than it should. The skin beneath my tattoo is scarred, making the eleven almost look bubbled.

"Look what you've done," he sighed. "You've ruined your pretty skin!"

I hear his voice again as if he's in the room with me. My thumb rubs harder over the numbers, but they stubbornly remain.

"Come on," I whisper, raking my hand over my skin and glaring at the black digits still holding strong. I dig my nail into one of the numbers, pressing into it as if to peel the tattoo away like a sticker. My skin breaks, my nail embedding into my flesh, but the tattoo stays put, looking the same as the day Peter Harris forced it upon me.

Defeated, I drop my hand.

I don't bother looking at the rest of my body. I don't care if I'm thin or fat, have cellulite or don't, if my stretch marks are faded or purple. I never see any of those things when I take in my naked appearance. My tattoo is too much of an attention seeker to allow that.

Turning my back on my reflection, I plunge into the scalding bath and push myself underwater. I'm tempted to hold my body down there to see how long it takes for my survival instinct to kick in, but I stop myself.

Normal people don't test drowning themselves in the bath, I remind myself.

Leaning against the wall of the tub, I will myself to give into the healing power of the water, but no matter how many 'relax and rejuvenate' products Joel loaded into it, the liquid does nothing to calm me. I thrash about, trying and failing to get comfortable, before heaving my soaking body out of the bath.

"Where's your panic alarm?" Joel asks when I pad into the living room wrapped in a towel.

"Don't start," I sigh, flopping onto the sofa beside him. "You know I don't want to wear it."

"But Conrad –"

"Joel, please. I can't do this right now," I plead, my eyes glossy with tears.

Joel nods even though I know there's more he wants to say. "Your phone rang twice while you were in the bath. It's not stopped buzzing with messages, either."

I check my phone and wince at the long list of notifications waiting for me. It seems like every person I know is reaching out. I'm grateful for the time they've taken to message me, but I can't help wishing that they weren't reaching out about the one thing I don't want to talk about.

"I don't know if I've got the energy to deal with all this," I say.

"Whatever you need to do is fine, Han. No one's expecting you to reply right now."

I know Joel's right, but as I skim over the kind messages, I give into the demands of my notifications and dial Tanya's number.

She picks up on the second ring. "I'm so glad you called me back! I wanted to see how you were doing," she says.

"I'm fine, thanks."

"You don't have to be strong for me, Hannah, you know that."

"I'm not trying to be strong. I'm trying to keep going."

"Well, however that looks for you, remember you're not alone in this, okay? You are surrounded by love and people who want to be here for you. I hope you see how true that statement is at tomorrow's meeting."

I stop picking at a loose thread on my towel and blink. "But Tanya, I'm not coming to the meeting tomorrow."

There's a pause before Tanya speaks again. "Hannah, with everything that's going on, do you think that's wise? Now more than ever you need a strong support network around you. Where better to find that than with your friends? We want to be here for you. Let us."

My heart twists at her words. "I really appreciate it, Tanya, I do, but I don't think now is the time to be moving backwards."

"Coming to a meeting wouldn't mean moving backwards. Seeing how much people care for you is vital right now. Plus, Riley would love to see you again."

Riley. Her name punches me in the gut. A low blow from Tanya, one that annoyingly seems to work.

"Today's been tough, I know," Tanya continues. "Let's take the pressure off this conversation. The offer to attend tomorrow's meeting is there if you want it. It will always be there if you want it. Take tonight to think it over. I'll send you the access code, just in case."

"Tanya —"

"Promise me you'll think about it?"

"I promise I'll think about it," I sigh.

"Thank you. Now I'll let you get on with your evening, but I really hope we see you tomorrow, Hannah," Tanya says, then we say goodbye and hang up.

"What did Tanya want?" Joel asks.

I lean back against the sofa, my limbs heavy with sadness. "She wants me to go to the Saturday meeting. She thinks it's for the best."

"And what do you think?"

"I don't know. Maybe she's right? She's always known what's best for me before."

"Hannah, the only person who knows what's best for you is you," Joel says, pressing a kiss onto the back of my hand. I nuzzle into him, breathing in the faint scent of washing powder on his shirt. "Do you want to go?"

"I don't know what I want, other than for things to be back the way they were," I admit. "I want to be normal again."

"Normal doesn't exist."

"You know what I mean. It's... I... I was so ready to stop being number eleven. I was so ready to be myself again."

"Hannah," Joel soothes, his lips against my hair. "You're so much more than number eleven. You always have been."

I smile in response, but my smile is hollow. It's so easy for Joel to say those words, but I know what they are – a beautiful lie. Just like it's part of my skin, the number eleven is part of my life and always will be.

The *Speculation.*

Conrad closes his eyes and sees Peter Harris before him. Years might have passed since they were last in each other's company, but Conrad's memories of the man whose vile acts tormented the entire country are so vivid they could have happened yesterday. The way Peter had grinned when Conrad finally placed the cuffs on him, the joy he felt at being one step ahead for so long written all over his face... he didn't seem to care that he'd been caught. Why would he when he'd already inflicted the damage he set out to?

And now someone's following in those same sick footsteps.

Conrad stops at his desk, allowing himself a moment to sit with his hatred before pushing it down again. The pause is only brief, but each millisecond counts. The time allows Conrad to fill his chest with air, iron out his worried brows and dress his features in competency and confidence.

Then, when his mask is in place, Conrad heads to the briefing room.

The bantering and chatter between Conrad's colleagues stops when he enters. It's almost as if someone has pressed mute on the scene. Conrad is used to the impact his presence has on people, no longer feeling the sting of not being invited to after-work drinks or never being asked how his weekend was.

He takes his place at the front of the room. Three whiteboards are lined up in a row, facing their audience. Conrad points to a photograph on the board beside him. Gabriella O'Hara. At least, Gabriella O'Hara from a few weeks ago, back before she was a maimed and brutalised corpse.

"I'm going to keep this briefing short because we have a lot of work to do," Conrad begins. "We have a grieving family wanting answers and a country that's about to be up in arms when they find out what happened to this girl."

Every eye in the room lingers on the image of Gabriella O'Hara. An image that was taken at her best friend Rose's fifteenth birthday party a few weeks ago. If you look carefully in the background of the picture, you can see the rose gold balloons and holographic pink streamers that decorated the event.

"Rose wanted an Instagramable backdrop at her party. Gabriella helped her pick it," Gabriella's mum said when she handed over the photo, then she dissolved into sobs that were so gut-wrenching, the memory of them kept Conrad awake later that night.

Conrad tacks another photo to the board. "And to this woman," he adds.

The second photo is of a woman named Trina Lamond. A twenty-six-year-old mother of three. A sex worker with tired eyes and limp hair known for bouts of disappearing then reappearing a few days later. Number Twelve, found in Armington Woods this morning. Formally identified by her fingerprints. They were on record thanks to previous arrests for petty theft. Her next of kin are being informed as Conrad speaks.

"Two bodies, two victims, murdered within a small geographical area in a short space of time. This suggests that, unless we stop them first, the person committing these crimes will act again soon."

After these words, a shudder travels through the room.

"If they're working this fast, then we need to work faster. To do that, we need everyone focused. We need to look at the bigger picture to find links and avenues for investigation. That's why we are all in this room right now – to work together to look at the bigger picture."

Some people shift in their seats, the intensity of the situation making them sweat.

Good, Conrad thinks. *Let them be uncomfortable. Let them realise early on that every moment spent working on this case will be a living hell.*

"These two murders bear an uncanny resemblance to the crimes of Peter Harris," Conrad states. "The killer even claims to be 'continuing the story' in notes that were found with both bodies. I know that every person in this room will understand when I say that we cannot allow more chapters to be added to that dark tale."

DS Fatima Rani, a woman Conrad would trust with his life, nods. Her display of unity encourages Conrad to continue.

"We are still waiting on some of the forensic reports from both bodies and crime scenes, but this is what we know so far."

On the blank whiteboard, Conrad draws a line, splitting it in two. Then on one half of the board, he makes notes as he speaks.

"The killer replicates aspects of what Peter Harris did to his victims. Each victim was numerically branded, with the brands continuing from the number eleven. I'm sure I don't have to inform you that eleven is a significant number because that was the number of women Peter Harris abducted before he was finally stopped. Ten lives lost, the eleventh impacted in a way that no one should experience."

Again, the room shudders. Conrad lets his colleagues sit in their unease for a moment before continuing.

"As well as the brands, the wrists of both victims were slit. Their bodies were bleached then left to be discovered in secluded areas. The methods of mutilation were again similar to that of the Peter Harris murders. For example, both Trina and Gabriella were struck on the head, with the blow breaking their right brow bone. We suspect the knowledge to inflict these wounds came from Nathaniel Clarke's book, but we don't know this for sure. With this in mind, we are re-interviewing Harris's associates.

People he worked with, people he socialised with. Anyone who knew him, we will speak to."

Conrad pauses before moving to the other half of the whiteboard. There, he begins to create a timeline.

"Trina Lamond was murdered first. Rough estimates are that she was killed six days ago but this should be confirmed later today. We do not know where Trina Lamond was abducted from, when the abduction happened or where she was killed."

Conrad lets his words settle. The blankness of them, the questions that surround every syllable, no answer in sight.

"We know that Gabriella O'Hara was walking home from school when she was abducted and that she was murdered on the same day she was abducted. We know that she was last seen alive on Fitzroy Street in Huntington and that, thanks to location data from where her phone was last active, Gabriella's suspected abduction site was Palmer Avenue. We know that Huntington is mostly rural-residential, meaning a distinct lack of CCTV in the area as well as traffic at that time. What I am guessing is that the killer knew that too."

Although everyone was listening to Conrad before, their attention now doubles.

"The locations where both Trina Lamond and Gabriella O'Hara's bodies were found follow the same pattern – remote and quiet with a lack of consistent foot traffic. Gabriella's abduction site was equally as isolated, and I'd guess that Trina's was too. The killer knows these streets well. They know where to strike so they aren't seen."

Conrad turns back to the room and puts the lid on his pen. It clicks shut, the sound sharp against the backdrop of silence.

"We need to figure out what bridges the gap between both sides of the board. Between Peter Harris and these current crimes."

"The killer knowing the city well... does this mean they're a local?" someone calls out.

"More than likely, yes," Conrad says. "At the very least, they're someone with a good knowledge of the area. We also need to factor into the situation that there were no signs of struggle on either Trina or Gabriella's bodies, which suggests they didn't fight their abductor. Then there's the issue of sedation. Both Trina and Gabriella were sedated, but Peter Harris never sedated his victims. He enjoyed the struggle, whereas this killer removes the struggle altogether. We need to ask ourselves – why would someone who's about to maim and murder sedate their victim so they would barely be alive to feel the pain?"

Fatima speaks first. "Maybe the person didn't want to hurt the victims."

"Doesn't want to hurt them, but wants to kill them? Yeah, right," Johnny Atkins, a new transfer with a habit of acting like he's got something to prove, scoffs. "Sedated victims are easier to move, plus they're less likely to cause a scene when being bundled into a car."

"How do we know the victims were sedated before they got into the car?" Fatima fires back.

"How else do you explain it? What, you think they got into the car through choice?"

"At this stage, we'd be naive to rule it out. The driver could be someone the victims recognised. They could have a job that people trust," Fatima says. There's a rise in tension as the thought that perhaps a police officer could be the copycat dances through everyone's mind. After all, they'd know about Peter Harris better than anyone. Conrad holds his composure despite the worrying thought.

"Surely that's a bit of a stretch," Johnny says, pulling a face at Fatima's idea.

"Maybe it's someone linked to Gabriella's school?" Sandra Hastings suggests, cutting into Fatima and Johnny's back and forth, an interruption Conrad's grateful for. "A staff member driving home at the same time, someone who knew where Gabriella was going. Someone Gabriella trusted enough to get into their car."

"Why would Trina Lamond get into their car though?" Johnny asks.

"Maybe there's a link between them, something we've not thought of."

"Between a schoolgirl and a prostitute?" Johnny retorts, his scorn prickling Conrad's skin.

"Links can be found in lots of places, if you bother to look," Conrad says, shutting Johnny down with an icy glare. "Hastings, can you arrange another round of interviews with the staff at Gabriella's school? All staff this time, please. Rani, I want you to be in charge of interviewing Trina Lamond's family and associates. Take Atkins with you. Teach him how to show some respect to the people we failed to protect."

As Johnny lowers his head, Conrad faces the rest of the room. "Anyone else have anything they'd like to contribute?" he asks.

A newer member of the team, Sasha Chen, raises her hand meekly. Conrad nods at her to speak. She tucks her inky hair behind her ears before she begins. "I think we need to look deeper into the Peter Harris link," she says. "There's got to be a reason why someone is copying him."

"Peter Harris made the country live in fear. Maybe someone wants to recreate that," someone at the back of the room responds, but Sasha chews her lip.

"I think there's more to it than that," she says, a blush burning her cheeks as she pushes herself to speak louder. "Peter Harris isn't the first killer that the country has feared, but he's one of the most famous. He's a celebrity in certain circles. There are online forums dedicated to him. People even want Nathaniel Clarke's book to be turned into a film. Maybe someone's seen what's happening as a way to make a name for themselves. It could be a loner, someone on the periphery, who thinks that killing is a way to break free of their isolation and become a legend in the corners of the internet they participate in."

As Sasha hides behind her hair to indicate that she's finished speaking, every head in the room turns to Conrad. "Forums, you say?" he asks. When Sasha nods, Conrad lets the information tick through his mind.

"I think Sasha's onto something with this," Fatima says. "You'd be surprised what people post on the internet under the guise of thinking an online pseudonym means there are no consequences in the real world."

Conrad couldn't agree more. "I want a team on those forums," he says decisively. "I want them looking for someone who sounds local, who has a knowledge of the killings and a tendency for the delusion Sasha speaks of."

"You'd need a strong stomach to face going on those websites," Sandra grimaces.

"We're all going to need strong stomachs if we want to solve this case. Two people have been murdered within a matter of days. We need to think smarter and work harder. We need to do it before another body turns up on our doorstep," Conrad says, the finality in his tone chilling.

From the front row, Ian Porter clears his throat. "If we're focusing on Peter Harris, what does that mean for Hannah Allen?"

At the mention of Hannah's name, Conrad tenses. He hopes the others didn't notice. "What about her?"

"Well, if someone is linking themselves to Peter Harris, shouldn't we put her under some kind of protection? They did leave copies of her missing poster with the bodies, after all."

Another detail that sends a shiver around the room. Even Conrad feels it, the hairs on his arms rising under his navy shirt in response.

"We've already taken security measures for Hannah's peace of mind," he says, "but we must remember that she is a twenty-four-year-old woman with a life to live. A life that has already been disrupted enough by Peter Harris."

"I know, but is a panic alarm and a few visits from the police enough?" Ian presses. "If we're operating under the idea that Nathaniel Clarke's book is instructing this new killer what to do, then surely this person is out for her?"

This time, Conrad bristles in a way that everyone notices. "We don't know that they're 'out for her'. Nothing that's happened has said that."

"Nathaniel Clarke's book said –"

"I know what the book said." Conrad hears the impatience in his voice and winces. "Look, Hannah Allen is a young woman who has been through an ordeal none of us can imagine. Bringing this into her life again is already causing a great deal of suffering. We don't need to traumatise her further and unnecessarily. We have eyes on Hannah, on her workplace and her home. For now, that is enough. The second that changes, we will act."

Conrad looks around the room, taking in the sea of faces before him. Most people are on his side, his confident delivery seeing to that, but one or two still look uneasy. The women in the team, the ones who were around when Peter Harris was roaming free. Women who will have been told to stay indoors, to go out in pairs, to keep vigilant, putting the onus on them to keep themselves safe from a man who hid in the shadows rather than society addressing the real issues behind these kinds of crimes.

"Hannah Allen will not be harmed," Conrad states. "I won't allow it."

Conrad's said those words to himself before. He said them the day the news broke of Hannah's disappearance. He said them the moment her distraught mother handed him a copy of Hannah's latest school photo to use in her missing poster. He said them every day between when she was taken and when she was found.

And now, all these years later, standing in front of an audience of his colleagues, he finds himself saying them again.

As the team files out of the briefing room, ready to plunge into the murkiness of this case, Conrad repeats those words internally until he allows himself to believe them. He just hopes that this time, he can make them come true.

Chapter *Eleven.*

Even though I spend all night and all morning promising myself I won't go, I still find myself at the Sisterhood of Support meeting the next day.

"You're back already!"

"I knew you wouldn't leave us!"

My fellow attendees' words when I stroll through the door hit me like arrows. I feign happiness, accepting their overjoyed greetings while bleeding on the inside.

"It's so good to have you back!" Amrita cries, wrapping me in a hug. She looks unusually dishevelled, but I don't have time to ask if everything is okay before she speaks again. "Are you here because of what's in the news?" she whispers into my hair.

I pull back. "What's in the news?"

Amrita angles her body to shut the others out of the conversation. "The dead schoolgirl? They're saying she was taken by someone copying Peter Harris. People think... Hannah, people think that 'The Ghost' is back."

Amrita doesn't need me to answer – the look on my face says it all.

"Oh, Hannah," she sighs. "I can't believe it's true. I'm so sorry."

Tanya chooses that moment to emerge from her office. She lights up when she sees me. "I knew you'd be here," she beams, her words making me curse myself for showing up at all.

"Of course she's here. She wouldn't miss out on the opportunity to make a dramatic entrance," Carla mutters, but I don't have the energy to care.

As the others filter in, I join the huddle and listen to Carla's stories about her night shifts at the care home she manages and Karolina's recount of what she bought in her latest online shopping haul. I find myself laughing along at their anecdotes, their stories bringing light into the darkness inside me, but then Tanya says it's almost time to begin and the darkness takes over once more.

As we move about the circle to find a seat, Danielle grabs me. "I knew you couldn't resist the lure of seeing us again," she grins, throwing her arm over my shoulder. "Whatever your reason for coming back is, please know that by doing so, you've made my Saturday a whole lot better."

"I'm glad my presence here has improved today for one of us," I joke as we grab a seat next to each other.

Paula sits beside Danielle, then leans across her to speak to me. "Are the rumours true?"

"What rumours?" Danielle asks.

"The girl who died, Gabriella O'Hara? I heard it's to do with Peter Harris. Apparently, another body's been found too."

Danielle glances at me and I quickly look away, but Paula doesn't give up on me that easily.

"Is it true? Is that why you're back?" she asks, fear dousing her features.

"I think we should let Hannah settle into the meeting before we fire such tricky questions at her, don't you?" Danielle interjects, shuffling her body so that it blocks Paula's intensity.

"Of course," Paula mutters, but her tension still ploughs through me.

Doing all I can to steady my wobbling emotions, I make eye contact with Amrita. She smiles and walks towards the empty seat beside me, but at the last minute, she dodges it, choosing to sit on the one after instead.

My hurt at the snub must be evident because Amrita takes my hand. "Tanya asked everyone to leave the seat beside you free for Riley."

As if conjured by her name, Riley enters the room. She's wearing another oversized outfit and a scowl, but when she catches my eye, her lips jerk upright. She takes the seat beside me without debating sitting elsewhere, a move that makes Carla sniff.

"Are we ready?" Tanya asks the room.

Instinct begs me to shout no, but as every other head in the circle nods, the meeting begins.

We start by listening to five minutes of gentle instrumental music. While we bathe in the sound with our eyes closed, Tanya walks around the circle, reciting affirmations in a soft, measured tone.

"You are worthy... your spirit is strong... you can learn to trust again... you are powerful..."

As she repeats the affirmations, her words seem to combine with the music. They flow through the air, running over my body and soaking into my skin until I feel them coursing through me with every beat of my heart, then the music fades until we are in silence.

"Whenever you're ready, open your eyes," Tanya instructs.

I hold on to serenity for a moment longer before peeling my lids apart. The lighting of the meeting room is dimmer now than when we first came in, Tanya's way of making the atmosphere cosy and intimate, therefore easier to open up in.

"Now it's time to go around the circle," Tanya says. "Please feel free to share if you wish to. A high, a low, a neutral. If you don't want to speak, that's okay too. We're all just grateful that you've shown up today."

"Here, here," some people whisper.

Tanya starts with herself, like always, to remind us that even though she is leading the circle, she is one of us. "I had a wobble this week. A moment where I didn't think I was making a difference."

"I hope you soon snapped out of that," Danielle interjects.

Tanya laughs. "I did, eventually, but it wasn't without spending a few hours wallowing in that thought first. The work we do here is tough in every way. It forces us to confront the worst things that have happened, to look at our past and to our future and shout, 'I am not afraid'. I suppose I felt overwhelmed by the enormity of that. I asked myself if the things I was doing and the choices I was making were helping people. If they were making the difference I wanted them to. In the end, I decided that's not for me to say. All I can do is wake up each day and try my best. The same thing we're all here to do."

We nod, Tanya's words impacting every one of us uniquely. Next, it's Karolina's turn to speak, then one by one, we go around the circle. The highs are high, the lows are low. There are tears, bursts of anger and chokeholds of grief, then moments of shining beauty, clarity and strength.

Then it's Danielle's turn, and my throat constricts as I realise I am next.

"Remember I told you about my bitch of a boss?" she begins, and the others laugh. I'm too tense to even raise a smile. "Well, this week she topped herself with her cruelty. She told a story about how her niece went to a club and some guy put his hand up her skirt. Apparently, the niece went to the bouncers and got the guy kicked out. Good for her, I say, but guess what my boss said? She said it was dramatic, that her niece was begging for attention."

A murmur of disgust travels around the room, even though none of us are surprised by the attitude of Danielle's boss. We've all had similar sentiments said to and about us.

"My boss said, 'It's not like she was raped or anything'," Danielle continues. "I had to bite my tongue. It was either that or lose my job, but sometimes I wish I could say something. I wish I could shout that it's not okay what happened to me, to her niece, or to any of us in this circle."

The room nods, Danielle's words igniting a fierce passion in people, but all I can think about is how any second now, it will be my turn to speak.

"I hate how people view violence as some kind of hierarchy," Amrita chimes in. "It's like there's this sick points system that judges how much care you receive, rather than people admitting that actually, any violation is a violation and it is wrong."

"Exactly," Danielle says. "It's bad enough that the thing happened in the first place, but then to have to fight to be heard, to be taken seriously? Well, that's an extra trauma none of us should have to go through."

Danielle's words receive a ripple of support and a thank you from Tanya, then the moment I've been dreading arrives. Everyone turns to me. I burn under the heat of their gaze, the questions they long to ask glinting in their eyes.

Why is she back?

What's going on?

Is everything okay?

I open my mouth to speak, but my words stay stuck in my throat. The more I try to force them out, the more they choke me.

Unable to push through, my head jerks to pass the opportunity to speak to Riley, but then I hear Tanya's voice. "It's okay, Hannah," she says.

Those words – how I've heard her say them in so many different contexts over the years. From 3am phone calls when I sobbed that I couldn't do life without my mum to nerves before telling Joel about my past, Tanya has guided me through every pivotal moment of my life.

And here she is, doing the same again.

Filling my lungs with air, I begin. "I didn't think I'd be here today. I didn't want to be," I admit. "Not because I don't want to see you all, but because I thought I was past discussing my pain like this. I didn't want to talk about it anymore, you know? But then... but then I was told that someone's abducting and murdering women. They're using Peter Harris's techniques. Copying him. Bringing that nightmare back to life."

Murmurs rumble around the circle, then a surge of love so strong it makes my head spin floods the room. I take in the sea of eyes shining with understanding until I feel tears in my own.

"Having the police back in my life and knowing this is happening is horrible, but for me, the worst part is that everything I worked so hard for feels like it's gone. It took ten years to get to a place where I didn't think about what Peter Harris did every day. I lived outside of those memories. I found a way to be Hannah again. A Hannah I liked, one I was proud of. But right as I was ready to put everything behind me, I find myself back here and needing to talk to you all more than ever. I feel like overnight I've lost ten years of progress, and that scares me." A tear rolls down my cheek, but I don't wipe it away. I don't need to in this circle.

"Oh, Hannah," Amrita says, leaning over Riley to take my hand. Beside me, Danielle takes the other. Others in the circle speak, sharing kindnesses that nestle into my soul.

"After what you've been through, to sit here today and be so strong? Well, you're an inspiration to us all."

"You're doing great. Be kind to yourself."

"Thanks, everyone," I sniff. "I just want to be me again, you know? Me before Peter Harris came into my life."

Tanya leans forward, resting her elbows on her knees. "Tell me something you liked about yourself from that time of your life."

I blink. Revisiting memories of the girl who once lived in me is like watching old home videos of a deceased loved one. You can see them. You can hear them. You can feel the energy they emitted and the space they took up, but they're gone. You can't get them back, no matter how many wishes you make or how many times you watch the footage.

"What did you like about yourself, Hannah?" Tanya asks again.

I close my eyes and allow myself to think back beyond the moment my life forked in a direction no one would have predicted it would take. Teenage Hannah in all her curious, giggly glory.

I used to make up dances with my friends. Silly, repetitive routines that we'd perform in front of the mirror. I had three best friends – Holly, Cassidy, and Ravneet. We were terrible dancers, but we loved music. Any music, even the classical stuff Holly's dad played on the odd occasion he'd drive us to school. Cassidy had the biggest bedroom out of the four of us so we went to her house the most. I had a crush on her older brother, Xavier. I once made a joke about one of the teachers at school that made him laugh so hard, he snorted water out of his nose.

"You're funny," he said. I wore that word like a badge of honour on my lapel. I remember writing about the exchange with Xavier in a diary I kept at the time, reliving it like it was the greatest moment of my life.

The memory makes me smile. "I was funny. I liked that about myself."

"Well," Tanya says, "you're still funny, Hannah. You've had me in stitches on many occasions. What else did you like?"

"I was kind," I say. "One of my friends, Ravneet, told me I was the kindest person she'd ever met. After what happened, her parents didn't like us hanging out together. They thought I was too troubled, but Ravneet found a way to send me a letter. She told me to never lose my kindness because of what happened. I think of that letter every time I feel myself wanting to snap at an irritable customer. It's one of my most treasured possessions."

I gulp down my wobbling emotions as I think of Ravneet's heartfelt words, stored safely in the memory box I keep under my bed. I haven't read the letter in such a long time, but I remember it word for word. Her scrawly handwriting, the spelling errors, the sparkly pink gel pen she'd used to put her thoughts on paper. The innocence of her delivery contrasting sharply with the content she was writing. Content she only learned of because Peter Harris forced everyone who knew me to grow up sooner than they should have.

"You've been kind to me on many occasions," Tanya says.

Beside her, Dipti nods. "The brownies you bring might not be kind to my waistline, but you, Hannah? Well, you're always kind."

"See?" Tanya says. "You haven't lost that part of yourself. Far from it, and I'll bet there are many other things you haven't lost too."

"It's hard to see those things right now," I admit.

"Of course, but all your friends at Sisterhood of Support are here to remind you how great you are. What you're feeling is valid, Hannah. Healing is never linear, and it's certainly not when the past crops up as it has done for you. But you are still you, and you always will be. Certain traits may dilute, others may grow, but that's life. That's the same for everyone regardless of trauma, but no matter what, you are a person who has built a fabulous life despite the most difficult of obstacles being put in your way. No one can take that away from you."

"Especially not someone who doesn't have the imagination to come up with an original way of murdering someone," Riley quips, her remark so dry and so unexpected that a bubble of laughter bursts from me.

Riley smirks at my response and lets out a snort of laughter herself, which only makes me laugh harder. Danielle, Dipti and Amrita join in too and, before I know it, the entire circle is laughing. The hysteria is contagious, although I'm sure if you asked us, no one would be able to explain why we are laughing.

"I guess being a copycat does show a lack of creativity," I giggle.

Danielle claps me warmly on the knee. "It's good to see you smiling again, Han. Serial killer humour, who'd have thought it?"

"Well, I didn't find it funny at all," Carla says haughtily, but I ignore her sour face. That eruption of laughter is what I needed. It reminds me that even if everything has been turned on its head, not all is lost. After all, where there's laughter, there's life.

Chapter *Twelve.*

"See you next time, Hannah," Amrita calls over her shoulder as she rushes to collect her sons from their babysitter. I don't correct her. I don't know if I need to. There's as much of a chance of me coming to the next meeting as there is me skipping it.

Beside me, Danielle slides a fur coat over her jumper. "Fancy going for a walk?"

"Thanks, but I'm going shopping," I reply, an answer I didn't know I was going to say until I said it. Once the words are out there, though, they make sense. Nice clothes are the layer that makes me feel like I can face the world. With everything chipping away at that confidence, reinforcing it with a new steely layer is vital.

"I wish I could come with you," Danielle sighs. "I'm still paying off the last dress I bought!"

I smile politely, and then I hear a voice behind me. "I'll come with you."

Surprise must be written all over my face when I turn around because Riley's cheeks flood with colour.

"Sorry, I shouldn't have invited myself. It doesn't matter."

"I'd love to go shopping with you," I rush before Riley's embarrassment sends her running.

"Are you sure?"

"Definitely," I reply, and I'm surprised to hear how much I mean it.

"I'd be careful going shopping with Hannah," Danielle warns. "She tells you that you look great in everything, then you end up spending double what you thought you would and walk away thinking you're the most beautiful woman in the world."

Riley hides a faint smile behind her hair. "Sounds great. Mum will be outside. I'll just let her know I'm going out."

As Riley leaves to speak to Sarah, Danielle pats me on the back. "You're doing a good thing there. She admires you."

"It's only shopping, it's no big deal," I shrug.

"Keep telling yourself that," Danielle replies with a wink, then she leaves.

When she's gone, I sling my handbag over my shoulder and go to find Tanya so I can say goodbye. She's talking to Carla but stops when she sees me approaching. "Leaving so soon?" she asks.

"I'm heading for a bit of retail therapy with Riley."

"Oh, how wonderful! I'm glad to see the two of you getting along so well."

Carla smirks. "Riley might as well enjoy this one-to-one time with you while she can. After all, you're only going to abandon her when you decide to stop coming to meetings again."

Her snide comment would upset me if it weren't for Tanya's even more upsetting response. "Oh, Hannah won't be abandoning anyone. She'll be back again, I'm sure."

The meeting has drained me too much to fight back against Tanya's assuredness. I say goodbye and trail outside where I find Riley and Sarah in a tense huddle in the corridor. They break apart when they see me, Sarah plastering on the fakest of smiles, Riley on the verge of tears.

"Is everything okay?" I ask.

"Mum wants to drive us into the city," Riley replies, her tone acidic.

"It's forecast to rain. I don't want you getting wet while waiting for public transport, that's all," Sarah says, her ability to lie the worst I've ever seen.

I look from Riley's scowl to Sarah's desperation and back again before mustering all the enthusiasm I can find. "A lift sounds great!"

Both Riley and Sarah exhale, then we exit the building together, Sarah's footsteps too close for comfort for Riley, Riley's shoulders too rigid for Sarah's peace of mind.

Sarah's car is exactly as I expected – a bulky silver four-wheel drive that she's uncomfortable driving. There's a car seat and a cluster of brightly coloured toys in the back, indicating Riley has a younger sibling she's not yet told me about. A discarded school bag sits on the backseat, a physics textbook poking out of the top. These small snapshots of information fill in the blank spaces around Riley, hinting at the person who exists outside the walls of the meeting room.

"Where would you like dropping off?" Sarah asks as she starts the ignition.

"Anywhere that's away from you," Riley mutters, but not quietly enough that we all don't hear her. Sarah flinches, but her fake smile holds strong.

"As close as you can get to the high street would be great, thank you," I reply, then we set off.

Sarah talks for the entire journey, but about what I couldn't say. I intercept with a nod or an 'Is that right?' now and then, but Sarah's relentless chatter would have carried on even if I'd been mute. It's almost a relief when she pulls up outside a new boutique called Firefly and we have to get out.

"Thanks for the lift," I say as I slide out of the backseat. Riley's two steps ahead of me, standing on the pavement and simmering with anger.

"No problem," Sarah says before looking past me towards her daughter. "Text me when you want picking up, Riley. Riley?" Sarah looks as if she's about to unclip her seatbelt and dive out of the car to make sure

Riley heard her.

"I'll make sure she does," I reply.

Sarah makes eye contact with me and so much is said in that look. *Please don't hate me for fussing. Please make sure she texts me. Please keep my baby safe.*

I nod in answer to all those pleas, and then Sarah finally relaxes enough to leave. As her car peels away from the curb, I turn to Riley. "So, where do you fancy starting?"

With Firefly right in front of us, that's where we begin. The clothes are not styles either of us would pick. There's no oversized, 'fuck you, world' outfit for Riley, and everything is too 'I'm going to get wasted in a nightclub' for it to project the vision of togetherness I'm aiming for. Still, we wander the store, selecting items and holding them against our bodies.

"I wonder what my mum would say if I came home with this," Riley grins, grabbing a lime green crop top that's so small it looks like it would fit an infant, not an adult. "I think her head would explode."

I laugh and pick up a baby pink mini dress with a cut out navel. "I think she might like this colour more."

Riley giggles and circles the rack, hunting for another item, then stops suddenly. Her eyes fix on a dark red, velvet bodycon dress. She strokes it, her fingertips light against the fabric. "I was wearing something like this the night it happened," she whispers.

I swallow hard, watching as Riley's eyes glaze over. I know she is no longer in Firefly with me, but in her memories of that night. Of the feel of that dress against her skin and the terror that overcame her as the unthinkable happened.

I approach quietly so I don't disturb her. "It's a beautiful dress, Riley. Definitely the nicest thing in the store."

"Pretty, isn't it? Mine was green, not red. It was my first grown-up party dress. My dad told me it was too short, even though it was longer than all my friends' dresses."

I smile, even though there's nothing to smile about in this situation. I've read about protective dads in magazines and books. Dads who said, 'Be home on time or else', who policed their daughter's wardrobes and stayed up late worrying about what time they got home. My dad was never in the picture to do that for me. Even if he was, Peter Harris stole me before I had my first grown-up party dress for him to object to.

Riley clears her throat, but even then, her voice still comes out hoarse. "When my parents told me I couldn't go to the party, my dad even said, 'You'll have to save your slutty dress for another occasion'."

"Well, for what it's worth, I think you'd look beautiful in a dress like this."

Riley smiles a wry smile. "I felt it, at the time. Now I want to burn any dress I see that reminds me of it." Riley lets go of the dress, her hand curling into a fist. "They've never said it, but they don't have to. My parents think that by wearing that dress, I invited what happened."

The weight of responsibility hits me square in the chest as I realise the power my response will have, but I don't back down. I've been where Riley is, on the receiving end of the ignorant things people say. I know how that blame hurts. I know how it changes how you see yourself and the world, and I refuse to let Riley do this to herself.

"Riley, nothing you did or said or wore made it happen. The person who did it made it happen. They're the one with the responsibility. They're the one in the wrong."

"I wish someone could make my parents see that," she says, her teary eyes meeting mine. "Can we go to a bookstore? I'd like to get lost in someone else's world for a bit rather than be in mine."

There's so much more I want to say, but instead, I nod. Leaving the velvet dress behind, we head to Fairfellow Books, a local literary institution that's survived the rise of online shopping and e-readers. The scent of freshly brewed coffee and ink on paper waves us into the store. An instant peace washes over me as soon as my foot crosses the threshold.

Even Riley's shoulders relax.

"I could spend hours in here," I say wistfully.

"You're here with me, that might happen," Riley jokes. "I spend more time in books than I do in the real world."

We mosey around, reading blurbs and passing each other books that sound interesting. I learn that Riley wasn't joking when she said she spends most of her time reading. She's well-read, much more than I am, even with Stefan's help. She enjoys books in all genres, writers old and new. For the first time, I truly see the person beyond what happened. For the first time, I see Riley.

We're browsing the 'T' section in the fiction area when Riley excuses herself to go to the bathroom. "I'll be around here somewhere," I reply, indicating to the rest of the store we've still to explore.

When she's gone, I wander through the fiction section taking photos of books with cover art I like to show Stefan, then I head into the non-fiction section.

That's where I see it.

Facing cover first, a bestseller sticker slapped on the top corner - '*Peter Harris and The Unlucky Eleven*'.

My legs move on autopilot, leading me to his tattooed image. My eyes trail over the book cover, skimming the extract from one of the many five-star reviews it received – "*A chilling insight into the mind of 'The Ghost' himself – unputdownable*" – before plucking the book from the shelf. It's heavy in my hands, almost as if the misery contained inside it weighs down the pages. I turn it over to read the blurb of the book that changed everything. The book that Conrad tells me someone is using as an instruction manual for murder.

"What are you doing with that?"

I jump at the sound of Riley's voice, a guilty flush covering my cheeks, but I don't put the book back on the shelf.

Riley looks at the book again, then at me. "Have you read it?"

I shake my head.

"Do you want to?"

My eyes fall on the cover once more. Peter Harris's mugshot, his tattoos, his cold, calculating eyes.

"I know this book isn't my story," I say. "I know Nathaniel Clarke wrote it to make money from other people's pain. I know it will be sensationalist and dramatic, and even then it will never be able to accurately describe what I went through. But still… still…"

"Still, you want to read it."

I nod. "The police think the new killer is using this book as an instruction manual. What if it contains the answer to who's doing this? What if when I read it, I can spot something the police can't? I mean, I lived through it, didn't I? I was the one it happened to. Surely I'm the one who's best placed to find clues in the book?"

"Maybe," Riley concedes. "But the question isn't if you can read it, it's if you're ready to."

My thumb brushes the cover, tracing over the embossed lettering of the title. "I don't know if I'll ever be ready to read it, but if I can help, then surely I should?"

Riley reaches out. For a moment, I think she's going to comfort me, but instead, she takes the book and walks away. I blink at her sudden departure and then look back to the shelf. There are only two copies of Nathaniel Clarke's book left. Two copies left because the book was so popular with people who could read it, shudder, and think, 'Thank goodness that wasn't me'.

Sighing, I walk away from Peter Harris's face and the memories it conjures, ready to leave Fairfellow Books, but when I scan the store, I can't see Riley anywhere.

My heart pounds. Sarah placed her trust in me to look after her daughter. Two shops in and I've lost her.

I head back to the fiction section and retrace our steps, hunting for the books Riley debated purchasing in case she went back to get them, but she's not there.

My pulse is in my throat, frantic and throbbing. I spin around, taking in the endless bookshelves and blank faces of strangers, none of them Riley.

"Riley?!" I call out. An elderly woman a few metres away jumps and shoots an irritated glare in my direction, but I don't care. I'd scare everyone in the store if it meant finding Riley.

Just as I'm about to call her name once more, I spot Riley walking towards me, a Fairfellow Books bag swinging in her hand. I almost fall to my knees with relief.

When she reaches me, Riley holds the bag out. "I wouldn't exactly call this a gift, but I didn't want you to spend your own money on it."

I take the bag and peek inside. Nathaniel Clarke's book looks back at me. "Riley, you didn't have to buy this."

"I wanted to. This way, Nathaniel Clarke doesn't get a penny from you."

A swell of emotion overcomes me. I don't fight it. I pull Riley into a hug, tears sliding down my cheeks as I whisper 'thank you' to her again and again. At first, Riley's body is stiff in my arms, but then I feel her shudder and break. She chokes on a sob, and I squeeze her tighter.

I know we must look strange – two women crying in a bookshop – but I don't care. This hug feels like healing. This hug, exactly what both of us need.

Chapter *Thirteen.*

Two hours later, Sarah collects Riley. She offers me a lift home, but I politely decline. Riley waves goodbye as they drive away, and then I'm alone.

A gust of wind sweeps through the city centre. I shiver and debate what to do next. The paper handle of the Fairfellow Books bag digs into my flesh. I thumb it, letting the coarseness scratch my skin, then my body takes matters into its own hands. It walks me away from the busy streets of the city towards Derwent Park.

I smile at its location of choice. Derwent Park is one of my favourite places. On paper, it should be somewhere I'm on edge. It has no CCTV and is secluded and sparsely populated, but the park holds too many precious memories for me to feel anything other than comfort in its presence. We came here so frequently throughout my childhood that Mum would joke it should be renamed 'Allen Park'. Whenever I come here, I feel close to her. As I walk through the wrought iron gates at the entrance, a foolish part of me can't help but hope that I'll see her waiting for me on one of the benches.

I make my way down the tree-lined pathways, hunting for the perfect spot to sit in solitude. A dad plays football with his son and daughter on the grass. He cheers as their little legs pound the ground, chasing a bright yellow ball. I continue past them, a jubilant shout of 'goal!' echoing behind me.

I find the perfect bench at the top of one of the park's many hills. It sits alone, looking out across the city. The veins of the streets stretch out before me, tiny dots of people and cars moving towards their destination of choice. Life in all its glory, proudly on display, close but out of reach.

Taking a seat, I pull the book out of the bag and thumb the pages, the fat stack of paper carrying the weight of a thousand nightmares.

This is it, I tell myself. *There's no going back from here.*

Once I read these words, I can't unsee them or lie to myself that being 'Hannah Allen' doesn't matter. But more than that, by reading this book, Peter Harris will no longer be a grey, murky shadow from my past, but a fully coloured-in person. I'll read quotes directly from him. I'll discover his insights and learn his thought patterns. I'll hear his version of my story.

Before I can talk myself out of it, I open the book to a random page.

When the identity of 'The Ghost' was finally revealed, there was a sense of disbelief up and down the country. For sixteen months, people had imagined a cloaked, mysterious, isolated figure. Someone who hid in the shadows. Someone so hideous, so full of evil, that they must live on the edges of society.

But Peter Harris was none of those things. In fact, to all who knew him, Peter Harris was a normal man.

One of the many things that shocked people about Peter Harris was that he didn't 'look' like their interpretation of a serial killer. He didn't look like someone who held sadistic, archaic views on women, or like a person who needed to abduct and rape women to have sex with them.

Handsome is an almost reductionist way to describe Peter Harris. To put it simply, he is a genetically blessed man. Many who knew him reported thinking he could have been a model, albeit an alternative one thanks to his heavily tattooed skin.

"I worked with Peter on and off in hospitality for a few years. He

always ended up with the biggest tips at the end of the night, and most of the time a stack of phone numbers too. He had these blue eyes that women couldn't resist," Frankie Coleman, a former colleague of Peter Harris, said. "When we'd work the closing shift at The Royal Oak, more often than not Peter went home with a woman. When it all came out, I thought there had to be a mistake. There's no way someone like Peter could be 'The Ghost'. There was no way he'd abduct women to sleep with them. He didn't need to."

*But, as Frankie Coleman and the rest of the world would find out, Peter Harris **was** the person responsible for these heinous crimes.*

I flick ahead, silencing Frankie Coleman and his disbelief that someone attractive could be a monster. That mindset makes me want to scream.

Bending the spine of the book, I settle on a page halfway through.

"She was my mum. She wasn't number seven. She wasn't someone who deserved what happened because she went for a walk on her own. How can people think that? And worse still, how can they say that to me as if they think that's something I want to hear? I was an eight-year-old kid who found out her mum was never going to come home. An eight-year-old kid who went to school and heard people say my mum was irresponsible, that she didn't keep herself safe. Keep herself safe? She went for a walk. A walk, like she did every day. Like she should have been able to without being murdered."

Bella's eyes shine with indignant tears. I can't help but ask her what she would say to the people who lay blame for what happened at Freya Moran's feet.

"I'd tell them to fuck off," Bella states bluntly. "If you think that's okay to say to me after what that man did, then you are not worthy of my time. You are not worthy of saying my mum's name. Freya Moran was my mum. That's what I want her to be known as. My mum, the best mum I could have wished for. The mum I'll forever be heartbroken to have had

stolen from me."

I snap the book shut, crushing it to my chest as if I can squash the words out of print.

Number Seven. Freya Moran. Bella Moran, her little girl, now a young woman who, somewhere in the back of her mind, is still waiting for her mum to return home from a walk.

The ache in my chest deepens. I drop the book to my lap, the cover blurring through my tears.

You don't have to do this, I think. The thought glimmers before me but it's soon shrouded in darkness. Whether I read this book or not doesn't change the fact that someone is out there, continuing the story. Someone has taken this insight into Peter Harris's sick mind and resurrected his reign of terror. Somewhere within these pages could be the reason why, and a way to stop it.

It takes everything in me to do so, but I go back to the beginning of the book and read it from page one. Then, on page two-hundred-and-thirty-seven, I reach my chapter.

Number Eleven

Two months after Amanda Powell was abducted, Peter Harris selects his final victim. Walking home from school in the regulation navy blue Parkwell High uniform was fourteen-year-old Hannah Allen.

Soon the entire country would be able to describe that uniform and every aspect of her teenage appearance in detail. Light brown hair in a loose ponytail, matchstick legs in long, white socks that were no doubt slipping down her shins after a long day of studying. The epitome of innocence that lured Peter Harris in when he first saw her walking down Clifton Crescent.

"She was a vision, there's no other way to describe her," Harris admits. "I was drawn to her. She wasn't like the others... she was pure."

The youngest of his victims by nine years, Hannah Allen had recently joined the school netball team. Inside her school bag, officers would find a pink diary with the names of her best friends scrawled on the front page. The day after she was bundled into Peter Harris's car, she was due to attend an appointment with an orthodontist.

In the eyes of the law, Hannah Allen was a child. A child whose life was about to be changed forever thanks to the actions of one man.

Hannah Allen took the same route home every day. She had done since the start of the school year, her mother able to work full-time again now she could trust her teenage daughter to travel to and from school on her own. A journey that took fifteen minutes, five of which Hannah walked with a friend, the rest she walked alone.

That day, there was no reason for Hannah to think she was unsafe. Harris's victims had all been over the age of eighteen. They had all been in various vulnerable positions – drunk on a night out, waiting for the last train home, taking a shortcut through a park at night... but walking home from school? The idea of danger in that seemed ludicrous.

But for Hannah Allen, the idea wasn't ludicrous at all.

Described by friends as a quiet, kind girl, those attributes would be the things that Peter Harris noticed. The purity he confessed attracted him to Hannah in the first place. Those traits resulted in Hannah being abducted, but they were also the things that ultimately saved her life.

From the start of our interview, it's clear that Peter sees Hannah differently from the rest of his victims. When he talks of her, his eyes mist over. The anger and hatred he had for the others isn't there. You could almost argue that, despite his prison uniform and the multitude of angry tattoos decorating his skin, he looks like a lovesick schoolboy.

I lower the book, nauseated. It's not the dramatic flair of Nathaniel Clarke's writing that sickens me, but the insinuation in his words. His writing almost justifies what Peter Harris did as an act of adoration, but what about my feelings? My childish, fourteen-year-old feelings?

My eyes trace the word 'child'. I want to grab a pen and circle the word a million times, highlighting it so furiously that the nib of the pen cuts through the page. A child - that's what I was. That's all there is to it. An adult man is not a lovesick schoolboy, no matter how Nathaniel Clarke frames it.

Inhaling deeply, I build up the courage to read on.

"There was something different about her," Peter admits. "I suspected it from the moment I saw her, but as soon as we spoke, I knew it was true. She was so shy, so wide-eyed. She didn't scream or fight back like the others. She just cried. There was such innocence in that. I had to have her."

There's a smile on Peter's face as he says this. Again, he looks like a man recounting the story of his first love. It's tempting to be drawn into his version of events, this charismatic man detailing a moment of ultimate connection. Only when I remember who he is talking about, I recoil.

"But you didn't treat her differently to the others, did you?" I ask. "You hurt her."

Instantly, Peter clouds over. "I made mistakes with Hannah, I admit. I tattooed her like the others, but I shouldn't have. She wasn't like them. She didn't deserve to be ordered. No, Hannah Allen wasn't like the others at all. She was special."

It's clear that Peter believes this to his core. While he has no remorse for what he did to his other victims, in Allen, he romanticises what happened whilst she was his captive.

"I feel like I was the first person to listen to her, you know? The only person she could open up to. We had a bond that people could only ever dream of."

I find myself looking into the eyes of a deluded man. A man who truly believes his version of events, even when he has been told explicitly that they are not true.

'I was scared that if I didn't speak, he would kill me. Now I'm scared to

talk to anyone, even my mum' – words from Hannah Allen's victim impact statement. Words that were read aloud in court, recited on the news, and printed in newspapers across the world.

When I mention Hannah's victim impact statement, Peter bangs his fist on the table so hard my drink spills.

"I don't care what they said in court," he hisses, the monster that took the lives of so many bubbling to the surface. "We had a connection. She trusted me. Sure, she didn't speak much at first, but eventually I got her talking. When she did, it was like I was the only person in the world. She was happy in my care. She wanted to be with me deep down, I know she did."

"Even if she told the court otherwise?"

"The court case was a joke. The police convinced Hannah to lie, but the truth is that what we had was special. When we made love, it was beautiful."

When I point out that Hannah was just fourteen when she was abducted, making their 'lovemaking' statutory rape, Peter Harris looks unfazed. "Call it what you want, but I know the tears she shed afterwards were tears of love. I was her first... how could she not love me?"

The burn of my tears almost blinds me, the sickly feeling flowing through my veins torture, but I read on, hunting for answers through the trauma of these words.

For the first time in all our meetings, I feel a chill whilst sitting in Peter's presence. The unhinged monster that graced the cover of every newspaper is no more present than when he talks about Hannah Allen. Mistaking her tears for love, her silence for complicity, and her fear for intimacy. The more I try to get Peter to see that Hannah was a victim, the more he tries to convince me otherwise. The more he asserts his adoration, the more he unnerves me.

Peter Harris doesn't strike me as a man who has any understanding of what he has done. If anything, he strikes me as a man who would do it all again if it meant he could get close to Hannah once more.

I read that last paragraph twice. My chin quivers, begging me to close this book, but I can't stop. Now I know Peter Harris doesn't believe our story to be over, I need to read on.

I lean closer to Peter even though every part of my brain tells me to back away from him. "If she mattered to you, then why did you hurt her?"

Peter looks shocked at this question. "I didn't hurt her. I would never hurt her."

Immediately, the scars on Hannah's wrists and ankles from being bound flash through my mind. "She was tied up with gardening wire -"

"I didn't want her to run away."

"She had cigarette burns on her arms —"

"She wasn't eating. I had to get her to eat or she'd be sick. That was her punishment for not doing what she was told. I did it for her own good."

"You didn't let her leave the room. She had to go to the bathroom in a bowl in the corner —"

"Like I said, I didn't want her to run away."

I point out the lack of love in this, but Peter snaps.

"You don't understand. You weren't there. When she first joined me, she would have run away if I didn't stop her. She'd been told I was a monster, but I knew with time she'd see I wasn't. She'd learn I only did what I did to those other women because they deserved it, but she didn't. She was made for me."

The way Peter's eyes gleam as he says this highlights what a psychopath he is. The brutalisation of the women before was sickening, but sitting before him as he deludes himself that his crimes against a child were an act of love is a whole new level of hideousness.

Something inside me wants to break him. I want him to realise what he did was wrong, so I do the only thing I can think of to hurt him — I tell him what has become of the woman he was so sure would be his forever, now happy and settled in a committed relationship.

The silence after I speak is booming. For a moment I wonder if I've made a mistake. Peter flexes his fingers, the tattoos on his knuckles expanding and contracting at the movement, then his piercing eyes lock on mine.

"So she turned out to be like the others after all," he says.

Peter sits with his disappointment, stewing in it until it transforms into anger. The blackness in his eyes returns. I find I feel more comfortable in his presence this way than when he was lit up by his one-sided love.

Suddenly, Peter lets out a bitter snarl. "I should have seen it coming. They always disappoint you in the end, don't they? Maybe there should have never been a Lucky Number 11 after all."

"What do you mean by that?" I ask, even though I know what his answer will be.

"Isn't it obvious? Hannah Allen deserved to die. She deserved to die like the rest of them."

Those words tip me over the edge. I lean over the side of the bench and empty my stomach of its contents. Vomit burns the back of my throat, the semi-digested remains of my breakfast splashing my shoes, but I don't have the brain capacity to care. Not after what I've just read.

Conrad was right – this book is an instruction manual for a killer. It tells them Peter Harris's methods and motive, but more than that, it tells them who one of their victims should be... me.

Chapter *Fourteen.*

I throw the book in the bin and leave Derwent Park, passing the father and his two children once more but barely registering their existence. Every step I take punches the same fearful thought throughout my body - Peter Harris wants me dead and somewhere, someone out there is going to make his wish come true.

My legs move quicker, racing through the city towards the bus stop. The hairs on the back of my neck stand on end the entire journey home as if I'm being watched. Behind me, someone listens to music through headphones, the volume so high I can hear the tinny beat.

When the familiar streets near my apartment come into view, I get off the bus and power myself home. Once inside, I slam the door shut behind me and test the lock twice to see if it will hold.

"I've just got in too, how good is that timing?" Joel calls from somewhere inside.

I don't answer him. Instead, I go to the bedroom and locate my panic alarm. I pull it over my head and grip the plastic casing, but still my heart pounds.

"How was shopping?" Joel asks as he enters the bedroom.

"It was good," I lie, the words slipping seamlessly from my lips. "I didn't buy anything, but it was nice to window shop."

"At least you had a nice time. How was the meeting?"

"As good as could be expected."

Joel eyes me sceptically. "Are you okay? You seem... off."

I push myself to smile. "I'm fine. It's just been a long day, that's all."

Joel doesn't push it. For the millionth time in our relationship, I'm thankful for his ability to give me space. "Have you seen the news?" he asks, his tone trying and failing to sound nonchalant.

"No, but Amrita told me they've publicly linked the killings to Peter Harris."

Joel nods, but it's clear from the look on his face that there's more to tell.

"Is my name mentioned?" I ask.

"Once or twice," Joel replies, an answer I know means a lot more than that.

My fingers itch to pull out my phone and see what's been written, but I stop myself. *Your focus needs to be on moving forward, not crumbling*, I think, but no matter how many times I repeat that sentence, I can't forget Peter Harris's words - '*She deserved to die like the rest of them*'.

When Joel goes for a shower after dinner, I give in to temptation. Curling up on the sofa, I grab my phone and search 'Gabriella O'Hara'. An article by Raja Kaling is one of the first hits.

BREAKING: 'The Ghost' Returns
By Raja Kaling

With the body of missing schoolgirl Gabriella O'Hara found and the identity of a second victim confirmed as sex worker Trina Lamond, the entire country faces a petrifying new reality – a murderer is on the loose. Not only that, but police sources have confirmed that whoever is responsible for the crimes terrifying the nation is taking inspiration from one of Britain's most notorious serial killers, Peter Harris.

It was just over ten years ago when women everywhere were living in fear of Peter Harris and his devastating killing rampage. Nicknamed

'The Ghost' for his ability to evade police detection, Harris abducted a total of eleven women over a sixteen-month period. Only one lived to tell the tale - Hannah Allen, also known as 'Lucky Number 11', a title earned thanks to her miraculous escape from Harris's clutches.

But it looks like this nightmare is coming back to life, for Hannah Allen and for women up and down the country.

I skim the rest of Raja's article, snarling at every hyperbolic sentence until I reach the end and see the comments. All 1326 of them.

Wendy273: The return of 'The Ghost'... I can't believe this is happening again. When will it stop?!

Timtim: Lock away your daughters. There's a madman on the loose!

FunJaney67: Poor Gabriella O'Hara. Just a schoolgirl! What did the other one expect, doing that job? Still, RIP

AntiWokeWarrior: If there's someone else killing people, doesn't this mean they've got the wrong guy? Been saying this all along... Peter Harris is INNOCENT

I read the last comment again, waiting for the letters to make sense, but they never do.

Innocent.

Innocent... how the word burns my retinas.

I want to reply to *'AntiWokeWarrior'* and ask them if they'd like to listen to me talk about my time with the 'innocent' Peter Harris. Ask them to look me in the eye when I've finished speaking and say he's innocent then.

But as I begin to type, it's something else I am writing. Not a response to *'WokeWarrior'*, but the words 'Peter Harris innocent'.

The first thing I see when the results of my search load is Peter Harris's mugshot. With his eyes on mine, the number eleven on my stomach fires into life as if I am being branded here and now. I feel every score of the needle, the ink going too deep because I'm recoiling from his tattoo pen of torture.

I scroll past his picture and scan the other search results, reading newspaper headlines and excerpts from press releases about Nathaniel Clarke's book. The further I scroll, the less official the websites become. Soon, I'm faced with a list of chat rooms and conspiracy theory threads. Extracts from web pages screaming phrases like '*set up by the police to keep men down*' and '*he did what we all wish we could do*' jump out at me.

As terrifying as it is to read these viewpoints, I know I'm in the right place if I want to learn more about the people who look up to that man. People who would potentially carry on his work.

Trembling, I click on the first promising-looking link.

BigDaddee101: Peter Harris is a HERO. The man stands up for a man's biological right to dominate and becomes a victim of the feminist agenda. This is a NATIONAL DISGRACE! Women need to learn that if they divorce, flaunt themselves for the world to see or reject like it's a sport, then they get what's coming to them. NO SYMPATHY!!

My stomach flips, but my repulsion only grows when I read the fifty-six replies.

MrToxic: Tell me u dnt rspct the guy 4 wot he did. Btches get stitches…lollllll

Kingp1n7: FRAMED to keep the feminazis happy. What next – getting locked up just for being a man?

The more I read, the angrier I become. The more I read, the more I see why Sisterhood of Support exists. A sickness breeds in society. It seeps into the water. It bleeds into courtrooms and meetings and HR departments and schools.

"Are you okay?"

Joel's unexpected interruption breaks me from my thoughts. I turn to the doorway where he stands, dripping wet from his shower and wrapped in a navy blue towel.

"You're shaking like a leaf!" he cries, rushing to my side, but he stops when he sees my screen. His face pales. "What are you doing?"

"I…"

When I can't find the words to answer him, Joel takes my phone from me. He's barely begun to read before he sucks in a breath. "Hannah, this is toxic."

"I know, but I wanted to hear what people thought."

"On the darkest corners of the internet?! No good can come from going on these websites, Hannah. You're only going to scare yourself."

I don't tell Joel that I'm already terrified. Instead, I watch as he puts my phone in a drawer as if it being out of sight will make me forget what I've read.

"That's enough of the internet for today, okay?" he says. "Let's do something nice. How about we watch a film? There are loads of new releases for us to dissect."

Even though I can't think of anything worse than watching a group of people live in a parallel reality with happy endings and neat resolutions, I nod.

For the rest of the day, I follow Joel's wishes. I don't search for Peter Harris or his fans, but it doesn't make a difference. I don't need to read their threats to know they're out there, wishing I was dead. Worse still, I know one of them is working to make that wish come true. They're coming for me like Peter Harris wants them to, something no film or time away from my phone can make me forget.

Chapter *Fifteen.*

Everything is heavy as I get ready for work the next morning. Even my fingers feel like they're carrying the weight of the last few days. I layer my makeup to cover the grey tinge to my skin as best I can, but the stream of restless nights is catching up with me. I glare at the skin underneath my eyes, hating it for betraying the true torment within.

Ellen does everything but gasp when I arrive at Break Time. "Hannah," she says, pulling me to one side. "Go home. Seriously, it's okay. We're always quiet on Sundays."

I shake my head. "I want to be here."

Ellen chews her lip. "But, Han, you look awful."

"Gee, thanks," I try to joke, but there's an edge to my voice.

"You know what I mean. I'm worried about you, sweetheart. I can see how tired you are underneath all that makeup."

"Ellen, I need to keep busy. Please, I need to be here."

Ellen scans my face for a sign of doubt, but I refuse to let her find one. After a moment, she caves. "Fine, you can stay, but if you need to go home or if you want a break, let me know, okay?"

I nod to appease her, but I won't be calling in that favour. Early shifts and extra breaks are a slippery slope that leads to not leaving bed. I already dropped out of school and turned down attending university because of what happened – I refuse to let my past make me lose a job I enjoy too.

Right here, right now, I make a vow – I am not leaving work until the end of my shift. This is my job, my life, and my routine. No one is going to take that away from me.

To my credit, I manage to plough through the day, serving with a smile and even earning a ten-pound tip from one customer. Another two police officers check in on me after lunch, a short, cordial visit that I don't allow to ruin my working flow. I keep my head down and my hands busy. Little routines like knowing how long to froth milk for and the right amount of cocoa to dust on a hot chocolate keep my mind away from where it wants to stray.

"You're on fire today," Stefan comments at one point. "I don't think I've ever seen you work so hard!"

I catch Ellen's eye. She winks and I feel myself come alive. *See? Things are okay*, I think, and for the first time in a while, I believe it.

But twenty minutes before Break Time closes, my new-found conviction is swept away when the front door opens and in walks the last person I want to see.

"What are you doing here?" I ask, but as soon as I register Conrad's strained face, I realise I don't want to know the answer to that question.

"Is there somewhere I can go with Hannah? Somewhere private?" he asks, staring past me to direct his question to Ellen.

Ellen's eyes are wide and fearful, but she nods. "Through here is best," she says, leading Conrad to the backroom. She stands in the doorway and looks at me to follow him.

Even though my entire body screams at me not to, I comply.

"I'll leave you to it," Ellen says. She tries to catch my eye before she exits the room, but I avoid her gaze, choosing to focus on Conrad instead.

The backroom is only big enough for us to store our personal belongings and have breaks in one at a time, so Conrad's broad frame fills the space. Even his height is too large, his head almost grazing the ceiling. Everything about him being here seems wrong, his dark clothes out of place against the green walls and cutesy décor.

When we are alone, Conrad takes a seat at the rickety table for two. The chair squeaks beneath his weight. "Take a seat, Hannah."

I don't move. "Why are you here?"

"Hannah, please –"

"Why are you here?"

Conrad's features fall into an indecipherable mask. "This won't be easy for you to hear, Hannah, but you asked me to keep you up to date with the investigation, so here I am. In the early hours of Saturday morning, a student was abducted on her way home from a night out."

My legs give way and I collapse into the chair opposite Conrad. "It's happened again?"

"We think so, yes."

The room spins, and for not the first time in my life, I find myself wishing that Ellen had painted it anything but green.

"What happened? Who is she?"

Conrad hesitates, but he knows better than to withhold information from me now. "Her name is Harriet Warren. She's a nineteen-year-old student. She was last seen at the Onyx nightclub on Harrow Street."

Harriet Warren, a name I will never forget. A student, just like Stefan. Harrow Street, a mere five-minute walk away from where I am at this very moment.

"Harriet had a falling out with her friends while at the club. They assumed she went back to another friend's house, but when she wasn't home by Saturday lunchtime, they got worried. They called around and realised Harriet hadn't gone home with anyone else. No one has seen or heard from her since the early hours of Saturday morning."

The impact of Harriet's disappearance passes through my mind. Classmates who will head to lectures on trembling legs. Friends who will forever carry the burden of wondering what would have happened had they not got into a silly argument. A family who will have received the worst call they could ever get.

So many lives ruined by one moment, one person.

"I don't understand how this can be happening again," I say, rubbing my temples. "I thought Peter Harris was in prison."

"He is, Hannah. This isn't him."

My heart pounds in my ears as I ask the question that's plagued me since Conrad first reappeared in my life. "Are you sure?"

Conrad doesn't break eye contact. "Positive. Peter Harris will spend the rest of his life behind bars."

"So there really is someone copying him," I exhale.

Conrad nods glumly and hangs his head, allowing me time to process the news.

I think of Nathaniel Clarke's book, of Peter Harris's wish that he had finished the job of murdering me, and shudder. "I don't understand, Conrad. It wasn't this quick last time. Peter Harris waited weeks, sometimes months, between victims. How can there be so many women missing one after another?"

"That's what we're trying to figure out. Remember, the person doing this might use similar methods to Peter Harris, but they aren't the same person. They're someone who... well, they're someone who has been inspired by him."

Inspired by Peter Harris... I frost over at the thought.

"Unfortunately, Peter Harris is a figure some people look up to," Conrad continues. "His actions and justifications for committing his crimes have influenced criminals before. Not to this extent, but they have."

I lean back in my chair, suddenly exhausted. "I don't understand why someone would want to be like him."

"The fact that you don't understand means you're a good person." Conrad clears his throat and leans closer. "When I say to you that these killings aren't the same as before, I mean it. The timeline of the disappearances is one thing, but there are other significant differences between what Peter Harris did and what is happening now."

"Like what?"

Conrad hesitates. "This is strictly confidential, Hannah, okay? What I'm about to tell you cannot leave this room."

"Conrad, who am I going to tell? It's not like I'm shouting about this from the rooftops."

My logic strikes a nerve with Conrad because he nods. "Well, for starters, none of the victims have been sexually assaulted."

I blink at these words. "None?"

As Conrad shakes his head, my chest constricts.

"But I thought Peter Harris killed women to show them how pathetic their right to say no was? He wanted to remind men to dominate. 'Fuck the feminists' is what he said at his trial, right?" The words are thick in my throat, but I've said them. Peter Harris's warped reasoning and the sickening excuse for why my childhood was robbed. "Why would someone copy his methods but not his motive?"

"Again, that's something we're working on answering, but it's clear that not everything we know about Peter Harris applies this time. For example, this person sedates their victims at or around the time of abduction."

The news wobbles my core. I try to fight off the memory of hammering against the boot of Peter Harris's car in a desperate attempt to free myself as he drove away with me, but it holds strong. It's like I'm back there, trapped in those dark, claustrophobic confines, Peter Harris's gym bag at my feet, the stench of his stale sweat choking the air.

"Peter Harris never sedated me," I whisper. "He made sure I was awake for everything."

"As I said, this is someone new," Conrad says softly. "They're copying some of his techniques, but not all of them. The sedation and lack of sexual motive are examples of this."

"If their motive isn't sexual, then what is it?"

"Right now, we're exploring different avenues and –"

"Conrad, why are they killing these women?"

Conrad holds my gaze, his eyes blinding me with the truth he doesn't need to say for me to know.

"You don't know, do you?" I whisper. As Conrad inflates his chest, ready to spin another falsehood to pacify me, I find myself interrupting him. "Conrad, please. After everything we've been through together, please don't lie to me."

Conrad folds in on himself. "Honestly, Hannah? Right now, we have no idea."

We sit in the density of Conrad's admission, the words clogging the atmosphere until they suffocate us. How can they not? If the detective in charge of the case has no idea what's going on, what hope is there for Harriet Warren? What hope is there for me?

Are people scared yet? As scared as they should be? As scared as living in this world should make them?

Or are they doing what they always do, what you always do, and living in wilful ignorance? Coddling themselves with new clothes and takeaway dinners as if things will be fine because they can make them look that way on social media. Turning a blind eye because the bad stuff isn't happening to them.

But the thing is, Hannah, you can't turn a blind eye because this is happening to you.

Are you scared yet?

I imagine you must be, but are you as scared as you should be? Probably not. Even with everything falling apart around you, even with me waiting in the wings, you're probably still telling yourself it will all be okay.

Well, you're wrong about that.

Just like the others, you will fall into death's abyss soon enough. I will leave you with no choice but to.

But more than that, soon you will accept that things are not okay and never will be, no matter how much you try to convince yourself otherwise. That's the beauty of the truth - sooner or later, it gets through to you. Sooner or later, you realise how fucked we all are. How there is no escaping the inevitable.

And your death by my hands is inevitable.

So I ask again, Hannah – are you scared yet? Because you should be.

Chapter *Sixteen.*

Conrad offers to drive me home. As reluctant as I am to have my independence disrupted further, I still say yes.

We leave work when Break Time closes to the public. Robbie waves when he notices me on the street, but his smile disappears when he sees Conrad and all his seriousness beside me. He ducks his head into his coat and watches us walk to Conrad's car from the corner of his eye.

Once we're driving, I take the opportunity to pepper Conrad with questions. "Have you looked into the people who know Peter Harris? Is there a cellmate who's recently been released or a friend who's been visiting him for years?"

"No, there's no one like that."

"Did Harriet have a boyfriend or girlfriend she could be staying with? Maybe a secret one her friends didn't know about?"

"No relationship, no secret."

"And nothing weird happened to her before the night out? No threats? No psycho ex?"

"Other than the argument in the club, no."

"What about her phone, have you tracked that?"

"Unfortunately for us, the battery died when she was in the club."

"Have you checked CCTV? Or -"

"Hannah," Conrad sighs, pulling up outside my apartment. "I know you're worried, but trust me when I say we are doing everything we can to find Harriet and whoever has taken her."

I pick at the hem of my coat. "I know you're doing everything you can," I say. What I don't add is that everything he can do clearly isn't enough.

Conrad glances at my apartment building. "Do you want me to walk you inside?"

"I'm fine. Thanks, though."

We share a smile, our first in forever.

"Take care, Hannah. I'll be in touch if I hear anything, okay?"

I leave the vehicle and keep my pace measured as I walk towards the front door, aware that Conrad hasn't driven away yet and won't until he knows I'm inside. When I reach it, I wave to him to project an air of confidence that says, 'Everything is fine'.

With my key in the lock, Conrad sets off. When he's gone, I open the door and step into the building.

I stop abruptly.

Another note has been left on the doormat.

Every hair on my body bristles, the folded white paper stark against the dark backdrop of the doormat.

Everything is okay. It's just a note, my brain says, but the pounding in my chest suggests otherwise. I glance back outside and check the end of the street, confirming that Conrad is now gone. I gulp, feeling much less self-assured than I was a few seconds ago.

Ordering myself to be brave, I pick up the piece of paper and unfold it to unveil a ballpoint inking of a person with a manic grin. The text scrawled above their head reads, '*I LOVE THIS GAME - DO YOU?*'

A cool, creeping sensation trickles down my body.

Like before, the writing is chunky and childlike, and the drawing is poorly executed. I flip the paper over to see if anything else is written on it, but the rest of the page is blank.

"Are those children at it again?"

I jump and look to the source of the voice. Arthur, another resident of the building, shuffles towards me. I always like bumping into Arthur - he tells me the best jokes he's heard at the community centre coffee mornings he attends and in return I take him a bundle of cookies whenever I bake - but at this moment, I've never been happier to be in his friendly presence.

"You've seen the notes too?" I ask.

Arthur nods. "Found three so far myself, all very strange. I tell you, that woman needs to control her children. These tricks of theirs are getting out of hand."

My eyes wander to the door of apartment one. "Do you think they're the ones doing this?"

"Who else would be silly enough to pull a stunt like this?" Arthur sighs, shaking his head. "Those boys make you wonder what the world will look like in twenty years' time. Anyway, I'd better head to the supermarket before it gets dark. Say hi to Joel for me."

I hold open the door for Arthur then look down at the note once more. It does look like something a child would draw, plus, if my time at Sisterhood of Support has taught me anything, it's that sometimes I let my paranoia win. What's to say this isn't one of those occasions?

"Oh, Hannah, before I forget," Arthur says, turning back to me. "There was a woman here today asking about you. She gave me this and I kept it to show you." Arthur locates his wallet in the breast of his coat and pulls out a small rectangular card. I recognise it instantly - Raja Kaling's business card.

My heart pounds as I take it from him. "Did you say anything to her?"

"Oh, I'm too old for gossip, especially about a friend, but she buzzed everyone in the building. She seemed to really want to talk to people. I thought you'd want to know."

With that, Arthur leaves. I watch the front door close behind him then look back at my hands. The creepy note sits in one, Raja's business card in the other. Two frustrations disturbing the already rocky foundations of my life.

Before I can talk myself out of it, I pull my phone out and dial Raja's number.

"Hello, this is -"

I cut in before Raja can finish her sentence. "You've been trying to talk to my neighbours?"

"Hannah, how wonderful to hear from you." There's a smile to Raja's voice, one I would love to wipe from her face.

"Stop with the false niceties, Raja. You're harassing me and I want you to stop."

"Come on, Hannah. You know how this goes. I'm only doing my job."

"Oh, please! Your job is not to hound me. What are you hoping to find out from my neighbours, anyway? I barely speak to half of them!"

"Well, you aren't exactly forthcoming with giving an interview, so what choice did I have? I had to get creative. It's my job to report on things people want to know about and you, Hannah Allen, are someone people most definitely want to know about."

Her words ignite a fire in the pit of my stomach. "There's a killer out there. Surely that's where your attention should be, not on me?"

"Hannah, whether you like it or not, you're part of what's going on. It's my job to unpick why and to tell that story."

"You're disgusting," I snarl. "Leave me and my neighbours alone, okay?"

With that, I hang up, screw both papers into a tight ball, and dash upstairs to the safety of home. Only with a killer on the loose and Raja on my doorstep, home feels less safe than ever.

Chapter *Seventeen.*

I'm on the early shift with Ellen the next day. Usually, a 6:30am start on a Monday would make me groan, but today I'm happy to be busy from the moment my eyes open. Busy means less time to worry about Harriet Warren, Raja Kaling and the unknown person who is killing in the name of the man who wishes me dead.

"I can already see three regulars making their way up the road," Ellen comments as she goes to unlock Break Time's front door. "Looks like it will be a busy day!"

Her prediction is right. From the moment we open, Break Time is heaving, meaning there's no time to sit with my thoughts. The only moment I'm not entirely focused on work is when I glance at the clock and wish it was ten so Stefan would be here to help ease the demand of a constant stream of customers.

I'm busy clearing empty plates when a conversation between two women at the next table stops me in my tracks.

"Have you heard another one is missing? A student this time."

I balance a mug on top of a precarious stack of plates, doing my best to ignore the rattling they make thanks to my shaking hands.

"Terrible, isn't it? They're saying these girls disappearing is just like what happened with that Peter Harris fella," the woman with red hair replies.

"God, I hope not! Do you remember what it was like back then?" her blonde friend asks. "All anyone ever talked about was 'The Ghost this' and 'The Ghost that'. Everyone was cancelling plans and fussing to check if you'd got home okay. It was awful!"

I blink, praying I've misheard the conversation, but as the blonde woman continues, she only makes things worse.

"I was newly single at the time. Trust me when I say that a serial killer on the loose does nothing for your love life!"

The redhead tips her head back, laughing. "Molly, you can't say that!"

"What? I'm serious! Do you have any idea how many times my dad would tell me not to go on dates in case it was with 'The Ghost'? If it was up to him, my love life would have been as dead as... well, as dead as those girls!"

The crassness of the woman's words explodes inside me. Her friend sets down her latte, oblivious to my anguish. "Peter Harris is in prison though, isn't he? So it can't be him."

"Doesn't mean he's not involved somehow. He had a lot of fans, didn't he? Both men and women from what I remember, which is strange if you ask me. I mean, didn't he do it because he hated women?"

"Well," her companion says, biting her lip as though she is about to say something she shouldn't. "I know what he did was evil, but he was a looker, wasn't he? I'd have got in his car of my own accord if he'd stopped me!"

I inhale sharply, the air hitting my lungs like opening a window on a frosty morning. The women don't look up from their conversation, too engrossed in their gossip to notice the effect of their words on anyone around them.

"Don't sit there all innocent now, Molly!" the redhead giggles. "You can't honestly tell me you didn't see his photo and think the same?"

"You've got me - those tattoos and those eyes? I wouldn't have kicked him out of bed."

As the pair descend into riotous laughter, I turn away, worried that if I listen to them any longer, I'll scream. I carry the soiled plates away on trembling legs, praying this day won't get any worse, but when Stefan arrives any hope of my good mood reappearing vanishes.

As soon as I see him, I know something is wrong. "Stefan?" I ask, but he ducks into the backroom without replying.

Ellen catches my eye and shrugs, but I can't brush Stefan's mood off as easily as she can.

"That's four pounds eighty, please," I say to the customer in front of me. When their transaction goes through, I head into the backroom where I find Stefan on his phone. He jumps when he sees me, a guilty flush warming his cheeks. "What's wrong?" I ask, but instead of replying, Stefan shrinks away from me.

I see the lies he debates telling me flashing in his red-rimmed eyes, a sight that sounds alarm bells in my mind. Stefan is the most honest person I know. The fact that he doesn't feel he can come to me with the truth sets my stomach swirling.

"Stefan, you're worrying me now. What's wrong?"

Stefan crumples. "Harriet Warren..." he whispers, then he shakes his head as if he can't continue.

"Do you know her?"

Stefan nods. "We aren't good friends, but we sit together in Contemporary Fiction. We worked on a project together a few months ago. She's really nice, Hannah, and now she's... now she's..."

I don't push Stefan to finish his sentence. Instead, I wrap his slender frame in my arms. "I'm so sorry."

Stefan tightens his grip around my body, holding on as if I'm his lifeline. We cling to each other for a moment before Stefan sniffs and pulls away. "I didn't want to say anything because of what happened to you, but it's so scary. Everyone's terrified. It's all over social media, look."

Stefan turns his phone to me, where a Facebook page called *'Find Harriet Warren'* is loaded. Harriet's face stares at me from the screen. There's something eerily familiar about her, although I'm sure I don't know her.

Maybe it's because of how much she reminds me of myself. Long, light brown hair, not too dissimilar to my own at that age. Big brown eyes, slightly crooked front teeth, and a smattering of freckles across the bridge of her nose. She looks so young, so vivid.

And now she's come face to face with a serial killer, just like I did.

I flick through the information accompanying the photo, reading over Harriet's physical profile and last known whereabouts. There's speculation she tried to take a shortcut home through Peel Park and that's where she was taken, a fact that wraps my spine in ice. Peel Park is about twenty minutes away from my apartment. I've walked there, sometimes with Joel, sometimes alone, and now it looks like the killer has walked there too.

To know that they've been twenty minutes away from the place I eat, watch TV, and sleep... my insides turn to jelly.

When I'm done reading, I view the rest of the photos of Harriet. The screen fills with various images of her on nights out, one of her with a cluster of girls on a summer holiday, and a painful to look at collection of family snaps. I study them for the longest time. It looks like Harriet grew up with her dad and two younger brothers. They seem close. A photo of Harriet with her arm around her siblings is particularly agonising to see. Harriet's brothers look at her with such adoration and love. I don't need to know anything about them to know that they will both grow up too soon because of what's happened.

There's a lump in my throat when I hand Stefan his phone back. "They'll find her. She'll be okay," I say, but as Stefan meets my gaze, we both know I don't believe that.

"How can this be happening, Hannah? Why would someone do

something like this?"

"I've been asking myself that every day," I admit.

Stefan's shoulders slump. I pull him in for another hug, partly for his benefit but partly for mine too. I need something to anchor me in reality so my mind can't drift into its worries. Stefan leans his body onto mine, the weight of his pain pressing through me.

"I don't know what to do," Stefan whispers, his voice catching. "I don't know how to make things better."

I open my mouth to reply, but someone coughs behind us. We break apart and find Ellen in the doorway, blushing as if she's intruded on something private. "Sorry to interrupt, but there's a queue," she says.

"Of course," I reply. With one last glance at Stefan, I follow Ellen back into Break Time. My mind, however, doesn't come with me. It stays with Harriet Warren and her crooked smile, wondering if her brothers are ever going to see her again.

The *Villain.*

There's a hush around the station. There had been ever since it was announced that another young woman had been taken. Another person snatched on their way home. Another life that, if he was honest with himself, Conrad already knew was gone.

He sighs and looks at the papers before him. Forensic and post-mortem reports, their findings making him want to weep. Printed copies of statements for him to scrutinise, reports about the last few years of abductions or attempted abductions in the area. Notes he's jotted down, ideas that have come to him about leads he might want to pursue. And finally, stacks of information about the figure Conrad is adamant is central to it all - Peter Harris.

The name alone makes Conrad break out in a cold sweat. The figure of many people's nightmares, elusive for so long, thanks to Conrad's failures.

Fatima appears at the side of his desk carrying two cups of tea. Conrad doesn't notice her approaching, or register the mug she sets down for him. He only looks up when she speaks. "You doing okay?" she asks.

"Another one's missing, Fatima, how do you think I'm doing?" As soon as the words leave Conrad's mouth, he regrets them. When he meets Fatima's gaze, she sees the apology in his eyes and nods.

"I thought you'd want to know that Hannah's doing okay. A bit rattled, but okay," she informs him. "A squad car checked in on her a few minutes ago."

"Good, that's good." Hannah's safety is a consolation. A small one in the grand scheme of things, but a consolation no less.

Conrad feels Fatima's eyes on the papers surrounding him. He knows she'll suggest he takes a break, as always. He won't listen, as always.

"Why don't you –"

"Fatima, I'm not taking a break."

"I wasn't going to say that. I was going to say why don't you talk to me? Throw some ideas around. We can see what sticks."

As Fatima pulls up a chair beside Conrad's desk, he distracts himself by shuffling a stack of papers so Fatima can't see how much this means to him.

"So, what have you got so far?" she asks.

"Peter Harris is the centre of this, that I'm sure of," Conrad states. "But how and why? What's his connection to what's happening?"

"You think he's communicating with someone?"

"That would be almost impossible. He makes no phone calls and responds to no letters, despite receiving many."

"It always amazes me that people want to talk to creeps like that," Fatima shudders.

Conrad doesn't share her horror. He's been around too long for those kinds of things to surprise him anymore. "He's always had a lot of fans. Fantasists who admire what he did, people who find him attractive."

"You'd think the ten murders would put people off him even if he was pretty, hey?"

"Clearly not. Peter Harris is almost a celebrity these days. The media calling him 'The Ghost' gave him some kind of mythical status, and that book didn't help. So many people have read his story now. So many people have seen his photograph."

"Let me guess – they fell for his blue eyes?"

"Spot on," Conrad says with a shake of his head. "But it's more than that. Some people think he was right to do what he did. Have you seen the comments on the articles about these murders? They're horrible and they're posted on mainstream news sites, so you can only imagine what the conspiracy theories are like. We have a team on different forums and chat rooms, reading posts to see what information they can coax out."

"They're going to need counselling after doing that job."

"Tell me about it. I need counselling after reading their findings, and I only get the highlights," Conrad jokes feebly, then he rakes his fingers through his hair. "There's nothing concrete, Fatima, that's the issue. All we've got to go on is that this person knows what Peter Harris did, potentially thanks to Nathaniel Clarke's book, and a hunch that they're a fan. That's it. Whoever is doing this blends into the crowd so inconspicuously we aren't noticing them. And their victims are disappearing so fast. It's like every time we find the glimmer of a lead, someone else is taken and we have to put all our effort there."

Fatima studies a printout on the table. "Phone records are a dead end, right?"

"That's right. Trina Lamond was between phones, Harriet Warren's died in the club and Gabriella's was turned off or broken at her abduction site. No personal belongings or items of clothing have been found either, so it looks like whoever is doing this isn't ditching the victim's stuff. It's all so strange, Fatima. It's like these women meet the killer and then… well, it's like they vanish."

"Vanish then show up dead a short while later."

"Exactly. Even DNA is drawing a blank. The bleach on their bodies impacts findings, and the women have no skin under their nails and no marks to indicate a struggle. It's like they don't even fight their attacker."

"They're sedated, right?"

"Yes, but it's been suggested that the sedation happened when they were in the car. That raises the question of why they got into the vehicle in the first place."

"What about CCTV?"

"We're looking through it now, but there's so much to collate and view, and we still don't know where Trina Lamond was abducted from. Harriet Warren and Gabriella O'Hara are just as difficult to trace. We've tracked Harriet heading towards Peel Park, then we go dark. There's no CCTV in there or on the streets around. She goes into the park but never comes out. It's the same with Gabriella O'Hara too. She was walking home in a rural residential area. The only CCTV around there is home installations, and they're usually pointing at garage doors, not the road. We've teams scouring footage around these sites, of course, but so far, we've not seen anything suspicious."

"What about anyone driving at the time of both Gabriella and Harriet's abductions?"

"There are forty-seven vehicles on the road within a twenty-mile radius of the abduction sites around the times both victims were taken. We're tracking and interviewing those vehicle owners as we speak."

"Well, there you go. That's a lead."

"A loose one with a lot of admin to get through for potentially little result. Just because someone was driving around the time the women were taken, it doesn't mean they're the killer."

"No, but it also doesn't mean they aren't."

Conrad knows he should acknowledge Fatima's sentiments and all their uplifting efforts, but his shoulders are too weighed down by the enormity of the task before him to move.

"Conrad, we'll find something. We always do. You always do."

Conrad shakes his head, deflecting the niceties that he doesn't deserve. "But how many women will be taken before then? How many will die?"

"You can't think like that, Conrad. You're doing all you can."

"But look around you, Fatima. It's not enough."

Fatima reaches out, her hand hovering over Conrad's for a second before she decides better of it and uses it to tuck her hair behind her ear instead. "Take a break, okay? You're tearing yourself in two with this."

With that, Fatima leaves him. Conrad watches her go, knowing that he won't take her advice. He can't. It's not okay to him that someone else might die along the way to unpicking this web. It's not okay to him that Peter Harris is once again pulling the strings.

Fatima wasn't there the first time, but he was. He saw the fear. He lived it. Countless nights he lost to raking over the details of Peter Harris's crimes, the clues buried like an endless riddle. Conrad can't let that happen again. He can't.

Conrad locates a photo of the man whose face he has come to know as well as his own. The blue eyes, the tattoos, that smug, self-assured arrogance. How Conrad hated him the first time. How he loathes him the second.

I will find who is causing the same pain you did, he swears to the photo. *I will find them, and I will destroy them before they can destroy anyone else.*

With that, Conrad scrunches the photo into a ball in his fist, compressing it tight as if it were Peter Harris himself he was obliterating.

Chapter *Eighteen.*

My eyes stay glued to Stefan for the rest of the day as he makes his way around Break Time without the sparkle he usually glimmers with. No one seems to notice the change in him, but to me, he leaks sadness like radiation. The blue walls of the café dim, the paintwork peeling in his presence.

I only make it to lunchtime before the elastic band of my heart snaps. "Here," I say, holding out a plate with a brownie on it as he had done for me. "Take this and have a break."

Stefan nods, his smile not quite reaching his eyes, but he does as he's told. He sits by the window and takes mechanical bites of the brownie, swallowing it as if it hurts to eat.

"He'll put customers off my brownies eating them like that," Ellen jokes.

My lips twitch in response, but Stefan's devastation is no laughing matter to me. From the corner of my eye, I watch him slip his phone out of his pocket to check for updates on Harriet. I don't have the heart to tell him that there will be no updates, not unless it's finding a body.

I turn away from Stefan, unable to stomach watching him crumble, only to look back a second later when he shouts my name. He leaps to his feet so quickly he knocks his brownie to the floor. The plate smashes, the clatter cutting across the café like a guillotine.

"What's wrong?" I ask as Stefan rushes towards me.

"It's been online since 8am, but I've only just seen it now," he says, thrusting his phone under my nose.

Then I see what all the fuss is about.

Someone has shared a photo of me at work on Twitter. The image has been taken by a person near the front of the queue, with me smiling from behind the counter as I greet the next customer. Break Time's logo is clear in the background.

Dread rolls down my body as I notice that I'm wearing the same clothes in the photo as I am now, meaning the photo was taken this morning.

"Are you okay?" Stefan asks, but I barely hear him. I'm too focused on reading the accompanying caption - *'It's Hannah Allen! Is there still a reward attached to finding her? LOL!'*

Then I notice the worst bit… the photo has been shared over two thousand times.

I almost can't believe it. Two thousand people have shared my face and my workplace with their followers. Two thousand people haven't stopped to think of the potential implications of this privacy violation.

My throat closes as I read the responses.

Damn, she's hot! I always wondered what she'd grow up to look like. Shame she'd be so messed up after what happened…

I went to school with Hannah and she was lovely! You should delete this. She's been through enough!

This is DISGUSTING! How could you share this photo?! You should be ashamed of yourself!!!

Wonder if she still has her 11 tattoo. Now that's a photo I'd like to see!

I burn from head to toe, but I can't figure out if it's from anger, embarrassment or something else entirely. I skim over the comments, each one chipping away a chunk of my confidence, until I see a response from the person who posted the image in the first place.

Bro, she was so easy to find! Read this earlier and it clicked where I'd seen her before #thebadassbarista

Linked to his comment is an article written by none other than Raja Kaling.

Could 'Lucky Number 11' Hannah Allen Hold the Secret to Finding Peter Harris's Copycat?
By Raja Kaling

With yet another innocent woman plucked from the streets, sources in the police force say that officers in charge of the investigation are 'thinking outside the box' when it comes to catching the culprit. Reportedly, top of their list is to involve Peter Harris's sole survivor Hannah Allen, AKA 'Lucky Number 11', in the investigation.

Allen, now 24, was just fourteen years old when she was abducted on her way home from school by Peter Harris, a serial killer so elusive he was dubbed 'The Ghost'. She was tortured, sexually assaulted, and branded with a numerical tattoo, an act that became known as Peter Harris's calling card.

Six days after she was taken, Hannah Allen was found alive in the basement of Peter Harris's home after a tipoff from a member of the public, making her the only survivor of his murderous rampage. Police now believe that she may hold the secret to finding the new copycat killer.

"Hannah doesn't want to be known as Peter Harris's victim," a friend who wishes to remain anonymous told us. "But I know if she could help with what's going on, she would. She wouldn't want anyone else going through what she did."

It's easy to understand why Hannah wouldn't want another woman to share the same fate she did. Her ordeal horrified the nation, with her incredible survival story earning her the nickname 'Lucky Number 11'.

Even though her story is known by many, Hannah prefers to live a quiet life these days. After making a statement to the press two weeks after she was found, she has since refused to speak publicly, including turning down sharing her experience in Nathaniel Clarke's bestselling book, 'Peter Harris and the Unlucky Eleven', published earlier this year.

Little is known about the simple life Hannah has chosen to live. Shortly after being rescued, she removed herself from mainstream school, choosing to be educated at home instead and cutting ties with all who knew her.

"It was tough to lose Hannah," Cassidy Richardson, Hannah's former best friend, said, "but after what she went through, I understood why she isolated herself. I imagine getting through each day was tough enough without going to school and being reminded of how her life was so different to everyone else's."

Home schooling and trauma didn't impact Hannah's education too much. She successfully scored a string of good grades, her marks so high she was in the top five percent of achievers in the country.

However, despite being offered scholarships by numerous higher education institutions, Hannah now spends her time working as a waitress at a student-favourite café famed for their brownies. "She's a good waitress. Quiet and kind," long-standing customer and lecturer Roy Peterson said.

While Hannah's job prospects might not be as lucrative as her childhood dreams had hoped, thankfully her ordeal hasn't impacted her romantic life too much. Ex-boyfriend Charlie Everett, with whom Hannah had a two-month fling aged nineteen, described her as, "Not the girl your mum would want you to marry, but one who was fun to hang out with."

Now in a relationship with graphic designer Joel McGiven and reportedly hunting for their first home together, one might say Hannah is trying to live a normal life – but can 'Lucky Number 11' ever live such a thing? And, with everything going on right now, should she be allowed to when she could hold the key to finding Harriet Warren alive?

My vision turns red, a flurry of energy surging through my veins that's so strong I could crush Stefan's phone. Everything seems so seedy when written by Raja's hand. Even Cassidy's words about understanding my withdrawal shine with belittlement thanks to Raja's spin.

None of what is written rings true to how hard I have worked to get to where I am. There's no mention of the sleepless nights, the panic attacks, the struggles with physical intimacy, or the night terrors that plague me even now – just a cruel quote from an ex-boyfriend who promised me the world and didn't deliver.

My mind spins. How can Raja give so many blatant hints about where I work? Who is the anonymous friend she spoke to?

And, most painfully, is she right – can I never have a normal life after what happened to me?

"Hannah?" Stefan pushes, wrapping his arm around my waist and moving me away from the counter. "Come to the backroom with me. People are staring."

Those words pull me from my trance. I look up to find a queue of customers that weren't there before, their alarmed eyes fixed on my pale, sweaty face. I open my mouth to reassure them, but then I catch a woman whispering to the man beside her.

"I told you if we came here, we'd see her. That's her. That's Hannah Allen."

Suddenly, it's all too much. I push past Stefan and sprint into the backroom, away from the prying eyes and whispers, but no matter how far I run, hushed chatter will always follow me. I'm Lucky Number 11, right? It comes with the territory.

Chapter *Nineteen.*

I don't try to pretend I can stay at work, but even if I wanted to, Ellen gives me no choice in the matter. She bundles me into a taxi and thrusts twenty pounds into the driver's hand. Far too much for the fare, but from the concerned look on her face, I know she doesn't care about the money. She just wants me home and safe.

"Take care, okay? And don't come in for the rest of the week if you're not up to it," she says before closing the car door. As the taxi peels away from the curb, I wave goodbye and watch Ellen shrink into the distance.

"Tough day?" the driver asks, glancing at me in the rear-view mirror, but I don't reply. I don't dare open my mouth in case the wail trapped between my lips breaks free.

My phone buzzes inside my pocket, Joel's name flashing on the screen. I let the call ring out then look at the rest of my notifications. Five missed calls from Joel, three from Tanya, as well as messages from everyone at Sisterhood of Support. Even Joel's mum has tried to get in touch with me.

They've probably all seen Twitter, I think miserably. *Or the article.*

My organs shrivel. I can't decide which is worse – the violation of the photo or Raja's twisted version of my life. I wonder how many people up and down the country will be talking about me, about my love life, about how I could be linked to what's going on.

Tears blur my eyes as my phone lights up again, Tanya's name on the screen. This time, I accept the call. "Hannah, it's so good to hear your voice," she exhales down the line. "How are you?"

"I'm not great," I admit, and then the tears start to fall. "I'm sorry," I cry, but I'm not sure who I'm apologising to – Tanya for starting the conversation so upset, the taxi driver for sobbing in the back of his car, or myself for breaking when I promised I wouldn't.

"We never have to apologise for our emotions, okay?" Tanya soothes. "Talk to me."

"What's there to say?" I sniff. "I'm back in the news and some sicko is carrying on from where Peter Harris left off. What's to say I'm not going to be next?"

"Hannah, you can't think like that."

"How else am I meant to think? Nathaniel Clarke wrote in his book that Peter Harris wants me dead. Besides, when I didn't think like that, when I walked home from school thinking everything was okay, look what happened."

"Where are you now?" Tanya asks.

"In a taxi, on my way home from work. Why?"

"Why don't I meet you at your apartment? We can have a cup of tea and a chat."

"I don't want to take your time –"

"Hannah, you could have every minute of every day if you wanted. I'm here for you whenever. I will always look after you."

"You can't look after me forever," I say, wiping my eyes with my sleeve. "No one can. Maybe I need to accept it – I'm going to end up dead like I should have been back then."

"Hey!" Tanya's voice is sharp. "I don't ever want to hear those words come from your mouth again, you hear me? I'm coming over. We are going to go for a walk. We will look at the freshness of the flowers, take in the colour of the sky, and appreciate the life we have. We will walk and walk until you know you are not alone and that in this world is where you belong."

"Thank you," I whisper, hoping to convey in those two words how much I appreciate her.

When the taxi drops me off at home, I wait for Tanya in the foyer instead of going upstairs. I'm not ready to go home and face Joel's pity, although a hug from him is all my body craves. I text him saying '*I need a bar of chocolate and some time alone*' so he doesn't worry. His reply is understanding and sweet, two things I've come to expect from the man I love.

A few minutes later, my phone lights up with a message from Tanya saying that she's outside.

"You'll have a speeding ticket coming your way after getting to me so quickly," I say as I climb inside her car.

"I was in the area," she replies, then she smiles confessionally. "And maybe I did go a little over the speed limit to get to you sooner."

Tanya drives us to Derwent Park. As she pulls into the car park, I try to push the last time I was here out of my mind, but Peter Harris's words still come to me.

Hannah Allen deserved to die.

Gulping, I unclip my seatbelt and scan my surroundings. An elderly man walking his dog, a crowd of teenage boys laughing together, two mums pushing prams. They all look so normal, so unsuspecting.

But then again, so did Peter Harris.

"Everything okay?" Tanya asks.

"Yes," I lie, then I slip out of the car.

Side by side, Tanya and I set off walking. "Beautiful day, isn't it?" she says.

I look up at the sky, bright blue despite it being winter. "It's not bad."

"Mother Nature has gone to the trouble of giving us a blue sky, and you say 'not bad'. Remind me never to ask you to review Sisterhood of

Support," Tanya laughs.

"I'd be kinder in my review of you."

"I hope so. You know, I might take you up on that offer. Especially now I'm thinking of expanding the program."

I stop and face Tanya. "You are?"

"Yes," she replies, and I see it in her eyes – the gleam of excitement. "What we have now is great, but it could, and should, be so much more. Poor Karolina takes two trains and a bus to attend meetings – that's not good enough. Support shouldn't be that difficult to obtain. The sad reality is that there are a lot of people who could do with a community like ours. A lot of women who are going to work, running households, raising children, struggling with addiction or living their life with a torrent of pain beneath the surface. A lot of women who need a space full of people who understand. We can provide that space, but only if we expand."

"Tanya, this is amazing! You're going to help a lot of people."

"That's the plan," Tanya says before setting off walking once again. I follow her, taking in her purposeful stride and confidence. For the millionth time in my life, I'm floored by this woman who turned the worst experience she had into a channel to help others.

"Would you run the other group?" I ask.

"I think so. I'd want to be part of setting it up, at least."

"What would happen to the Sisterhood of Support here?"

"It would continue. It's too vital a service not to. Here, let's take a seat." Tanya gestures to a bench opposite the children's playground. We sit together and watch toddlers running wild.

I try not to think of the little girls in that crowd, and how, at some point in their life, they might experience some kind of sexual harassment or violence.

"You know, Hannah, I was hoping you'd assist me with running the expanded version of Sisterhood of Support."

If I hadn't already sat down, my legs would have given out on me.

"You want me to help?"

Tanya nods. "Who else knows the program better than you? Who else is a better advocate for excelling against all odds?"

"Tanya, look around you. Look at my life right now. I'm barely surviving, never mind excelling."

Tanya's face twists. "Maybe this wasn't the best time to bring it up with you, but I've been thinking about it for a while. You'd be wonderful at something like this. I believe in you, Hannah. I believe you have the power to make a difference. Just look at Riley. A few meetings with you and she's blooming. Your presence impacts people more than you realise."

I struggle with Tanya's comments. I'm not blind to how Riley is around me, or how sometimes when I speak in the circle, the others take my words with a weight that they don't take other people's. When I downloaded those university prospectuses a few weeks ago, I'd looked at the psychology courses, wondering what it would take to be like Tanya and help someone when they were on the edge of giving up.

But I'd also been ready to leave Sisterhood of Support. I'd been ready to be someone new, someone no longer bound to Peter Harris.

"Tanya, I appreciate you thinking of me, but I don't want my life to be defined by what Peter Harris did. I don't want his actions to overpower mine."

"Owning your story isn't letting Peter Harris have the power. It's reclaiming it. It's taking back the life that is rightfully yours."

"But my story isn't my own. What's happening right now proves that. You only have to look at the newspapers to see that my story is in the hands of people like Raja Kaling. It's in the hands of a copycat killer."

Tanya rests her hand on top of mine. "This was the wrong time for me to raise this with you. You've got too much going on, but know that this offer is there. Know that I have every faith in you. Please think about it. Me and you, working together to help survivors find their voice and their place."

"Tanya…"

"Just think about it."

I nod and Tanya's face breaks into a smile. She squeezes my hand, and I squeeze hers back. This small, steady hand has held mine so many times. Sometimes I wish it would never let me go.

Chapter *Twenty.*

The next morning, I wake determined not to let anyone, Raja included, stop me from living my life the way I've worked so hard to. Fuelled by that notion, I peel back the duvet and climb from bed.

"Where are you going?" Joel asks groggily.

"I'm getting ready for work."

Joel flicks on the bedside lamp. "You're going in today? Even after what was posted online?"

"Yes." I hold eye contact with Joel, challenging him to tell me otherwise.

"Let me make you breakfast then," he says, throwing back the duvet. "You'll need energy for a big day."

While Joel makes breakfast, I get ready. I use my best hair products, lather my most luxurious moisturiser on my skin, and pick a new shirt to wear. Facing my reflection in the mirror, I'm ready to fight back.

"Breakfast's ready!"

Following the sound of Joel's voice, I head to the dining table where I find a plate of pancakes waiting for me. He's even arranged fruit into a smiley face on top of the stack.

"This is almost too cute to eat," I joke as I skewer a strawberry.

If Joel has any apprehension about my day, he doesn't show it. He kisses me goodbye, makes a joke about trying not to forget anyone's order, and then waves me off. His confidence provides me with the extra boost I need to leave home on steady legs.

The sky clings on to the last scraps of darkness as I make my way towards the bus stop, my breath fogging before me.

"Freezing, isn't it?" a man says as I join the queue.

"I can't remember the last time it wasn't," I joke, grateful for this small, innocent slice of human interaction, but then the man's eyebrows furrow.

"Do I know you from somewhere?" he asks.

I shake my head and turn away so I don't have to witness the moment my identity registers in his brain. When the bus arrives, I take a seat at the back, as far away from him as possible.

A few minutes later, familiar scenery outside the window warns me I'm almost at work. I hop off the bus, ready to face the day, but as soon as my feet hit the pavement, I'm bathed in flashing red and blue lights.

Flashing red and blue lights coming from outside Break Time.

My feet catch on each other as I race towards the scene. Grabbing the first police officer I see by their fluorescent coat, I shriek, "What's happened?!"

The man backs away, his eyes wide and full of alarm.

"What's happened?!" I repeat. I'm seconds away from shaking him when I hear a voice I recognise.

"Hannah, it's okay!"

I turn to find Ellen rushing towards me, her face tight with worry. Surveying her body for any sign of damage, I race to her side.

"It's okay, I'm okay," she says. I throw my arms around her, thanking the universe for keeping her safe, but when I see what's over her shoulder, my blood turns to ice.

Break Time's windows have been obliterated, sharp shards of glass littering the floor and tables. Inside has been ransacked – chairs thrown across the room, pictures pulled from the walls, display units that are usually full of baked goodies now cracked.

As my hands fly to my mouth in horror, Ellen reaches for me. "It's okay, Hannah. It looks worse than it is."

"It's… it's ruined!"

My words make Ellen fold in on herself. "The insurance will cover it. The main thing is that no one was hurt, right?" she smiles, but her smile doesn't meet her eyes.

"Ellen…" I begin, but I don't know what to say.

"It's not that bad. Nothing a lick of paint and some new windows can't fix." There's a heart-wrenching sadness in Ellen's voice despite the calm she is trying to project. My gut twists as I realise she's putting on a brave face for me. Me, Hannah Allen, whose identity is shared online one day and whose workplace is ransacked the next.

"What happened?" I ask thickly.

Ellen faces Break Time, her features falling into distraught resignation. "I have no idea. I got a notification saying the alarm was going off, so I came in early. It was like this when I got here."

Side by side, we take in the destruction she means by 'this'.

"Was it a robbery?" I ask.

"That's the strangest part – no money was taken from the till. It's like whoever did this just wanted to cause chaos. At first, I thought it was mindless idiots. Vandals, you know, but when I saw the note –"

"What note?"

Ellen suddenly shifts her body away from mine, a shutter closing down over her expression.

"Ellen, what note?" I demand.

I sense her debating what to say before she fixes her eyes on me. "I don't want to scare you, love, but it was a note for you."

The world around me tips off-kilter. "What did it say?"

"It said, *'Time to say goodbye to everything you love. You won't be so lucky this time'*."

Chapter *Twenty-one.*

As I take a stumbling step backwards, Ellen reaches for me. "Hannah, it's going to –"

"Please don't tell me it's going to be okay," I whisper. "Look around you, Ellen. What part of this is okay?"

Ellen glances back at Break Time, the business she has poured her heart and soul into for so many years, and her face cracks with pain.

"This happened because of me," I say.

"Hannah, no –"

"It did! It happened because you hired me. If I didn't work here, if you didn't know who I was…"

Ellen grabs me by the arms. "Don't go down that path, Hannah. No matter what, I wouldn't change hiring you. Break Time could be broken into one hundred times, and I'd still never regret that choice."

"You don't mean that."

"I do. I *do*."

My chin wobbles dangerously. Ellen might mean what she says, but that doesn't stop guilt from consuming me. So many lives are being impacted because of what's happening. Trina Lamond, Gabriella O'Hara, Harriet Warren, everyone who knows and loves them, and now the people in my life too.

"Try not to worry too much, okay? The police will find the person who did this," Ellen continues. "Robbie saw them -"

"He did?"

Ellen nods. "The smash of the window woke him up. He's given a statement about what he saw."

I follow Ellen's line of sight to where Robbie is standing, flanked by two police officers, his shoulders hunched inside his coat. When Robbie senses he's being watched, he looks up and offers me a small wave.

I don't return the wave. Instead, I rush to him. "You saw who did this?"

"Yeah. I mean, kind of," Robbie says, shifting on his feet.

"What do you mean, 'kind of'?"

"It was dark, Hannah. He had his hood up and was wearing all black, but I saw him running away."

My breath comes out ragged. "It was a man? A man did this?"

"I think so, yeah. I mean, it could have been a woman."

"You don't know if it was a man or a woman?"

Robbie runs his fingers through his hair in anguish. "I don't know, Hannah, I don't know! I couldn't see their face, but I think it was a man."

"You think..." I groan, trailing off miserably at the uselessness of Robbie's description before desperation takes over me once more. "What else did they look like? What else can you tell me?"

"They were skinny, I guess. And... and I don't know much more than that. Like I said, it was dark -"

Frantically, I reach out and clutch the front of Robbie's coat. "Please, Robbie, I need you to think. What did you see?!"

A booming voice interrupts my interrogation. "Everything okay here?"

I jump at Conrad's sudden presence. Robbie uses my surprise as an excuse to pull himself free of my grip.

"Everything's fine –" Ellen begins, but I cut across her.

"It's the killer, isn't it? They did this."

Conrad stiffens, then a hostile professionalism takes over him. "We don't know that, Hannah."

"Come on, Conrad. Take a look around you," I snap, indicating to the destruction beside me. "Who else would it be but the killer?"

"That is one avenue of inquiry, but at this stage, we can't rule anything out."

"But they left a note for me? You think it's them, don't you? Surely you do?"

"Hannah," Conrad sighs, taking me by the elbow and leading me to the side. "I need you to stop scaring our witness and I need you to trust me. We are doing everything we can."

"But everything you can isn't enough!" I shout, the words bringing with them a fresh onslaught of tears. "This person should be caught by now. They shouldn't be smashing up my work and hunting for their next victim."

"We don't know that this is the same person."

"Who else could it be?" I cry, my shrill tone slicing through the early morning air. "Ellen's livelihood is in pieces, Conrad! This isn't fair to her or to anyone who works here. Being my colleague shouldn't mean something like this happens."

"Hannah, you need to stop torturing yourself. There's no blame on you for what's happened here. Go home and look after yourself. Let the police figure out what's going on. That's their job, not yours."

"And it's my job to what, watch my life get torn apart? Try not to get killed?"

My words weigh heavy on Conrad. "Hannah, you have to trust me. You have to trust the police. We can drop in on you more often, we can park someone outside your home, we can even move you to a safe house. We can do whatever you need to feel safe, but you have to trust us."

After everything, trusting the police is the last thing I feel like I can do, but I don't have the energy to fight Conrad on this anymore. Blinking away my tears, I nod.

"Why don't I get an officer to drive you home?" he offers but I shake my head.

"I don't want my neighbours to see me coming out of a police car."

"A taxi then?"

I nod. Appeased, Conrad turns to one of the officers and indicates for them to sort me out with a ride home. I stand with Ellen while I wait for a car to arrive. All the while, regular customers and nosy bystanders approach us to ask what happened.

"Random attack," Ellen shrugs, pushing her shoulder in front of me to shield me from the worst of their inquisition.

"I can't believe it!"

"People these days! What's happened to the world, eh?"

Their shock and horror wash over me. All I can focus on is the ruins of what was once my place of work. A small, shabby café that had empowered me in more ways than I could have ever dreamed of.

I remember feeling so sick with nerves on my first day at Break Time that I almost bailed on my shift.

"You can do this," Tanya said when she called to wish me luck. Her voice held so much belief in what she was saying it convinced me it was the truth. I entered Break Time with my head held high, and from that day forward, my life and my confidence improved. I spoke to strangers, I learned new skills, I allowed myself to make friends. I even interacted with people I knew before Peter Harris changed my life, old schoolmates or friends of my mum's who would come in for coffee or breakfast. There was a time when I'd have avoided those people at all costs, but that apron, that counter, gave me the confidence I needed to say, 'I belong here'. Break Time wasn't just a job to me - it was a pathway back to feeling human again.

Remembering all that my job has given me makes me so numb I barely notice my taxi arriving.

"Time to go, Hannah," Ellen says, steering me towards the vehicle.

I follow her instructions, my legs heavy like lead. Before I get into the taxi, I try to catch Robbie's eye, but he avoids my gaze. Part of me wants to go back to him and apologise for being so frantic earlier, but I don't move. There are too many people watching, too many police officers who would stop me from approaching their witness.

Ellen opens the car door for me. "Look after yourself," she says before leaning closer. "Whatever that detective says, I get the feeling you might need to."

With that, Ellen walks back towards her ruined business. I stare after her, her words of warning ringing in my ears.

Chapter *Twenty-two.*

In the taxi, I type a message to Joel to let him know what's happened, but I don't send it. I'm not ready to have to explain what I saw or relive the trauma of witnessing Ellen's pain.

With a sigh, I go to lock my phone, but a message from Stefan that was sent yesterday catches my eye.

Whoever wrote that article should be sued... they practically named Break Time! How many other universities have a lecturer called Roy Peterson and cafés next to them that are famous for their brownies? Anyway, hope you're okay. Hot chocolate on me next time you're at work x

I read Stefan's message twice until the words ignite inside me. He's right - Raja Kaling told the world where to find me, and the killer listened.

Sparks of rage ping from the flames inside me as I open Raja's article so I can read every cruel, intrusive word again. They seem to cut deeper today, the thoughtlessness of them so brutal they bring tears to my eyes.

Then I see something I didn't notice yesterday – the comments underneath.

That poor girl! She went through what no one should have to. Leave her alone!!

Wot hapened 2 her scared me 4 life! I dn't fink I'd survive it. Bet Hannah wishes she woz ded

I can't believe this is happening again. It was terrifying enough the first time around

Oh, bore off, Hannah! It's anything to get into the papers with this generation. Next thing we'll find out she's on some crap reality TV show. Attention seeking much?

There it is – the ugliest side of life as 'Lucky Number 11'.

I lock my phone as if a black screen can erase the last comment from my mind, but it doesn't. Strangers giving their opinions on me, however cruel or negative, is my reality once more. Raja has made sure of that.

Anger bubbles in the pit of my stomach. I hear the hiss of its fury, feel it rising through me. It's too hot to ignore, the truth too potent to push away - my life is being ruined by someone else, again. Someone who is forcing me into the role of victim without thinking about how that might make me feel. Someone whose irresponsible writings have caused my workplace to be destroyed, and the lives of all who work there impacted.

And the saddest part is, when Raja finds out about Break Time being attacked, she won't feel bad. She'll just write about it. An over-the-top article describing the destruction, the fear, and the horror. She won't think about the responsibility she bears as she types her clickbait headline, presses publish and moves on to the next scandal.

Nothing about Raja's role in this is fair. I worked hard to craft myself in a way that was nondescript, plain, and passable. I was the girl who sat next to you on the bus. I let you in front of me in the queue at the supermarket. I was the woman trying on the latest styles in the changing room beside yours. Then Raja Kaling burst onto the scene, and suddenly customers whisper about me and strangers on the internet accuse me of begging for attention.

Clenching my hands into fists, I turn to the driver. "Sorry, can we make a detour and go to The Daily Reporter offices instead?"

"Do you have an address?"

After finding the address online, we change course, no longer heading towards home but towards the person responsible for taking a match to the last normal thing I had in my life.

By the time we pull up outside the sleek, high-rise offices of The Daily Reporter, I'm overflowing with fizzing anger. I slam the door of the taxi behind me and march into the marble-clad foyer.

A heavily made-up brunette behind the reception desk beams at me. "Welcome to Dawson Tower. How may I help you?"

"I'm here to see Raja Kaling. She works for The Daily Reporter."

The woman blinks at my tone, her lips pressing together like a parent pretending they're not irritated when their child misbehaves in public. "Do you have an appointment with Miss Kaling?"

"No, but if you say that Hannah Allen is here to see her, I'm sure she'll buzz me straight up."

The receptionist cannot hide her horror upon hearing my name. "Of... of course, Miss Allen. I'll call right away." She types a number into the phone beside her with a shaky hand and speaks softly down the line, tilting her body as if shielding herself from the misery I remind her of. "Hannah Allen is here to see Miss Kaling?"

A few seconds later, she hangs up.

"Take the lift to the eleventh floor. Miss Kaling will meet you there."

"Thank you," I say, because I refuse to have this horrified stranger tell people not only did she think I had a wild temper, but that I was rude too.

I jab the call button of the lift so hard I break my nail. When it arrives, I climb inside, the mirrored doors sliding shut to show how distressed I look. Pale everywhere but my cheeks, which are pinched pink with fury. Raja doesn't know what's coming her way.

Pressing the 'eleven' button and smirking at the irony of that number, I'm whisked towards my fate.

As soon as I step out of the lift into a large, open-plan office, Raja pounces. "Hannah! It's great to see you again," she gushes, but her friendly tone falters when she sees my face of thunder.

"You," I yell, stabbing my finger in her direction. "Who do you think you are?!"

Every head in the office snaps around to look in our direction.

"Do you know what's happened because of your stupid article?" I shriek. "Break Time has been attacked!"

Raja blinks. "What?"

"That's right! One day after you share a million clues about where I work, it's been targeted. Windows smashed, place destroyed - ruined, all because of you!"

"I'm sorry to hear that," Raja says. Her diplomatic tone sets off a firework of fury in my chest.

"That's all you have to say? Are you kidding me? My boss has had her business ransacked! Who do you think you are, dropping hints about my life like there are no consequence for your actions?"

"Hannah, it's in the public's interest –"

"It's in the public's interest to know where I work?!"

As Raja takes a small step backwards, a middle-aged man in a smart suit approaches us. Seeing the slick, patronising expression on his face is like pouring lighter fuel on an open flame.

"Ladies, perhaps we should take this conversation somewhere a little less public?" he says, putting his hand on my back to steer me away.

"Don't touch me!" I shout, and the man leaps back, holding his hands up as if to protest his innocence.

With the suited man by her side, Raja's confidence returns. "Look,

Hannah, I'm just doing my job. Surely you understand that?"

"Your job is to report the truth, not to hound me or out me to the world. You've led the killer right to my door!"

"Now that's a very big accusation, Miss Allen, one you may want to reconsider making," the man says sternly, and at this moment I hate him more than I hate Raja.

"I don't need to reconsider anything. You're the ones who need to reconsider the things you put into the world."

"Look, we want our readers to -"

"I don't care about your readers or what you want! I just want to be left alone, is that too much to ask for?" I shout, furious with myself for the wobble that appears in my voice.

"People need to know –"

"No!" I cry, hot tears spilling down my cheeks. "No, they don't! They don't need to know anything about my life!"

"People care about your story, Hannah," Raja says. "My job is to report the facts so things like this never happen again. If people understand what you went through –"

"But no one will ever understand! They won't know what it was like to be in that house or to have to rebuild your life after it was ruined! I was a child, Raja. A child who grew up to be an adult who just wants to live a normal life. Do you honestly think you're doing something good by dragging me back into this? You're ruining my life. You're no better than Peter Harris."

As Raja flinches, I take a moment to study her clear, line-free skin and try-hard energy. She's young, I realise. Young like me. She could have been someone in my year at school. She could have been a friend.

Or, in an alternate life, she could have been the one walking home from school as Peter Harris pulled up to the curb.

"How old are you?" I find myself asking.

Raja swallows before she answers. "Twenty-four."

"The same age as me then, only look how different our lives turned out. You got to be innocent at fourteen. You got to be innocent at fifteen. My guess is that your first kiss was with someone you chose, not a murderer. You probably stopped having nightmares when you were a child. Me? I'll have them until the day I die."

Raja's forehead furrows, but I don't stop.

"Do you have scars? I do. Do you want to see them?" I pluck at my sleeve to reiterate my point.

Something flashes in Raja's eyes, only this time it's not the promise of a juicy story I see, but fear.

"Do you want the exclusive look, or will seeing them make it too real for you?" I continue. "Will I stop being a story and become a person? Well, guess what? I AM a person. This is my *life*. You want to blast me all over the internet like I'm nothing but a headline, but I am someone. Someone like you. Someone who could quite easily have been you. Think about it - 'Raja Kaling, Lucky Number 11'. Would you want that published for the world to see? Would you want to be reminded of it every time you get your life on track? Because that could have been the way it worked out. All that's separating me from you is a roll of the dice."

I watch Raja lower her head, a dark curtain of hair covering her face. For a second, it looks like I've got through to her. For a second, I am jubilant... but then Raja speaks.

"Hannah," she says in a small voice. "I'm just doing my job."

I shake my head, scanning the office and taking in the face of every curious spectator. "Whatever you need to tell yourself to get to sleep at night," I say, then I head for the lift and leave them all behind.

Chapter *Twenty-three.*

The comedown of adrenaline after my argument with Raja makes for a rough taxi ride home. However much I try to convince myself that going to The Daily Reporter offices was a good move, in reality, it's probably made things worse. Raja will only come after me more now. And if she doesn't, then the others in her office will. I'm too juicy a story not to pursue.

Slumped in my seat, I lose myself in worry, but when the driver slows to a stop and gasps, I'm dragged from their clutches. Following his line of sight, I look out of the window and find a small crowd of journalists and photographers poised outside my apartment building, their eyes hungry for an exclusive. Large, black cameras hang around their necks, ready to snap candid shots of Hannah Allen, all grown up.

My heart drops like a stone down a well.

"Am I okay to stop here?" the driver asks, his eyes flicking to mine in the rear-view mirror.

I open my mouth to tell him to take me somewhere else, but I have nowhere to go. "Here's fine," I croak.

The driver looks at me again, his eyes brimming with sympathy. "I can walk you to the door, if you'd like?"

I shake my head. A photograph of me is bad enough, but a photograph of me needing assistance to get into my own home? I can see the headline now – '*Lucky Number 11: Still Broken After All This Time*'.

"Thank you for the offer, though," I say as I fumble for the door handle.

"You'll get through this," the driver says, his sudden, unexpected burst of kindness stopping me in my tracks. "Things will get better once the story dies down."

His words bring tears to my eyes. I nod at him in a way that I hope shows my gratitude, then I exit the vehicle. As soon as the car door shuts behind me, the photographers turn. Their eyes light up with the promise of pound signs, then their cameras are on me.

"Hannah, how are you feeling about what's going on?"

"What would you say to Peter Harris?"

Their questions hit like bullets. I push my head down and cover my face, but it's no use. They snap me, the click, click, click of their cameras narrating my journey to the front door. Elbowing my way through the huddle, I dodge the questions and voice recorders that are thrust under my nose.

"Do you think Peter Harris has connections to the outside world?"

"Do you think whoever is doing this is going to target you too?"

Panic balloons inside my chest as my hand gropes around the bottom of my bag for my keys. My fingers connect with my purse, a stray lip balm, an old receipt, but not a set of keys. The swelling of dread inside me rises until it pushes against my windpipe.

"Is there anything you'd like to say to Harriet Warren's family?"

"Do you think the police are doing enough to keep women safe?"

"Are you scared, Hannah?"

Beads of sweat prickle on my forehead. My back is damp, my fingers are clumsy, and the intrusive pack of media wolves is uncomfortably close, but finally, my middle finger connects with the metal loop of my keyring. I snatch the keys out of my handbag and thrust the right one into the lock, then I spill into the foyer of the building.

The journalists don't follow, but I know they want to. If legalities would allow it, they'd chase me all the way up to my front door.

I slam the door behind me as if that fixes all my problems, but the outline of the hungry crowd is visible through the frosted glass. Their questions are muffled now, but not inaudible. I blink it all in, stumbling backwards... then I see it.

Another note.

A bigger one this time, an A4 piece of paper rather than a small, torn-off scrap.

As soon as I see it, I know something isn't right. Finding these notes hasn't been right all along.

Despite every instinct telling me to do the opposite, I pick up the paper and open it. As soon as I see what's on it, my hand flies to my mouth to hold in a scream.

There, printed in the centre of the page, is a copy of my missing poster. The same missing poster that's been found alongside every one of the copycat killer's victims so far. Next to the printed version of my smiling, fourteen-year-old face is a cartoon version of the image, only this time there are Xs where my eyes should be.

Then, written underneath in block capitals, are the most terrifying words I have ever read. Words that prove once and for all that the notes I've been finding aren't the work of our resident pranksters and never have been:

ARE YOU SCARED YET, HANNAH? YOU SHOULD BE.
READY OR NOT, I'M COMING FOR YOU

You can't pretend everything is okay now, can you? Not now you know how close I am. How close I've always been.

How does it feel to know I've been outside your home, I wonder? To know that I've watched you scurry to work on early mornings and been there when you come home at night, trailing down the footpath with an invisible burden on your shoulders?

How does it feel to know that I've been in the shadows the whole time, watching, waiting?

I wonder if knowing that will finally break the illusion you live under. The one that says that after what happened, life can go back to normal.

Normal? That word shouldn't even be in your vocabulary.

You treat life like it's a game of all-consuming make-believe, of fantasy lands blurred into reality and masks to hide behind. And boy, do you hide!

Well, you can't hide anymore. I'm going to tear that mask from your face and expose you to the harsh truth. The truth you discovered aged fourteen, then tried to run from.

Really, you should be thanking me. Your game of ignorance needs to end so you can wake up to your destiny, to the character you were always meant to be - the one whose death redirects the trajectory of the world.

Because that is how this ends – with death. There is no alternate ending, no rewrite, no luck that can save you, just what is meant to be. And what is meant to be, Hannah, is that you will die.

So, keep an eye out next time you go outside. You never know if I'll be watching. Chances are, I probably will be.

Chapter *Twenty-four.*

The voices outside the bedroom are muffled, but the tension of their conversation carries through the door. I curl into the fetal position and will it all to go away, but a knock on the door tells me that's wishful thinking.

"Hannah?" comes Conrad's low voice. "Hannah, I'm coming in."

Somewhere inside me, a voice panics that yesterday's clothes are on the floor instead of in the laundry basket, but that worry is soon drowned out by the hideousness of the reality I now find myself in. Let Conrad judge me. Let him see that there is mess in my life. What's the point in pretending otherwise?

As Conrad steps into the room, Joel's apologetic face hovers over his shoulder. I flash him a small smile to let him know I'm not angry at him for letting Conrad in. I knew after I called Joel and asked him to come home from his meeting in the city that there would be no way I could hand over the note and leave it at that.

Conrad looks as out of place in this environment as I've ever seen him. He hesitates at the end of the bed, debating sitting on it to talk to me, but he quickly shoots down that idea. He settles with perching on the window ledge, the light from the world outside framing him like a halo.

"How are you doing?" he asks.

"I've seen you twice in one day, how do you think I'm doing?" I joke, but when Conrad responds to my comment by looking at his shoes, I realise my sarcasm didn't land the way I wanted it to. "I didn't mean that how it sounded. You're just usually the bearer of bad news."

"Trust me, I wish that wasn't my role," Conrad replies, an admission I appreciate. "We've spoken to your neighbours. Three others have reported finding notes by the front door. They all did the same as you – assumed they were nothing serious and threw them away."

My bloodshot eyes stare at Conrad, waiting for his words to make me feel better.

"Why didn't you tell me about the notes before, Hannah?"

His question hits me square in the chest. I toy with the edge of the duvet while I try to find the answer. "I didn't want them to be related to what's happening," I admit. "It's silly, I know, but I didn't want this in my life so I told myself they were a prank. I thought if I said that enough, then it would be the truth. I didn't want to admit that a serial killer had been outside my home, toying with me for weeks."

"There's no reason to think this is the work of the killer, Hannah. There could be lots of reasons why these notes have ended up here."

I almost laugh. "Oh yeah? Like what?"

"Maybe you were right all along and it is someone playing a prank. Maybe someone read about you in the paper and wanted to rattle you. Maybe... look, it's not worth dwelling on the possibilities. That's my job, not yours. All you need to know is that we are taking this seriously and that you are safe."

"Please, Conrad, can we stop with the lie that everything is okay?"

"I'm not..." Conrad begins, but he trails off when he sees the steely look in my eye. "You're right - things are concerning. Why these events seem to be circling you, I can't say, but what I can say is that every eye in the police force is watching over you."

"Every eye in the police force, yet no one saw strange notes being delivered to my apartment."

"If it would make you feel better, I can arrange for officers to be stationed outside or move you to a safe house or -"

I shake my head furiously. "I'm not leaving my home. I'm not letting this killer take something else from me."

"Hannah," Conrad sighs, but I don't want to hear it.

"This is my life, Conrad. I can't lose control of it. I can't go through that again. If this killer is after me -"

"You don't know if that's what's going on here."

"Don't I? You know as well as I do that the person sending these notes is the killer. It can't be anyone else, otherwise how do you explain the notes I found before today? Or the fact that they used my missing poster? No one outside of the police knows that the killer's been doing that."

"I know it's scary, Hannah, but it's my job to deal with facts. Right now, the fact is that someone has been sending you alarming notes. Yes, there is a chance that it could be the perpetrator of the murders, but there's also a chance it could be someone else entirely. The missing poster in this note could be a coincidence. After all, it's one of the only photos of you out there."

"Not anymore. Did you see the photographers lined up outside?"

A grimace takes over Conrad's features. "Unfortunately I did, but I've done what I can to move them on."

"What's the point? They'll only come back tomorrow. Face it, Conrad - this is just the start of the story. This killer is finishing off what Peter Harris started, you know it and I know it, so can we stop pretending that everything is okay?"

"You don't —"

"Conrad," I sigh, the exhaustion of defeat weakening my muscles. "Look around you - it's happening again. You need to stop pretending you can keep me safe. Stop pretending you can fix this. If you couldn't last time, why is this time any different?"

Conrad gets to his feet suddenly, a vein in his forehead throbbing. "I promise you, Hannah, I am going to find who is doing this. I am going to stop them. Peter Harris will not win again."

I hold Conrad's gaze, willing myself to believe him as much as he wants me to, but I can't. Not when history has proven otherwise. "Please close the door on your way out," I whisper, pulling the duvet to my chin and closing my eyes to signal that we are done.

I sense Conrad hesitate, battling with himself over what to do next, before his heavy footsteps inform me he's leaving. I hear him tell Joel to lock the door, to keep his panic alarm close, and to call if we need anything. All instructions that are meant to make me feel safe, but don't.

Chapter *Twenty-five.*

The remnants of the super-size chocolate bar Joel brought me after asking, 'A hug and a chat or a bar of chocolate and some time alone?' melts beside me. I look at it and smile. I couldn't believe how big the bar was when Joel brought it into the bedroom.

"When did you get this?!" I marvelled, holding the impressive, weighty slab in my outstretched hands.

"The other day."

"How have I never spotted it in the cupboard?!"

"What can I say, I'm good at hiding things," Joel replied with a wink, then he left me alone to stuff my face with chocolate, a choice I now regret.

Fighting against the sickly sensation currently flipping my stomach, I pad into the living room where I find Joel working. I watch him for a moment, taking in the smooth movement of his hand as he brings a graphic to life.

Joel looks up. "Feeling better?"

"Much, although my lack of self-control when it comes to chocolate isn't putting me in the best mood."

"Who needs a good mood when you have good chocolate," Joel jokes. "I've got to go back into the city for another meeting in a bit, but I was thinking, why don't you go for a walk while I'm out?"

"And get photographed all the way?" I grimace.

"Conrad moved the photographers on."

"They'll be back," I reply, the bitterness in my voice souring the air around us.

"Well, when they are, I'll tell them to fuck off, but for now, enjoy the freedom. It's not good for you to be cooped up inside like this."

Even though I don't want to hear it, I know Joel is right. I've lived in fear of leaving home before. I know how that dread can take over until your world becomes so small it can be contained within four walls.

"Maybe," I say.

"You should change that 'maybe' to 'definitely'. Mum's called three times offering to come over and look after you. I'd get outside while you can. Who knows what trash she'd force you to watch otherwise," Joel teases.

I laugh at the thought of Jackie sitting in our living room and trying to engage me in a conversation about the latest dating show she's obsessed with. "She means well," I reply.

"She does, even if her version of meaning well means spending four hours watching TV that's so mind-numbing your brain melts out of your ears," Joel laughs. "For what it's worth, I think you should get out for a bit. Conrad said Break Time was going to be shut for a few days. You could look for something to do during that time. Maybe buy some new books? Or remember how you said you wanted to try painting? We could get you some paints."

"What if I discover I have an artistic talent that rivals yours?" I joke.

Joel comes to me and wraps his arms around my waist. "Then I'd proudly shout about your work from the rooftops."

I lean into Joel and rest my head on his chest. "I might go for a walk later. For now, I just want to be around you. Is that okay?"

"Of course," Joel replies, kissing the top of my head.

For the next hour, we coexist in harmony until it's time for Joel to go to the city for his meeting. "Are you sure you'll be okay without me?" he asks as he adjusts his tie in the hallway mirror.

"I'll be fine," I reply. "I've got some chocolate left, what more could I need?"

Joel laughs then reaches for his coat. "We should have a movie night sometime this week," he says. "I'd suggest having one now if I didn't have this meeting to go to."

"Cancel it. Who needs a job anyway?" I joke, but when a sudden urge to ask Joel to stay punches me in the ribs, I realise I'm not joking. I don't want him to leave. I don't want to be alone in this apartment.

Sweat prickles my brow as Joel checks the time on his phone. "I'd better go, but call me if you need me, okay?" he says, giving me a peck on the cheek and reaching for the door handle.

"Will do. Have fun," I reply, waving goodbye as he dashes out of the apartment.

As soon as he's gone, I wish he'd come back.

Gnawing my lip to stop myself from crying, I slide the security chain in place and face my home. The apartment is different in Joel's absence. Colder, more menacing somehow. Shadows appear in my peripheral vision, danger lurking around every door frame, only when I look properly, there's nothing there.

I wrap my arms around myself and head into the living room, hunting for something to do. I skim the bookshelf, but nothing appeals to me. I check our plants, luscious, green and not in need of watering. I'm about to give in to my tears when my phone buzzes with an '*I love you*' text from Joel. The few seconds it takes to respond fill me with purpose, but then my reply is sent and I'm back to oppressive loneliness.

I turn on the TV to fill the silence, only to turn it off again straight away. The noise covers up other sounds too much. Anyone could creep up on me and I wouldn't hear them until they were beside me. By that point, it would already be too late.

Doing my best not to imagine a killer inside my home, I glance at the time. Joel has only been gone for five minutes. It will be at least two hours before he's home again. Two hours to spend alone. An all too familiar anxiety rises through me at the thought.

For the first few years after I was found, I couldn't be home alone. Every time I was, I had a panic attack, so I did everything I could to make sure I was never by myself. Mum left her job to home school me so I had no reason not to be glued to her side, and it wasn't like either of us went anywhere. I was too terrified to go out, and Mum was too scared to leave me.

Eventually, thanks to the help of my mum and Tanya, I could be alone for half an hour, then an hour, then an evening. By the time I met Joel, I was able to stay overnight at someone's house. I could use public transport by myself rather than needing to be taken door to door by someone I trusted. I was able to live a life that was more normal than anyone would have ever believed possible.

I can't let that progress be for nothing.

Forcing myself to move, I root through a drawer until I unearth a mindfulness colouring book Joel got me for Christmas. Sitting at the dining table, I get to work. My heart hammers but I focus on the pinks and blues I've chosen to fill in the outline on the page. I'm careful not to go out of the lines, to follow the curves of the shapes and focus on my breathing.

I'm as calm as I could be when the intercom buzzes.

The sound electrocutes me. Flushing hot and cold all over, I turn my gaze to the white box on the wall where the call button flashes on and off, on and off.

I let the intercom ring out, but a second later, it rings again.

Gulping, I stand on jelly legs and tiptoe towards it. "Hello?" I whisper into the speaker.

"Hannah? It's me, it's Stefan."

As soon as Stefan's voice registers in my brain, my legs weaken with relief. "Stefan! What are you doing here?"

"I thought I'd lend you some books so you don't go crazy doing nothing for the next few days."

I can't help but smile. "That's so kind, thank you! Come on up."

I buzz Stefan into the building and throw open the apartment door. He pounds the stairs, taking two at a time until he reaches my front door. My heart soars at the sight of a familiar, friendly face, then flies even higher as I laugh when Stefan points to my panic alarm and says, "Nice necklace."

"This old thing? I've had it for years," I joke as I usher him into the apartment.

"Why are you wearing that, anyway? I thought only old people had them to get help if they fall."

"It's a panic button. If I press it, the police will come. They think it will solve all my problems."

"And will it?"

"Well, it's solved the issue of not knowing how to accessorise," I joke. "Want a drink?"

When Stefan nods, I head into the kitchen to grab him a glass of water, then join him in the living room. I find him standing by the bookcase, studying framed photographs of me and Joel. He lingers on a snapshot of us when we first met, our arms around each other as we enjoyed a picnic on the beach.

Stefan senses my presence and turns around. "This is a nice place. Much better than the student halls I'm in."

"Thank you. It's usually a lot tidier than this, but I didn't think I'd have company today."

"Sorry to drop in on you like this, although some might say an afternoon spent with me is a good thing."

"And who would those people be, exactly?" I tease.

Stefan laughs and we take a seat on the sofa. He drops a bursting carrier bag into the space between us.

"Did you bring every book you own?!" I marvel.

"Nope, only the best ones." Stefan takes the books out one at a time and holds them as if they are priceless works of art. "I thought I'd bring you a mix of genres to suit any mood."

"Stefan, this is far too kind!"

Stefan blushes, thumbing the corner of a copy of *The God of Small Things*. "What can I say, I like talking to you about books."

I eye the impressive stack. "Well, judging by this pile, we'll have a lot to talk about."

"Exactly! Although if there is something else you want to talk about, we can. I know there's a lot going on right now for you," Stefan says, fixing his gaze on me.

I take a book from the pile - a copy of *The Book Thief* that's in such pristine condition it looks brand new - and turn it over in my hands. "To be honest, I'd like to talk about anything but what's going on."

"Deal. Harriet's all anyone is talking about at uni. I could do with a break from the sadness myself," Stefan admits, then he selects a book. "So, *1984*. Have you read it?"

I don't know how long we sit together, flicking through books, but time passes in a blur. I laugh for what feels like the first time in forever. Most importantly, I don't once think of what is going on outside of this moment.

That is, until Joel comes home.

I'm laughing so hard I don't hear his key in the lock. I don't hear the door close behind him or his shoes hitting the floor as he slips them off by the welcome mat. In fact, the first time I'm alerted to his presence is when he stands in the living room doorway, his face set in silent fury.

"Joel," I say when I spot him. "Stefan has brought me some books to read while Break Time is shut. Isn't that kind?"

Joel says nothing. He looks from Stefan to me and back again, his mouth a firm, straight line. I blink him in, distracted only when Stefan stands up. "I've heard so much about you. Nice to finally meet you," he says, stretching out his hand for Joel to shake, but Joel doesn't take it.

Stefan's hand seems to hover for an eternity, but Joel doesn't retract his snub. "Been here long?" he asks gruffly.

"An hour or so," Stefan replies, putting his hands behind his back.

Joel lets out a 'huh' noise that's so blunt my toes curl. "Joel," I begin, but at that very moment, Stefan clears his throat.

"I'd better go. Enjoy the books, Han."

"I'll see you to the door," I reply, jumping to my feet. As I walk past Joel, I shoot him a furious glance, but he looks as angry with me as I do with him.

When we're in the hallway, I grab Stefan's arm. "I'm sorry about Joel. He's normally so friendly, but he's really stressed with everything that's going on," I say, but even to my ears, my excuse sounds weak.

"It's fine," Stefan replies with a tone that suggests it's anything but fine. "I'll see you soon, Hannah. Take care of yourself."

I wave goodbye and watch Stefan flee down the stairs. When he's out of sight, I sigh and shut the front door.

"What the hell, Hannah?!" Joel shouts as soon as the door clicks in place.

I jump at his outburst, then flood with anger. "Why are you shouting at me? It should be the other way around! You were so rude!"

Joel looks incredulous. "Rude?! Stefan should be thankful I didn't drag him out of the apartment! There's a killer out there, Hannah, and I come home to find you've invited a stranger into our apartment. How am I meant to react?"

"He's not a stranger – it's Stefan! I work with him every day."

Joel folds his arms across his chest, the hostility of the gesture riling us both up further. "So? I'm sure people worked with Ted Bundy every day, and look at what he did."

"Joel, be serious," I scoff. "Stefan is not a serial killer!"

"You know that for sure, do you?"

"Stefan is my friend. His visit was innocent!"

"Oh yeah? Has Stefan ever visited you before?"

My forehead creases at the irrelevance of his question. "No."

"Did you invite him over?"

"No, but –"

"Has he ever dropped you off at home after work?"

"No."

"So if he's never visited before, you didn't invite him over, and he's never given you a lift home, then how the hell does he know where you live?"

I open my mouth to fire a response back, but Joel has got me. Suddenly, his questions make complete sense, and suddenly I'm more terrified than ever.

"Maybe… maybe Ellen gave him our address," I stammer, but Joel shakes his head.

"Your boss would give out your address despite all the rules about data protection, would she? And she'd do that at a time when her business has been attacked and threatening notes have been sent your way?"

As I continue to falter, Joel pounces on my indecision.

"How long have you worked with Stefan, exactly? A few weeks? A few months?"

"Almost a year," I reply in a small voice.

"Almost a year, okay. So where did Stefan go to school? Does he have any siblings? What's the name of his best friend?"

My eyebrows furrow, but I'm not mad at Joel - I'm mad at myself. I can't answer his questions because I don't know the answers. Stefan and I talk about books and work and studying, but real stuff, deep stuff? That never comes up. I mean, he didn't even know who I really was. Joel's right – Stefan is practically a stranger.

"Don't you find it bizarre that the second I leave, he comes over?" Joel continues. "I mean, was it simply good timing that you were home alone for a catch up, or was he watching the apartment, waiting for me to go? Maybe he's been keeping his eye on you for a few days now, or how about a few weeks? That's enough time to leave weird notes lying around, right?"

"Joel, stop," I whisper tearfully, but Joel's on a roll now, too controlled by anger to see how his words are killing me.

"Eyes on you at work, eyes on you at home… Stefan is really making sure he gets you where he wants you! Did you ever –"

"I said stop!" I roar, tears now streaming down my face. "You've made your point - I can't be trusted on my own!"

"Hannah, that's not what I meant. I'm just trying to keep you safe," Joel argues, but I don't want to hear it. I push past him, heading into the bedroom and slamming the door so hard that the walls of the apartment ricochet. Sliding my body down the door, I sit heavily on the carpet, a wail escaping me.

"Hannah," Joel calls, trying to open the door, but I press hard against it with the flat of my back. "Hannah, I'm sorry! Please let me in. I didn't mean to shout! I was just worried, I'm sorry!"

Joel's pleas ring out over the sound of my sobs, but I don't budge. Instead, I sit and cry for the friendship I thought I had and the naivety that could have got me killed.

The *Centre.*

Conrad's eyes burn. He'd call it tiredness, but the word doesn't do justice to the exhaustion humming through his body. How could it be any other way, though? How can he rest when all around him, lives are being destroyed? When he'd seen the terror in Hannah's eyes and promised her it would be okay?

The Peter Harris Horror Story – Part 2

He'd read that headline earlier. His lips had curled at the media's unrelenting ability to turn something as horrific as a killing spree into some binge-worthy gossip column, but even Conrad couldn't deny the truth in those words. This was a horror story, the scariest one of all.

Conrad's bloodshot eyes rest on the corkboard before him. A map sits on the right-hand side of the board, specific points marked with red pins. Potential abduction spots, last known sightings, and locations of the bodies found so far. Harriet Warren's whereabouts are still unknown, but Conrad knows that won't last for long. Soon there will be another red pin on that board, another body found.

But the mystery of who's doing this? Well, that's the opposite, and Conrad has no idea when that will change.

It's so different this time. The killer is acting faster, snatching victims at an almost reckless speed. Part of Conrad suspects this person wants to be caught, even if they've been clever in how they clean the bodies and where they abduct people from.

Conrad looks at the photo of Harriet Warren that's pinned to the corkboard. It was taken less than a year ago on her eighteenth birthday. In the original image, her arm is around someone's waist. The police cropped the other person out, zooming in on Harriet's features in the hope that someone would recognise her wide eyes and dimples and come forward. That hasn't happened yet, but there's still hope.

Hope. How Conrad clings to it, even when everything around him says not to.

He's not the only one. The person in the other half of the photo, the man cropped from the image, is Harriet's dad. Markus Warren. The last time Conrad saw him, his stubble was scraggly, his hair unwashed. He'd taken a printed version of the photo down from his living room wall to show Conrad. When he permitted Conrad to circulate it to the media, it was clear Markus didn't want to let it go. "It's one of my favourites," he confessed.

Even though they'd used a digital version of the photograph, Markus was adamant the police should take the hardcopy, just in case. Anything to find his little girl. Conrad had taken the framed photo, kept it for a day, then made sure it was hand delivered back to Markus. He didn't want Markus to think he didn't understand how much that photo, and the person in it, meant to him.

Deep down, Conrad knew that when they did find Harriet, it would be her body they came to Markus with. From that moment on, that photo would take on a new, even more precious significance, but for now, let Markus live with hope.

Clearing his throat before emotion gets the better of him, Conrad moves his attention away from Markus and Harriet and on to the list of what is known about these murders. It's depressingly short, but he starts with the post-mortem evidence.

Trina Lamond and Gabriella O'Hara both died from blood loss due to lacerations to the wrists, the same final injury Peter Harris inflicted upon his victims. There were other significant injuries to their bodies too, such as the numbers carved into their skin. Their wrists and ankles were marked as if they'd been bound, the same technique Peter Harris used.

But then it gets strange. While the killer copies Peter Harris's methodology, they change key parts.

While Peter Harris wanted his victims to endure every second of their ordeal, this killer sedates them from the start. A needle to the neck, the puncture mark indicating the wound was inflicted fast and with force. The sedative wasn't strong enough to be lethal, but it was enough that Trina and Gabriella would barely be alive to feel the pain of their torture.

The sedative they were injected with was made from a mix of diluted anti-anxiety medication and sleeping pills. A tough lead to pursue when a vast number of the population is on some form of medication thanks to a global pandemic, a string of lockdowns and a major cost-of-living crisis.

Conrad skims over the rest of the 'know for certain' list, the bullet points so arbitrary they make him want to throw the piece of paper across the room, then he reads Gabriella O'Hara's post-mortem report once more. He stops at the words that shook him to the core the first time he read them – Gabriella O'Hara was already dead when most of her injuries occurred, meaning her wrists were slit first.

Conrad sits back in his chair, asking himself the same question that has been keeping him awake for days now - what kind of murderer kills someone first, then tortures them?

A worm of unease wriggles in Conrad's gut, warning him that this killer is something new. Something he's not encountered before.

When his eyes can no longer focus on the words before him, Conrad lifts his gaze back to the photograph pinned in the centre of the corkboard…

Peter Harris.

His nemesis, still toying with Conrad as he had done all those years before.

How many more lives will be ruined by that man, Conrad wonders. He hates himself for thinking like that, but he can't help it. The way Hannah looked at him when he told her she was safe... the memory pierces his soul. It was a promise he wanted to make, one he wants to keep.

One Hannah has every right not to trust.

Conrad locates Hannah's photo on the board. It's a recent one, not the one from her missing poster, although when Conrad looks at Hannah, he still sees the child he first met. The one who cowered in the corner as he made his way down those basement stairs, disbelieving that Conrad was coming to save her when all she'd known during her time there was captivity and pain.

Conrad stares at her photo until his vision blurs. He waits for something to come to him through the haze, only everything remains unclear.

But he knows there's something there. Some link between Hannah and Peter and whoever is doing this. Some thread he's yet to pull.

Conrad makes a vow here and now in his dimly lit office – he will work late every night if he must. He will question every citizen, review every hour of CCTV in existence. He will do whatever he can to keep the schoolgirl he was supposed to save out of harm's reach. He failed her once before, but he refuses to do it again.

It's a race between him and the killer, Conrad knows that. He just prays that this time, he won't be too late.

Chapter *Twenty-six.*

It's been a long time since I found myself counting down the minutes to a Sisterhood of Support meeting, but I find myself doing exactly that.

Too ashamed to face Joel despite his constant apologies, I hide in the bedroom and torture myself over my stupidity. Like all trips into self-loathing, I go out of my way to make it worse. I search my name online, reading articles about me and the comments underneath. One particularly sticks with me, written by Raja Kaling and proof that showing up at her work did more damage than good.

The True Cost of Life as 'Lucky Number 11'
By Raja Kaling

With the recent spree of abductions and murders officially linked to Peter Harris, the country's thoughts have understandably turned to Harris's sole survivor, Hannah Allen.

Allen was just fourteen when she was abducted on her way home from school. Her missing poster haunted parents' nightmares for years, but what has become of the girl whose story of survival captivated the nation?

"Hannah keeps herself to herself," a source close to her said. "She has a small circle of friends, most of whom she met at a support group

for survivors of violence. Other than that, she doesn't really have anyone. She's found it hard to connect with people who don't understand what she went through. As much as she tries to be normal, there's a line drawn between her and the world."

The rest of Hannah's life seems to agree with this statement, indicating the true cost of surviving a serial killer. Despite being offered numerous university scholarships, Hannah shunned higher education and, up until recent years, hadn't held down a job.

"For years, Hannah Allen was one of the most recognisable names and faces in the UK," Nathaniel Clarke, author of the bestselling novel 'Peter Harris and The Unlucky Eleven', said. "With that in mind, how could Hannah ever live a normal life? What public-facing role could she do without being recognised?"

Maintaining healthy romantic relationships could also be described as something Hannah struggled with. One ex-boyfriend even went as far as describing her as 'a psycho'. "She slept with the bedside light on and cried if I stayed out later than I said I would. Who can live with someone like that? It was stifling."

I give up on the rest of the article and don't bother reading the comments. I know they will only be a toxic mix of pity and judgement, with people pouncing on the careless and cruel 'psycho' label that's been placed upon me.

I don't need to question who is responsible for that quote. Those words come from the mouth of Tommy Ridley, a boy I met at a nightclub, one I deluded myself into believing could save me from my sadness. I tried hard to find comfort in his taut abs and hot and cold behaviour, but comfort was the last thing on Tommy's mind.

When I met him, I was lost. Everywhere I looked, I was surrounded by reminders of how lonely I was. Mum had just passed away. The friends I had from school I'd left behind, and Sisterhood of Support was a space I confined to meetings and meetings alone. Whenever I went out, I came back to my empty childhood home, a space I'd shared with my mum my entire life, now reserved solely for me.

Everything around me said that being in a relationship would make me whole again. Every film I watched, every song I listened to, every magazine article that told me how to 'be the girl all the guys fall in love with'... I consumed that media. I believed it wholeheartedly.

I bought a slinky dress that was a 'must buy' for the season. I layered makeup on until I looked like an entirely different person, then I went to a club called Cube where I drank artificially-coloured shots and swayed along to loud, aggressive music.

Then I met Tommy.

I pretended I'd lost my friends in the crowd, and he told me he'd look after me until I found them. We never found my imaginary friends, and in him, I never found someone who would look after me.

For three whole months, I pretended Tommy's heavy-handed touch and penchant for rough sex didn't make me want to cry. For three whole months, I pretended I was okay with being ditched so Tommy could go out with his friends. I told myself it was okay that he only invited me over late at night, that his laughter when I asked if I could sleep with a light on wasn't cruel. For three whole months, I silenced my body and my mind because letting Tommy use me was better than being alone.

Then Tanya asked if he made me happy and I burst into tears. I wasn't stupid - I knew the 'relationship' was wrong. Songs and films never described what I was experiencing, and every time I cut away chunks of my soul to please him, I knew I'd lose myself forever if I wasn't careful.

"Am I supposed to be upset?" Tommy said when I told him I didn't want to be with him anymore. "You're a psycho anyway."

Judging by Raja's article, it looks like Tommy has continued to mislabel me as that ever since, a truth that reopens a wound inside me I'd fought for a long time to close.

There are no notes on the doormat when it's time to leave for the

Sisterhood of Support meeting, but a few photographers are camped outside. Not as many as before - Conrad must have scared them away - but enough that it still feels like an intrusion.

I hang my head the entire bus ride to avoid being recognised and reply to a message from Joel's mum and one from Danielle, who will be late for the meeting again.

Lateness is loveable, right? she jokes.

As I reply to her, a text comes through from Stefan asking if I've started reading the books he brought yet. My body tenses at his name, but I type a breezy response that betrays no hint of the tension Stefan's visit created or the darkness of Joel's insinuations.

For the first time in a long time, I arrive at Sisterhood of Support twenty minutes early. Stepping into the meeting room, I blink at the sight of Tanya and Riley standing in a friendly huddle.

"You're back!" Tanya cheers.

I nod. "I'm a little early."

"Me too," Riley says, shooting Tanya a coy glance.

"Well, I'm glad you're both here," Tanya says. "I baked some muffins earlier with Danielle, so there's lots of tidying for me to do in the kitchen. You two can set up in here, if that's okay?"

"Let me guess, chairs in a circle?" Riley jokes.

Tanya laughs. "You've got it!"

Tanya bustles into the kitchen at the side of the meeting room while Riley and I begin to form the circle.

"It's good to see you again," Riley says.

"You too. I'm glad you've given meetings a chance."

"They help," Riley admits sheepishly. "Even setting up is kind of therapeutic. It gets you in the headspace for what's to come. Like, I look at the circle and know that soon I'll be talking about the worst thing, but then the chairs will be cleared away and everything will be put to the side."

"I've never thought of it like that," I say, looking around the room at the orderly structure we are creating, "but you're right. It helps to unpack it all and then put it away again."

"Exactly," Riley nods. "How are you, anyway? I'm guessing things are pretty shit for you right now."

"I've been better," I shrug.

Suddenly, Riley stops what she's doing and fixes her gaze on me. "Will they always only remember what happened to us? Is that all we'll ever be to people?"

Riley's words rattle me. I know she's looking to me for comfort, but I can't lie to her, or myself. "I hope not," I reply, "but who knows? All I can say is, I wish they'd forget about me. I wish it more than anything."

Riley takes a step towards me, but as she does, the meeting room door buzzes open and Carla, Paula and Amrita enter.

"Oh great, you're here," Carla says, her tone iced with disappointment.

Amrita ignores her and comes to me with her arms wide open, squeezing me into a hug that smells of floral soap and cleaning products. "Am I happy to see you! Although I've got to say, as beautiful as you are, I thought we were past your face being on the news every day," she jokes, nudging me in the hip until I laugh.

We finish the circle as a group, chatting while we work. More people arrive and Tanya brings an assortment of drinks and snacks in from the kitchen, then we stand together, eating, talking and waiting for the meeting to begin. Amrita shares details of the new meds she's been prescribed for her insomnia then Karolina tells us about a promotion she's up for at work.

Minutes before the meeting is due to begin, a red-faced Danielle arrives. "I've got a stitch from running up the stairs so fast," she pants.

"I bet! Treat yourself to a muffin. Tanya said you both made them earlier. They're great," I say.

"Thank you. I'm not sure Tanya wanted to combine baking with therapy when we met today, but I bet she's not regretting the choice now," Danielle jokes as she selects a chocolate chip muffin from the refreshments table.

"These muffins are rivalling the brownies you usually bring, Hannah," Amrita teases. "We should have a tasting competition and see which we prefer. I'm happy to be a judge!"

Lightness and laughter fill the air, then Tanya calls for the meeting to begin. I sit between Riley and Danielle, my new, unspoken place in the circle. Once the guided meditation is complete, we move around the group, each person sharing the stories they have saved for this space.

"Remember I told you I'd met someone online? Well, we had plans to meet this week, but then he Googled me. He cancelled an hour before the date then messaged to say he didn't think he could handle my 'emotional baggage'. My emotional baggage... as if what happened was my fault. As if I want to carry this."

"I went clothes shopping in an actual shop this week. I can't remember the last time I did that. I stood in front of the changing room mirror in my underwear and looked at myself. Truly looked at myself. Do you know what? I didn't cry. Even in that horrible lighting, I didn't think I looked bad. That's never happened before."

"I'm here, aren't I? I made it to this meeting. I haven't had more than two glasses of wine a night for the last week either, and I went to the supermarket twice. That's something. That's progress."

Even Riley speaks, sharing a short anecdote about how she went to a friend's house for dinner. I watch her with admiration, only it turns to dread when she finishes speaking and all eyes land on me.

"Hannah," Tanya says gently. "How have you been?"

"You all watch the news, right? You know how I've been," I joke, turning to Danielle in the hope that Tanya will move on, but she doesn't. She keeps her calm, encouraging eyes locked on me. "It's been tough," I finally admit. "I feel like I'm in danger."

The room shivers at my words.

"I can't shake the feeling that it's only a matter of time before... well, before this killer gets me. I don't feel safe anywhere. Even Break Time was broken into. The police tell me I'm safe, but I believed that once before, didn't I? Look where that got me."

Everyone in the room nods. Sisterhood of Support, a place where we learned the hard way that the people we're taught will save the day don't always fulfil that role.

"I've tried to push on, tried to pretend I'm fine and stick to my normal routine, but it's getting harder. I can't be on my own without panicking, but being around other people makes me just as tense. I don't know who to trust. I don't even trust myself. I mean, a friend showed up at my apartment and I didn't even think about not inviting him inside, only when Joel asked me how he knew where I lived, I couldn't answer him."

"If this person is a friend, it makes sense that you wouldn't turn them away," Amrita says.

"I know, but I should have asked how he knew my address. I didn't think to check. It's like I've lost the ability to spot danger. Sometimes I wonder, did I ever have that ability? After all, Peter Harris abducted me."

"Being abducted wasn't your fault, Hannah. We did a lot of work on this when you first came here, remember?" Tanya reminds me.

"I know but..." I bite my lip as a swell of pain inflates inside me. "Maybe it was my fault. Maybe I could have walked home a different way or screamed for help. Maybe... maybe I could have saved myself." I lower my head but then a hand slips in mine. Pale, slender, scratched.

I look up at Riley, and her fingers squeeze mine. "None of what happened is your fault, Hannah," she says.

A murmur of agreement rings out around the circle.

"Riley's right," Tanya says. "Deep down, you know she is. It's been a long time since you blamed yourself because you know that you are not, and never were, to blame."

My tears make it difficult to swallow. "I know you're right, but I've still gone back to torturing myself about it. I don't trust my brain anymore."

"However far you feel you've slipped, know how far you have come. Know that you're surrounded by friends and love. You are strong, Hannah. Stronger than you will ever know." Tanya's words shine like a beacon. I hold them close, afraid of what will happen if I let them go.

The conversation moves on. More tales are told and more moments of vulnerability are shared until it's time for the meeting to end.

While we pack away, I realise that Riley was right - the weight of the circle lifts as the shape is deconstructed and the chairs are stacked. The formal structure gone, our secrets safe with each other.

When everything is tidied away, I go to leave with Danielle, but Tanya calls after me. "Hannah, could you stay behind for a minute?"

I say goodbye to Danielle and hover on the periphery until it's only me and Tanya left in the room.

"How are you doing after today's meeting?" she asks.

"Good. Better than I was before I came, anyway."

"I'm glad to hear it. Now, I wanted you to stay back so I could offer you a ride home. I didn't want the others to hear and think I had a favourite," Tanya jokes, even though we all know that's what I am to her.

Temptation draws me in, but I shake my head. "Thanks, but I think I need to get the bus. I need to prove to myself that I can do it."

Tanya beams. "What a good idea! The offer is always there if you need it, though. Don't forget that."

I thank Tanya, then leave Sisterhood of Support. Even though it's dark, even though I'm alone, I don't allow self-doubt a second to sink in. I power myself to the bus stop with my hands balled into fists inside my coat pockets.

When I'm safely on the bus, I check my phone and find a voicemail from Ellen.

"Hi, Hannah! Just calling to let you know that I'm using Break Time's closure as an opportunity to give the place a makeover. The police have finished scoping it as a crime scene, but repairs are still needed. We can't open to the public until they're done, but I thought I'd use the time to update the paintwork and get new furniture. I'm going to be in tomorrow working on the new look with Stefan if you'd like to join us."

The voicemail has barely finished before I'm dialling Ellen's number. "I'll be there," I say as soon as she picks up.

If Ellen is reluctant to have me back, she doesn't show it. She cheers as she agrees to me coming in, then we hang up.

I can't fight my happiness as I hop off the bus, my smile only faltering when a gust of wind chills my bones. I wrap my coat tighter around myself and pick up my pace.

Somewhere behind me, someone laughs. I flinch and look over my shoulder to find two women walking arm in arm. My panic was for nothing though, because they're not even looking at me. The taller woman says something, making the other laugh again.

My pounding pulse subsides, but only slightly. I keep moving, keep focusing on thoughts of home to drown out the encroaching creep of anxiety.

Headlights from passing cars highlight my presence on Robson Lane, but when I turn onto the next street, an eerie quiet hits me. No one is driving along this dark residential road. Doors are locked and curtains are drawn, an armour blocking out the world and the cold it brings.

You're fine, you're fine, I repeat to myself, but each time my knees knock, I lose all sense of conviction in those words.

Bare-branched trees loom overhead, their skeletal fingers poised to scoop me up, as I listen to the silence of the night. The only thing disturbing the peace is the sound of my footsteps against the pavement. The pace is rhythmical, even, and fast, but then I hear it… a car behind me.

A car behind me, their tyres rolling slowly.

Too slowly.

Chapter *Twenty-seven.*

I pick up my pace, but the car increases its speed to match mine. My heart judders in my chest as the vehicle encroaches, my hands coiling into fists that I pray will be strong enough to save me should I need to use them. I move quicker, my feet catching on the paving stones as nerves make me clumsy.

Then suddenly, headlights illuminate the way before me, which only means one thing… the car is getting closer.

My feet burst into life. They slap against the damp pavement, faster and faster, but still not quick enough. My heart beats in my throat, each pound of my pulse begging me to save myself from whoever is following me.

As I race towards home, the engine of the car growls louder, fighting to keep up with me. I tear along the pavement, my legs moving so fast they could burn a hole in the ground.

"Hannah!"

A ragged half-scream, half-wail bursts from me upon hearing my name.

"Hannah, stop!"

Through the searing rush of adrenaline, the voice registers in my brain. I know that voice.

I trust that voice.

Slowing to a stop, I turn to find Tanya's head sticking out of the driver's window of the car pulling up beside me. "I'm so sorry! I didn't mean to scare you," she says sheepishly. "I was just following you to check you got home okay. Not as subtly as I'd hoped, clearly."

Lightheaded from the rush of adrenaline, I lean against the garden wall behind me and press my hand to my chest. My heart races beneath my palm. "You followed the bus?"

"Guilty," Tanya says with a confessional grimace. "I wanted to know you were okay. You've been so shaken recently."

"Well, now I'm more shaken than ever," I try to joke, but there's a snappiness to my response. Tanya looks down at her lap and my stomach twists. "I didn't mean it like that, Tanya. You just... you really scared me."

"I know, I'm sorry. You were never meant to know I was there."

"Put it this way, you'd make a terrible spy."

Tanya's lips flick as she levels her gaze with me. "Am I forgiven?"

Part of me wants to say 'no', but all that fear has drained me of any fight. I force myself to smile. "Of course you're forgiven. Now go home before my neighbours accuse you of stalking me."

Tanya laughs and restarts her car. "Thanks for being so understanding. Goodnight, Hannah."

I wave goodbye then watch Tanya's car shrink into the distance until it's gone, then I walk home, my legs still jittery from the chase.

Joel's working at the dining table when I get in, his eyes puffy and tired from a day spent staring at a screen. I decide not to tell him about Tanya following me, but I do tell him about going back to work tomorrow. He's so supportive of the decision that if I didn't love him already, I'd fall for him all over again.

"A slice of normality will be good for you," he says.

I'm half tempted to reply, 'Even if Stefan is there?', a tumble-weed-inducing joke if ever there was one, but my joke has more of an impact on me than I thought. It knots my stomach and warns me that I too find Stefan's appearance at my home suspicious. And if I find him suspicious, then maybe Stefan might be someone to fear.

The thought sits on my chest all night, making sleep impossible. I toss and turn, twisted in tangled bedsheets until my alarm demands I leave the cosiness of bed.

"Have a good day," Joel mumbles, then he rolls over and drifts back into sleep.

As Joel's lips part to exhale gentle snores, temptation begs me to follow his lead and fall back into the arms of sleep, but I shake it off. I've been down the road of skipping plans before, and it wasn't pretty. If I miss work today, missing it tomorrow will be even more tempting, then before I know it, leaving the house will become a task so colossal I won't do it.

Throwing back the duvet, I force myself out of bed and get ready for the day. I'm so busy focusing on making sure I don't give up on going to work that I don't even think about what I'm opening the front door to, but as soon as I leave my apartment building, reality confronts me like a shock of electricity.

"Hannah, have you anything to say to Harriet Warren's family?"

"Peter Harris is reportedly reading the news from prison. Is there anything you'd like him to know?"

I stumble backwards, blinking in the fresh swarm of journalists and photographers on my doorstep, more here today than ever before.

"What do you think happened to Harriet Warren?"

"How are you feeling? Are you scared?"

Keeping my head low, I push my way through the intense crowd. Halfway down the path, a photographer forces his camera in my face, the flash blinding.

"Stop!" I shout, but they don't hear me. Even if they did, they wouldn't listen.

Covering my head with my arms, I duck low and fight my way through. When I reach the road, I burst into a run. Most of the photographers stay behind, happy with their shot, but one decides to follow me, his battered trainers doing all they can to keep up with my frantic pace.

On Robson Lane, I slow to a walk and catch my breath. All the while, the photographer takes pictures of me. I stare ahead, doing all I can not to look at him as he snaps away.

An elderly couple are already at the bus stop when I reach it, two bags of groceries at their feet. Their eyes widen as they watch me arrive with a photographer in hot pursuit, then my identity registers with them.

"That's her, isn't it?" the old man whispers, not quietly enough. "That's Hannah Allen."

The woman's grey eyes land on me and I bite my cheeks, looking ahead as if studying the house opposite the bus stop can stop me from crying. Suddenly, the woman steps in front of me. "I think you've got enough photos now, don't you?" she says to the photographer.

He lowers his camera and shrugs. "Just doing my job, ma'am."

"And what a wonderful job you have. I'm sure your parents are very proud," she snarls, then she puts her arm over my shoulder and steers me away from the man and his intrusive lens. "Now piss off," the old woman shouts over her shoulder, a move that's so unexpected I can't help but laugh.

The elderly couple insist I sit with them on the bus. They tell me the story of how they met and discuss their love of travel, and the simple goodness of the conversation refuels me. I'm almost sad when it's time for me to leave them behind.

When the bus stops for me to get off, the old woman squeezes my hand. "Have a great day, dear. A great day like you deserve."

Her words give me the confidence I need to face the world head-on.

When I step off the bus, I look for Robbie, but he's not there. A nagging worry grows in me when I notice his stuff has gone too. I wonder if he's been back to this spot since the break-in. I wonder if he feels safe to do so, especially after he caught a glimpse of the person responsible for it.

Shaking myself from those thoughts, I continue down the road towards the familiar orange and blue sign of Break Time. The windows are boarded up, but the open door broadcasts the sound of bustling activity inside.

"Hey," I call out as I step over the threshold.

"Hannah!" Ellen cries, dropping the leg of a chair she's assembling to greet me. "I've missed you!"

"It's only been a few days," I laugh, "but I've missed you too. Have you been here long?"

"Only about half an hour," Stefan says, appearing from the backroom and leaning against the counter. My heart flutters at the sight of him, but I try not to show my panic. "Ellen's providing unlimited coffee. I thought I'd get here early to make the most of her generous offer. One of us must, seeing as you don't like it."

"I'm hoping copious amounts of caffeine means he'll build the flatpack quicker," Ellen says with a cheeky wink.

"Now that sounds like a challenge! I'll put my stuff in the backroom and we can have a competition to see who builds furniture the fastest," I joke, then I dodge Stefan and step into the backroom. It's piled high with new furniture and kitchenware, the space so tight I feel like I need to inhale to move around it.

Weaving my way around a stack of boxes, I go to hang up my coat, but as I do, I knock Stefan's satchel from an old chair. The bag lands with a thud, the contents spilling across the scuffed linoleum.

"Shit," I whisper. I crouch to pick everything up but freeze when my eyes rest on something sticking out of the satchel.

Nathaniel Clarke's book.

A book the killer is using as an instruction manual for murder.

A book that has somehow found its way inside Stefan's bag.

Chapter *Twenty-eight.*

Disbelief chokes me as I reach for the book. I need to feel it in my hands for this moment to be real, but even when I've picked it up, it still seems like a bad dream.

Why would Stefan have a copy of Nathaniel Clarke's book? It doesn't make sense. He didn't even know about Peter Harris until I told him.

Swallowing my fear, I examine the book. Stefan usually takes such good care of his books, but not this one. It's clearly an often-read text, with frayed edges and a creased spine. Corners of pages throughout the book are downturned to mark them as ones to return to, a sight that dries my mouth. What could Stefan possibly find so interesting that he wanted to remember where to go back and find it?

I open the book at a random bookmarked page and gasp... it's the start of the *'Number Eleven'* chapter.

My chapter.

I flip the book over, trying not to flinch at every sign informing me that this book has had its contents devoured more than once. To pick up tips, maybe? The thought solidifies in my stomach.

Biting back a shudder, I open the book once more and a familiar piece of card slips out. It flutters to the floor and lands beside Stefan's lunch. I pick it up, losing Stefan's page but also losing my mind over what I see.

Raja Kaling's business card.

I blink twice, but the facts don't change. At some point in time, Stefan had taken one of Raja's cards. Worse still, he kept it. I think back to the quote from a friend referenced in one of Raja's articles. Surely Stefan wouldn't betray me like that?

Looking at the objects in my hands, I'm not so sure.

Suddenly, the door to the backroom opens.

"Hey Hannah, do you want a hot –" Stefan begins, but when he sees what I'm holding, he can't finish his sentence.

We stare at each other for what feels like an eternity, the world on pause while we figure out what to do next.

"Hannah, I can explain," Stefan rushes, but I cut across him.

"Explain what, why you're reading about the serial killer who hurt me or why you're holding on to the card of a journalist who's hounding me?"

"It's not what you think. Please, hear me out," Stefan begs. He steps towards me, but I jump to my feet and back away, hitting into a stack of boxes behind me in the process. Stefan's face crumples. "Don't look at me like that, Hannah. I was only trying to understand what you went through."

"And you think reading this book will help you understand that? It isn't my story or my experience – it's a book profiting off my pain!"

Stefan's cheeks burn. "You have to understand, Hannah, I didn't know who you were or what had happened to you. I wanted to learn about it so I didn't say or do the wrong thing."

"Having this book is doing the wrong thing!"

"I'm sorry! I never meant to hurt you."

"Well, you've not done a very good job of that," I fire hotly, furious with myself for the swell of tears I can feel building inside me.

"Please, just listen to me," Stefan pleads. "I bought the book when Harriet went missing. Everyone was talking about Peter Harris and what he'd done, but I had no idea. I read it once and –"

"You've read this book more than once, Stefan."

"Okay, maybe I went back and read over some parts."

His words taste like bleach in my mouth. I take a step forward, holding the book in the air. "Do you realise that the police think the killer is using this book as a guide for murder? Do you have any idea how owning it makes you look?"

Stefan flinches. "Are you saying you think I'm responsible for these murders?"

"I don't know, Stefan, are you?"

"Hannah, you can't be serious!"

"It's not that weird of a theory. You know me, you know Harriet Warren. The place we both work was attacked. You're reading this book for fun –"

"Nothing about reading that book was fun!"

"But you still did it!"

Stefan slumps in on himself, his body brimming with self-loathing, but I'm past the point of caring for his upset. All I can feel is the weight of this book in my hand and the horror of what it could mean. There's a worrying trend here, one I can no longer ignore.

I level my gaze with Stefan. "How do you know where I live?"

Stefan blinks. "What?"

"That day when you visited me - how did you know where to go? I've never told you my address. You've never been to my apartment before, but you knew where it was. How?"

The blush creeping up Stefan's neck deepens, so dark he almost looks ill. "Hannah –"

"How do you know where I live?!"

Stefan doesn't answer me, and I get bored of waiting for him to confess. I march towards him and push the book hard into his chest. "I don't know who you are," I whisper icily.

"Hannah, I'm your friend."

"Some friend," I snarl. I go to walk away, but Stefan grabs the top of my arm to stop me. The sharp pain of his bony fingers digging into my flesh makes me gasp. I look at his hand grasping my skin then into his eyes, eyes that are clouded with anger.

The eyes of a stranger.

Ellen chooses this moment to rush into the room. Stefan lets go of me like I burn to touch as soon as she appears, the rage dousing his features suddenly masked.

"What's going on in here?!" she cries. "The whole street has probably heard the two of you shouting!"

I don't have the words in me to explain the situation when my brain is still struggling to make sense of it. "Ask Stefan. I'm sorry, Ellen, but I can't be here. Not around him," I say, then I use her interruption as an opportunity to flee.

Stefan calls after me, but I don't turn around. My legs propel me away, not stopping until I'm far from Break Time. They lead me to Derwent Park, the manicured gardens and intricate gates welcoming me inside.

I collapse onto a bench and go over the events of the morning, but everything about them is jarring. The Stefan I know would never read that book. The Stefan I know would never sell a story about me… would he?

I sit until my bum is numb. Strangers pass me by without a second glance, but I'm so lost in thought that I barely notice anyone else's existence but my own. The only constant keeping me in reality is the buzzing of my phone in my pocket. Calls I know will be from Stefan.

When grey clouds roll in and droplets of rain begin to fall around me, I check my notifications. I was right - Stefan has left countless messages and voicemails. I ignore every single one.

There are missed calls from Ellen too, ones I also ignore. I'm not ready to talk to her about working alongside Stefan, although that's assuming I still have a job after walking out like that.

Chewing my lip to stop myself from crying, I open my contact list to call Tanya, but as I do, my phone comes to life. This time, it's not Stefan or Ellen's name on the screen - it's Conrad's.

"Hannah, where are you?" he asks as soon as I answer the phone.

"I'm in Derwent Park, why?"

"I need you to leave right now. I need you to go home."

Terror bites my throat. "Why?"

There's a beat of silence so full of tension I almost hang up. "We've found Harriet Warren. We've found her body."

Chapter *Twenty-nine.*

I grip the bench, leaning forward as the weight of the news presses against my back. Another woman, gone. Another life extinguished before it even started.

Another victim claimed by the killer.

I want to take some time to sink into this moment and let the gravity of the news crush me that little bit more, but Conrad speaks again. "There's more to what we found, Hannah. I need to see you so I can tell you about it."

"Can't you tell me over the phone?"

Conrad must hear something in my voice that worries him because he speaks to me in a calm, measured way. "No, Hannah, I can't. It's best I say it to your face, so I need you to go home, okay? I'll meet you there. Can you do that for me?"

"I... yes, yes I can."

"Good. I'll see you soon. And Hannah? Don't talk to anyone, don't trust anyone, just... just go straight home."

Conrad's words ring in my ears long after the call has ended, but I follow his instructions. I take a taxi home and find him leaning on the hood of his car outside my apartment when I pull up. For a moment, he's too engrossed in his phone to notice I've arrived. His frown lines appear deeper than ever as he stares at the screen, his fingers working furiously to respond to a message.

The sound of the taxi door closing behind me alerts Conrad to my presence. He looks up and pushes himself from his car. "How was your journey?" he asks.

"Uneventful," I reply as we make our way towards the building. "Did you get rid of the reporters? There were loads outside this morning."

"I did. They won't be coming back again if they know what's good for them."

I smile, but I don't share Conrad's certainty on that one. Unlocking the front door, I gesture for Conrad to go inside, but he insists I go first.

Once we're ascending the stairs towards my apartment, I address the elephant in the room. "So, you've found Harriet's body. Was it... was it like the others?"

"I'll tell you more when we're inside," Conrad replies, an answer that only increases my paranoia. "Is Joel home?"

I shake my head. "He had to go into the office today. Do you want me to ask him to come home?"

"No, that's fine. It's probably better if I speak to you alone."

Another answer that traps me in the jaws of terror. Clumsily, I unlock the door to my apartment and we step inside, Conrad's frame once again too big for the space he finds himself in. For a moment, we stand in awkward silence, neither of us quite knowing what to do from here.

"Would you like a drink?" I offer.

"A glass of water would be good, thanks."

Conrad goes into the living room while I get him a drink. Dirty breakfast pots greet me from the countertop, waiting to be stacked into the dishwasher. Hastily, I tidy them away, relieved that Conrad hadn't followed me into the kitchen to discover the mess.

I take Conrad a glass of water then sit on the armchair opposite him. "Thanks," he says. He takes a drink, gulping as if he hasn't had water in days. I study his grey, sallow skin and wonder if maybe that's actually the case.

Clasping my hands together so I have something to hold on to when everything falls apart, I address him. "Are you ready to talk now?"

Conrad lays a coaster on the coffee table and sets his glass on top of it, then his eyes lock on mine. "As you know, we found Harriet's body. With it, we found a note. A note addressed to you."

I find myself nodding as if this somehow makes perfect sense.

Conrad reaches into his coat pocket and pulls out a piece of paper. "I have a copy of it here," he says. "I've done my best to keep you out of what's going on, but I'm afraid that's not possible anymore. I hate to do this to you, Hannah, but I need you to read this note. I need you to tell me what you think because there's no denying it now - you are at the centre of what is happening."

A chill travels down my body. I grip on to my composure, the bones of my hands crushing against each other as they fight to cling on despite this moment of turbulence.

"I need you to read this note and see if you can think of anyone who might have written it," Conrad says, holding the piece of paper in his outstretched hand.

My breath catches in the back of my throat as it dawns on me what Conrad is saying. "You think I know the killer?"

Conrad doesn't reply, just waits for me to take the paper from him.

It trembles as I accept it, the words jumping up and down on the page. I recognise the handwriting immediately. "It's the same writing as the notes I found on the doorstep," I say.

"I know," Conrad replies, a confirmation that somehow makes everything worse.

Inhaling to steady my nerves, I read.

Hannah - are you still pretending you're over all this Lucky Number 11 nonsense like usual, or have I finally got through to you?

It's almost time for game over. It's coming for you. I'm coming for you.
Ready or not... I'll see you again soon

I read the note once more, then I drop it onto the coffee table, secure in the knowledge that I will never have to read it again to know what it says. Those words will stay with me forever.

The truth screams inside me until my ears ring... they're coming for me. Whoever it is, they're coming for me.

"Does this message mean anything to you?" Conrad's gentle question drags me from the thorns of fear.

I swallow hard and shake my head.

Conrad points to part of the note. "This line, *'Are you still pretending you're over all this Lucky Number 11 nonsense like usual'* is of particular interest. Plus, they say they will see you again soon. The language used seems to indicate... well, it seems to indicate –"

"That they know me already."

"Exactly. Hannah, I know this is a hard question, but is there anyone you think it could be? Anyone at all?"

"Conrad, do you have any idea what you're asking?" I say, wrapping my arms around my body. "You're asking me if I know anyone who could be a serial killer."

"I know, Hannah, I know."

I blow a long, steady stream of air out of my mouth. "The honest answer is no. No, I don't think I know a serial killer."

"How about anyone with a link to Peter Harris? Perhaps someone who might have an interest in him?"

"Do you honestly think I'd befriend someone like that?"

A moment of silence rings out, one that's only interrupted by the faint sound of a phone buzzing. I don't need to look at my phone to know it's Stefan calling again.

Stefan who lends me books and makes the best hot chocolates.

Stefan who knew where I lived without being told. Stefan who has a copy of a book about Peter Harris. Stefan who knew Harriet Warren when she was alive.

Robbie's words about thinking he'd seen a man attack Break Time echo in my mind.

"Actually, there is someone," I hear myself say.

Conrad's head jerks upright. "Who?"

I breathe and will myself to be strong because once I say these words, I can never take them back. "Stefan from work. He showed up here unannounced the other day, but I've never told him where I live. I found a copy of Nathaniel Clarke's book in his bag too."

"He's the kid who said he didn't know who you were, right?"

I nod. "There's something else too. Harriet Warren was in his class at university."

Conrad's eyes widen. I don't need him to say it for me to know it's true – he thinks there's a chance that Stefan could be the killer. Right here, under his nose the whole time, serving cake and coffee with a smile.

"Thank you, Hannah. I'll make sure we speak to Stefan today," Conrad says before glancing at his watch. "I should go. Do you want me to call anyone before I do? Joel? Tanya? Another friend, perhaps?"

"No, I'm fine."

"Are you sure you'll be okay on your own? Like I've said before, we can move you -"

"Conrad, I'm fine," I lie, the words the only answer I am prepared to give.

Ignoring Conrad's hesitancy, I lead him out. At the door, he points to my neck. "Put your panic alarm on and always keep your phone on your person. I'll have mine with me. If you need anything, call."

"Thank you," I say as I open the door for him.

When Conrad steps out into the hallway, he turns back to me. "For the next few days, I need you to be extra careful. Trust no one until we can get to the bottom of this, okay?"

With that, Conrad walks away.

As soon as he's out of sight, I slam the door shut then run to my bedroom. Locating my panic alarm on the bedside table, I throw it over my neck. I wrap my hand around the smooth shape, waiting to feel comforted by it, but that feeling never comes.

For the first time in a long time, I wish my mum was here. I wish she could stroke my hair from my face and fill me with much-needed reassurance like she did so many times after I was found.

"You are strong. You are capable. You can get through this," she would whisper, repeating those words until I believed them. I say them to myself now, but in my fear-filled voice, they seem false. I give up on self-soothing. In that defeat, the silence of the apartment swells, but then it's interrupted by a knock at the door.

Frown lines etch into my forehead. I didn't buzz anyone into the building for them to be at my front door.

Before I have time to question it further, another knock rings out.

Creeping to the doorway of the bedroom, I glance down the hallway. "Conrad?" I call, but there's no reply.

Another knock sounds, this time a pound as if made by a closed fist. The aggression of the sound makes me jump, but I put one foot in front of the other until I reach the door.

Plucking up the courage to see who's there, I press my palms against the door to steady myself as I rise onto tiptoes to look through the peephole. Through the small circle of glass, my eye locks on the figure outside my home.

Stefan.

Stefan is on the other side of the door.

Chapter *Thirty.*

I stumble backwards and trip over a pair of Joel's discarded trainers left in the middle of the hallway. I land on the floor with a thud, a searing pain shooting up my wrist.

"Hannah? Hannah, is that you?" Stefan calls from the other side of the door.

Hearing my name leave his lips chills me to my core. "Go away!" I shriek, the shrillness of fear dousing every word.

"Please, open the door. I want to explain!"

I fight the urge to cover my ears with my hands to blot out the sound of Stefan's voice. "I don't want to hear what you have to say! Leave! Leave before I call the police."

"The police? Hannah, this is crazy!" Stefan protests. "You can't seriously think I had anything to do with this?"

When I say nothing, Stefan bangs on the door again.

"Hannah, please! Talk to me!"

I haul myself to a standing position, wincing as I put weight on my injured wrist. "Stefan, this is your last chance – leave or I will call the police."

"What the… Hannah, it's me. It's Stefan. I'm your friend."

"A friend wouldn't have that book," I retort.

"A friend would if they were trying to find out about their friend's past. A past they had no clue about up until a few days ago!"

Stefan's words push me over the edge. I press the red button on the panic alarm as if my life depends on it, willing Stefan and his reminder of the past to go away, just go away.

"Please hear me out," Stefan pleads. "Do I have to break down the door to get you to talk to me?"

My bottom lip quivers as I imagine Stefan bursting through the door and confronting me with no barrier between us to keep me safe. "Just go, Stefan. Please," I beg.

"No, not until you speak to me! Come on, Hannah, I thought we were friends! How could you think I was a killer?"

In the distance, I swear I hear sirens, but Stefan's shouting drowns them out.

"I've left Ellen sorting Break Time on her own to come here and talk to you," Stefan continues. "Let me in! I don't want to argue with you."

"The police are on their way," I reply tearfully. "You need to get away from my front door."

"You've called the police? Is that a joke?" Stefan cries, but neither of us is laughing.

Summoning every ounce of strength I have, I will myself to look through the peephole once more. When I do, I see Stefan again, only this time his cheeks are burning with indignation. He stares back through the peephole like he knows he's being watched.

"You've got this all wrong," he says. "You don't know what you're doing."

Somewhere outside, the wail of sirens rings out louder. Stefan must hear them too because a toxic mixture of disbelief and rage flashes in his eyes. He hits the door so hard I feel it shake.

"You're not giving me the chance to explain," he shouts, but his shouts don't scare me anymore, not now I know the police are on their way. Not when there is something I need to ask him before they arrive.

"Did you do it? Did you kill those girls?" I ask.

There's a pause before he replies. "Hannah, why are you asking me this?"

"That's not an answer, Stefan," I say, pushing myself to act braver than my wobbling chin makes me feel. "You know where I live despite never being told. Weird notes have been left at my house and Robbie thinks he saw a man attack Break Time. It's not that crazy to think it could be you, so I'm asking you now - did you do it?"

I don't get to hear Stefan's answer because the intercom interrupts our conversation by ringing. Backing away from the door, I rush to it. "Hello?" I shout into the speaker.

"Miss Allen? It's the police," replies an authoritative voice.

I buzz them into the building then collapse to my knees as adrenaline drains from my body. In the background, heavy footsteps pound the stairs, then come the shouts of 'police'.

"What the..." I hear Stefan gasp, the anger in his voice replaced by fear.

Pressing my head into my hands, I sob as the commotion in the hallway begins. I listen to Stefan get pinned to the wall against his will. I hear a male officer telling him to be calm and Stefan's shouts of innocence as he begs me to intervene. Then I hear his pleas and protests grow softer as he's taken away.

When the world outside falls silent, there's a gentle knock at the door. "Hannah, it's me," comes Conrad's voice from the other side.

Wiping my eyes with my sleeve, I go to the door and unlock it. Conrad sweeps into the apartment, his features softening when he sees my red-rimmed eyes. "I was only a few streets away when you pressed the alarm," he says. "You did the right thing, Hannah. Are you okay?"

"I'm fine."

Even though he knows I'm lying, Conrad doesn't push it. "I've asked one of the officers to let Joel know what's happened. He's on his way home. I didn't think you'd want to recite the events of today more than is necessary."

"Thanks. I owe you," I reply.

"You owe me nothing, Hannah, but I do need to ask you something, and I want you to think about your answer carefully before you make any decisions. Are you comfortable staying here tonight, or would you like us to relocate you?"

I look around my living room. The sofa cushions are squashed from multiple movie nights. The illustration of a giraffe my mum drew when she found out she was pregnant with me hangs beside the bookcase. There's a chip on the skirting board by the door from when I knocked into the wall with the coffee table when we first moved in. My space has been tainted by threatening notes and Stefan's intrusion, but this apartment is my home. Outside of the house I spent my childhood in, it's the only home I've ever known. Cushion by cushion, vase by vase, flatpack by flatpack, I have built it as my place of comfort. Once upon a time, I thought I'd lost the ability to do that forever.

"If I leave my home, I let whoever is doing this win," I say. "Besides, Joel will be here with me."

"And you're happy with that?"

I tilt my head. "Why wouldn't I be?"

"No reason," Conrad replies, but there's an edge to his tone that unsettles me.

Still, if Conrad thinks I'm making a mistake, he doesn't say so. He just sits with me and asks about the books on my shelf while we wait for Joel to come home. There's an ease to being in each other's company that isn't usually there. It's almost nice. If anything, I'm a little dismayed to have our time cut short when I hear Joel's key in the lock.

Joel rushes to my aid when he sees me and I collapse into his arms. He presses my body tight against his, so close I can feel his heart pounding in his chest. I squeeze him harder, my way of letting him know that everything is okay, but over Joel's shoulder, I catch Conrad's eye.

Don't trust anyone, his stare tells me, and suddenly Joel's embrace is claustrophobic.

I pull out of the hug, feigning a smile. "You didn't have to rush home for me."

"Are you kidding? You've had the worst day imaginable! Of course I'd want to be here for you."

Conrad clears his throat and uses Joel's presence as his excuse to leave.

"So soon?" I reply, alarmed to notice how much the thought of Conrad's departure panics me.

"I need to be there to interview Stefan," he replies.

The thought of Stefan sitting on a cold, hard chair in a police station interview room, being questioned about the most hideous of crimes, flashes in my mind. My stomach brews, churning with the intensity of the vision. "I'll walk you to the door," I say, leading Conrad out before I'm sick on the living room carpet.

When we are alone, Conrad comes close and lowers his voice. "Remember, be careful for the next few days, Hannah. Go to your support meetings, keep your panic alarm on you, but most of all trust no one, and I mean no one. Do you understand me?"

"Conrad, I -"

"Do you understand me?" Conrad repeats, his tone final.

Fraught, I nod, and then Conrad opens the front door. He offers me a brisk wave before walking away, leaving me alone with a man he's just warned me not to trust.

Chapter *Thirty-One*

I hover at the doorway until I feel Joel behind me. "Why don't we go for a walk?" he suggests. When I jump at the sound of his voice, he comes to me, brimming with concern. "Hannah, you're shaking."

"It's been a big day, that's all," I dismiss.

"I know, that's why a walk might help. A break from the apartment could be just what you need."

I think of the outside world, so bright, so intimidating, so full of unknowns. Joel must see my reservations because he speaks again.

"I won't let anything happen to you, Hannah. I'll be with you every step of the way." Joel rests his hand on the small of my back, but with Conrad's words still ringing in my ears, the gesture doesn't fill me with peace like it would have once upon a time.

But however jittery I feel, I know that Joel is right - a change of scenery is what I need. I push myself to get ready, wrapping myself in thick layers so my clothes can provide the hug I so desperately need, then we set off.

The winter sun is blinding as we step outside. I wince, the onslaught of light burning my raw-from-crying eyes.

"Look at that sky," Joel comments. "It looks to me like better days are coming." He slips his hand inside mine, but his grip isn't tight enough to stop me from feeling like I am floating away.

The more we walk, the more aware of other people I become. They're everywhere, glued to their phone or talking loudly to the person beside them, their words laced with aggression as they rant about public transport being late or the cost of the weekly shop. Each step is a sensory overload, the sky too bright, the air too cold. As we walk, Joel squeezes my hand now and then in an attempt to reassure me, but the infrequent pulsing jolts me with panic every time.

We make it three streets away from home before the merry-go-round of colours, stares, and faces gets too much. "Joel, I can't," I say, coming to a stop.

"What's wrong?"

"I... I just can't," I stammer, turning back and heading towards home. Within seconds, my walk breaks into a run. Before I know it, I'm tearing down the street as if I'm being hunted.

"Hannah! Han, stop!" Joel shouts after me, but I don't listen and I don't stop, not even to check for traffic before running across a road. Car horns beep furiously and someone leans out of their window to shout at me, but still, I run.

"Hannah, be careful!" Joel hollers, but there's nothing careful about my need to flee. I must get away from here, from him, from everyone.

Rounding a corner, our apartment building comes into view in the distance. My heart bursts at the serenity it promises. I run faster, ignoring the quizzical stares from every person I race past and the tightening in my chest as I push my body too hard.

Blood thumps through me, the pounding of my heart painful by the time I reach the doorway, but I don't care because home is at my fingertips. I wrench the handle of the front door, but it doesn't budge.

Locked.

Of course it's locked.

I pat my pockets to find my keys, but my fingers don't find their bulky shape. Then I remember – I didn't bring mine with me, Joel did. I'd trusted him to be at my side the whole time, never once thinking I would ditch him in a wild panic.

My heart is in my throat as I look around, suddenly aware of how out in the open I am. Exposed in a doorway with no way of getting to safety inside.

Anything could happen.

Anyone could hurt me.

My lungs constrict. I open my mouth to breathe but it's as if all oxygen has been vacuumed out of the atmosphere. The more I try to find it, the less there is.

Gasping for air, I clamber for the intercom to alert a neighbour that I need help, but I'm too shaky to press the buttons. I watch my fingers flail, too unsteady to reach out for assistance.

As the walls of my throat close in on themselves, I fall to my knees.

I'm going to die, I realise. *Right here, right now on this doorstep, I am going to die.*

The grey paving stone blurs before me, the colour of the day draining away with every choking non-breath I fight to take.

Then I hear footsteps behind me.

It could be someone coming to save me.

It could be someone coming to kill me.

All I know is, at this moment, I couldn't care either way.

A pair of hands grip me. Strong hands. Hands I don't fight against. They turn me towards them, and a familiar face appears before me.

"Breathe, Hannah," Joel instructs, his tone measured and calm. "You're having a panic attack. You're okay but you need to breathe."

"I… I can't," I gasp but Joel grips me tighter.

"Yes, you can."

There's something about the steadiness of his voice that breaks through to me. I cling to Joel, my grip so tight I must be bruising him, but he doesn't flinch. He holds me and breathes with me, in and out, in and out.

His dark eyes bore into mine and, despite Conrad's words of warning, I trust him.

I find air again. It comes back to me in short, sharp bursts, then full, desperate gulps. My chest relaxes, my hands steady, and, propped up by Joel, I make it back to the apartment.

"You're safe now. You're safe," Joel repeats as he sits with me on the sofa. He rocks me back and forth, pressing kisses into my forehead, but no matter what Joel says, no matter what he does, I can't shake the feeling that this won't be the last time I am gasping for air.

The grains of sand are well and truly slipping through the hourglass now. Oh, how they flow. They flow until there is no more to give.

They flow until the end.

I know you feel it too. I can see it in your eyes, despite what you tell yourself or what you choose to believe from the soothing words of others. You can't shut out the overwhelming sensation warning you that your luck is running out. That soon it will be time for us to face our final showdown.

This was always meant to be how it ended for you, you know that as well as I do. That's why I chose you. Who else could be my final victim? I mean, just look at your history – the girl who survived the unsurvivable. It wouldn't be called that if you were meant to live past it, would it?

Like with the others, I'm doing you a favour. In your case, I'm finishing your story the way it was intended to go. I'm setting you free. By coiling our lives together, I'm finally giving you the thing you crave most – peace with the past, acceptance over what happened, and the courage to step away.

The legacy I am adding to your name... it's incredible. This bond will connect us forever. A beautiful thought, don't you think? From the day we face each other for the last time, our names will be said in unison. My name said as much as yours, your name as much as mine. Two stories intertwined, two people conjoined, the ties unbreakable even in death.

So, when my blade slices your skin – and it will – give into it. Sink into the moment. Look me in the eyes, the last eyes you'll ever see, and thank me.

I'm going to set you free, Hannah. Cut by cut, I'm going to set you free.

Chapter *Thirty-two.*

With terror underpinning my every move, the next day I do something I haven't felt the need to do in years – I ask Tanya for a lift to the Sisterhood of Support meeting. "Of course! I can take you home too if you'd like?" she offers.

"That would be great, thanks," I reply, and with that, I seal my regression back to Hannah Allen, petrified of everything and mistrustful of everyone.

While I wait for Tanya to arrive, I do everything I can to distract myself from what is going on in the outside world, but nothing works. Even reading doesn't help. Stefan loaned me these books. Stefan who is talking to the police at this very moment, suspected of murder.

When Tanya texts to say she's outside, I slip on my shoes with such enthusiasm I'm surprised I don't break them.

Joel leans against the living room doorway, watching me get ready to leave. "Mum's asked if we want to go to hers tonight. I've said no, but if you want, I could meet you after the meeting. We could go out for dinner or to the cinema or something."

The thought of being in a crowded room surrounded by strangers makes me bristle. "I'd rather have a night in," I dismiss, but then I catch the sadness on Joel's face. "We'll get back to doing things like that again one day, I promise."

"Hannah, it's not missing out on a meal or the cinema that I'm bothered about. It's you feeling like you can't do those things. I wish I could fix this for you. I wish -"

Inside my pocket, my phone buzzes with another text from Tanya. Joel hears it too. An artificial brightness takes over his face, one so false it makes my heart hurt.

"We can talk about this another time. Go to your meeting. Have fun," he says.

I hover for a moment, but Tanya's calming presence calls to me. I leave Joel behind and race to Tanya's car before my mind has a moment to waver about going outside.

As always, Tanya's reassuring smile works its magic, and my erratic heartbeat begins to find its rhythm again. "Thanks for picking me up," I say as I clip my seatbelt in place.

"Of course! I'd do this every meeting if you wanted me to."

I smile, knowing just how true that statement is.

Tanya lowers the volume of the radio as we set off. "So, how are you doing? Conrad filled me in on what's been happening. Your friend being questioned... that's got to be tough."

"It's not the best feeling, no."

"Eloquently put," she jokes.

Despite myself, I giggle. "You know what I mean. I can't imagine Stefan hurting anyone, but then never in my wildest dreams would I imagine someone copying Peter Harris."

"Well, sometimes the wildest dreams become unfortunate realities, but Conrad will find out if Stefan is or isn't guilty. Until then, all you've got to do is keep your head above water."

"You make it sound so easy."

"Oh, there's nothing easy about it, but advising someone to do it? Well, that's definitely easy."

I laugh then we sit in companionable silence until we reach Sisterhood of Support. We complete the set up together, then people start to arrive. I greet my friends, but my warmth isn't returned. Paula can't meet my gaze and Karolina barely responds to my 'hello'. Even Amrita seems off. I'm about to ask what's wrong when Riley loops her arm through mine and leads me to the side of the room. She slips her hand into her coat pocket and pulls out Raja Kaling's business card.

"Where did you get that?" I ask, dry-mouthed.

"She was outside. She stopped everyone before they came in and asked them for information about you."

The ground beneath my feet trembles as I take Raja's card from Riley. "She was here, outside Sisterhood of Support?"

Riley nods. "No one said anything to her but I think it's shaken people up. Being here is meant to be super secretive, you know?"

I understand exactly why the secrecy of Sisterhood of Support matters. The women who come here have experienced the worst. This is their safe space. It shouldn't be violated. Raja's articles have already made it so people could identify my place of work. What if she shares details about these meetings or the people who attend them? What if the people who hurt my friends find them once again?

I scan the room, taking in everyone's squared shoulders and tight expressions. "They're all terrified."

"They are, but it's not your fault. You didn't tell her to come here."

"I know, but still…"

"Try not to worry about it, okay? People might be a bit off with you tonight, but to be honest I think they just feel bad for you. Even if they're scared, they're protective of you."

I smile a weak smile. "Thanks, Riley. You're a real friend."

"Don't worry about it. You'd do the same for me, although hopefully you never have to," Riley says, then she leads me back to the others. I follow her, even though I'm not sure I should.

I keep my head low as I locate Danielle, who's arrived in the nick of time, as per usual. "Who stole your picnic?" she asks when I stand beside her.

"Sorry?"

"It means you look miserable. Everything okay?"

At that moment, Carla shoots me a look that can only be described as one that could kill. "Everything's fine," I lie, a sentiment I repeat to myself as we take our seats for the meeting.

To my surprise, no one mentions Raja, even though it's clear people want to. It's like there's an unspoken agreement that her presence was traumatic for everyone, and no one wants to add to that by calling it out, not even Carla. I breathe a little easier knowing that no one's going to blame me for Raja's intrusion, but still, an underlying tightness clings to my lungs. When Tanya calls time on the session, I'm so tense that my calves scream as I stretch them to stand.

Danielle puts her coat on then fights a yawn. "Need a ride home?"

"I'm good, thanks. Tanya's giving me a lift."

Carla overhears the exchange and rolls her eyes. "Of course she is," she snaps before marching out of the room.

Danielle grimaces. "One day, that woman will learn to lighten up."

"Can it be one day soon?" I joke weakly.

"Hang in there, okay? Things will get better," Danielle says. She hugs me before leaving, an embrace that means more than she will ever know.

When everyone has gone and only Tanya and I are left, I sigh a sigh so big I deflate.

"Tough night?" Tanya asks.

"You could say that. Did you hear about this?" I ask, handing Tanya Raja's card.

She doesn't even look at it before she nods. "I heard, yes."

"I think everyone hates me because of it."

"They don't hate you, Hannah, but an unexpected reporter's presence is bound to be alarming for people."

"There wouldn't be a reporter sniffing around if I didn't come here."

"There also wouldn't be as great an atmosphere if you didn't come here," Tanya says, then she looks around the room. Remnants of snacks are still laid out on the table and the last of the coffee needs to be poured away, but Tanya shakes her head. "Let's go. I think we could both do with a change of scenery."

Tanya links my arm and leads me away before I can protest.

"I swear, this winter is never-ending," she complains as we bundle into her car.

"A never-ending darkness seems appropriate right now," I joke. Tanya lets out a little laugh, then she starts the engine and we roll down the dimly lit streets of my city.

Familiar sights flit past my field of vision. There's something soothing about knowing these streets as well as I do, a peace that comes from knowing I could navigate the journey home blindfolded or tell you the name of every shop on the high street.

"I've got a question for you, Hannah," Tanya says when we stop at a red traffic light. "How come you never moved away after everything that happened here?"

Whatever I was expecting Tanya to ask, it wasn't that.

"Why did you stick around?" she continues. "After all, everyone here knew who you were. Everyone knew what happened."

"Thanks for reminding me," I mutter.

"I'm serious. Tell me why."

I sigh as I look out of the window once more. The humanities block of the university is to my right, an archaic building with grand architecture and an impressive flight of stairs leading up to the ornate front door. When Mum and I would walk past it when I was little, I'd let go of her hand and run up those stairs. Standing at the top and looking back at her, I felt so grown-up, so invincible.

"It's my home," I reply eventually. "It's where I grew up. For the longest time, when it was just me and Mum, I was happy here. It's a place where I have memories, most of them of life with her, most of them good. I know something bad happened here, but I love where I live. I didn't want to leave it behind."

"What a beautiful answer. You had something you loved and you didn't let what happened take it from you. You could have moved elsewhere and started over somewhere new, but you didn't. You chose to stay because you're a fighter, Hannah. You always have been."

"I don't know about that," I reply, shifting in my seat.

"How can you look at the last ten years of your life and say otherwise? You battled every day to stand where you are now. Times might feel tough at the moment, but you've got yourself through tough times before and you will again. That all starts by being honest with yourself. Recently whenever I see you, you pretend everything is fine, but torment is written all over your face."

"I'm trying to keep going. I don't know what else you want me to do."

"I want you to keep going while also being true to what you're feeling. There are some things we can't hide from, however much we wish we could. Trying to only causes more damage in the long run. Don't bother with pretence, Han. There's such strength in vulnerability. There is power in admitting you're scared."

"You want me to admit I'm scared? Tanya, I'm terrified."

"So be scared. Acknowledge that feeling. With what you're going through right now, it's okay to be scared."

"It's so much more than that, though. Conrad told me not to trust anyone. Where does that leave me? Where does that leave my life?"

"In your hands, Hannah, where it should be. Ask yourself this - what do you think of Conrad's advice?"

"I think he's right," I admit. "I saw the note they found on Harriet Warren's body. Whoever's doing this is someone I know."

"So does that mean you can't trust the people in your life?"

"Of course it does. One of them could be a serial killer."

Tanya smiles reassuringly. "You have a good heart, Hannah. You have good instincts. Trusting people is a choice, one only you can make."

"I'm not sure I have a choice in this situation."

"There's always a choice," Tanya says as she turns right, my apartment building now in sight. She pulls over. "Can I give you some advice to override Conrad's? I think that maybe, instead of trusting no one, you need to learn to trust yourself."

I almost laugh. "You want me to trust myself? Me, the woman who has had a murderer tailing her for the last few weeks and didn't notice?"

"Yes! Trust yourself! Wonderful, brilliant you. The person who got you through this the first time."

I shake my head. "You got me through it, Tanya. Without you, I'd still be lying in bed in a dark room, hating the world."

This time, it's Tanya's turn to shake her head. "No, Hannah, where you are now, this life, it's all yours. Everyone who said you couldn't carry on after what you survived, every person who told you you'd never find love or a job? You proved them wrong. You took every step. *You* built your life. I want to hear you say it. I want to hear you say, 'I made it'."

"Tanya..."

"I can't hear you!" Tanya cheers, cupping her hand around her ear.

Giggling, I recite her words.

"Louder!"

"I MADE IT!" I shout.

Tanya whoops and beeps the horn of her car, much to the annoyance of the neighbours, I'm sure, but I'm too light from her love to care.

"Thank you," I whisper.

"Anytime. Now, go inside and have a lovely evening with your lovely boyfriend."

At the mention of Joel, my stomach squirms.

Ever in tune with my feelings, Tanya tilts her head. "Do you think Joel is someone you can't trust?"

I don't even have to think - I shake my head. "He's never given me any reason not to trust him."

"Well then, you know my advice."

"Trust yourself?"

Tanya nods. "You'll be okay. You'll both get through this and come out of the other end stronger than before."

She sounds so sure of those words that I believe them too. Flashing her one last grateful smile, I climb out of Tanya's car. A cold breeze wraps around my legs and I rush to the front door, desperate for the warmth within.

"Remember – trust yourself!" Tanya hollers after me before driving away.

With her words still ringing in my ears, I head to my apartment. There's a chill in the air that's reminiscent of the cold outside, one that makes me shiver as I remove my coat.

"Joel?" I call out into the silence.

There's no reply. I wander from room to room in search of him, but only inanimate objects greet me. I pause at the dining table, my fingertips brushing the top of his closed laptop.

"Joel?" I call again, feebly this time.

My heart drums in my chest as I check my phone, but other than an '*I love you*' text sent when I left home earlier, there's nothing from Joel waiting for me. I message to ask him where he is, but ten minutes later, no reply has come through.

Chewing on my bottom lip, I sit on the sofa and press my nails into the cushions.

He's fine, everything is fine, I repeat to myself, but with every second that drags by, my belief in those words wavers.

You should have taken Conrad's offer of relocation, the darkest side of my brain snarls. *Now who knows what's happened to Joel.*

My grip on the sofa tightens as visions of Joel unconscious somewhere, a halo of blood pooling around his head, take over until they're all I can see. They're so realistic that my nostrils flare as the metallic scent of blood infiltrates them. I shake my head to rattle the vision out of my mind, but it holds strong.

"Joel?" I call out again, even though I know there will be no response.

Half an hour later, after pacing the room so furiously I could have burned a hole in the carpet, the front door opens.

I rush into the hallway where, sure enough, Joel's hanging up his coat. He blinks when he sees me bounding towards him.

"You seem –" he begins, but I don't let him finish his sentence. Instead, I throw myself into his arms as if this is the last hug we will ever share. "Hey," Joel says into my hair. "What is it? Are you okay?"

"I thought something bad had happened to you," I whisper, burying my face into his neck and inhaling his scent.

Joel's body deflates with sympathy. "Oh, Hannah, I'm sorry. I went to see my mum. She's been worried about us so I thought I'd better see her, that way she doesn't show up unannounced one day and insist on cooking dinner for us."

I laugh at Joel's joke, Jackie's appalling cooking a bullet we've managed to dodge a lot over the years.

"I didn't mean to worry you," Joel continues. "I thought I could get there and back before you'd get home."

"I'm earlier than usual. Tanya gave me a lift," I explain, then I lean out of the hug so I can see Joel's face. "We should do something nice tonight."

"How about we watch a film together and cuddle under a blanket?"

"Sounds perfect."

Grinning, Joel throws his arm over my shoulder, and we head back to the living room.

The opening credits of a documentary we've wanted to watch for ages have only just started when my phone rings. I straighten up when I see who's calling.

"It's Conrad," I say. Joel gives my hand a reassuring squeeze, passing along the boost of confidence I need to answer the phone.

"I'm just calling with an update," Conrad explains when I ask if everything is okay. "We've talked to Stefan all day. Hannah, it's not him."

I sink into the sofa. "Are you sure?"

"Positive. He has an alibi for the night Harriet Warren was abducted. His housemates have confirmed he was studying in his room all night."

"Studying in his room? So they didn't actually see him?"

"Hannah," Conrad sighs. "He has an alibi. It checks out. Plus, he was working when Gabriella O'Hara was abducted. Ellen sent me a photo of the rota. It's written in black and white – Stefan was working that day."

"He could have called in sick."

"Do you remember him calling in sick?"

I open my mouth, but I don't know what to say. I can barely remember what day it is, never mind life before a copycat killer derailed everything.

"He has alibis, Hannah," Conrad says, pulling me back into the conversation. "Plus, he's a student. Where would he take the bodies, back to student halls? It's not him."

"You really think so?"

"I really think so."

I chew my lip, psyching myself up to ask the most painful question of all. "Does he… does he hate me?"

"Hannah, you're scared. People make mistakes and rash judgements when they're scared."

"So that's a yes then," I say with a sad smile.

"Look, why don't you save worrying about this for another day? You and Stefan will patch things up, I'm sure of it, but right now you've bigger things to think of, like making sure you're okay."

"You're right. Thanks, Conrad. I appreciate the update," I reply, then we say goodbye and hang up. I rest my head in my hands, doing all I can not to think about how my relationship with Stefan will never be the same again. How could it be? I falsely accused him of murder.

"What did Conrad want?" Joel asks.

"To tell me that it's not Stefan."

Joel blinks. "Not him? Not the person who stalked your home and showed up at your door in a fit of anger?"

"He was upset, Joel. I accused him of killing three women."

"Only because everything points to him being responsible for all this."

"Well, he has alibis."

"So? Alibis can be faked."

Joel's words strike me across the face. "What do you mean by that?"

He runs his fingers through his hair. "Nothing, it was a careless, throwaway phrase, I'm sorry. Besides, if Conrad says it's not Stefan, then it's not Stefan. That's all there is to it." Joel sighs and squeezes my shoulder. "He'll find who it is soon enough, okay?"

Joel's words land heavy in the pit of my stomach, but I nod as if he's right. "Let's not let tonight be ruined by this," I say. "Let's still have our date night."

I've barely finished my sentence before Joel flushes with giddiness. "Yes! I'll open a bottle of wine," he says, dashing out of the room. I watch him go, the ghost of a smile on my lips, then I reach for my phone and text Stefan. The message is only two words long, the only words I can think of to say.

I'm sorry x

Then, with a bone-rattling sigh, I take Raja's business card from my pocket and write another text before I can talk myself out of it.

It's Hannah. Meet me tomorrow, Derwent Park, 10am.

I read over the message, waiting for my brain to wake up and stop me from reaching out to the woman who has intruded on all aspects of my life, but it does the opposite. It tells me that the message needs to be sent.

It's like Tanya said - I need to trust myself. Raja might be the last person I want to speak to, but she might also be the best. After all, everyone knows there's a serial killer out there, but only a handful of people know it's a serial killer who is somehow connected to me. To unmask them, I need someone on the outside looking in. Someone who has interrogated every inch of my life.

To unmask the killer, I need Raja's help.

Chapter *Thirty-three.*

I wake to find Joel's arms around me. There's a comfort to the weight of them that allows me to breathe again. We stay huddled together for the first hour of the day, swapping stories and laughing until our stomachs ache.

Joel leaves the bed to bring us both a glass of orange juice. When he returns, he perches beside me. "So, what do you fancy doing today?"

"I'm meeting Danielle at ten. We're going for a walk."

"Very nice. Maybe we could do something when you're back?"

"Definitely," I confirm, but as I take a sip of juice, I wonder why I didn't tell Joel what I'm really doing this morning. It's not like he wouldn't be supportive of my meeting with Raja. Joel's never not cheered on any of my decisions before, even ones he disagrees with, but still, something warned me not to tell him. The orange juice turns bitter in my mouth as I try to digest what that warning could mean.

I shower and put on a new dress. It's one I'd reserved for special occasions, an impractical outfit for a walk on a cold day even when paired with tights, but I don't change. I need a layer of confidence-projecting armour so I can brave meeting Raja.

Before I set off, I check my phone for a response from Stefan. Unsurprisingly, I find none. Pushing down the sting of disappointment, I kiss Joel goodbye and make my way to Derwent Park.

Even though I'm early, Raja's already waiting by the entrance when I arrive. Wrapped in a smart coat and wearing high heels, she gives off the impression of someone who's always on duty. Usually I'd hate her for it, but today I'm glad to see her ever-present professionalism.

She spots me approaching and doesn't conceal her happiness. "Morning, Hannah. I must say, I was surprised to receive your message," she says when I reach her.

"Not as surprised as I was when I sent it."

The corner of Raja's mouth flicks into a smile. "Shall we walk?"

I nod, then we enter the park. Raja buys us both a drink from a café by the entrance. My fingers wrap around the takeaway cup, grateful for the warmth of the hot chocolate within.

"So," Raja begins as we set off walking. "I don't imagine you wanted to meet to share book recommendations?"

"No, not exactly."

"Which means we're here because…"

"We're here because the murderer is someone who knows me, and probably someone I know too," I say. The words leave my mouth surprisingly easily for ones that detail such a horrific truth.

Raja blinks, but she doesn't look surprised. "How do you know that?"

"Because the killer left a note with Harriet Warren's body."

"All the bodies have had notes, Hannah. They're a printout of your missing poster -"

"Not this one. This one was a handwritten message addressed to me."

This gets Raja's attention. "What did it say?"

"I'm not here to swap notes on this case like gossip, Raja," I sigh. "I'm here because I need your help. Someone I know is murdering people, and they're coming for me next. I think you can help me figure out who it is."

"Why me?"

"Because you're relentless when pursuing answers and you've already canvassed every inch of my life."

"So you think I've already met the killer?"

"Yes."

"Wow," Raja exhales. She spots a bench nearby and takes a seat, her confident swagger now diminished ever so slightly. "Do the police think you know the person as well?"

"They do now. This note convinced them. Whoever is doing this knows all about me. They knew where I lived. They sent notes to my home before the killings even started."

Raja's eyebrows dart towards her hairline. "The police kept that quiet."

"Believe it or not, Raja, your sources won't tell you everything."

"Touché," she grins. "So, am I looking for someone who knows both you and Peter Harris?"

"I don't know. Surely the police will have thought of that already?"

"Maybe, but to be honest the police have been so focused on how this all linked to Peter Harris that they've barely stopped to think there could be a different angle to it. I think your friend, the great DI Conrad Wallace, has let his own need to win when it comes to Peter Harris get in the way of objectivity."

My eyebrows furrow. "What do you mean by that?"

"Well, from the start of this case, the police have thought of you as being part of Peter Harris's story rather than as him being part of yours. This note might have made them look at you and your life now, but they should have been doing that from the start. They're so far behind where they could have been."

"Do you really think so?"

"Of course. I mean, look at it this way - the police started this investigation by thinking anyone who had read Nathaniel Clarke's book was a potential suspect. Do you have any idea how many people that is?"

I grimace. "More than I'd like to think."

"Exactly. Part of being a journalist is looking at a story from all angles and deciding which is the best hook. The best hook isn't always the easiest, most obvious one. In this case, Peter Harris and his internet fanbase are the easiest, most obvious answer."

"Well, what are your theories? What do you think is going on?"

Raja takes a sip of her coffee. "I always thought it was someone who knew you, or someone who was obsessed with you. Someone who saw the tenth anniversary of what happened as a way to connect with you."

"By killing innocent women?"

"By getting your attention."

Raja's words send a shiver down my spine. I wrap my coat tighter around myself to fight off the chill.

"The police looked at the victims as if they were linked to Peter Harris. Trina Lamond was a sex worker like Phoebe O'Shay, Gabriella O'Hara was a schoolgirl like you, and Harriet Warren was a university student like Bettina Frankhurst. But if you look at the killings in relation to you, there's a different pattern."

The hairs on my neck stand to attention. "What's that pattern?"

"Well, it's almost like the killer has drawn a ring around your life and is getting closer to you with each victim they take," Raja explains. "Harriet Warren was a student at the local university. She knew your colleague, Stefan. She came into Break Time now and then. One of her last photos on Instagram is of a breakfast she had there."

I think back to Harriet Warren and how her face had seemed vaguely familiar. "What about Gabriella O'Hara? What's her connection to me?"

"You really don't read the news, do you?" Raja sighs. "Gabriella attended the same school you did when you were abducted. She was even in the same year group."

My throat constricts as these twisted connections are drawn. "What about Trina Lamond?"

"She lived on the same street where you spent the first four years of your life. They might not seem like much, but these little details are still a connection. If you look at the murders with that pattern in mind, then the next victim is going to be someone closer than the last until eventually, the killer reaches you."

Raja's words coil around my neck until I can't find air. The park blurs, the edges of my vision closing in.

Raja pushes my hot chocolate towards my mouth. "Take a drink. It will help with the shock."

The sugar hits me like a truck, but she's right, it helps. "I never realised how close things were to me," I whisper. "I mean, I know the killer was sending me notes, but I thought it was just to mess with my head. But this? This is a whole other level of toying, one I can't believe no one's mentioned to me before."

"Like I said, the police have focused their efforts in a completely different direction. It's hard to spot connections if you aren't looking for them."

"Or being told about them. The only thing I knew was that Harriet had classes with Stefan, and I only heard about that through him."

Raja's eyebrows raise again. "The police didn't tell you any of this? Not even about Gabriella going to the same school as you?"

"No. They've been trying to keep me out of it. Trying to protect me."

"Well, it seems to me that the best way of protecting you is finding out what links you to the killer before it's too late, not pulling wool over your eyes."

I set my gaze on Raja. "Well, what else have you found out?"

"What do you mean?"

"Come on, Raja. You've been outside my home, my support meetings, and my place of work. You must have some idea as to who the killer is?"

Raja mulls over my question. "I mean, I have leads, sure."

"What are they?"

"Hannah," Raja laughs. "You want me to go through every possible link to you? We'd be here for hours."

"Let's talk for hours then."

Raja eyes me. "You're being serious, aren't you?"

"This is a matter of life and death. I've never been more serious about anything."

Raja nods slowly. "Alright, theory time it is. First of all, I looked at the people in your life and how they might link to Peter Harris. He was a man who worked in hospitality. A man with an irregular shift pattern who had multiple roles across multiple venues. He's in his late thirties now. A good chunk of the women who attend your support group are of a similar age or older. They probably went on nights out to the clubs and bars he worked at. He could have even crossed paths with your boyfriend."

I blink. "Joel?"

"Sure. Peter Harris was a barman. Joel's almost thirty, so ten years ago he'd have been almost twenty. Judging by his social media, he used to be quite the party animal. That's plenty of opportunity for the pair to have met."

"Surely he would have told me if he'd met Peter Harris?"

Raja shoots me a pointed look. "Is it that hard for you to believe that people aren't always honest with their partner? I mean, surely you've kept secrets from Joel?"

I think about how right now, Joel is under the impression that I'm meeting Danielle for a walk, then press my thumbnail into my finger so hard it bleeds. "What else?"

"Your boss, Ellen, has worked in hospitality all her life. So did Peter Harris. I'm sure there will have been a crossover at some point."

"You think Ellen knew him?" I ask, but as I do my phone starts to ring. "Sorry," I say, pulling my phone out to see who's calling.

"Anyone important?"

"Just Tanya," I reply, ending the call.

"Ah, Tanya - the all-important leader of Sisterhood of Support."

There's something about Raja's tone I don't like. "What do you mean by that?"

She shrugs. "Well, if we're looking for a motive, don't you think it's a bit strange that these killings started at the time you were about to leave her little project? Tanya's star attraction, no longer there to inspire others."

"What do you –" I begin, but I'm cut off by my phone ringing again. I sigh as Tanya's name flashes on the screen once more. I end the call abruptly, but then I notice three missed calls from Conrad and a message from Tanya queued in my notifications.

Please pick up. It's urgent x

A sickly sensation of dread rolls down my body.

"Everything okay?" Raja asks. I open my mouth to respond, but as I do, my phone bursts into life once more.

"Hannah, where are you?" Tanya's voice is frantic when I accept the call. I dig my nail deeper into my flesh, the pain searing enough to momentarily drown out my internal panic.

"I'm in the park. Why, what's wrong?"

"I... I don't know where to begin." As Tanya chokes on a sob, everything around me shifts. I've never heard her so rattled before. Tanya is the person who takes everyone's emotions and untangles them so that they make sense. She is calm, steady, and unflappable.

She is not the person on the other end of this line.

"Tanya, what is it?"

As Tanya gulps, I steel myself, praying that whatever she tells me won't be as bad as I'm imagining.

"It's Paula. She didn't make it home from yesterday's meeting," Tanya replies. "We think... Hannah, we think Paula's been abducted."

Chapter *Thirty-four.*

Tanya tells me there's an emergency Sisterhood of Support meeting in an hour for anyone who might need it after hearing the news about Paula. From the way my knees are trembling, I know I am one of those people. Tanya offers to pick me up from Derwent Park, then the phone goes dead, the silence buzzing in my ear.

I'm acutely aware of Raja staring at me. I see her lips moving, but what she's saying I have no idea. All I can think of are Tanya's words... 'We think Paula's been abducted.'

"Hannah," Raja shouts, snapping her fingers in front of my face until reality whooshes back into focus. "Is everything okay?"

I don't know what to say. I rub my temples, the light of the day blinding me.

"Do you need to go home?" Raja asks.

"No, Tanya's picking me up from here."

"Why, what's happened?"

I look into Raja's eyes. The hungry glint of a story is there, but there's fear in them too. I blink as if seeing Raja for the first time. She might be a journalist who's plagued my life, but she's also a woman who knows what it's like to decide it's too dark to walk home alone through fear of what could be hiding in the shadows. Like most women, she won't be able to count how many '*let me know when you're home safe*' texts she's sent and received in her lifetime.

"Someone from my support group has gone missing," I say.

Raja inhales a short, sharp intake of breath. "Who?"

"Paula."

"Paula Anderson?"

"You know her?"

"I know about everyone at your meetings, Hannah."

"Then you know what's happened to them, and you know you need to help me protect them. Raja, I need you to look into what's happening deeper than you've ever looked into anything before. I need you to use all the knowledge you've gathered and utilise every connection you have to see who you think this killer could be."

Raja can't hide her surprise. "I have your permission to dig into your life?"

"Dig as deep as you like," I say as I stand up. "Dig up anything and everything. Who knows how many lives could depend on it."

Raja chews her lip, looking nervous for the first time since I met her. "Are you sure you want me to do this? You might not like what I find."

"It's either I find out from you, or I find out when I'm face to face with the killer. I know what I'd prefer."

With that, I rush past Raja and head back to the entrance of Derwent Park.

Tanya arrives a few minutes later. Her expression is pinched, her face red from crying, even if she's doing her best to act as if she's anything but upset. "You okay?" she asks when I get into the car.

I nod. "You?"

"Yes," Tanya replies, her calm tone forced. "Worried about Paula, of course, but I'm okay."

"What's happened?" I ask once Tanya sets off.

"Paula's sister, Karen, rang me this morning. She'd been trying to get hold of Paula all night. They usually check in with each other at the end of the day. It's a comfort for them after everything Paula's been through, but no matter how many times Karen called, Paula didn't pick up."

An ominous, icy fingernail traces my spine. "Did you go to the police?"

"Of course. I called Conrad as soon as I finished speaking with Karen. He went around to Paula's house. No one was home so he spoke to the neighbours. They hadn't seen Paula since she went out to yesterday's meeting. You know Paula, Hannah. She's a creature of habit. She comes to meetings and goes home. She doesn't... vanish."

"Could it be Neil?" Neil is Paula's ex and the reason she attends Sisterhood of Support in the first place.

Tanya shakes her head. "Neil is in Spain. It can't be him."

"It's the copycat, isn't it?" I whisper, my eyelashes suddenly spiked with tears.

"We don't know that," Tanya replies, but the edge of fear in her voice tells me everything I need to know. "All we can do is sit tight and wait for the police to do their job. In the meantime, we have a meeting to attend and a room full of people who need our support."

I gulp at the thought of walking into the meeting room and feeling every eye on me as people wonder if Paula's disappearance has anything to do with her connection to me.

With those thoughts on my mind, I sit in silence for the rest of the journey. When we pull up outside Sisterhood of Support, my eyes trace the building, my confidence wavering with every brick that passes my gaze.

"Come on," Tanya says, getting out of the car and not giving me another second to wallow in self-doubt.

My teeth chatter as I follow her inside, but I can't tell if it's from the cold or the dreaded anticipation of seeing a gap in the circle where Paula usually sits.

Like a mind reader, Tanya turns to me. "Set out the chairs as normal. Leave one for Paula, just in case."

I follow her orders, the clink of metal chair legs against the wooden floor echoing into the tense silence. Ten minutes before the meeting starts, there's a knock at the door. Two police officers stand on the other side of the glass.

As my jaw drops, Tanya lets them in. "Sorry, I didn't think to send you the passcode," she says, ushering them inside.

"We need police protection now?" I ask as the officers invade the space that's supposed to be gentle, healing and free.

"No, but Conrad and I thought it might be best to have some officers attend today's session to put people at ease. It's good to have them here if anyone has any questions." Tanya smiles brightly to convince me that everything is okay, but there's nothing okay about seeing those neon jackets and stiff uniforms in the meeting room.

Over the next few minutes, people start to arrive. Everyone wears the tell-tale badges of fear – wide, alert eyes, a trembling lower lip, and tense shoulders.

As soon as Amrita enters the room, she seeks me out. "Come here," she says, drawing me close. I breathe in her heady perfume, grateful for the solidity of her physical touch.

"I can't believe it," I whisper into her hair.

"Me neither, but we've got each other, okay? I'm so glad Tanya called this meeting. It's good to know we're together in this."

I nod but over her shoulder, Carla catches my attention. The accusation shining in her eyes takes my breath away. I bow my head, a move that Amrita takes as me struggling with emotion, and she pats the top of my arm.

When Tanya announces that it's time for the meeting to begin, we take our seats. I sit between Riley and Danielle, then curse myself for setting up Paula's chair, even though I was instructed to. Its vacancy screams.

Once we are all seated, the two police officers retreat into a corner, but their presence has never felt more imposing. Everyone's eyes dart to them, their concern rising with every panicked glance.

"This is so fucked up," Riley whispers, but I don't have time to respond before Tanya clears her throat.

"Let's begin," she says. "I want to start this meeting by acknowledging the concern we are feeling, as well as thanking you all for showing up today. The love you are demonstrating by being here has never been more appreciated."

People reach for each other, uniting themselves with Tanya's sentiments.

"I also want to acknowledge the presence of the police in this room and the complexities this brings for many of us," Tanya continues. "Please be assured that their presence here is simply to offer you peace of mind, and to reassure you that everything is being done to protect the women of this city."

The room bristles. After years of hearing lines like 'not enough evidence to prosecute' and not always being taken seriously when reporting violent crimes, there's a general mistrust towards the police at Sisterhood of Support. But right now, trusting them is all we can do. They're the only hope we have for finding Paula alive and well.

"We need to use this space as we feel we must, so the floor is open for whatever conversation you would like to have. We can talk about Paula, we can talk about our week, we can talk about reality TV, it doesn't matter. All that matters is that every single person in this room knows they are not alone right now."

The room falls silent, waiting for someone to take the leap and start this meeting that no one wishes they were attending.

Everyone's eyes are on their laps until Carla clears her throat. "I'd feel much better if *she* wasn't here," she says, her tone spiked with so much acidity Amrita gasps.

I don't need to look at Carla to know who she means. I feel her eyes on me, the fiery gaze of her loathing burning my skin.

"Excuse me?" Tanya responds, but she heard Carla. We all did.

"Her," Carla spits. "Hannah. *She* is the reason Paula is missing."

"Carla —"

"Don't 'Carla' me," Carla snaps, whipping her head around to face Tanya. "We know she's your passion project, but she's a danger to us all."

I shrink into my seat, wishing the plastic could swallow me whole.

Carla addresses the circle. "I tried to warn you all when that reporter was sniffing around, but nobody would listen to me. We all had to defend 'poor little Hannah'," she mocks. "But who's defending us? Who's defending Paula?" Carla cries before turning to me. "Go home, Hannah. You're not welcome here."

"Hey!" Danielle cuts in.

"That's enough, Carla," Amrita says. "Hannah didn't ask for this."

Their protests only rile Carla up more. "Are you seriously defending the person who brought this tragedy to our doorstep?!"

"Carla, I know emotions are running high –" Tanya begins, but Carla scoffing silences her.

"Of course emotions are running high – look who's missing!" Carla jabs her finger towards Paula's empty chair to highlight her aching absence. "I don't care if you're friends with Hannah, I really don't. I'm sure you've had great chats in the past, but can you honestly tell me that you feel safe with her around?"

A booming silence echoes out into the room. I look around the circle and not one person meets my eye. They actively look away, staring at their hands, their shoes, the floor - anywhere but at me.

"Is that how you all feel?" I ask, my voice catching as I speak.

"I don't," Riley jumps in, but she's the only one.

Carla rolls her eyes. "Come on, kid. You're not even slightly worried that being her friend will end with you in the next body bag?"

Riley opens her mouth to argue, but she falters.

Carla sits back in her seat, triumphant. "Exactly. We all know what it's like to live through something horrific. We don't need to go through it again for Hannah Allen."

"That's enough," Tanya says firmly. "Hannah is as welcome here as everyone else."

"Who's welcoming her?!" Carla cries, waving at the subdued circle. "Even if they aren't saying it, everyone knows that Paula's disappearance is her fault!"

"Carla, there -"

"Tanya, please don't fight my battle for me," I interrupt, a move that makes Carla laugh.

"Tanya's always fighting your battles, Hannah, haven't you learned that yet? We're sick of it, and we're sick of you. Everyone's thinking it, even if they're not saying it - you've put us in danger, Hannah. It's time you do what you've been saying you will for a long time and leave. No one wants you here."

There's a collective intake of breath as if no one can quite believe what has been said. Even the police officers shift on their feet, glancing at each other and wondering if they should do something to stop this verbal attack, but it's too late. The line has been drawn, my presence so clearly unwelcome.

"That was too far, Carla," Amrita says, shaking her head, but her sadness does little to diminish my upset.

"I can leave if it makes you all feel better," I say, standing and collecting my things with as much dignity as I can muster when I'm fighting back tears.

"Hannah, please," Tanya says, the professionalism in her voice slipping.

"It's fine, Tanya. Whatever makes people comfortable," I say, but really it's anything but fine. I take one last look around the circle, studying the downcast gazes and blushing cheeks of my friends, then I walk out of Sisterhood of Support and don't look back.

Chapter *Thirty-five.*

The man on the screen takes a bold step towards the blonde woman before him. He reaches for her waist, and she falls into him, her lithe body collapsing into his strong, capable arms.

"I've waited forever for this," he says, then he pulls her in for a passionate kiss. Dramatic music swells as the camera circles the couple, then the screen fades to black, and the credits roll.

"That was... interesting," Joel says politely, turning off the television. "Did you enjoy it?"

I shrug because in all honesty, I couldn't describe any of what we've spent the last ninety minutes watching. My eyes might have been on the screen, but my brain was most definitely elsewhere.

On the sofa beside me, my phone buzzes. Another notification from someone at Sisterhood of Support. Another message of guilt, another plea asking if I'm okay.

I turn my phone over, not ready to respond. It's not that I'm mad at them – I completely understand that their need to feel safe comes above all else - but more that I'm hurt. Hurt that my life has come to this.

As my phone buzzes again, Joel sighs. "Another apology?"

"Another one joining the long list, yes."

"Good. They should be reaching out and begging for your forgiveness."

I nod, but only because nodding is easier than explaining that I don't think my fellow attendees should be blamed for being momentarily ruled by their fear. Trauma is like that – sometimes, it grips you even when you don't want it to, even when you know better.

"I still can't believe Carla spoke to you like that," Joel says with a shake of his head. "In fact, I can't believe Tanya let her speak to you like that."

"Tanya keeps the space open for us to speak freely, and that's what Carla felt she needed to fill it with. I can't blame her for that, not when she's so scared."

"But fear doesn't give her the right to be a dick." Joel slams his mug on the coffee table so hard I'm surprised it doesn't shatter. Even he looks shocked by his outburst. He gulps his tension away before reaching for me. "I'm sorry it's been such a shit day. You don't deserve it."

Smiling sadly, I curl under Joel's arm and breathe in the minty scent of his body wash, my body softening ever so slightly until the peace of our embrace is interrupted by a phone call. I peel out of the hug to check who it is.

"I'm going to take this," I say when I see Riley's name on the screen. I leave Joel on the sofa and head to the bedroom to talk in private.

"I just wanted to check you were okay after what happened earlier," she says when I answer the call. It was... well, Carla was completely out of order. We all told her that after you'd left. I wish you'd been there to see everyone stand up for you."

"That would have been nice."

"Well, trust me, everyone told her to back off. Carla didn't say a word for the rest of the meeting, then all anyone could talk about was how they wished you hadn't left."

"I bet Carla loved that," I joke.

"I don't think it was her favourite topic of conversation, no," Riley laughs. "But at least now I've told you what happened, you know how much we all love you."

"I do, thank you," I say, then I let out a groan. "Do you ever wonder how we ended up here? Why us? What did we do to deserve this?"

"Oh, only every day."

We sit in this admission for a moment, the words seeping into the layers of our skin like rain on parched ground.

"Does it get better?" Riley asks, unable to mask the glimmer of hope in her voice.

"Yes," I reply, and I realise that I'm right. Someday, somehow, life finds a way to remind you it's worth living. The thought of waking up each morning doesn't fill you with dread, until one day, it's the moments of laughter you pay attention to, not the moments of fear or doubt.

I just hope that day arrives for me soon.

"I should probably go - Mum's calling me," Riley says.

"Of course. Thanks for calling, Riley. I really appreciate it."

"Anytime. You've been a real friend to me. I wanted to be the same to you."

When the call ends, a swell of gratitude overcomes me. For the first time, 'Lucky Number 11' doesn't seem an inaccurate descriptor for my life. I am lucky - lucky to know the people I do.

But then I remember… someone in my life is the killer. As soon as that thought enters my mind, whatever warmth Riley's call brought fades. Trapped in the vice of my fear, the faces of the people I know and love shapeshift until I'm no longer sure who I see when I think of them. I shake my head, willing myself to vanquish my toxic thoughts, but the more I try to force them down, the faster they grow.

Suddenly, there's a knock at the door. I jump so violently that my phone slips out of my hand. It clatters to the floor, falling through the gap between the bed and the bedside table.

"Hannah, have you finished with your call?"

My mouth is too dry to speak, but I manage to force words out. "Yeah, you can come in."

Joel pushes open the bedroom door. "I was thinking, why don't we get a takeaway tonight? I'm not sure either of us feels like cooking."

My stomach spasms at the thought of food. From down the side of the bed, my phone buzzes again. Another person reaching out to me. Another friend trying to make amends.

Another potential suspect to be wary of.

Shaking myself from the arms of paranoia, I beam at Joel. "A takeaway sounds great!" I enthuse, then I follow Joel out of the bedroom, wishing that silencing my worries was as easy as walking away from a discarded phone.

Chapter *Thirty-six*

We order a curry each, then share them half and half. While we eat, we talk about work, Joel's mum's new car, house hunting and holiday plans. We talk about everything other than the big, black serial killer shaped cloud hanging over us, but its presence seeps into my every thought.

Halfway through clearing away the remnants of dinner, the intercom buzzes. I check the time. "Someone calling this late can't be good," I grimace.

Joel squeezes my arm as he brushes past me, then answers the intercom so I don't have to. "Who is it?" he asks.

"Joel, it's me. It's Tanya."

Joel looks back at me, his eyebrows creased in loving concern.

"I've been trying to contact Hannah for the last hour. I've been calling and calling and... look, I need to speak to her. I feel horrible about what happened at the meeting."

Joel opens his mouth to reply on my behalf, but I march over to the intercom and respond myself. "Come on up, Tanya," I say, then I buzz her into the building.

Joel watches me, dumbstruck. "After everything that happened today, you want to speak to her?"

"She'll be upset, Joel. She'll need to talk."

"So? She let a room full of people attack you. How can you be okay with her after that?"

The well-timed sound of Tanya knocking at the door stops me from responding. Wordlessly, I leave Joel to let her in.

"Oh, Hannah," Tanya exhales when she sees me, then she practically collapses into my arms. "Thank you for speaking to me," she whispers into my hair.

"Of course. Come in," I say, moving to the side to let her into the apartment.

Tanya leaves her coat on as she walks through to the living room. She finds Joel clearing away dinner, his features fixed in a frosty glare. "I hope I'm not interrupting?"

"It's fine. We've just finished," I say.

"Well, whatever you've had, it smells delicious," Tanya says, then she sits on the sofa. When I sit beside her, she takes my hand in hers. "Hannah, I feel terrible about what happened earlier."

"Honestly, you don't have to -"

"But I do, Hannah, I do. Sisterhood of Support is supposed to be a safe space for everyone, and tonight I failed to provide that for you. I never wanted you to leave, but I also didn't want you to have to deal with an unprovoked attack. By letting you go, I thought I was doing the right thing. I thought... I thought..."

Tanya's face crumples, and my chest pulls at her distress. "You did the right thing," I soothe. "It was best for me to leave. That way, everyone could speak without worrying they'd upset me."

"Still, it wasn't nice for you to sit through that."

"No, it wasn't," Joel says. I flinch at his comment, but Tanya doesn't react.

"You've every right to be mad about how Hannah was treated, Joel. It was unacceptable, but that's why I'm here. I came to apologise and to reassure Hannah that she's welcome at Sisterhood of Support and always will be." Tanya turns back to me. "I promise, Hannah, you will always have a safe space with me. I will always, always be here for you."

"She has other people she can speak to, not just you," Joel says, his voice carrying with it an arctic chill.

I open my mouth to apologise for Joel's snappiness, but Tanya speaks for me. "Of course she does, and I know how much Hannah values your support. You've been brilliant throughout this, Joel."

Joel nods curtly, but the undercurrent of tension in the air goes nowhere. The moment teeters on a knife-edge. I ransack my brain for something, anything, to say to pull it back on track, but then Tanya straightens her back and stands up.

"Now I know you're okay, I'll leave you to your evening," she says. "I'm running some one-to-one sessions at my house tomorrow. If you want to pop around, you know where I am. Show up whenever. Even if I'm with someone else, I'll make time for you."

"You don't have to do that," I reply.

"Anything for you," she says, then with one last squeeze of my hands, Tanya leaves. I watch her go, a strange tightness in my chest growing with every step she takes in the opposite direction to me. When the front door closes behind her, I feel lonelier than ever.

Joel leaves the living room without saying another word. A few seconds later, the sound of banging plates and cutlery rings out from the kitchen. Joel's coolness travels through the air, and I psych myself up for the argument that I know is to come.

Following the noise, I head into the kitchen where I find Joel scraping scraps of curry into the bin. "I know you're upset about what happened at the meeting, but you didn't have to be so rude," I say.

Through the back of his t-shirt, I witness Joel's shoulders lock with tension. For a moment, he continues discarding the congealed curry, but then he slams the plate he's holding onto the counter. The knife and fork skid across the surface, dregs of curry sauce splashing everywhere.

Joel turns around, his entire body fizzing with manic energy. "Considering everything that's been going on recently, I think I held it together quite well, actually."

"Tanya was just doing her job," I sigh.

"Her job is to help you, not make things worse! You were devastated when you came home today, Hannah. I watched you cry for almost half an hour. She could have stopped that from happening, but she didn't."

"She -"

"Please don't make excuses for her," Joel says. He tips his head back and stares at the ceiling until his anger fades to make way for something much worse - devastation. "Do you have any idea how hard it is to watch you go through this?" he whispers. "To know that no matter what I do or say, it's not enough? That I can't take your pain away? And the worst part of it all is that you don't even let me try. You want everyone else but me. I would never let what happened today happen to you. Tanya did, yet she's the one you want to speak to."

"It's not like that," I protest, but Joel shakes his head.

"It's exactly like that. Hannah, you are the person I love most in the world. The person I want to spend the rest of my life with. I notice every time you treat me like a stranger. I notice it, and every time it breaks my heart."

With those words, Joel crumbles in a way I've never seen before. I go to him, holding his head in my hands and pulling his forehead so it rests on mine. "I love you, okay?" I say, pronouncing each word forcefully so he hears how much I mean them. "I love you so much, but what's going on isn't normal relationship stuff. It's complicated and horrible, and something very few people understand. Those people all attend Sisterhood of Support."

"I want to understand. I want to help."

"But I don't want you to understand. Understanding means you know what it's like to live through the worst. If anything, I'm happy you're separate from this. I don't want to talk to you about my past, I thought you understood that? I thought you knew why I kept that side of myself for Sisterhood of Support?"

"I do, I did, but everything feels like it's changed." Joel chokes on a sob, his long, dark eyelashes soaked with tears. "I just want to make it better for you."

"Joel, there's no way to make this better and no rule book on how to deal with this. We've just got to put one foot in front of the other and try not to trip each other up."

A pathetic joke, but it does the trick because Joel snorts on a laugh.

"Come here," I say, and I pull him towards me. As we hold each other tight, I look over Joel's shoulder and spy the messy evidence of his anger when he threw the plate. I almost can't believe it of him, can't believe it of us. We're not people who shout at each other or break in such a volatile way. We're not people who are so twisted with tension that they don't know where to turn or who to trust.

Whoever is doing this, they're winning, I think sadly as my eyes trace over the sauce-splattered tiles. *They're tearing your world and the people in it apart, bit by bit.*

The worst part of that admission is the knowledge that I have no idea how to stop them.

Chapter *Thirty-seven.*

Joel leaves me in bed the following morning. I coil the duvet around my body and drift into a dreamless sleep, one I'm roused from a few minutes later when Joel shakes my shoulder. "I've got a message from Conrad," he says. "He wants to speak to you. Have you lost your phone?"

I think back to my call with Riley. "I dropped it yesterday," I reply, then I reach down the side of the bed. When I pull my phone out, the screen is black, the battery dead.

"You can use mine to call him back," Joel says. I take his phone to check why Conrad wants to speak to me, but the message just reads, '*Please have Hannah call me as soon as she can*'. I press dial, trying not to feel concerned about the abruptness of the text, or the potential reasons for it.

"Thanks for calling me back," Conrad says. "I only have time for a quick chat but I wanted to tell you the news - we've taken someone in for questioning. Hannah, we think we've found them. We think we've found the killer."

Instinctively, I reach for Joel, who takes the phone from me and puts it on loudspeaker so we can both hear what's being said.

"You've found them?" I ask.

"That's right, we believe we have," Conrad confirms.

As a beaming smile spreads across Joel's face, I take a moment to catch my breath, then I ask the scariest question of all. "Is it... is it someone I know?"

"It doesn't look that way," Conrad says. "I can't share too much information because the person hasn't been charged yet, but with the evidence we have already and the evidence we're still finding, it's looking increasingly likely that it's them."

I nod, but the news still doesn't sink in. "How did you find them?"

"We've had officers canvassing online forums about Peter Harris. There was one particularly vocal member who mentioned knowing Peter Harris when he was younger. He wasn't on any of our contact lists from the time of the original murders, but he posted how he believed Peter Harris had been framed, the usual conspiracy theory stuff. We'd been tracking his comments, and then he posted that he was behind the attack on Break Time."

Joel grips my hand tight. "He's admitted to smashing it up?" I ask.

"He posted online that he did, yes. We're hoping to get a formal confession today, but we took his prints when we brought him in. They match the ones we found at the scene."

"Wow," I breathe. "I... I don't know what to say."

"You don't have to say anything, Hannah. I just wanted to give you an update."

"I really appreciate this call, Conrad," I say, and I mean it. My bottom lip trembles as the thought that this nightmare might finally be over appears before me. "Has he told you where Paula is? Is she safe?"

"We don't know yet, but I'm sure we will soon."

Disappointment claws at my insides. I close my eyes and try to give in to the relief of the moment, but something wriggles inside me, nagging that this conclusion is too good to be true. "Are you sure it's him, Conrad? The notes made out like the person knew me?"

"As I said, we've not pressed any charges yet, but the evidence we have suggests it's likely it's him. When I know more, I will come back to you. Look, I need to go, but I wanted to tell you about the breakthrough. I know you've been keen for updates and… well, this is the biggest update there is."

I sit back and let Conrad's words wash over me. "I don't know how to thank you for ending this."

"You don't need to thank me, Hannah. This is my job. I'll be in touch later, okay? Take care."

We hang up and I give Joel his phone back. He takes it, watching my every move. For a moment, I don't know what to do, then I rest my head on Joel's shoulder. "It's over," I say. "It's really over."

The skin around Joel's eyes crinkles as he smiles. "You got through it, Hannah. You did it."

I let out a small, disbelieving laugh. "I… I don't know what to say."

"How about 'woooo'?!" Joel says, then he leaps into the air, jumping up and down as if he's won the lottery. I giggle at his outlandish behaviour, but even when witnessing his jubilation, the news still won't sink in. Joel sees my uncertainty and re-joins me on the bed. "Conrad wouldn't have called unless he was certain he'd got the right guy."

"I know."

"He wouldn't build your hopes up for nothing."

"I know. I just… I…"

As my sentence trails off, Joel brushes my cheek with his thumb. "Do you want some time alone? I won't be offended if you do."

"I don't know what I want. I don't know what to think."

"Why don't you go for a walk and clear your head?" Joel suggests. I nod, the thought of fresh air and open space more appealing than I can put into words. "Do you want me to come with you?"

I shake my head. "Thanks, but I want to go on my own. Reclaim the city as my home, you know?"

"Sure," Joel nods. "Well, I'll be waiting with a hug when you get back."

We share a kiss then Joel leaves me to get dressed. I pull on whatever clothes are nearest, no longer thinking about constructing an armour I can face the world in. For the first time in a long time, I feel okay stepping out exactly as I am.

There are no photographers outside when I leave my apartment building. No police cars, no journalists, just damp grass in need of a cut and parked cars lining the street.

Setting off walking, I trust my muscle memory to do what it thinks is best to reacquaint me with the place I no longer want to fear. It leads me through the city, past the university and the shops, then finally to Derwent Park. I stroll along the tree-lined paths, heading towards the bench at the top of the hill. The place where I'd read Nathaniel Clarke's book, my body compelled to go there and have this nightmare come full circle.

In the distance, I spot my bench, but someone's already sat on it. They're wrapped up warm in a pink coat, their eyes fixed on the view of the city ahead.

As I draw closer, I realise that I know them. I slow to a stop, but it's too late. "Hannah?" they call, then they do the unthinkable - they shift along the bench to make room for me.

I blink. Conrad might have caught a serial killer, but Carla inviting me to join her might end up being my biggest news of the day.

"You want me to sit with you?" I can't help but ask.

Carla shrugs, but the blush creeping up her cheeks betrays her. Instead of making her squirm, I accept the offer. Once seated, I look at the city before me. My hometown in all its cloudy, rundown glory. It might not be as impressive as a New York skyline, but there's something to this view. A peace that only the sights of home can bring.

Carla sits with me for a moment before speaking. "I suppose I should apologise for how I treated you the other day."

"You should only apologise if you mean it."

Carla lets out a laugh. "Maybe I shouldn't apologise then. I meant what

I said. I did at the time, anyway."

"It's okay. You were scared."

"I was, yes," Carla admits. She looks at her hands, hands that confess they belong to someone with the nervous habit of picking their skin.

I've never seen Carla's hands up close before. Never seen the damage she inflicts upon herself. I guess that's what happens when you keep each other at arm's length – you never see the other person's pain or their point of view.

"I understand, Carla. You don't need to apologise."

"I do. I think I sometimes forget that you didn't ask to be the name that the world knows. I forget that in all this, you've been scared too."

At that moment, two young boys run past us chasing a football. Their mother shouts after them to be careful, but they barely hear her. They're having too much fun, their riotous giggles ringing out across the park.

Carla beams. "Kids are the best at that age."

"I'll take your word for it."

"Are children not on the cards for you?"

"Maybe one day, but not yet. I've always wanted children, but the events of the last few weeks have made me reconsider my plans a little."

Carla nods. "I suppose it's hard to want to bring something so innocent into the world when you've been through what we have. If I hadn't already had Josh before I met Harold, I don't think I'd have dared to have children at all."

"Exactly. The idea of having children and having to explain who I am terrifies me," I admit.

"Oh, your children seeing who you are is terrifying with or without experiencing the trauma we have, trust me."

We watch the older of the two children kick the football between his brother's legs. The younger boy shouts in protest, his bottom lip wobbling. Just as he's about to turn to his mother and ask her to intervene, the older brother kicks the ball back to him. It's such a simple gesture, but for some reason, it brings tears to my eyes.

"It's strange to think Harold was small and innocent like that, once upon a time," Carla says softly.

"It's strange to think that Peter Harris was."

Wordlessly, Carla reaches out and takes my hand. The move is as unexpected for her as it is for me. We look at our hands curled together, then smile.

"I never thought we'd sit together like this," I joke.

Carla blushes. "I know a lot of the blame for that falls on me. For what it's worth, I'm sorry."

"I told you, you don't need to say sorry."

"But I do, Hannah. I want you to understand that my issue isn't with you as a person, but it's hard going to Sisterhood of Support and having you and your story seem more important than anyone else's. So many of us had to fight to be heard, never mind believed. I know you didn't create that favouritism, it's just... well, it's hard to be around."

"Trust me, if I could have it any other way, I would."

Carla laughs. "Wouldn't we all give anything to not need to attend those meetings? But the thing is, they matter. Sometimes it was like you didn't want to be there with us."

"That's because I didn't want to be there. Surely you don't really want to attend?"

Carla's eyes trace the horizon. "If I could redo my life, of course I'd make it so I never had to attend a meeting in the first place, but do-overs don't exist. I have to make peace with the way things turned out. What happened was the worst thing I've ever experienced, but out of it, I managed to find a community. Week after week, I show up somewhere that provides me with friendship and care. How many people have that in their life? More than that, how many survivors have that? In a way, despite what happened, I'm lucky. I'm lucky because after I went through hell, I had people who helped me rebuild my life on the other side. I'm lucky because I found a place where my story and my friendship could help someone else."

"I never thought of it like that."

"Because you didn't want to be part of the group, not really."

Now it's my turn to be sheepish.

"I'm not trying to make you feel bad, Hannah. There's no blueprint for how to live after what you went through, and no one can blame you for wanting to act like Peter Harris doesn't exist. You've worked so hard to move past your trauma and you've done an amazing job of that, but maybe the next thing you can do is accept the part the past plays in your life. Who knows what could happen if you did. I mean, look at Riley. Look at the difference you've made there."

"I've not done anything."

"You've been there for her, Hannah. Everyone can see the difference that's made. Maybe it's time you opened your eyes and saw it too."

I follow Carla's gaze to the edges of my city, the world as far as I can see it. A world Peter Harris tried to take from me.

A world Tanya reminded me I could refuse to be removed from.

"I need to go," I say suddenly.

Carla blinks. "Already? You've only just sat down."

"There's someone I need to see, but thank you, Carla. This has been lovely. I mean it - really, truly lovely."

"Really, truly lovely, that's my middle name," she jokes.

We hug goodbye, a hug I suspect will be the first of many from now on, then I set off walking with a pace and purpose I've not had for a long time.

The *Admission.*

Conrad clasps his hands together and instructs himself to stay calm, but at this stage, it's almost impossible. Calling Hannah had set something off inside him, a buzz of hope that was too loud to ignore.

Fatima was less than pleased that he'd made that call. She said he should have waited until after the interview, and maybe she was right, but Conrad argued that he wanted to keep Hannah up to date with developments. The way Fatima eyed him told him she saw through that excuse.

Still, from the moment Conrad heard the relief in Hannah's voice, he felt like he was riding some kind of wave. The idea that this nightmare could end right here, right now, with the man before him? Well, it's almost too exciting to pretend otherwise.

Vince Mayhew is exactly the kind of creepy that Conrad has come to expect from a man who dedicates his spare time to toxic internet chat rooms. A man who blames the world for the failures in his own life, especially the romantic ones.

Vince Mayhew is small and slight. A man Conrad has no trouble believing would need to sedate his victims to overpower them.

At a glance, Vince looks normal enough, with his neatly pressed collar, precisely cut hair and wire-rimmed glasses, but there's something about him that makes you relax when not in his presence. Conrad can't tell if it's the way his eyes bulge slightly, the quietly frantic air about him, or the fact that his nails are cut so far back they look sore, but something is unsettling about Vince Mayhew, all right.

Or maybe, Conrad thinks as he looks into Vince's pale eyes, *maybe what's unsettling about Vince Mayhew is that I suspect him of murder.*

The evidence is there, published on the internet under Vince's pseudonym – MayhemMayhew04.

Smashed up Lucky Number 11's café late last night... did the message get across to you yet, Hannah? Your luck is running out. You are next. Do you need me to say it again? YOU ARE NEXT!

Then the other posts, not direct confessions but equally as implicating.

Another one's dead. One less to worry about.

How is it that all these so-called victims are always 'innocent' or 'full of life'? Of course that's what their family would say. How about they tell the truth? These women were SLUTS

One day you'll know my name. One day you'll be thanking me. Maybe that day has already come...

These disgusting posts, shared and celebrated on the darkest corners of the internet.

Conrad doesn't consider himself a violent man, but there's something about Vince that brings out a rage in him. A rage that screams, how the hell can a person have such vile views? And not just that, but how can they use those views as a twisted justification for committing the worst crimes?

Then there's another rage inside Conrad, one he knows he will never be able to extinguish - the rage that it's taken him this long to find Vince

Mayhew, and that more bodies have been added to the pile in that time. A rage Conrad will direct at himself later when Vince Mayhew is locked in a cell and Conrad has no one else to hate but himself.

But right now, Vince is here, in this room, sitting on a blue chair opposite Conrad, a smug smile on his face. A smile Conrad itches to wipe away.

Vince cracks his knuckles, clicking his fingers into place one by one. Each snap is a bullet tearing through Conrad's patience. "Mr Mayhew," Conrad says when Vince is on his fourth finger, no longer able to stomach the sound of bones cracking and all the connotations that sound brings. "Where were you on the night in question?"

"Where are any of us at any moment?" Vince shrugs. "This big old rock we're stuck on? The one that's tumbling around the sun – where is it? What does being on it mean?"

"I'm not here to discuss philosophy with you, Mr Mayhew. I'm here to discuss your whereabouts on the occasions four separate women were abducted."

"My whereabouts… my whereabouts… now that's a tough one." Vince taps his fingers on the table, pausing as if he's pondering, but Conrad knows this is all an act. A deliberate provocation, even. In some sick way, Vince Mayhew is enjoying this.

Conrad has never hated anyone more.

"Do you mean the whereabouts of my physical body or the whereabouts of my spirit?" Vince asks, grinning as if he's told a joke only he knows the punchline to.

Fatima jumps in, a move Conrad is grateful for. His expression might have been composed, but inside he was seconds away from grabbing Vince's neat little collar and using it to pull him across the desk.

Fatima slides three photographs taken from CCTV towards Vince. "This is your taxi, correct?"

"Who knows? Photo editing software is getting smarter by the day."

Fatima ignores his riddle-like teasing. "And that's you, in the driver's seat?"

"I don't know, do you have a clearer picture?"

Fatima's hands curl into fists. Vince watches them coil, his wet lips twisting into a smile. He opens his mouth to speak, but Conrad leans forward on the table, addressing Vince before he gets the chance to rile them up any further.

"It's very simple, Mr Mayhew. You can cooperate with us now, or you can cooperate with us later. Now is easier for both of us. Later means us knocking on the front door of your house. It means trawling through that computer of yours. It means us asking everyone you know and love about what you get up to. It means showing them the things you write. Your colleagues, your neighbours, even your mother."

Vince's eyes flick from Fatima to Conrad. "Why does she need to see that?"

"Well, you won't play ball with us, and we need to get information from somewhere. This is a murder investigation, after all. Murder is a very serious crime, with very serious consequences. We can get a warrant to search your home like that." Conrad clicks his fingers, the snap cracking like a whip across the quiet room.

"Your poor mother," Fatima grimaces. "I wonder what she'll think when she sees us on her doorstep?"

"I didn't do it." Vince's words come out fast, desperate.

Conrad smirks. He's heard that line from guilty men before, many, many times. "That's not what it says online…"

"I wanted to join in with the banter, okay? The café, yes, I did that, but the other stuff? The murders? That wasn't me. I didn't even know Peter Harris back then. It's all lies!"

Conrad sits back in his seat, enjoying the rhythm of the conversation now Vince no longer feels like he's in charge. "So you expect me to believe that you attacked Hannah Allen's place of work and left a note attached to her missing poster, but you weren't the person leaving similar notes at her home or with the bodies of the victims?"

Vince blinks. "I... I didn't know about the notes at her home or the ones with the bodies. I thought it would scare her if I used a picture of her missing poster, but I never... I never thought –"

"It's funny, you people always come in here with all the bravado in the world," Conrad cuts in. "Acting like you're one step ahead, but you're not. Eventually, we break you. Eventually, we expose you for who you are. And then, when you get sent to prison, you see how worthless your 'I don't care' act is."

"I didn't do anything! You can't send me to prison," Vince says, his voice catching on the last word.

"I wouldn't be so sure about that. And when you get there?" Conrad whistles and pulls a pained expression. "It's not a fun time, is it, Fatima?"

"It's not a fun time at all," Fatima agrees.

"There's a name for people like you in prison," Conrad says as he leans closer towards Vince. "A name for people who think and act like you do."

Vince sticks his chin out in defiance. "A hero."

Conrad laughs. "A hero? Not quite. Out here in the real world, when someone's committed crimes like these, they aren't given a hero's welcome. That's what you keyboard warriors don't realise when you spend all your time in your toxic chat rooms, letting your brains turn to mush so they can be warped by the sickest views – in the real world, people don't like people who hurt children. And Gabriella O'Hara? Well, she was most definitely a child."

Vince's chin dimples, the sign of a wobble. The sign that something Conrad said has chipped through his bravado.

"Now, Mr Mayhew, are you going to cut the act and talk to us, or do we have to continue this song and dance until it's time for you to be sent away?"

Fate chooses that moment to let someone knock at the door of the interview room. Vince flinches at the sound, still too under the terrifying spell Conrad has cast for him to realise that the interruption will give him time to regroup and continue with his lies. Conrad ignores the intrusion too, but a few seconds later, the knock sounds again. He grinds his teeth as he mentally prepares the furious rant he will shout at whoever is responsible for knocking when he's not finished in here.

But then the door opens.

Conrad blinks, wrongfooted by the gall of someone interrupting his interrogation.

"Conrad?" Millicent says. Millicent, a junior who should know better than to barge in like this. "You're needed."

"Now?"

Millicent's eyes flick to Vince before settling back on Conrad. "Now," she confirms.

With a sigh, Conrad suspends the interview. He leaves Vince to his nervous lip licking and exits the room. Once in the corridor, he glares at Millicent. "This better be good," he snaps.

Millicent says nothing but instead drops a stack of papers in his hands. "What's this?"

"A log from the taxi rank Vince works for. The sat nav system they use tracks their drivers' journeys, routes and all."

Conrad flicks through the papers, unsure what there is to see here other than the potential association of guilt. Vince Mayhew, a driver for a well-known, trusted local taxi rank. Would it be so hard to think that a schoolgirl caught in the rain or a tipsy teenager upset after an argument with her friends might accept a ride so they could get home quicker? Probably not, but Conrad's sure he will find out from Vince soon enough.

His patience runs short, the pages before him meaningless when his mind is still in the interview room with Vince. "So?"

Millicent stops his frustrated riffling and points to a page. "These maps show Vince's routes the night Harriet Warren went missing."

Conrad pays attention now. He scans the information before him, his face draining of colour with each second that passes, not that Millicent notices. She's too busy flicking through the rest of the papers until she stops on another page.

"These next few pages show the routes he took around the time Gabriella O'Hara was abducted. He was in the area, yes, but look where he went. Look at the timestamps."

Conrad looks, then he gulps, a movement that's painful thanks to his dry throat. "Is there any way these can be doctored?"

"No."

"Could he have given his tracker to someone else?"

"No, and we already know from CCTV that Vince was driving his taxi. These are the routes he took. He finished work at 4am the night Harriet was abducted. He completed six journeys after the estimated time of her disappearance, something he couldn't have done with a body in the back of his car."

Millicent stops there, letting her words hang in the air.

"You know what this means, don't you?" she says, a question so redundant it makes Conrad want to scream. "Vince might have attacked Break Time, but as for the murders? Well, it looks like we've got the wrong person."

As the walls of the station fall in on him, Conrad closes his eyes and thinks of only one thing - Hannah. The person he called when his hunger to end this once and for all got the better of him.

The person stepping out into a world she thinks is safe, all the while a killer is one step behind her.

Sometimes I think you're the only person who would understand why I've had to do this. You might not want to, but deep down, I think you would. After what you've lived through, after what you've seen, how could there not be a part of you that understands how I got here?

You'd understand why you had to be part of this too. There's no one else but you. After all, you're the perfect victim, the lucky survivor, the name everyone knows. There's no other way to look at it - the end of your life is the most fitting end to this story.

I see so much of myself in you. That's why I know you'd understand me. The way my brain ticks constantly, the way destruction calls to me like an old friend, the way my patience feels like a taut rubber band waiting to snap... you'd understand.

Over the years, many doctors have told me I'm sick. 'It's understandable', they say, 'Let us help. Work with us, not against us.' I've been sceptical of authority figures for a while now, especially ones in uniforms who say they're going to make it better, but sometimes I think the doctors might be right. Maybe there is a sickness in me.

Or maybe I'm just a person who has been pushed too far for too long.

I fantasise about the moment we no longer have to pretend around each other, the truth out there as your blood drips from my fingers. The moment the circle is complete and we are intertwined forever. Our names, our stories, our lives – connected, always.

I think about what you'll say. How you'll look at me. How your shock and anger will give way to one thing – understanding.

Because I know you will understand. I know you will know why I had to do this.

You have to die, Hannah, you know that. Thanks to Peter Harris, you've always known that. You might have lived your life, prolonging the inevitable, but you've known death has been following you ever since that day.

Well, I'm here to write 'the end' now. I'm here to finish what was started. I'm coming for you.

In fact, I'm already here.

Chapter *Thirty-eight.*

The last of the winter sun beats down on me. Soon, it will be spring, a season of new beginnings. The timing couldn't be more perfect for what I'm about to do.

I walk down Darling Drive, passing a row of terrace houses with sash windows until I reach the one with the purple door. I remember the first time I came to this house. My mum practically forced me down the path. Now I'm here of my own accord, ready to accept my future.

I use the big, brass knocker to rap on the door and then listen for the sound of footsteps. Sure enough, after only a few seconds of waiting, I hear them.

Tanya cheers my name when she sees me on her doorstep. "I'm so glad you decided to come over," she cries, throwing the door wide to invite me inside.

The house hasn't changed much the entire time I've known Tanya. It's as welcoming as ever, with the same plush, neutral carpet lining the floors, the same evocative artwork decorating the walls, and the same inviting furniture in every room. And, as always, somewhere in the house, a vanilla candle is burning.

Before I get lost in my memories, Tanya leads me to the kitchen. This is the one room that's been transformed thanks to a renovation two years ago. It's now sleek and modern, with a large, stone-top island in the middle of the room and double doors leading out to the garden. The garden, Tanya's pride and joy, is as well-groomed as ever, like something straight from the pages of a magazine.

"I was about to make a cup of tea. Do you want one, or have you still not acquired a taste for it?" Tanya jokes, opening a cupboard to grab a mug.

"I'm still firmly anti-tea, I'm afraid."

"One day I'll get you drinking it. It's my mission in life!" Tanya says as she flicks the kettle on. The sound of boiling water fills the kitchen. In its bubbling chaos, I find the courage to say part of the news I came here to tell her.

"Conrad called me earlier. The police think they've found the killer."

Tanya stops what she's doing and turns to me. "Wow," she breathes, then her face breaks into a smile. "This is wonderful news! You must be so happy."

"I am. At least, I think I am. I'm still a little numb," I admit.

"Why numb?" Tanya asks as she continues to make her drink.

"It just doesn't feel real. The last few weeks haven't, to be honest. My feet have barely touched the ground. One minute I've been scared, the next in denial, the next furious at the world."

"Hannah, you've handled this situation with grace and dignity."

"I don't know about that," I dismiss, but Tanya shakes her head.

"Don't dodge the compliment. You survived the unimaginable then the unimaginable happened again. Through it all, you kept your head held high. You should be proud of yourself."

"Maybe," I reply. "What's happened has got me thinking, though, about my life and the direction I want it to take."

Tanya approaches the breakfast bar and leans her forearms on the countertop, a mug of tea encased in her hands. "Well, that sounds interesting. Have you arrived at any conclusions?"

"I have. Your offer for me to help expand Sisterhood of Support? I'd like to take you up on it, if it still stands."

I've barely finished my sentence before Tanya shrieks. "Hannah, of course it still stands!" She rushes to my side and throws her arms around me. "This is amazing news!"

"I'm glad you're happy," I giggle.

"Happy? You're not leaving me anymore - I'm over the moon! In fact, I'm so far over the moon I can no longer see it!" Tanya jokes before pulling out of the hug. "I have to know, what brought about this change of heart?"

"A few things, really. How helping Riley made me feel. Something Carla said. Even everything that's been going on has helped, in a way. I've spent so many years trying to pretend my time with Peter Harris didn't happen and believing that because of it I'm now another person altogether. I don't want to do that anymore. I want to reclaim my identity. No 'Hannah Allen Then' and 'Hannah Allen Now', just me, exactly as I am. I thought that meant leaving Sisterhood of Support forever, but I'm starting to think it means the opposite."

"Hannah, I don't know where to begin. This is everything I've ever wanted for you," Tanya says, her eyes shining with happiness, but our joy is interrupted by a knock at the door. The sound cuts the atmosphere cleanly open.

"Talk about timing," Tanya groans, glancing at the clock on the wall. "That will be Danielle arriving for her one-to-one. You stay here, I'll get the door, but this is amazing news, Hannah. Truly amazing!"

Grinning, I watch Tanya leave the room. Her excitement stays with me, bouncing off the walls and confirming everything I need to know – this is the right choice.

As the front door opens, I go to make a cup of tea for Danielle, turning around only when I hear voices drawing nearer.

"I'm sorry we'll have to push our one-to-one back," Tanya says.

"It's no bother," Danielle replies as she enters the kitchen. She catches me making her a drink and beams. "Well, you know how to make a woman feel welcome."

"I'm hoping making you a drink means you'll forgive me for crashing your session. I'm sorry, I didn't realise you were booked in at this time."

"Please, my day will be even better now I've seen you," Danielle says, then she looks at what I'm doing. "Sorry, Han, but I only drink herbal tea. Tanya got some tea bags especially for me. Sit down, I'll make it myself."

"Are you sure?"

Danielle waves me away from the kettle. "Honestly, I use this kitchen more than I use my own. Go, sit."

Following her instructions, I settle back onto the stool and watch Danielle manoeuvre about the room with such familiarity I feel like I'm in her home.

"Well," Tanya beams. "Isn't this lovely, the three of us together! Shall we open some biscuits?"

"Do you really need us to answer that question?" I joke. Danielle laughs and opens a cupboard, knowing exactly where to locate Tanya's sweet treats.

"You've come at a good time, Danielle," Tanya says, taking a sip of her drink. "A celebratory time, in fact!"

"Oh yeah? What are we celebrating?"

"Hannah's no longer leaving us. And, better than that, she's agreed to help me expand Sisterhood of Support!"

Danielle drops the packet of biscuits she's holding, looking from Tanya to me and back again, her mouth agape. "She's... she's what?"

"She's going to help me expand Sisterhood of Support! Isn't that wonderful? There are so many people out there who need our community. I couldn't do it on my own, and thanks to Hannah, I won't have to. What a team we're going to make!"

Tanya reaches across the counter and grabs my hand, our joy combining to become an unstoppable swell of happiness. I turn to Danielle, waiting for her to be swept up in the current with us, but when I look at her I don't see happiness at all. I see red splotches on her neck and chest, her mouth opening and closing, and her eyebrows pointing into a frown.

When she finally speaks, her words blast me open.

"Are you fucking kidding me?!"

I flinch at Danielle's outcry, my nails digging into Tanya's skin.

"I come to every class you put on, tell you every thought in my brain, but still, you're picking *her*?" Danielle snorts a bitter laugh. "Well, that's just typical!"

"Danielle, is everything okay?" Tanya asks, a question that makes Danielle shriek.

"How can you ask me if everything is okay after what you've just said?! She doesn't even want to be part of your stupid group anymore!"

Tanya lets go of my hand, a move that feels like taking a bat to the gut. Out of the corner of my eye, I watch her approach the ball of fury standing in her kitchen.

"Danielle, sweetheart," Tanya begins, reaching out to offer comfort, but Danielle pushes her hard in the chest.

"Don't touch me!"

Tanya holds her hands up to show Danielle she's not coming closer, but all I see is my mentor standing exposed and vulnerable in front of someone I do not recognise. Someone whose eyes are glinting in a way I do not trust.

"What do I have to do to be good enough for you? To be good enough for anyone? Did my beatings not last long enough? Are my scars not deep enough?" With that, Danielle rolls up her sleeves to show the tracks of scars lining her arms, some the consequence of years of self-harm, others the remnants of her ex's violent temper.

"Danielle –" Tanya begins, but at that moment, Danielle snatches a knife from the knife block on Tanya's kitchen island.

The sudden escalation is petrifying. Tanya takes a step backwards and

I leap to my feet, the stool I was sitting on skidding across the floor behind me. I've never been more aware of how far away an exit is or how not having my phone makes me powerless to seek help.

"Do I need to cut deeper, to bleed more?!" Danielle shouts as she takes the knife to her flesh, the silver blade resting against her pale skin.

"Don't!" Tanya shouts, but her protest is futile. In one swift movement, Danielle slices her arm, sending crimson blood spilling from the wound.

"Are you happy now?" Danielle directs her question at me, her eyes wet with tears as she puts the blade against her skin once more. "Does that put me on 'Lucky Number 11' level or do I need to cut again?"

I'm too shocked to speak, but Tanya isn't. "Danielle, let me help you," she says. She grabs a towel and goes to Danielle, bundling it around her wound. I want to scream at Tanya to back away from Danielle and the knife that's glinting in her hand, but my words stay stuck in my throat.

"This is deep. It might need stitches," Tanya says, a sentence that makes Danielle scoff.

"So now you care about me. Only when I'm hurt, only when I'm bleeding, do I match up to the invincible Hannah Allen." Danielle spits my name with such venom it hurts to hear. "Everyone acts like you're so special, Hannah, but you're not. We all went through hell, not just you."

"Danielle," Tanya says, but the warning tone in her voice reignites Danielle's fury. She pushes Tanya once more, sending her stumbling backwards. The towel that was compressing Danielle's cut slips to the floor, the red of her blood a stark contrast against its white fibres.

"After everything that happened, you wanted to act like it hadn't," Danielle hisses. "Like you could live a normal life while the rest of us had to be tortured by what we went through."

"I never —" I begin, but the sound of my voice infuriates Danielle so much that she slams her fist onto the counter.

"Don't deny it! You never wanted to be at Sisterhood of Support! You listened to our stories as if they were an insult to be around, then

Nathaniel Clarke's book came out. The way you talked about it... it was like it was the worst thing to happen to you."

"That book was one of the worst things to happen to me!" I protest. "Do you honestly expect me to be happy that strangers read about the worst moments of my life before they go to bed?"

"You don't get it, do you? You complain that people are interested in your story, but what about the rest of us? The ones who don't get books written about them? The ones no one believes? People don't understand if getting out of bed feels like too much for us. People don't want to help or make things easier, they just want us to shut up and disappear."

"No one wants you to disappear," Tanya says, but Danielle is so upset she doesn't hear her.

"You have no idea what it's like, Hannah. When you cry, the world is there with open arms and tissues. When I cry, I'm left alone. Even my family tell me I should move on from what happened, like forgetting it is that simple. I live my life, day in, day out, with this weight on my chest that I can never talk about, pretending I'm fine when I'm not. It crushes me every day and no one notices! No one cares!"

"Danielle, lots of people care," Tanya attempts to soothe, but Danielle shakes her head.

"They don't, not really. You're the worst of all. Inviting me to your little group, letting me spill my guts, and all the while you only care for what she has to say."

"That's not true."

Danielle laughs. "Of course it's true! She's Hannah Allen. She's the headline star." Danielle's icy glare fixes on me once more. "You were the perfect victim, Hannah. The little, lost schoolgirl. Everyone cared about you. Everyone wanted to make it better, but me? I was in my mid-thirties, average looking, and childless... they weren't bothered. They never are when it comes to people like me. Paula lost a fucking eye and do you know what she got? Not even half a page in the local paper! But you,

Hannah, you were front page news. You still are, for fucks sake!"

"So what, you want to be Lucky Number 11?" I ask hotly, my eyes prickling with tears.

"I want what I went through to matter! I want to be anything, anyone but myself!"

With that, Danielle reaches for her mug of tea and launches it across the room. I flinch as it hits the wall behind me, shards of porcelain and splashes of molten liquid flying everywhere.

"Danielle, sweetheart -" Tanya begins, but Danielle screams and raises her hands to her head to shut out Tanya's voice.

"My ex made me wish I was dead, but what happened after was just as bad," Danielle sobs. "The police interviewed me like it was my fault. They asked if I spoke to other men, if I provoked him, then guess what? My ex didn't even get charged. 'Not enough evidence', the police said, as if my scars appeared by magic, but they threw every resource in the police force behind you, Hannah! Your pain mattered, but I was expected to carry mine alone."

As Danielle chokes on her tears, I'm silenced by the ugly truth in her words. I've sat through enough Sisterhood of Support meetings to know that not everyone was lucky enough to have Conrad fighting for them or a mum who never let them doubt they could make it through.

"I think we should all take a moment to stop and breathe," Tanya says, but Danielle shoots her a look so full of hatred that it freezes my heart.

"Stopping and breathing doesn't fix anything, Tanya, you know that as well as I do. I've taken the pills, I've gone to the meetings. I've done everything a 'good survivor' is meant to do and none of it helps. None of it makes people stop and think, 'Maybe it's not the woman's fault for wearing a short dress or having a life outside the walls of her home. Maybe there's something wrong in the world that we need to address'. None of it makes me forget what happened or makes people believe survivors! Well, maybe after what I've done, people will believe us.

Maybe now they're paying attention, they'll care."

My legs lock as the glint in Danielle's eyes tells me everything I need to know. "You," I breathe, my terrified voice barely a whisper. "You're the killer."

Danielle tips her head back and scoffs. "This is what I'm talking about! Everyone makes out like you're so special, Hannah, but you've only just realised I'm behind it all."

"I don't understand," I say, shaking my head as if to dislodge the truth from my brain. "How could you do this?"

"It was easy," Danielle shrugs. "All I had to do was go into work and say I had car trouble and I could access a range of rental cars. Ones I could return the next day and get cleaned with no questions asked. Ones the police wouldn't spot on CCTV because I made sure never to use the same car twice. You know, if you put a child's car seat in the back, it's amazing how many people don't hesitate when taking you up on the offer of a ride home."

"I don't mean how could you physically do it," I cry, the chilling details of Danielle's crimes making waves of nausea roll over me. "I mean how could you actually do it? How could you hurt people?!"

"Look around you! Women around the world are hurt on a daily basis, but people are so numbed to the news that they barely even react anymore. What choice did I have? People needed something to happen that was so shocking they had no excuse but to face the truth. Besides, I'm not you, Hannah. No one listens when I speak. I went to the police covered in cuts and bruises and they still didn't believe me."

"That doesn't make what you've done okay!"

Tanya steps in front of me in an attempt to de-escalate the situation, but my anger won't allow me to be shielded. I step forward, disbelieving tears filling my eyes.

"This is sick, Danielle. You knew what it felt like to be hurt, and you still went out and killed those women."

"Don't twist this," Danielle snaps, the red blotches on her neck darkening. "You know as well as I do that most people only listen when they're forced to. They only talk about this violence when there's a body. What else was I supposed to do?"

"You were supposed to do anything but become a killer!"

"Hannah, take a breath. I think we all need a moment to calm down," Tanya interjects, reaching for me, but I brush her away.

"Calm down? Tanya, she killed Paula! She killed innocent women with lives and hopes and dreams!"

"Stop saying it like that," Danielle shouts. "I had to make people listen somehow! I had to make them think!"

"And the only way you could do that was by murdering people?!"

Danielle's chin wobbles, but she stands firm. "It's not murder if the crime is committed for a good reason."

The obliviousness of her words reverberates through me. "What reason can you give for any of what you've done that would excuse the cruelty of it? You've tortured me for weeks, Danielle. Sent notes to my home as if this was all some sick game!"

"I sent the notes because I knew the media would go wild for details like that. It wasn't about you, Hannah. It was about getting as many headlines as possible. The more headlines there are, the more people pay attention."

"This is madness!" I cry. "Danielle, think of what you've done. Think of all the people up and down the country who are terrified because of your actions. Think of Paula who saw you as a friend -"

"I was Paula's friend! You know how hard it was for her to go outside after what she went through. She didn't want to live like that. I stopped her pain!"

"You didn't stop anything! You just caused more hurt."

My words injure Danielle. She steps back, blinking. Tanya reaches for my arm to stop me from saying anything else, but I'm too lost in my rage to follow her instruction.

"You're a killer, Danielle. There's no other way to say it - you are a *killer*," I spit.

"Don't call me that," Danielle whispers.

"But it's true! You killed people! You hurt them -"

"They didn't feel a thing, I made sure of that! I put them to sleep first."

"You tortured them -"

"No!" Danielle shouts, raising her hands to her ears to block out my voice. "They were asleep! They felt nothing!"

"You *killed* them."

"I saved them! Saved them from living in a world where someone could attack them and they'd still somehow be blamed! Trina Lamond was covered in bruises when I met her, did you know that? And Gabriella O'Hara was a schoolgirl - who knows what could have happened to her when she grew up? Harriet Warren -"

"You can't justify this!" I explode, anger swelling inside my chest as I think of Danielle's victims, of their families, of the terror I've lived in for the last few weeks. "You're not a saviour – you're a killer. You hurt people like your ex hurt you."

Something happens when those words leave my mouth. The atmosphere shifts and a steeliness takes over Danielle's features, one that quashes my anger and fills me with even more fear than before.

"I did what I had to do to make people pay attention," Danielle says, her eyes lit up with an uncontrollable fire. "And I'll do it again until they have no choice but to listen."

The hum of Danielle's fury fixes me to the spot, the knife in her hand the only thing I can focus on. As her chest rises and falls with her heavy breathing, Tanya takes a step forward. She stands between us, but Danielle's rage seems to penetrate through her.

"Danielle, I can see you're upset. Why don't we all go into my living room to sit and talk about this?"

"I don't want to sit and talk! That's all we ever do. Sit and talk, sit and talk, but what does that change? What does that fix? Do you know how many women are sexually assaulted each year in this country? Do you know how many are murdered? Talking doesn't change anything when no one is listening."

"Talking is tough, I know, but it's the start of healing and –"

"I don't want to heal - I want to stop hurting! I want this to be over!"

With that, Danielle lunges for me.

"Danielle, no!" Tanya shouts. She grabs Danielle's arm that's holding the knife, struggling to keep it back. My brain screams at me to move, to run, to help, to do anything but stand there immobilised.

"Fuck you!" Danielle screams. She pushes Tanya backwards and as she stumbles away, Danielle lashes out with the knife.

It all happens so fast, yet it seems like I'm watching the situation unfold in slow motion. The fury contorting Danielle's face, the desperation in Tanya's eyes, the knife intent on claiming a victim.

And, as the blade slices through Tanya's throat, the knife gets its wish.

Chapter *Thirty-nine.*

As Tanya's blood sprays across her pristine kitchen tiles, an animalistic scream bursts from my lips. She falls to her knees, her hand grasping the deep wound gouged into her flesh. Blood darker than any I've ever seen before pools from between her fingers.

"Tanya!" I shriek.

Rushing to Tanya's aid, my fingers fumble at her split throat, but no matter what I do, the blood keeps coming.

"It's okay, it's going to be okay, I promise!"

I hear myself repeatedly saying those soothing platitudes, ones Tanya has said to me many times before, but I don't remember telling myself to speak. I don't remember anything but the way the knife sliced so easily through Tanya's throat.

"Shit!" Danielle shouts, but I barely hear her over the pounding in my ears.

Tanya opens her mouth to speak, but no sound comes out. I press harder on her neck, but it doesn't stop the warm, sticky blood from coating my fingers.

Then Tanya locks her eyes on mine, and in them, I see something that will haunt me forever - defeat.

"Danielle, what did you do?!" I cry, turning to face her.

"I didn't mean it!" Danielle yells, her expression as horrified as mine. "She wouldn't stop talking. Neither of you would stop talking!" Tears stream down Danielle's face. She looks at Tanya then folds forward, resting her hands on her knees as if to stop herself from being sick.

"You need to call an ambulance. Please," I beg.

"I... I can't!"

"Please, Danielle. She's dying."

"Don't say that! I didn't mean to hurt her!"

"But you have, Danielle, you have," I sob. "If you don't get Tanya some help soon, you'll have killed her. You'll have killed the woman who has gone out of her way to help so many others."

My words flick a switch in Danielle. She watches Tanya struggle to cling to life, her erratic breathing slowing until suddenly, she pounces forward and pushes me to the floor.

Shrieking, I tumble backwards, my head hitting against the side of the fridge as I fall. I wince at the impact, but all feeling drains from my body as the woman I once viewed as a friend stands above me with a blood-soaked knife in her hand.

"Danielle," I breathe.

"Save it, Hannah. Don't make this harder than it already is."

"But Tanya –"

"She's going to die, yes."

It's like the centre of my chest is wrenched away at those words. I look at Danielle, waiting for her to shake her head or change her mind about calling an ambulance, but she holds my gaze, unwavering.

"No!" I cry. My body moves to go to Tanya's aid, but Danielle points the knife at me.

"There's nothing you can do to change what's about to happen, so please don't try."

With me no longer stemming the flow of her blood, Tanya makes a gurgling sound like the remnants of washing-up water swirling down the sink. My limbs jerk to reach her, but Danielle kicks me hard in the chest and I fall back once more.

"She'll bleed out soon," Danielle says. "It usually only takes a few minutes. It's that way with the wrists, at least. I wonder if it will be the same for you."

Our eyes lock, and for one blissful second, the whole world seems to stop, but then Danielle breaks the illusion by laughing.

"Did you think I was going to let you walk away? You're too important for that, Number 11. You have a pivotal role in what happens next."

My mouth dries at the determination in Danielle's voice. "What do you mean?"

"I can't get the amount of attention I need for people to start taking all survivors seriously without you. You see, your death? Well, that would get the entire world talking." Danielle eyes me up and down. "Don't look at me like that. Death was always going to be your ending. You can't stay lucky forever."

Danielle doesn't allow me a split second to react to what she's said before she lunges for me. I try to move away, but she's too fast. Her strong arms wrap around my body, pulling me tight against her, then she grabs a chunk of my hair and uses it to drag my head backwards, leaving my throat exposed.

I scream, fighting to wriggle free of her grip and protect my vulnerable flesh, but then Danielle rests the knife that's dripping in Tanya's blood against my cheek. As soon as the blade touches my skin, I stop moving.

"You understand why I have to do this, don't you? Why I have to carve you open and show the world that they need to fight for change?" Danielle whispers, her hot breath tickling my cheek. She moves the knife around my face, leaving trails of blood in its wake.

From the floor beside us, Tanya tries to speak, but the sound comes out all wrong. Blood bubbles between her fingers, puddling around her body until red is all I can see.

"Danielle, don't," I beg, pushing back against her body, but she holds me strong.

"I'm not a bad person, Hannah. I've been pushed to this, you see that, don't you? You can only silence someone for so long before they scream."

Through the blur of my tears, I look at Tanya. Her spirit dims before me, the light in her eyes fading. It's too much to witness. I jerk my body in an attempt to free myself, but all that happens is my knees slide in a pool of blood. I try not to think of how the thing that's causing the dampness soaking into my jeans is the life force slowly draining out of the woman who has been there for me through every high and low point in my life.

Danielle presses her mouth against my ear. "What happened to you is no more important than what happened to me –"

"I never said it was!"

"No, but you were treated as if it was. People believed you. They never believed me, but after this, they will. After this, they'll never forget my story."

With that, Danielle digs the knife into my cheek. I scream as it scores my skin. Danielle shivers like she relishes the sound, then in one swift motion, she moves the knife to my neck. Even with blood trickling down my cheek, all I can focus on is the knife and the chill of its blade against my skin.

"Please, Danielle, don't," I beg, but it's like she can't hear me.

"Do you have any idea what it's like to be torn in two by someone else's actions and for it not to matter? To never get justice for what you endured? To not be pretty or innocent enough for the front page?"

Danielle moves the blade to my chest. She holds it above my heart, the tip cutting into my skin.

"Last week, a woman called Catarina Abimbola was murdered by her husband. I bet you've never heard of her. People were too busy writing about the missing girls to care about her. It's wrong!"

"That doesn't mean you turn to murder," I sob. "There are other ways –"

"There is no other way! Don't you get it? I tried everything else. None of it worked. None of it made it better for people like me. Then that book came out and I took my chance."

"Your chance to what, to kill?"

"To make a difference! For years I sat beside you, a friend you could count on, but you were going to walk away. Pretend I didn't exist, pretend it never happened, as if I could ever be that lucky. What happened haunts my every waking moment. It's branded on me more than any tattoo ever could be."

Danielle grabs my shirt and lifts it, exposing my number 11. Instinctively, I flinch, but that doesn't stop her. She lowers the knife and uses it to trace the lines of my tattoo.

"You want to be rid of this. You don't even realise how lucky you are to have it."

"Please," I whimper, but Danielle doesn't register my voice.

"I'd give anything for this number. Anything to have the world notice my pain. Anything for them to believe me."

I open my mouth to respond, but I don't get the chance to start my sentence before Danielle stops me from speaking altogether. In one sudden movement, she plunges the knife into my stomach, right between the ones of my tattoo.

Chapter *Forty.*

For a moment, I'm so shocked that I forget to breathe, but then a burst of excruciating pain hits me and I choke on a desperate, jagged gasp of air. Lowering my eyes to my abdomen, I stare in horror at the handle of the knife that's sticking out of my flesh, the blade embedded deep inside me.

"Dan... Danielle," I gasp, but then she does the unthinkable – she pulls the knife out and lets me go.

I fall forward, doubling over and clutching my stomach as blood spills from my body.

"No one's going to forget me now," Danielle says, then she kicks me in my side. I collapse onto the floor, my cheek resting in a crimson puddle, a metallic-scented mix of mine and Tanya's blood invading my nostrils.

I can't believe it will end like this, laid on Tanya's kitchen floor, killed by a friend after ten years of battling to survive.

A sob rises in my chest, but it gets stuck there as terror takes over when I feel Danielle's hands on me once more. She turns me on my back, Tanya's crisp white ceiling coming into view, then she kneels beside me.

"Me and you, Hannah," she whispers. "United by the worst thing a person can do to someone else. Our names, our stories, as valid as the other."

With that, Danielle raises the knife above her head, ready to bring it crashing down into the centre of my chest.

This is it, I think. *My luck has run out.*

As I close my eyes and accept my fate, a myriad of images plays in my mind, a slideshow created just for me. Break Time's chipped paintwork and smiling regulars. Joel curled beside me in bed on a Sunday morning. Tanya cheering me on when I first stayed at a friend's house overnight. My mum's tight, all-encompassing hugs. The bedroom she decorated purple for my ninth birthday. Hot chocolate and marshmallows. A surprise date night, a stranger letting you on the bus first, smiling at the sound of people around you laughing even though you don't know the joke. All the little things that add up to make life wonderful.

My life. The life I fought to have.

The life I don't want to lose.

I open my eyes to beg Danielle to spare me, but as I do, I realise opening my eyes was what she wanted me to do. That way, she can watch me go.

As she lowers the knife, Danielle's face splits into a wide, beaming smile. The happiest smile I've ever seen. The last smile I will ever see. In the split second before the impact comes, I close my eyes and pray. I pray Joel knows how much I love him, pray Stefan will forgive me, pray that whatever comes next brings me peace.

I wait for the slick, sharp slice of flesh, but it never comes.

Instead, I feel a wet spray on my face and hear a startled gasp.

It takes every ounce of courage I have, but I open my eyes to find Danielle's throat hanging open. A river of red runs down her neck and chest, staining her shirt.

Danielle drops her knife, gargling as she spills her contents across the kitchen floor. Her eyes lock on mine, no longer full of malice, but shock instead.

Suddenly, she falls forward. I scramble away from her fall path, escaping just in time before Danielle crashes to the floor beside me. Her jaw jerks as she tries to speak, but I'm not sure I have it in me to hear what she has to say.

I turn away, not wanting to witness Danielle's life fade to nothing, then I see her.

Tanya, collapsed in a heap, so pale she's almost completely white. A blood-soaked knife sits in her barely-there grip.

"Tanya," I cry, reaching for her, but she shakes her head.

"Go," she mouths. For a moment, my brain doesn't compute her instruction, but as she nods encouragingly at me, I understand what she's asking me to do.

"No, please. It can't end like this," I whisper, but as Tanya mouths 'go' again and my stomach screams in agony, I know that I don't have a choice but to comply.

My chin wobbles at the finality of this moment. There will be no holding Tanya until she takes her last breath. No reassuring her that she isn't alone. No thanking her for everything she has done for me. Neither of us has time for any of that. All I can do is take Tanya's bloodied hand and press a kiss into her skin, hoping that the gesture goes some way to showing her how much she means to me, this woman who has saved my life more times than I can count.

Then, with one last squeeze of her hand, I let her go.

Using every scrap of energy I have left, I drag myself to my feet.

The pain from my stomach is blinding as I stumble out of the kitchen, a trail of blood decorating the floor behind me. I force myself to keep moving, keep heading towards the light peeping through the glass in Tanya's front door. My movements are slow and sluggish, but my will to survive is strong.

Gripping the door handle with my red-stained hand, I twist it open, then I fall into the outside world.

"Help!" I scream, staggering onto the street. "Someone, please, help me!"

My vision swims, the street swirling in and out of focus. I order my left foot to take another step, but the energy it takes to complete the movement depletes me. Suddenly, I crumble to the ground, the tarmac on the road scratchy against my skin.

As the edges of my vision close in, flashes of activity flicker past my eye line.

Someone opening their front door.

Another person running towards me.

A car pulling up, their frantic breaks screeching.

Someone shouting to call an ambulance.

Someone telling me it will be okay. Someone who sounds an awful lot like Raja Kaling.

My eyelids flutter as I cling to those words, the ones Tanya has said to me so many times. The ones she said because she believed in me too much to let me give in.

The ones I said to her as I held her dying body in my arms.

The pain of remembering Tanya's lifelessness hurts more than my stab wound. I hear the ghostly echo of her words in my head, telling me that it will be okay, but as the wail of sirens rings out in the distance, I give in to my pain. My eyes slide into the back of my head, unable to focus on anything but how much this hurts, and then everything goes black.

The strange thing about all this is not knowing how it ends. Prison? Undoubtedly, but outside the confines of the legal system, what will happen to me? Will I become a figure of hate, or will people understand why I had to do this, however uncomfortable it makes them feel?

Will it make people talk, make people think, make people listen when we say enough is enough?

Will people start to believe us?

Will they care?

Will any of it matter?

*It must matter. It **must**. The people I took can't have died for nothing. What drove me to do this must be heard. Change needs to come. The world can't carry on like this anymore.*

You might hate me for what I've done, Hannah, but you also know me. The real me. You know my story, and you know how the world we live in does everything it can to ignore stories like mine. You know I couldn't continue waking up every day, doing nothing with my rage, as if everything was okay. Couldn't listen to people say 'not all men' when nearly every woman I know has experienced violence at some level. Couldn't listen to people tell me things I should do to keep myself safe as if I was the one to blame, not the person committing the crime. Couldn't let the world look at what happened to you as an anomaly when violence like that happens every day, up and down the country, to all kinds of people.

Even thinking of the injustice of it all makes me want to scream.

I want to scream, I want to scream, I want to scream. I wake up every day screaming on the inside, but no one hears me. No one hears, no one believes, no one cares, and nothing changes.

Well, this is me screaming on the outside. This is me joining you in the ranks of the ones they talk about, Hannah. Another name that the whole country knows. I had to take your story and add mine to it. It was the only way they'd hear me. How depressing is that? To have my story heard, I must add more pain to it. To make people listen, I must take more lives, instil more fear, become both a victim and a perpetrator.

But at least, after everything, they'll hear me. They'll have no choice but to hear me.

So, this is me shouting until my lungs burst that I am here and I have had enough.

*I have had **enough**.*

Eighteen Months *Later.*

Ashton, the realtor, picks up the documents and beams. "It's official – you're now homeowners! Congratulations."

"We did it!" Joel cheers, throwing his arms around me. Together, we float on a cloud of ecstasy.

"I think you might be the happiest people to have ever signed on the dotted line," Ashton jokes. "I'll take the paperwork to my manager and leave you both to have a moment. Congratulations again."

When Ashton exits the room, Joel grabs me once more. "I can't believe it, Hannah. We're homeowners, actual homeowners!"

I think of the three-bedroom semi-detached house with its neat garden and modern ensuite, and how it's now ours. After months of searching and months of me saying, 'We can't live there' without being able to pinpoint a reason why, we finally found a place I feel safe. A place I'm ready to call home.

"Does this mean we're grown-ups now?" I ask, pulling a horrified face.

"I'm afraid so. Although we can still be immature grown-ups, right?"

"I don't want to be any other kind," I reply, then I kiss Joel. Our bodies melt together in blissful contentment. When we pull apart, I wipe my lipstick from Joel's lips then glance at the time. "I have to go. You're okay to finish up here, aren't you?"

Joel nods. "I'll meet you at Gus's Place when your event's finished, okay? Mum's coming with me, so don't worry about picking her up, and the table's booked under Conrad's name."

Wriggling my coat on, I laugh. "Is there a clearer sign of someone being new to retirement than them feeling the need to organise everything?"

"Hey, Conrad's punctual nature is our gain."

I smile because lots of things about Conrad's retirement have been our gain, not least the unconventional friendship that has blossomed between us.

It's hard to meet people who can relate to what I've been through, but as the lead detective on each case, Conrad fits that bill. We meet every two weeks at Break Time. Usually, we sit by the window and Robbie, Ellen's replacement barista of choice after I left, brings our drinks to us. I've learned more about Conrad in those meetups than I ever thought I would.

Now when I think of the name 'Conrad Wallace', I don't see someone who let me down. Instead, I see a man who tried his best, who worked a tough job under the worst pressure, and who lives with the guilt of getting things wrong every day.

"Speaking of punctuality, Stefan said he might be late," Joel adds. "He's stressed about his dissertation. I've said I'll proofread it when he's done, so hopefully that calms him down."

"That's kind of you."

Joel shrugs. "Stefan is a friend."

I smile at the truth in those words. A few weeks after I was released from the hospital and when I finally felt up to visitors, Stefan came around to the apartment. We talked about everything. It turns out, Ellen had given him my address, thinking nothing of it as we were friends. On top of that, he really did think that reading '*Peter Harris and the Unlucky Eleven*' would help him understand my story, and I really did wrongly accuse him of murder. Somewhere in the middle of all that, we made peace with each other, and then Joel joined the conversation too. Beers were had and bonds were made. Now, we're an inseparable trio. Joel and Stefan are even talking about writing a graphic novel together, with Stefan in charge of the words and Joel the artwork.

"I'll see you all there," I confirm, then I kiss Joel goodbye and leave Hart and Johnson Realty.

Riley jumps from the bench outside when she sees me exit the building. "How did it go?"

"It's official – the house is ours!"

"Hannah!" she squeals, hugging me close. "This is amazing news!"

"I know, but we'd better go to the launch. We can celebrate the house later. Are you ready?"

Riley looks down at her outfit, a bright pink power suit that she looks incredible in. "Ready and looking good, right?"

"Oh, very!"

Linking arms, we walk to my car, another new thing in my life. No one's more surprised about it than I am. Anxiety used to tell me that being in charge of a vehicle that could crash at any time was terrifying, but I've discovered I love driving. There's something freeing about it. Sometimes, when memories hold me in their chokehold so tightly I can't sleep, I take myself for a solo drive around the city. I glide through the empty streets until the hammering in my chest slows, then I head back home and climb into bed beside Joel, asleep in minutes.

Riley slides into the passenger seat, but I don't follow her straight away. Instead, I take a moment to look up at the sky.

"We did it, Tan. We got the house," I whisper, even though I know she already knows. She was watching over me when I signed the papers, I could feel it.

I close my eyes and think of her smiling face, but the image flickers, the last time I saw her distorting what I see. 'Go', she mouthed, and I did. I left her, and I'll never not feel guilty about the choice I made.

My new therapist, Ingrid, tells me I need to forgive myself for leaving

Tanya behind, that it was already too late for her, that there was no other option. I'm working on it. I suspect I'll always be working on it.

Blinking back tears, I get into the car. When I'm seated, Riley presents me with an empty water bottle I'd discarded in the passenger footwell. "I thought you were a neat freak?"

I laugh, but the laughter knots my stomach. Memories of being in Tanya's messy car, gentle music filtering through the speakers, fill my mind. How I'd taken those moments for granted. How I'd assumed I'd have the luxury of her wisdom, advice and care for the rest of my life.

I've not yet gotten used to how the smallest things can remind me of Tanya, something Ingrid assures me is normal. The other day I saw a jumper I thought she'd like. I bought it for her, even though she'll never wear it. I took the jumper home and cried into the soft fibres, then put it in a drawer and carried on with my day.

Riley senses what's on my mind. "She'd be so proud of you, Hannah," she says. "Today of all days."

Even through the haze of emotion, I know Riley's right. Her assurance is enough to push me to start the car.

I didn't walk away from Sisterhood of Support in the end. After everything, I couldn't. But more than not walking away from it, I couldn't let Tanya's dreams of expansion die with her. So here I am, studying psychology at university and one half of the team leading Sisterhood of Support to new heights.

Surprisingly, although not surprising at all if you know her, Carla is the other half of that team. After Tanya's death, Carla was a friend like no other. Uplifting when I needed her to be, vulnerable when the rawness of loss needed sharing, and motivating when I wanted to give up, she was one of the people who got me through the darkness. Now I can't imagine my life without her, and together we work to continue Tanya's legacy at Sisterhood of Support.

So far, we've opened a second location for in-person meetings and counselling, as well as launched a website where anyone impacted by violence can access support. While most of our open meetings are facilitated by survivors like Carla and myself, we also hire a team of qualified therapists for some meetings and all one-to-one sessions. Doing that helped to strike a better balance between creating a space where people could connect to those with a similar lived experience, while also offering more specialised, focused help.

"Have you thought about what you're going to say tonight?" Riley asks as we coast through the city.

"I've no idea," I admit. "Raja is hoping I'll give a speech, but I'm not sure I should. The book is all hers."

"Hannah Allen, forever the humblest person in the room," Riley jokes, but what I said is the truth – Raja has done all the work for '*Hannah Allen – Behind the Headlines*'. She's the one who deserves the mic, not me.

When news of what happened that day at Tanya's house broke, predictably the press went wild. A domestic abuse victim who became a serial killer with the goal of murdering the poster girl for surviving against all odds? It was too juicy not to write about!

The more details the media uncovered, the wilder the headlines became.

It turns out, there had been concerns about Danielle's well-being for a while. She'd received two written warnings from the rental car company she worked for, one for volatile behaviour and the other for unexplained absences. She was seeing Tanya three times a week on top of attending group meetings. In the last two weeks of her life, Tanya wrote in their session notes that she thought Danielle might need more help than Sisterhood of Support could offer. Unfortunately, Tanya never got the chance to push for that help.

But concerns that were never acted on are only part of the unnerving details of the crimes Danielle planned to perfection.

Unbeknown to anyone, Danielle had taken herself off the medications she was prescribed to help her deal with her insomnia, PTSD and anxiety.

She still collected the prescriptions, though. Only instead of using them for herself, she crushed and diluted them to make the sedative that knocked her victims into a near-dead state.

Chillingly, Danielle also wrote an online diary detailing her actions. The posts were auto-published three days after she died. She'd scheduled them to go live at a specific time, a move that I've been told shows she planned to kill me on that date. I try not to think about that fact, although sometimes late at night I don't do a good job of avoiding it.

I've never read what Danielle wrote, but I've overheard snippets and know that some posts were addressed to me. Maybe one day I'll read what she had to say. Maybe living it was enough. All I know is, quotes from her diary have been published in newspapers and on websites around the world. Her name and story are known by many now. In a way, she got her wish, although I'm not sure her actions are reported as she would have hoped.

'Psycho', *'Cold-Blooded Killer'*, *'Heartless Hound'*... none of the words people use to describe Danielle fit the woman I remember. The one who sat by my side for years under the guise of friendship. The one who looked horrified at hurting Tanya. The one who insisted, however misguided the notion was, that she had saved her victims.

But then I feel the scar on my stomach and remember that the deaths of five women happened at her hands, and I'm not sure what to think at all.

"I wonder what the journalists coming tonight are going to write about you," Riley says, chipping into my thoughts. "Although whatever they say, I'm not sure they'll beat my favourite nickname for you."

"What one is that?"

"Definitely 'The Girl Who Cheated Death Twice'. You've got to love the drama of that one!"

Riley's enthusiasm makes me smile, even if the nickname doesn't.

After that day at Tanya's house, I lost myself. Darkness was all I could see. I didn't feel like a survivor or a hero - I felt empty. I didn't want to speak to anyone. Anyone but Raja, my unlikely ally.

Raja was outside Tanya's house that day. She was the person I could hear telling me it would be okay. She had suspicions that the person responsible for the murders attended Sisterhood of Support.

"The truth often lies in unlikely places," Raja said when she visited me in the hospital. "Who was more unlikely than one of the people who endured fates like yours? After all, they knew you better than anyone. They knew all your routines and your secrets."

That day, Raja was going to speak to Tanya about how she vetted attendees. Only instead of having that conversation, she found me bleeding out in the middle of the road.

Raja was part of the group of people who saved my life. I've been told that if an ambulance had been called a minute later, the chances are I wouldn't have made it.

With that in mind, as soon as I felt strong enough to face what happened, I promised her an interview. "It's the least I can do after you saved my life," I said.

"Don't make me sound too noble, you might regret it," Raja joked, then she leaned closer. "The thing is, I'm not thinking of writing an article about this. I want to write a book."

Flashbacks of Nathaniel Clarke and his incessant hounding made me flinch.

Raja saw my reaction. "Not a book like that, I promise. It turns out, what you said when you came to my office got to me. I think it's time I used my talents for something more than clickbait. With your permission, I'd like to write your story, and Danielle's. I'd like to write about how everyone deserves to be heard."

After a bidding war between several publishers, we sold the rights to the book. All my royalties will go towards growing Sisterhood of Support, and ten percent of Raja's.

"Don't act so surprised," she said when she told me she'd be donating too. "I have a heart, you know."

A heart Raja does have, and a work ethic unlike anything I've ever seen. She's poured everything into this book and tonight, at the headquarters of Sisterhood of Support, we are hosting a pre-release party for it. The guest list is one of dreams – CEOs of major charities, MPs pushing for a safe, equal future, and other survivors.

As if remembering the room full of people waiting for me, I check my reflection in the rear-view mirror. I've finally gotten used to the scar on my cheek, another reminder of that fateful day. I look past it to the rest of my features, each one emphasised by a cosmetic layer. Red lipstick seemed like a good idea when I was getting ready, but now, against my pale skin, it reminds me of the white of Tanya's floor tiles and the red of her blood.

Riley watches me from the corner of her eye. "Stop stressing, you look great. More than that, you're doing something great. This book is proving Tanya right when she said our stories could help create change."

I swallow the lump in my throat and force a smile. "Well, it's about time things weren't only told from the perspective of the serial killer, right?" I joke as the Sisterhood of Support headquarters come into view. I swing into the car park behind the building, pulling into my usual spot.

"By the way, there's someone coming tonight," I say. "She's joining us at the next group meeting. Mariam Khan, I don't know if you've heard of her?" Riley shakes her head. "I was thinking, why don't you ask her to sit with you tonight?"

Riley's cheeks flush. "You want me to welcome someone new?"

"Only if you want to."

Riley nods, her attempt at nonchalance doing little to mask how thrilled she is at being given this responsibility. "I'd love to."

"Great! Now let's get inside before we're the last people to arrive at an event we're hosting."

Giggling, we exit my car and walk around the building. As we turn onto the street, I spot a small, skinny man with wire-rimmed glasses on the opposite side of the road. He's staring at Sisterhood of Support, his eyes narrowed like he's confronting an enemy.

My pace slows, my eyes fixed on this stranger and his bubbling hatred. He must sense he's being watched because he stops looking at the building and meets my gaze. A flicker of recognition passes through him. For a moment, I think he's going to shout something, but as soon as that flash of intention appears in him, it dies.

He turns and walks away, heading towards a taxi that's parked further up the road.

"Are you ready, rockstar?" Riley asks.

I pause to take in the red brickwork and factory-like windows of the Sisterhood of Support headquarters. I used to think this place was cursed by the misery it contained, but now when I look at it, all I see is a building. Bricks and mortar, it could be anywhere, but the people inside? They are something special. Something to keep coming back for. A group of women like no other, creating a safe, hope-filled space to share with each other. Everything Tanya worked tirelessly to build. Everything I am going to continue to grow in her name.

It's taken me a while to get to where I am today. A place where I accept that what happened is in the DNA of my life, but it is only one part of it. In a rainbow spectrum of my experiences, Peter Harris is just a minor blot. My courage, my strength, my vulnerability and my fight - they are large, vibrant splashes of colour.

Yes, I am 'Lucky Number 11', but I'm also a friend, a partner, a student, a reader, an ex-waitress, and the mentee of an incredible woman who I will remember until the day I die. I am my past, I am this very moment, and I am everything there is still to come.

Fuelled by those thoughts, I step across the threshold and into the next chapter.

Acknowledgements

As with my other books, this story deals with complex, emotional and potentially triggering issues. If you are reading these acknowledgements, it means you've stuck with what is at times a difficult read, so I want to start by thanking you for that.

This story has lived in me for a long time, but for a long time, I didn't feel ready to write it. It was too personal, too difficult, too daunting to commit to, but when a chain of real-world events made me want to scream 'enough is enough', I felt compelled to write the book you have just finished. As I listened to people victim blame and dodge acknowledging the deep-rooted misogyny behind certain crimes, I sat at my laptop and wondered, 'What would it take for people to believe survivors? If these crimes aren't shocking enough to result in meaningful change, what could be?'

From those questions, this story came to life.

While this book is a work of fiction, a lot of my own lived experience has gone into it. Like Hannah, I was sexually assaulted as a teenager. I hadn't had my first kiss, gone to 'grown-up' parties or had time to learn who I was. Because of what happened, I too was forced to grow up before I was ready to. Because of what happened, I too mourn the person I imagined I'd be, as well as feel incredible pride over the life I've worked hard to build in the aftermath.

To craft Hannah's story, I spoke to some of my feelings of being a survivor as well as took influence from a range of sources, such as coaching sessions I've attended, support resources I've used, and experiences people have generously shared with me. Living with the aftermath of a sexual assault is so personal - I never intend to or claim to speak for others - but I wanted this story to reflect some of the realities of carrying this trauma. I wanted to explore the bits that are hard to face - the anger you feel when people victim blame, the sense of a loss of self, the times you lash out at people you care about - but I also wanted to highlight the strength of vulnerability, how healing isn't linear, and how being a survivor looks like many different things.

Writing about this trauma wasn't easy, especially when for much of my life, like Hannah, I didn't want to think of what had happened. Thankfully, I have been lucky enough to meet many incredible people who supported me when I was ready to face up to it - my own version of Sisterhood of Support, if you will. To those people (you know who you are) - you showed me that bad things can happen, but it doesn't mean that everything after that must be bad too. Some of the lines in this book are things you've said to me, things that helped, so thank you for gifting me your wise words. I hope they help someone else too.

I'd also like to thank the people who have shared their stories with me and sensitivity checked this book. I really appreciate your advice about crafting Hannah, Danielle, and all the other characters impacted by violence. I hope that through the Sisterhood of Support attendees, I have shown the importance of an understanding community and that there is no one way to be a survivor. You are not the sum of your bad days. You can experience the worst and still build a life to be proud of. Create an amazing career like Amrita, find the joy in everyday routines like Hannah, be a friend like Riley, or a beacon of change like Tanya. Be whoever you want to be.

Now, on to some lighter acknowledgements!

There are people whose edits and insights made this book a million times better and for that, they deserve all the praise. First, I'd like to thank my mum, whose enthusiasm for this story was clear from the start. Laura Tennant and Laura Sheldrake - you have the sharpest eyes and best ideas! Jack, who assured me this was a story I needed to share, especially in the moments I doubted myself. Isa and Sara – you opened my eyes to a whole new way of looking at this book, thank you! And of course, to the team at Kingsley Publishers, who signed me for an 8-book deal during this time and kept me on track and motivated.

I'd also like to thank Christine and Nigel Carter, who were visiting Australia at the time I was writing Lucky Number 11, for their kindness and care. Notes were stuck to the living room wall and I was avidly typing away whenever I could, but you always made sure I took a break, went for walks and looked after myself - thank you. I can't wait to have you back in Sydney soon!

To the readers - the wonderful, wonderful readers! Over the last few months, it's been a pleasure to meet some of you in person (finally!). The support you have shown me is something I will never forget. In particular, I'd like to shout out every member of the 'Official Jess Kitching Reader Community' on Facebook, aka the kindest, most supportive group ever. You all give me so much, from words of encouragement to book recommendations to endless motivation - thank you.

Another thank you to Jack, who has lived with Hannah Allen and her story for so long that I'm sure she feels as real to you as she does to me! Thanks for being on this journey with me and for never letting me shy away from chasing my dreams.

And lastly, I'd like to thank myself for not giving up, even when I felt like it. Look how far you've come.

Author Bio

Jess Kitching is the bestselling Author of *The Girl She Was Before*, which was nominated for a Sisters in Crime Davitt Award and has been translated into Danish. She is also the Author of *How To Destroy Your Husband*.

A proud advocate for anti-bullying, sexual assault survivors and beauty diversity, Jess uses her spare time to discuss and raise awareness of these issues.

Originally from the north of England, she currently lives in Sydney with her fiancé.

Connect with Jess on social media

Instagram: @jesskitchingwrites

Twitter: @kitching_jess

Facebook: Jess Kitching Writes

Or her special readers group on Facebook:

'Official Jess Kitching Reader Community'

"I gulp as I stare at the stranger before me. Who is this man I had wanted to spend the rest of my life with?"

Cassie Edwards swore she'd never fall in love... then she met Jamie. He changed everything, and Cassie's never been happier.

But with less than one month to go to her wedding, Cassie discovers Jamie is cheating on her with his colleague. Blinded by rage, Cassie makes it her mission to seek revenge on the pair.

When Cassie looks deeper into her fiancé's life, she soon realises being faithful isn't the only thing he's lying about.

As her hunt for the truth takes her to some of the darkest corners of the internet, Cassie learns just how little she knows about the man she shares her life with. It leaves her wondering one thing – is Jamie someone she should destroy, or someone she should fear instead?

How far would you go to destroy your husband?

How to Destroy your Husband

By Jess Kitching

KINGSLEY

PUBLISHERS

The *End*

The clock over his shoulder tells me it's ten to three.

Ten to three, a time that used to be as inconsequential to me as any other but now could be the time of my death.

A bubble of laughter builds in me at the absurdity of the sudden importance of this moment. It fights to break free, but the way Jamie's hand crushes my windpipe tells me no sound will escape my lips even if I try allowing it to pass.

Who would have thought we would end up here? Here, on the day of our wedding, with the most beautiful dress I'll ever own now crumpled beyond recognition.

Here, with Jamie's hands around my throat, my life in his hands. This man I loved, now a stranger, and not just because of the murderous intent in his eyes.

How did it get to this?

How did we get to this?

For that there is only one answer.

<u>The First *Beginning*</u>

I first stopped believing in love five years ago thanks to yet another bad breakup, only this one wasn't mine. Over a Chinese takeaway one Saturday night, my best friend Lily wasn't presented with the engagement ring she'd been expecting, but instead received a bumbling apology from her teenage sweetheart Andy as he left her to 'discover' himself in Thailand.

Dumped, after everything, just like that.

Andy didn't even have the decency to clear his stuff out of the apartment they'd shared for the last two years. It would have been 'too painful', apparently. Instead, he asked Lily to box everything up and send it to his mum's house, a task he didn't stop to think might be 'too painful' for her as well.

After smashing his aftershave collection into a million indecipherable pieces and burning his beloved pit-stained football shirts, Lily called us from the foetal position on her bedroom floor. Half an hour later and armed with multiple bottles of cheap white wine, my best friends and I were sat beside her.

Obviously, the news shocked Lily the most, but Alisha, Laney and I were a close second. We'd known Andy since we were awkward year sevens battling acne and clueless about who we wanted to be when we grew up. Andy was our friend. He bought the first round of drinks on a night out and showed us flowers weren't only gifted when coinciding with an apology. He provided advice better than an agony aunt ever could. He was, in short, our idea of a good man, and one half of the only 'real' couple we knew. The kind of couple who hosted dinner parties and had matching kitchenware. The kind of couple you looked at and thought, 'Oh, so *that's* what all the films and songs are about'.

But when Andy turned out to be the villain of the story and not the romantic lead, it dawned on us that everything we thought we knew about love was, in fact, wrong.

"Eight years of my life I gave him!" Lily ugly cried, snot dripping from her upper lip. "I even went to the same university as him because he said he couldn't stand to be apart from me. Can't stand to be apart from me, huh? Thailand isn't exactly around the corner!"

"He's an idiot. They all are," Alisha sighed. With D-cup breasts, a bum that practically invented the peach emoji and an award-winning PR firm she built from scratch, Alisha was who most girls dreamed of being when they grew up.

However, according to the men she dated, she was also a vain, ruthless bitch... but only once they realised she earned triple what they did.

"Do you know what Andy said to me? He said he doesn't fancy me anymore. He said I don't make enough effort, but it's hard to want to dress up when the person you're with jabs your stomach and asks when you're due!" Lily pinched the roll of flesh above the waistband of her pyjamas to emphasise her point.

Despite being beautiful both inside and out, Lily was forever following the latest celebrity endorsed diet regime to try shrink herself to twiglike proportions. She had a smile that lit up a room and hair the exact shade of blonde many spent hundreds trying to emulate, but whenever Lily looked in the mirror, all she saw were flaws. The fact that Andy used her body image issues against her in their breakup poured lighter fuel on the already raging fire inside us all.

"He seriously said that? He was hardly Mr Perfect himself!" Laney cried.

"I know, but he was perfect to me," Lily said, then she threw her head back to release a gut-wrenching wail.

Alarm flickered across Laney's face. She opened her mouth to speak but with a subtle shake of the head, Alisha silenced her. In that silence, Lily cried. She cried with a rawness none of us could bear or imagine.

The three of us exchanged helpless looks over the top of Lily's head as it became glaringly obvious how out of our depth we were. This was a real, serious, grown-up heartbreak, the kind that defined a portion of someone's life. How could we help with that? Laney was going out every weekend as if she was still a student, Alisha was on a dating ban so she could focus on growing her business, and I was three months into dating a man I only heard from when he had no one else to hang out with. Never in the history of the world had there been a group of people so ill-prepared to fix the sudden disappearance of a lifetime of plans and the breaking of years' worth of promises.

Four glasses of wine in and Lily's tears were no longer cascading waterfalls, but sad, singular drops trailing miserably down her cheeks. "I just don't get it. Where did it all go wrong? What did I do to deserve this?"

"You did nothing," I soothed, but Lily shook her head.

"I give up! You can do anything and everything for them, be anything and everything they say they want, and it's still not enough. Do you know how many of Andy's socks I must have picked up off the floor during our relationship? Hundreds! I was like his personal cleaner, and he still left me."

"Andy didn't know how lucky he had it. In fact, they rarely ever do," Laney said, picking at her chipped black nail polish. "I mean, how many times do you hear about middle-aged men leaving their wives for someone younger because their wife doesn't look like she did when she was twenty-one? It's like women aren't allowed to age. Push out the children, remember the birthdays, book the appointments, sure! But get a few wrinkles or find a grey hair? No way!"

"Exactly!" Lily hiccupped. "The standards are too high. They're impossible to meet! You're supposed to have the body of a supermodel but still order a takeaway on a Friday night."

"And you've got to be edgy enough to stand out in a crowd, but not so edgy that their friends think you're weird," Laney added, rolling her heavily eyelinered eyes. "If one more person says to me, 'you're great, but you're just so… different' like it's a bad thing, I might scream."

"Don't forget money. You can't earn more than them because that's emasculating, but if you earn too little, you're not someone they can see a future with. You know, because someone who can't pay for half the meal isn't 'wife material'." Alisha air quoted the phrase with a bitter sigh.

"Wife material," I scoffed. "What even is that? Florals on one side to show their mother, leather bondage on the reverse?"

Laney and Alisha tittered, but Lily was too upset to even raise a smile. "See? It's hopeless!"

At this, Alisha put her arm around Lily's shoulders. "Lil, it's going to be okay! I know it doesn't feel like it now, but it will be. We've been through this before and we'll go through it again but one day, when it's our wedding day, we will look back and laugh. You'll have the man of your dreams, a man who thinks Thailand is overrated and knows where the clitoris is, and Andy will just be the name of someone you think you know but can't remember where from."

Lily's blue eyes glittered with hope. "You promise?"

"I promise. We all do, don't we?"

"Of course," Laney agreed, but my words stayed lodged in my throat, not budging even when Alisha raised her eyebrows to prompt me to nod along.

In that moment, I felt my spirit leave my body. It floated above the tragic scene, looking down at the four of us sat in an exhausted heap on the floor, wine soaking into the carpet and spinning ourselves a make-believe story with the same yarn we were gifted as little girls. 'One day your prince will come, but until then you're going to have to put up with peasants with commitment issues and a minor binge drinking problem'… it was bullshit!

I couldn't shake the feeling that we were doing Lily a huge disservice. Her future had been torn from her in the most brutal way, yet there we were, feeding her vague lines about being fixed by someone she'd yet to meet. We were bad friends for sending that message, even though every rom-com we'd ever watched had trained us to respond to a breakup in such a way.

In fact, when I thought about it, we'd been trained to respond to every part of a courtship-to-relationship timeline like that. Spewing half-baked sentiments about fate and soulmates as if they excused the appalling treatment we'd endure on the path to finding 'The One'.

I found myself wondering how many nights we had wasted over the years worrying if a man who played video games as frequently as a teenager loved us.

How many conversations had we had trying to decipher the meaning behind cryptic texts from our latest romantic prospect? Ones that were vague enough to keep us as someone they were 'seeing' but not harsh enough to make us realise we deserved better.

How many tears had we wiped from our eyes because of men who cringed at the mention of a period but expected us to smile after a cum shot to the chin?

I didn't need a calculator to work out the answer was too many.

As soon as this realisation hit, something inside me changed. I was never going to be the heartbroken girl again. My self-worth was never going to be pushed to the side so I could have someone to cuddle up to at night. I wouldn't suppress my annoyance when plans were cancelled at the last minute in favour of going to the pub with moronic mates. Never again would I pretend a supermarket bought gift voucher purchased on the way home from work was a good enough birthday present from a romantic partner. Forget *that*. That Cassie was dead.

Like a caged animal, I waited for the next one to come along and try it, just try it.

I didn't give up on dating altogether. I was open to the idea of meeting someone – I just expected my opponent to match my energy.

I played my part like society told me I was meant to. My stray hairs were torn out with wax strips and I spent too much money on skincare products that promised to make me beautiful. I stayed up late flirting on various dating apps and worrying if the photos I used on my profile gave the 'right' impression, but still I was repeatedly reminded of the truth Andy had shown us – love was a myth, one we were stupid for believing in.

I flitted from bad date to bad date, a merry-go-round of terrible experiences I wouldn't wish on my worst enemy, until eventually, spirit sucked dry, I snapped.

"I give up!" I declared one night over pizzas at Lily's. "I have a new rule – one date, one chance. If it's not flowing, then it's not happening. There shall be no second chances for 'it was alright' nights or mediocre conversation from me anymore."

"Good for you," Alisha agreed. "There's so much more to life than chasing romance, anyway."

"Spoken like a true career woman," Lily laughed. "Dating is meant to be fun! Don't take it so seriously."

"I'm with Lily on this one. Besides, don't you think the whole 'one chance' part is a bit harsh? I mean, what if they're having a bad day when you meet?" Laney replied through a mouthful of pepperoni.

"Laney, your last date was with someone who told you they'd been wearing the same t-shirt for the last three days, and you still met them again. If anything, I think we're not harsh enough."

The debate about my new standard continued all night, but the more dates I went on, the more evidence I had to prove the standard was wise to keep.

I mean, why would I want to spend another evening with Imran who listed what he believed to be his ex's physical flaws within the first hour we met? Or Peter who was vocal about the fact that he expected whichever lucky lady he married to give up work and take care of their children, no discussion on the matter? Or Hudson who was open to the point of being proud that he'd cheated on every girlfriend he'd ever had?

My conversations online weren't much better than the ones I had in person. I lost count of the amount of abuse I received on dating apps when I said I wasn't interested, never quite understanding how I could go from *'hey gorgeous'* in one message to *'you're an ugly bitch anyway'* in the next.

The longer my single status went on for, the more people seemed to think they had a right to comment on it, as if my lack of a romantic partner meant there was a fundamental flaw with my life.

My mum fretted with every friend she had that my dad passing away when I was five had scarred me for life. She never once stopped to think being alone was a choice I was happy with, one that didn't stem from the childhood trauma of watching her cry herself to sleep in an empty double bed for months on end.

Every aged relative mentioned my biological clock until it became a ticking timebomb narrating the 'lonely girl' label those relatives placed on me. It didn't matter that I wasn't emotionally or financially ready for children, or that I wasn't lonely. I was in my late twenties, single and childfree, therefore pity oozed from them every time we met. It was almost surreal, feeling whole but being questioned as if I wasn't.

"When are you going to settle down?"

"Have you met The One yet?"

"Well, you'd better get a move on... time's ticking for a woman your age!"

Everywhere I looked, all I saw were signs shouting that happiness meant being on the arm of someone else. The way you could buy hundreds of cards congratulating someone on their engagement, wedding, or pregnancy, but only a few lacklustre designs were available for celebrating a promotion or individual success. Cinema tickets were cheaper… if you came with another person. It was outrageous, but no one else seemed angry about it but me.

The more I looked at the world through this lens, the more cynical I became.

I watched as Alisha met Simon. Simon who wore retro cardigans because he misguidedly thought he could pull the look off. Simon who read TripAdvisor reviews like they were passages from The Bible. Simon who was punching not one or two leagues above his own but who was with a woman from a totally different sport.

I watched Alisha insist she was happy, that she had met 'The One', all the while wondering if what she meant was 'I've met The One Who Won't Leave Me'.

I watched as Lily flirted her way through flings with men and women who promised they would heal her broken heart, only to walk away a few weeks later once they'd got what they wanted.

I watched Lily claim she was happy, that Andy had done her a favour by allowing her to experience sexual liberation, all the while wondering if that was the case, then why was Lily still stalking Andy's social media? Especially now he was married to an American with a flawless tan and teeth so white they hurt your eyes.

I watched as Laney met Anton, fell head over heels and ditched her all-black ensembles and bright hair dye for cutesy tea-dresses and muted pink lipstick. Then, eight months later, I watched Anton walk out the door and back into the arms of his ex-girlfriend.

I watched, I waited, I simmered.

Then one night, out of the blue, I met Jamie.

Dating websites and hook-up apps would have you believe organic meetings don't happen anymore, but Jamie and I bucked that trend. The minute our eyes met across the heaving dancefloor, 80s party tunes blasting from the speakers and cheap vodka flowing through my veins, I knew he was going to mean something in my life. Call it fate, call it intuition, call it a good old-fashioned crush, but I just knew.

After his drunken friend hollered across the bar at me for the third time, Jamie approached me. His body was so close I could feel the heat radiating from him, but he kept a respectful distance between us. He never once put his hand on my waist the way some men do when they think loud music in bars gives them permission to touch you without consent or consequence.

"Sorry about my friend," he shouted over the music, the low pitch of his voice sending a flutter through my stomach. "I'd say he's not usually like this, but he's an embarrassment most of the time. I should ditch him, shouldn't I?"

Maybe it was the vodka talking, or maybe it was because I felt alive in his presence, but I hit the ground running. "You should thank him. If it wasn't for him, you wouldn't have had a reason to talk to me."

Jamie's twinkling eyes locked on mine. A current of electricity passed between us, one so strong I was surprised the power to the bar didn't short circuit. "You wanted me to talk to you?"

I bit my lip and gave a confessional nod. The next thing I knew, Jamie was buying me a drink.

Leaving Lily and Alisha at the bar, we sat together in a faded booth beside the dancefloor and fell into easy conversation about everything and nothing. After years of bland exchanges, I was finally sat opposite someone who wasn't afraid to share their deepest secrets in and amongst lighter titbits of information like their favourite food.

The sticky table in front of us and the sea of people on the dancefloor faded into insignificance until all I could see, hear, feel, and think of was the man sat beside me. The man who had a small scar on his left hand from a childhood bike accident and a laugh that made fireworks burst inside my chest. The man who was at once both a stranger and someone it felt like I'd known forever.

One by one, all the secret, closed off parts of me began to unlock. The weight of the cynicism I'd carried for so many years drifted away, and I softened into the moment until, quite abruptly, the lights in the bar came on to announce closing time.

Reality was jarring, unwelcome even. I remember blinking and wondering how it could possibly be time for the bar to close when Jamie and I had only just sat down?

But when I checked the time on my phone, it confessed that Jamie and I had been talking for the last three hours. The fizzing feeling I'd felt since I first saw him intensified, and I gulped in the acceptance that maybe I'd been wrong to shut down the idea of love quite so firmly.

Jamie's hand wrapped around mine as we manoeuvred towards the exit. I held on tight, dreading the moment I would have to let it go.

Bitter, frosty air assaulted me the instant we stepped outside, but my body barely had time to tremble before Jamie wrapped his coat around my shoulders. The gesture caught me off guard. I couldn't remember the last time someone had given me a strip of gum, never mind their coat on a freezing night. I looked into Jamie's big, brown eyes and melted, and in that puddle of my being, every doubt I ever felt simply evaporated.

"I don't want to leave you," Jamie confessed as we waited for our respective taxis.

"So don't," I replied, and that was it – that was the moment everything changed.

Overnight my fury disappeared. I didn't need to fight back or overrule whatever narrative was being forced upon me because I had a man who didn't want me to play a role other than his equal.

I had a man I couldn't imagine a future without. A man who donated a chunk of his salary to charity, who recycled, who volunteered at a homeless shelter on Christmas Eve. A man who was a teacher too, who understood the pressures of the job so did all he could to make my load easier to carry. A man who went for beers with my stepdad and took my mum shopping when her car broke down. I went on holiday to places like Paris and Rome and saw why everyone said they were romantic cities instead of scoffing at the sentiment. I received thoughtful gifts on my birthday and at Christmas and sometimes just because. My life was good.

No, it was *more* than good. I had a partner who liked my friends and friends who liked my partner back. I woke up to kisses that gave me butterflies almost three years down the line. My future felt like it was filled with endless possibility.

I gave into the happiness. I trusted it. I let myself get comfortable with the idea that this was to be my life – blissful, happy, loved. I noticed how much brighter the world seems when you're in love, how easy it is to get out of bed on a morning. My colleague Shari even called me a walking advert for romance, a badge I wore with pride.

With no clouds of fury blocking my vision, I noticed how Laney's sense of self was stronger than ever after her breakup with Anton.

I noticed how single Lily laughed more than she ever had when she was with Andy.

I noticed how Simon treated Alisha like a queen and gave into the idea that the two of them were happy together after all.

Smitten, I dived headfirst into love. That was the problem. That's where it all went wrong.

That's how I've found myself trying to digest the fact that even though I am to be married in less than one month's time, my teaching assistant Debbie's phone is in my hand and I'm staring dumbly at a photo of Jamie and his colleague Tara kissing.

Made in United States
North Haven, CT
04 September 2023

41137816R00203